CUJO

STEPHEN KING   Photograph © Dick Dickinson

There is a reason why Stephen King is one of the bestselling writers in the world, *ever*. As George Pelecanos says: 'King's gift of storytelling is unrivalled. His ferocious imagination is un-limited.' King knows how to write stories that draw you in and are *impossible to put down*.

King is the author of more than fifty books, all of them world-wide bestsellers, including the iconic, chilling classics *Cujo, The Dark Half, Pet Sematary, 'Salem's Lot* and *The Shining*. Many of his books and novellas have been turned into celebrated films, including *Cujo, Misery, The Shining* and *The Shawshank Redemption*.

King was the recipient of the 2003 National Book Foundation Medal for Distinguished Contribution to American Letters. He lives with his wife, novelist Tabitha King, in Maine.

HAVE YOU READ . . . ?

THE DARK HALF

For years, Thad Beaumont has been writing books under the pseudonym George Stark. When a journalist threatens to expose Beaumont's pen name, the author decides to go public first, killing off his pseudonym. But Stark isn't content to be dispatched that easily . . .

PET SEMATARY

Dr Louis Creed and his family have just moved to rural Maine. Near their house, local children have created a cemetery for dogs and cats killed on the busy highway. But deeper in the woods lies another graveyard, an ancient Indian burial ground whose sinister properties Dr Creed is about to discover . . .

'SALEM'S LOT

Author Ben Mears returns to 'Salem's Lot to write a book about a house that has haunted him since childhood, only to find his isolated hometown infested with vampires. Now Ben must gather the locals to combat the terrors before it is too late.

THE SHINING

Danny is only five years old but in the words of old Mr Hallorann he is a 'shiner', aglow with psychic voltage. When his father becomes caretaker of the Overlook Hotel, Danny's visions grow out of control. Somewhere, somehow, there is an evil force in the hotel – and that too is beginning to shine . . .

'Obviously a masterpiece, probably the best supernatural novel in a hundred years' - Peter Straub

By Stephen King and published by Hodder & Stoughton

NOVELS:

Carrie
'Salem's Lot
The Shining
The Stand
The Dead Zone
Firestarter
Cujo
Cycle of the Werewolf
Christine
The Talisman (with Peter Straub)
Pet Sematary
IT
The Eyes of the Dragon
Misery
The Tommyknockers
The Dark Half
Needful Things
Gerald's Game
Dolores Claiborne
Insomnia
Rose Madder
Desperation
Bag of Bones
The Girl Who Loved Tom Gordon
Dreamcatcher
From a Buick 8
Cell
Lisey's Story
Duma Key
Under the Dome
Blockade Billy

The Dark Tower I: The Gunslinger
The Dark Tower II: The Drawing of
the Three
The Dark Tower III: The Waste Lands
The Dark Tower IV: Wizard and Glass
The Dark Tower V: Wolves of the Calla
The Dark Tower VI: Song of Susannah
The Dark Tower VII: The Dark Tower

As Richard Bachman
Thinner
The Running Man
The Bachman Books
The Regulators
Blaze

STORY COLLECTIONS:

Night Shift
Different Seasons
Skeleton Crew
Four Past Midnight
Nightmares and Dreamscapes
Hearts in Atlantis
Everything's Eventual
Just After Sunset
Stephen King Goes to the Movies
Full Dark, No Stars

NON-FICTION

Danse Macabre
On Writing (A Memoir of the Craft)

STEPHEN KING

CUJO

HODDER

Copyright 1981 by Stephen King

First published in Great Britain in 1981 by Macdonald & Co

This paperback edition published in 2011

The right of Stephen King to be identified as the Author of the Work has been asserted by him in accordance with the Copyright, Designs and Patents Act 1988.

A Hodder Paperback

2

A CIP catalogue record for this title is available from the British Library

ISBN 978 1 444 70812 7

Typeset in Bembo by Palimpsest Book Production Limited,
Falkirk, Stirlingshire

Printed and bound in Great Britain by Clays Ltd, St Ives plc

Hodder & Stoughton policy is to use papers that are natural, renewable and recyclable products and made from wood grown in sustainable forests. The logging and manufacturing processes are expected to conform to the environmental regulations of the country of origin

Hodder & Stoughton
338 Euston Road
London NW1 3BH

www.hodder.co.uk

About suffering they were never wrong,
The Old Masters: how well they understood
Its human position; how it takes place
While someone else is eating or opening a window or
*   just walking dully along . . .*

— W. H. AUDEN, 'Musée des Beaux Arts'

Old Blue died and he died so hard
He shook the ground in my back yard.
I dug his grave with a silver spade
And I lowered him down with a golden chain.
Every link you know I did call his name,
I called, 'Here, Blue, you good dog, you.'

— FOLK SONG

'Nope, nothing wrong here.'

— THE SHARP CEREAL PROFESSOR

This book is for my brother, David,
who held my hand crossing West Broad Street,
and who taught me how to make skyhooks
out of old coathangers. The trick was so
damned good I just never stopped.

I love you, David.

Once upon a time, not so long ago, a monster came to the small town of Castle Rock, Maine. He killed a waitress named Alma Frechette in 1970; a woman named Pauline Toothaker and a junior high school student named Cheryl Moody in 1971; a pretty girl named Carol Dunbarger in 1974; a teacher named Etta Ringgold in the fall of 1975; finally, a grade-schooler named Mary Kate Hendrasen in the early winter of that same year.

He was not werewolf, vampire, ghoul, or unnameable creature from the enchanted forest or from the snowy wastes; he was only a cop named Frank Dodd with mental and sexual problems. A good man named John Smith uncovered his name by a kind of magic, but before he could be captured – perhaps it was just as well – Frank Dodd killed himself.

There was some shock, of course, but mostly there was rejoicing in that small town, rejoicing because the monster which had haunted so many dreams was dead, dead at last. A town's nightmares were buried in Frank Dodd's grave.

Yet even in this enlightened age, when so many parents are aware of the psychological damage they may do to their

1

children, surely there was one parent somewhere in Castle Rock – or perhaps one grandmother – who quieted the kids by telling them that Frank Dodd would get them if they didn't watch out, if they weren't good. And surely a hush fell as children looked toward their dark windows and thought of Frank Dodd in his shiny black vinyl raincoat, Frank Dodd who had choked . . . and choked . . . and choked.

He's out there, I can hear the grandmother whispering as the wind whistles down the chimney pipe and snuffles around the old pot lid crammed in the stove hole. *He's out there, and if you're not good, it may be his face you see looking in your bedroom window after everyone in the house is asleep except you; it may be his smiling face you see peeking at you from the closet in the middle of the night, the STOP sign he held up when he crossed the little children in one hand, the razor he used to kill himself in the other . . . so shhh, children . . . shhhh . . . shhhh . . .*

But for most, the ending was the ending. There were nightmares to be sure, and children who lay wakeful to be sure, and the empty Dodd house (for his mother had a stroke shortly afterwards and died) quickly gained a reputation as a haunted house and was avoided; but these were passing phenomena – the perhaps unavoidable side effects of a chain of senseless murders.

But time passed. Five years of time.

The monster was gone, the monster was dead. Frank Dodd moldered inside his coffin.

Except that the monster never dies. Werewolf, vampire, ghoul, unnameable creature from the wastes. The monster never dies.

It came to Castle Rock again in the summer of 1980.

★　　★　　★

CUJO

Tad Trenton, four years old, awoke one morning not long after midnight in May of that year, needing to go to the bathroom. He got out of bed and walked half asleep toward the white light thrown in a wedge through the half-open door, already lowering his pajama pants. He urinated forever, flushed, and went back to bed. He pulled the covers up, and that was when he saw the creature in his closet.

Low to the ground it was, with huge shoulders bulking above its cocked head, its eyes amber-glowing pits – a thing that might have been half man, half wolf. And its eyes rolled to follow him as he sat up, his scrotum crawling, his hair standing on end, his breath a thin winter-whistle in his throat: mad eyes that laughed, eyes that promised horrible death and the music of screams that went unheard; something in the closet.

He heard its purring growl; he smelled its sweet carrion breath.

Tad Trenton clapped his hands to his eyes, hitched in breath, and screamed.

A muttered exclamation in another room – his father.

A scared cry of 'What was that?' from the same room – his mother.

Their footfalls, running. As they came in, he peered through his fingers and saw it there in the closet, snarling, promising dreadfully that they might come, but they would surely go, and that when they did –

The light went on. Vic and Donna Trenton came to his bed, exchanging a look of concern over his chalky face and his staring eyes, and his mother said – no, snapped, 'I told you three hot dogs was too many, Vic!'

3

STEPHEN KING

And then his daddy was on the bed, Daddy's arm around his back, asking what was wrong.

Tad dared to look into the mouth of his closet again.

The monster was gone. Instead of whatever hungry beast he had seen, there were two uneven piles of blankets, winter bedclothes which Donna had not yet gotten around to taking up to the cut-off third floor. These were stacked on the chair which Tad used to stand on when he needed something from the high closet shelf. Instead of the shaggy, triangular head, cocked sideways in a kind of predatory questioning gesture, he saw his teddybear on the taller of the two piles of blankets. Instead of pitted and baleful amber eyes, there were the friendly brown glass balls from which his Teddy observed the world.

'What's wrong, Tadder?' his daddy asked him again.

'There was a monster!' Tad cried. 'In my closet!' And he burst into tears.

His mommy sat with him; they held him between them, soothed him as best they could. There followed the ritual of parents. They explained there were no monsters; that he had just had a bad dream. His mommy explained how shadows could sometimes look like the bad things they sometimes showed on TV or in the comic books, and Daddy told him everything was all right, fine, that nothing in their good house could hurt him. Tad nodded and agreed that it was so, although he knew it was not.

His father explained to him how, in the dark, the two uneven piles of blankets had looked like hunched shoulders, how the teddybear had looked like a cocked head, and how the bathroom light, reflecting from Teddy's glass eyes, had made them seem like the eyes of a real live animal.

4

'Now look,' he said. 'Watch me close, Tadder.'

Tad watched.

His father took the two piles of blankets and put them far back in Tad's closet. Tad could hear the coathangers jingling softly, talking about Daddy in their coathanger language. That was funny, and he smiled a little. Mommy caught his smile and smiled back, relieved.

His daddy came out of the closet, took Teddy, and put him in Tad's arms.

'And last but not least, Daddy said with a flourish and a bow that made both Tad and Mommy giggle, 'ze chair.'

He closed the closet door firmly and then put the chair against the door. When he came back to Tad's bed he was still smiling, but his eyes were serious.

'Okay, Tad?'

'Yes,' Tad said, and then forced himself to say it. 'But it was there, Daddy. I saw it. Really.'

'Your *mind* saw something, Tad,' Daddy said, and his big, warm hand stroked Tad's hair. 'But you didn't see a monster in your closet, not a real one. There are no monsters, Tad. Only in stories, and in your mind.'

He looked from his father to his mother and back again – their big, well-loved faces.

'Really?'

'Really,' his mommy said. 'Now I want you to get up and go pee, big guy.'

'I did. That's what woke me up.'

'Well,' she said, because parents never believed you, 'humor me then, what do you say?'

So he went in and she watched while he did four drops and she smiled and said, 'See? You *did* have to go.'

Resigned, Tad nodded. Went back to bed. Was tucked in. Accepted kisses.

And as his mother and father went back to the door the fear settled on him again like a cold coat full of mist. Like a shroud stinking of hopeless death. *Oh please*, he thought, but there was no more, just that: *Oh please oh please oh please.*

Perhaps his father caught his thought, because Vic turned back, one hand on the light switch, and repeated: 'No monsters, Tad.'

'No, Daddy,' Tad said, because in that instant his father's eyes seemed shadowed and far, as if he needed to be convinced. 'No monsters.' *Except for the one in my closet.*

The light snapped off.

'Good night, Tad.' His mother's voice trailed back to him lightly, softly, and in his mind he cried out, *Be careful, Mommy, they eat the ladies! In all the movies they catch the ladies and carry them off and eat them! Oh please oh please oh please —*

But they were gone.

So Tad Trenton, four years old, lay in his bed, all wires and stiff Erector Set braces. He lay with the covers pulled up to his chin and one arm crushing Teddy against his chest, and there was Luke Skywalker on one wall; there was a chipmunk standing on a blender on another wall, grinning cheerily (IF LIFE HANDS YOU LEMONS, MAKE LEMONADE! the cheeky, grinning chipmunk was saying); there was the whole motley Sesame Street crew on a third: Big Bird, Bert, Ernie, Oscar, Grover. Good totems; good magic. But oh the wind outside, screaming over the roof and skating down black gutters! He would sleep no more this night.

But little by little the wires unsnarled themselves and stiff Erector Set muscles relaxed. His mind began to drift . . .

And then a new screaming, this one closer than the nightwind outside, brought him back to staring wakefulness again.

The hinges on the closet door.

Creeeeeeeeeeee —

That thin sound, so high that perhaps only dogs and small boys awake in the night could have heard it. His closet door swung open slowly and steadily, a dead mouth opening on darkness inch by inch and foot by foot.

The monster was in that darkness. It crouched where it had crouched before. It grinned at him, and its huge shoulders bulked above its cocked head, and its eyes glowed amber, alive with stupid cunning. *I told you they'd go away, Tad*, it whispered. *They always do, in the end. And then I can come back. I like to come back. I like you, Tad. I'll come back every night now, I think, and every night I'll come a little closer to your bed . . . and a little closer . . . until one night, before you can scream for them, you'll hear something growling, something growling right beside you, Tad, it'll be me, and I'll pounce, and then I'll eat you and you'll be in me.*

Tad stared at the creature in his closet with drugged, horrified fascination. There was something that . . . was almost familiar. Something he almost knew. And that was the worst, that almost knowing. Because —

Because I'm crazy, Tad. I'm here. I've been here all along. My name was Frank Dodd once, and I killed the ladies and maybe I ate them, too. I've been here all along, I stick around, I keep my ear to the ground. I'm the monster, Tad, the old monster, and I'll have you soon, Tad. Feel me getting closer . . . and closer . . .

Perhaps the thing in the closet spoke to him in its own hissing breath, or perhaps its voice was the wind's voice. Either way, neither way, it didn't matter. He listened to its words, drugged with terror, near fainting (but oh so wide awake); he looked upon its shadowed, snarling face, which he almost knew. He would sleep no more tonight; perhaps he would never sleep again.

But sometime later, sometime between the striking of half past midnight and the hour of one, perhaps because he was small, Tad drifted away again. Thin sleep in which hulking, furred creatures with white teeth chased him deepened into dreamless slumber.

The wind held long conversations with the gutters. A rind of white spring moon rose in the sky. Somewhere far away, in some still meadow of night or along some pine-edged corridor of forest, a dog barked furiously and then fell silent.

And in Tad Trenton's closet, something with amber eyes held watch.

'Did you put the blankets back?' Donna asked her husband the next morning. She was standing at the stove, cooking bacon. Tad was in the other room, watching *The New Zoo Revue* and eating a bowl of Twinkles. Twinkles was a Sharp cereal, and the Trentons got all their Sharp cereals free.

'Hmmm?' Vic asked. He was buried deep in the sports pages. A transplanted New Yorker, he had so far successfully resisted Red Sox fever. But he was masochistically pleased to see that the Mets were off to another superlatively cruddy start.

'The blankets. In Tad's closet. They were back in there. The chair was back in there, too, and the door was open again.' She brought the bacon, draining on a paper towel and still sizzling, to the table. 'Did you put them back on his chair?'

'Not me,' Vic said, turning a page. 'It smells like a mothball convention back there.'

'That's funny. *He* must have put them back.'

He put the paper aside and looked up at her. 'What are you talking about, Donna?'

'You remember the bad dream last night—'

'Not apt to forget. I thought the kid was dying. Having a convulsion or something.'

She nodded. 'He thought the blankets were some kind of—' She shrugged.

'Bogeyman,' Vic said, grinning.

'I guess so. And you gave him his teddybear and put those blankets in the back of the closet. But they were back on the chair when I went to make his bed.' She laughed. 'I looked in, and for just a second there I thought—'

'*Now* I know where he gets it,' Vic said, picking up the newspaper again. He cocked a friendly eye at her. 'Three hot dogs, my ass.'

Later, after Vic had shot off to work, Donna asked Tad why he had put the chair back in the closet with the blankets on it if they had scared him in the night.

Tad looked up at her, and his normally animated, lively face seemed pale and watchful – too old. His *Star Wars* coloring book was open in front of him. He had been doing a picture from the interstellar cantina, using his green Crayola to color Greedo.

'I didn't,' he said.

'But Tad, if you didn't, and Daddy didn't, and *I* didn't—'

'The monster did it,' Tad said. 'The monster in my closet.'

He bent to his picture again.

She stood looking at him, troubled, a little frightened. He was a bright boy, and perhaps too imaginative. This was not such good news. She would have to talk to Vic about it tonight. She would have to have a long talk with him about it.

'Tad, remember what your father said,' she told him now. 'There aren't any such things as monsters.'

'Not in the daytime, anyway,' he said, and smiled at her so openly, so beautifully, that she was charmed out of her fears. She ruffled his hair and kissed his cheek.

She meant to talk to Vic, and then Steve Kemp came while Tad was at nursery school, and she forgot, and Tad screamed that night too, screamed that it was in his closet, the monster, the monster!

The closet door hung ajar, blankets on the chair. This time Vic took them up to the third floor and stacked them in the closet up there.

'Locked it up, Tadder,' Vic said, kissing his son. 'You're all set now. Go back to sleep and have a good dream.'

But Tad did not sleep for a long time, and before he did the closet door swung clear of its latch with a sly little snicking sound, the dead mouth opened on the dead dark – the dead dark where something furry and sharp-toothed and -clawed waited, something that smelled of sour blood and dark doom.

Hello, Tad, it whispered in its rotting voice, and the moon peered in Tad's window like the white and slitted eye of a dead man.

The oldest living person in Castle Rock that late spring was Evelyn Chalmers, known as Aunt Evvie by the town's older residents, known as 'that old loudmouth bitch' by George Meara, who had to deliver her mail – which mostly consisted of catalogues and offers from the *Reader's Digest* and prayer folders from the Crusade of the Eternal Christ – and listen to her endless monologues. 'The only thing that old loudmouth bitch is any good at is telling the weather,' George had been known to allow when in his cups and in the company of his cronies down at the Mellow Tiger. It was one stupid name for a bar, but since it was the only one Castle Rock could boast, it looked like they were pretty much stuck with it.

There was general agreement with George's opinion. As the oldest resident of Castle Rock, Aunt Evvie had held the *Boston Post* cane for the last two years, ever since Arnold Heebert, who had been one hundred and one and so far gone in senility that talking to him held all the intellectual challenge of talking to an empty catfood can, had doddered off the back patio of the Castle Acres Nursing Home and broken his neck exactly twenty-five minutes after whizzing in his pants for the last time.

Aunt Evvie was nowhere near as senile as Arnie Heebert had been, and nowhere near as old, but at ninety-three she was old enough, and, as she was fond of bawling at a resigned (and often hung-over) George Meara when he delivered the mail, she hadn't been stupid enough to lose her home the way Heebert had done.

But she was good at the weather. The town consensus – among the older people, who cared about such things – was that Aunt Evvie was never wrong about three things: the week when the first hay-cutting would happen in the summertime, how good (or how bad) the blueberries would be, and what the weather would be like.

One day early that June she shuffled out to the mailbox at the end of the driveway, leaning heavily on her *Boston Post* cane (which would go to Vin Marchant when the loudmouthed old bitch popped off, George Meara thought, and good riddance to *you*, Evvie) and smoking a Herbert Tareyton. She bellowed a greeting at Meara – her deafness had apparently convinced her that everyone else in the world had gone deaf in sympathy – and then shouted that they were going to have the hottest summer in thirty years. Hot early and hot late, Evvie bellowed leather-lunged into the drowsy eleven-o'clock quiet, and hot in the middle.

'That so?' George asked.

'*What?*'

'*I said, "Is that so?"'* That was the other thing about Aunt Evvie; she got you shouting right along with her. A man could pop a blood vessel.

'*I should hope to smile and kiss a pig if it ain't!*' Aunt Evvie screamed. The ash of her cigarette fell on the shoulder of George Meara's uniform blouse, freshly dry-cleaned and just put on clean this morning; he brushed it off resignedly. Aunt Evvie leaned in the window of his car, all the better to bellow in his ear. Her breath smelled like sour cucumbers.

'*Fieldmice has all gone outta the root cellars! Tommy Neadeau seen deer out by Moosuntic Pond rubbin velvet off'n their antlers ere the first robin showed up! Grass under the snow when she melted! Green grass, Meara!*'

'That so, Evvie?' George replied, since some reply seemed necessary. He was getting a headache.

'*What?*'

'*THAT SO, AUNT EVVIE?*' George Mear screamed. Saliva flew from his lips.

'*Oh, ayuh!*' Aunt Evvie howled back contentedly. '*And I seen heat lightnin last night late! Bad sign, Meara! Early heat's a bad sign! Be people die of the heat this summer! It's gonna be a bad un!*'

'*I got to go, Aunt Evvie!*' George yelled. '*Got a Special Delivery for Stringer Beaulieu!*'

Aunt Evvie Chalmers threw her head back and cackled at the spring sky. She cackled until she was fit to choke and more cigarette ashes rolled down the front of her housedress. She spat the last quarter inch of cigarette out of her mouth, and it lay smoldering in the driveway by one of her old-lady shoes — a shoe as black as a stove and as tight as a corset; a shoe for the ages.

'*You got a Special Delivery for Frenchy Beaulieu? Why, he couldn't read the name on his own tombstone!*'

'*I got to go, Aunt Evvie!*' George said hastily, and threw his car in gear.

'*Frenchy Beaulieu is a stark natural-born fool if God ever made one!*' Aunt Evvie hollered, but by then she was hollering into George Meara's dust; he had made good his escape.

She stood there by her mailbox for a minute, watching

him go. There was no personal mail for her; these days there rarely was. Most of the people she knew who had been able to write were now dead. She would follow soon enough, she suspected. The oncoming summer gave her a bad feeling, a scary feeling. She could speak of the mice leaving the root cellars early, or of heat lightning in a spring sky, but she could not speak of the heat she sensed somewhere just over the horizon, crouched like a scrawny yet powerful beast with mangy fur and red, smoldering eyes; she could not speak of her dreams, which were hot and shadowless and thirsty; she could not speak of the morning when tears had come for no reason, tears that did not relieve but stung the eyes like August-mad sweat instead. She smelled lunacy in a wind that had not arrived.

'George Meara, you're an old fart,' Aunt Evvie said, giving the word a juicy Maine resonance which built it into something that was both cataclysmic and ludicrous: *faaaaaat*.

She began working her way back to the house, leaning on her *Boston Post* cane, which had been given her at a Town Hall ceremony for no more than the stupid accomplishment of growing old successfully. No wonder, she thought, the goddamned paper had gone broke.

She paused on her stoop, looking at a sky which was still spring-pure and pastel soft. Oh, but she sensed it coming: something hot. Something foul.

A year before that summer, when Vic Trenton's old Jaguar developed a distressing clunking sound somewhere inside the rear left wheel, it had been George Meara who recommended that he take it up to Joe Camber's Garage on the outskirts of Castle Rock. 'He's got a funny way of doing things for around here,' George told Vic that day as Vic stood by his mailbox. 'Tells you what the job's gonna cost, then he does the job, and then he charges you what he said it was gonna cost. Funny way to do business, huh?' And he drove away, leaving Vic to wonder if the mailman had been serious or if he (Vic) had just been on the receiving end of some obscure Yankee joke.

But he had called Camber, and one day in July (a much cooler July than the one which would follow a year later), he and Donna and Tad had driven out to Camber's place together. It really was far out; twice Vic had to stop and ask directions, and it was then that he began to call those farthest reaches of the township East Galoshes Corners.

He pulled into the Camber dooryard, the back wheel clunking louder than ever. Tad, then three, was sitting on Donna Trenton's lap, laughing up at her; a ride in Daddy's 'no-top' always put him in a fine mood, and Donna was feeling pretty fine herself.

A boy of eight or nine was standing in the yard, hitting an old baseball with an even older baseball bat. The ball would travel through the air, strike the side of the barn, which Vic assumed was also Mr Camber's garage, and then roll most of the way back.

'Hi,' the boy said. 'Are you Mr Trenton?'

'That's right,' Vic said.

'I'll get my dad,' the boy said, and went into the barn.

The three Trentons got out, and Vic walked around to the back of his Jag and squatted by the bad wheel, not feeling very confident. Perhaps he should have tried to nurse the car into Portland after all. The situation out here didn't look very promising; Camber didn't even have a sign hung out.

His meditations were broken by Donna, calling his name nervously. And then: 'Oh my *God*, Vic—'

He got up quickly and saw a huge dog emerging from the barn. For one absurd moment he wondered if it really was a dog, or maybe some strange and ugly species of pony. Then, as the dog padded out of the shadows of the barn's mouth, he saw its sad eyes and realized it was a Saint Bernard.

Donna had impulsively snatched up Tad and retreated toward the hood of the Jag, but Tad was struggling impatiently in her arms, trying to get down.

'Want to see the doggy, Mom . . . want to see the *doggy*!'

Donna cast a nervous glance at Vic, who shrugged, also uneasy. Then the boy came back and ruffled the dog's head as he approached Vic. The dog wagged a tail that was absolutely huge, and Tad redoubled his struggles.

'You can let him down, ma'am,' the boy said politely. 'Cujo likes kids. He won't hurt him.' And then, to Vic: 'My dad's coming right out. He's washing his hands.'

'All right,' Vic said. 'That's one hell of a big dog, son. Are you sure he's safe?'

'He's safe,' the boy agreed, but Vic found himself moving up beside his wife as his son, incredibly small, toddled toward the dog. Cujo stood with his head cocked, that great brush of a tail waving slowly back and forth.

'Vic—' Donna began.

'It's all right,' Vic said, thinking, *I hope*. The dog looked big enough to swallow the Tadder in a single bite.

Tad stopped for a moment, apparently doubtful. He and the dog looked at each other.

'Doggy?' Tad said.

'Cujo,' Camber's boy said, walking over to Tad. 'His name's Cujo.'

'Cujo,' Tad said, and the dog came to him and began to lick his face in great, goodnatured, slobbery swipes that had Tad giggling and trying to fend him off. He turned back to his mother and father, laughing the way he did when one of them was tickling him. He took a step toward them and his feet tangled in each other. He fell down, and suddenly the dog was moving toward him, over him, and Vic, who had his arm around Donna's waist, felt his wife's gasp as well as he heard it. He started to move forward . . . and then stopped.

Cujo's teeth had clamped on the back of Tad's Spider-Man T-shirt. He pulled the boy up – for a moment Tad looked like a kitten in its mother's mouth – and set the boy on his feet.

Tad ran back to his mother and father. 'Like the doggy! Mom! Dad! I like the doggy!'

Camber's boy was watching this with mild amusement, his hands stuffed into the pockets of his jeans.

'Sure, it's a great dog,' Vic said. He was amused, but his heart was still beating fast. For just one moment there he had really believed that the dog was going to bite off Tad's head like a lollipop. 'It's a Saint Bernard, Tad,' he said.

'Saint . . . Bennart!' Tad cried, and ran back toward Cujo, who was now sitting outside the mouth of the barn like a small mountain. 'Cujo! *Coooojo!*'

Donna tensed beside Vic again. 'Oh, Vic, do you think –'

But now Tad was with Cujo again, first hugging him extravagantly and then looking closely at his face. With Cujo sitting down (his tail thumping on the gravel, his tongue lolling out pinkly), Tad could almost look into the dog's eyes by standing on tiptoe.

'I think they're fine,' Vic said.

Tad had now put one of his small hands into Cujo's mouth and was peering in like the world's smallest dentist. That gave Vic another uneasy moment, but then Tad was running back to them again. 'Doggy's got teeth,' he told Vic.

'Yes,' Vic said. 'Lots of teeth.'

He turned to the boy, meaning to ask him where he had come up with that name, but then Joe Camber was coming out of the barn, wiping his hands on a piece of waste so he could shake without getting Vic greasy.

Vic was pleasantly surprised to find that Camber knew exactly what he was doing. He listened carefully to the clunking sound as he and Vic drove down to the house at the bottom of the hill and then back up to Camber's place.

'Wheel bearing's going,' Camber said briefly. 'You're lucky it ain't froze up on you already.'

'Can you fix it?' Vic asked.

'Oh, ayuh. Fix it right now if you don't mind hanging around for a couple of hours.'

'That'd be all right, I guess,' Vic said. He looked toward Tad and the dog. Tad had gotten the baseball Camber's son had been hitting. He would throw it as far as he could (which wasn't very far), and the Cambers' Saint Bernard

18

would obediently get it and bring it back to Tad. The ball was looking decidedly slobbery. 'Your dog is keeping my son amused.'

'Cujo likes kids,' Camber agreed. 'You want to drive your car into the barn, Mr Trenton?'

The doctor will see you now, Vic thought, amused, and drove the Jag in. As it turned out, the job only took an hour and a half and Camber's price was so reasonable it was startling.

And Tad ran through that cool, overcast afternoon, calling the dog's name over and over again: '*Cujo . . . Cooojo . . . heeere, Cujo . . .*' Just before they left, Camber's boy, whose name was Brett, actually lifted Tad onto Cujo's back and held him around the waist while Cujo padded obediently up and down the gravel dooryard twice. As it passed Vic, the dog caught his eye . . . and Vic would have sworn it was laughing.

Just three days after George Meara's bellowed conversation with Aunt Evvie Chalmers, a little girl who was exactly Tad Trenton's age stood up from her place at the breakfast table – said breakfast table being in the breakfast nook of a tidy little house in Iowa City, Iowa – and announced: 'Oh, Mamma, I don't feel so good. I feel like I'm going to be sick.'

Her mother looked around, not exactly surprised. Two days before, Marcy's bigger brother had been sent from school with a raging case of stomach flu. Brock was all right now, but he had spent a lousy twenty-four hours, his body enthusiastically throwing off ballast from both ends.

'Are you sure, honey?' Marcy's mother said.

'Oh, I—' Marcy moaned loudly and lurched toward the downstairs hall, her hands laced over her stomach. Her mother followed her, saw Marcy buttonhook into the bathroom, and thought, *Oh, boy, here we go again. If I don't catch this it'll be a miracle.*

She heard the retching sounds begin and turned into the bathroom her mind already occupied with the details: clear liquids, bed rest, the chamber-pot, some books; Brock could take the portable TV up to her room when he got back from school and –

She looked, and these thoughts were driven from her mind with the force of a roundhouse slap.

The toilet bowl where her four-year-old daughter had vomited was full of blood; blood splattered the white porcelain lip of the bowl; blood beaded the tiles.

'Oh, Mommy, I don't feel good—'

Her daughter turned, her daughter turned, turned, and there was blood all over her mouth, it was down her chin, it was matting her blue sailor dress, blood, oh dear God dear Jesus Joseph and Mary so much *blood* –

'Mommy—'

And her daughter did it again, a huge bloody mess flying from her mouth to patter down everywhere like sinister rain, and then Marcy's mother gathered her up and ran with her, ran for the phone in the kitchen to dial the emergency unit.

Cujo knew he was too old to chase rabbits.

He wasn't *old*; no, not even for a dog. But at five, he was well past his puppyhood, when even a butterfly had been enough to set off an arduous chase through the woods and meadows behind the house and barn. He was five, and if he had been a human, he would have been entering the youngest stage of middle age.

But it was the sixteenth of June, a beautiful early morning, the dew still on the grass. The heat Aunt Evvie had predicted to George Meara had indeed arrived – it was the warmest early June in years – and by two that afternoon Cujo would be lying in the dusty dooryard (or in the barn, if THE MAN would let him in, which he sometimes did when he was drinking, which was most of the time these days), panting under the hot sun. But that was later.

And the rabbit, which was large, brown, and plump, didn't have the slightest idea Cujo was there, down near the end of the north field, a mile from the house. The wind was blowing the wrong way for Br'er Rabbit.

Cujo worked toward the rabbit, out for sport rather than meat. The rabbit munched happily away at new clover that would be baked and brown under the relentless sun a month later. If he had only covered half the original distance between himself and the rabbit when the rabbit saw him and bolted, Cujo would have let it go. But he had actually got to within fifteen yards of it when the rabbit's head and ears came up. For a moment the rabbit did not move at all; it was a frozen rabbit sculpture with black walleyes bulging comically. Then it was off.

Barking furiously, Cujo gave chase. The rabbit was very small and Cujo was very big, but the *possibility* of the thing put an extra ration of energy in Cujo's legs. He actually got close enough to paw at the rabbit. The rabbit zigged. Cujo came around more ponderously, his claws digging black meadow dirt, losing some ground at first, making it up quickly. Birds took wing at his heavy, chopping bark; if it is possible for a dog to grin, Cujo was grinning then. The rabbit zagged, then made straight across the north field. Cujo pelted after it, already suspecting this was one race he wasn't going to win.

But he tried hard, and he was gaining on the rabbit again when it dropped into a small hole in the side of a small and easy hill. The hole was overgrown by long grasses, and Cujo didn't hesitate. He lowered his big tawny body into a kind of furry projectile and let his forward motion carry him in . . . where he promptly stuck like a cork in a bottle.

Joe Camber had owned Seven Oaks Farm out at the end of Town Road No. 3 for seventeen years, but he had no idea this hole was here. He surely would have discovered it if farming was his business, but it wasn't. There was no livestock in the big red barn; it was his garage and autobody shop. His son Brett rambled the fields and woods behind the home place frequently, but he had never noticed the hole either, although on several occasions he had nearly put his foot in it, which might have earned him a broken ankle. On clear days the hole could pass for a shadow; on cloudy days, overgrown with grass as it was, it disappeared altogether.

John Mousam, the farm's previous owner, had known about the hole but had never thought to mention it to Joe Camber when Joe bought the place in 1963. He might have mentioned it, as a caution, when Joe and his wife, Charity, had their son in 1970, but by then the cancer had carried old John off.

It was just as well Brett had never found it. There's nothing in the world quite so interesting to a small boy as a hole in the ground, and this one opened on a small natural limestone cave. It was about twenty feet deep at its deepest, and it would have been quite possible for a small squirty boy to eel his way in, slide to the bottom, and then find it impossible to get out. It had happened to other small animals in the past. The cave's limestone surface made a good slide but a bad climb, and its bottom was littered with bones: a woodchuck, a skunk, a couple of chipmunks, a couple of squirrels, and a housecat. The housecat's name had been Mr Clean. The Cambers had lost him two years before and assumed he had been hit by a car or had just run off. But here he was, along with the bones of the good-sized fieldmouse he had chased inside.

Cujo's rabbit had rolled and slid all the way to the bottom and now quivered there, ears up and nose vibrating like a tuning fork, as Cujo's furious barking filled the place. The echoes made it sound as though there was a whole pack of dogs up there.

The small cave had also attracted bats from time to time – never many, because the cave was only a small one, but its rough ceiling made a perfect place for them to roost upside down and snooze the daylight away. The bats were another good reason that Brett Camber had been lucky, especially this year. This year the brown insectivorous bats inhabiting the small cave were crawling with a particularly virulent strain of rabies.

Cujo had stuck at the shoulders. He dug furiously with his back legs to no effect at all. He could have reversed and pulled himself back out, but for now he still wanted the rabbit. He sensed it was trapped, his for the taking. His eyes were not particularly keen, his large body blocked out almost all the light anyway, and he had no sense of the drop just beyond his front paws. He could smell damp, and he could smell bat guano, both old and fresh . . . but most important of all, he could smell rabbit. Hot and tasty. Dinner is served.

His barking roused the bats. They were terrified. Something had invaded their home. They flew en masse toward the exit, squeaking. But their sonar recorded a puzzling and distressing fact: the entrance was no longer there. The predator was where the entrance had been.

They wheeled and swooped in the darkness, their membranous wings sounding like small pieces of clothing – diapers, perhaps – flapping from a line in a gusty wind. Below them, the rabbit cringed and hoped for the best.

Cujo felt several of the bats flutter against the third of him that had managed to get into the hole, and he became frightened. He didn't like their scent or their sound; he didn't like the odd heat that seemed to emanate from them. He barked louder and snapped at the things that were wheeling and squeaking around his head. His snapping jaws closed on one brown-black wing. Bones thinner than those in a baby's hand crunched. The bat slashed and bit at him, slicing open the skin of the dog's sensitive muzzle in a long, curving wound that was shaped like a question mark. A moment later it went skittering and cartwheeling down the limestone slope, already dying. But the damage had been done; a bite from a rabid animal is most serious around the head, for rabies is a disease of the central nervous system. Dogs, more susceptible than their human masters, cannot even hope for complete protection from the inactivated-virus vaccine which every veterinarian administers. And Cujo had never had a single rabies shot in his life.

Not knowing this, but knowing that the unseen thing he had bitten had tasted foul and horrible, Cujo decided the game was not worth the candle. With a tremendous yank of his shoulders he pulled himself out of the hole, causing a little avalanche of dirt. He shook himself, and more dirt and smelly crumbled limestone flew from his pelt. Blood dripped from his muzzle. He sat down, tilted his head skyward, and uttered a single low howl.

The bats exited their hole in a small brown cloud, whirled confusedly in the bright June sunshine for a couple of seconds, and then went back in to roost. They were brainless things, and within the course of two or three minutes they had forgotten all about the barking interloper and were sleeping again, hung from their heels with their wings wrapped around their ratty little bodies like the shawls of old women.

Cujo trotted away. He shook himself again. He pawed helplessly at his muzzle. The blood was already clotting, drying to a cake, but it hurt. Dogs have a sense of self-consciousness that is far out of proportion to their intelligence, and Cujo was disgusted with himself. He didn't want to go home. If he went home, one of his trinity — THE MAN, THE WOMAN, or THE BOY — would see that he had done something to himself. It was possible that one of them might call him BADDOG. And at this particular moment he certainly considered himself to be a BADDOG.

So instead of going home, Cujo went down to the stream that separated Camber land from the property of Gary Pervier, the Cambers' nearest neighbour. He waded upstream; he drank deeply; he rolled over in the water, trying to get rid of the nasty taste in his mouth, trying to get rid of the dirt and the watery green stink of limestone, trying to get rid of that BADDOG feeling.

Little by little, he began to feel better. He came out of the stream and shook himself, the spray of water forming a momentary rainbow of breathless clarity in the air.

The BADDOG feeling was fading, and so was the pain in his nose. He started up toward the house to see if THE BOY might be around. He had gotten used to the big yellow schoolbus that came to pick THE BOY up every morning and which dropped him back off again in midafternoon, but this last week the schoolbus had not shown up with its flashing eyes and its yelling cargo of children. THE BOY was always at home. Usually he was out in the barn, doing things with THE MAN. Maybe the yellow schoolbus had come again today. Maybe not. He would see. He had forgotten about the hole and the nasty taste of the batwing. His nose hardly hurt at all now.

Cujo breasted his way easily through the high grass of the north field, driving up an occasional bird but not bothering to give chase. He had had his chase for the day, and his body remembered even if his brain did not. He was a Saint Bernard in his prime, five years old, nearly two hundred pounds in weight, and now, on the morning of June 16, 1980, he was pre-rabid.

*   *   *

Seven days later and thirty miles from Seven Oaks Farm in Castle Rock, two men met in a downtown Portland restaurant called the Yellow Submarine. The Sub featured a large selection of hero sandwiches, pizzas, and Dagwoods in Lebanese pouches. There was a pinball machine in the back. There was a sign over the counter saying that if you could eat two Yellow Sub Nightmares, you ate free; below that, in parentheses, the codicil IF YOU PUKE YOU PAY had been added.

Ordinarily there was nothing Vic Trenton would have liked better than one of the Yellow Sub's meatball heroes, but he suspected he would get nothing from today's but a really good case of acid burn.

'Looks like we're going to lose the ball, doesn't it?' Vic said to the other man, who was regarding a Danish ham with a marked lack of enthusiasm. The other man was Roger Breakstone, and when he looked at food without enthusiasm, you knew that some sort of cataclysm was at hand. Roger weighed two hundred and seventy pounds and had no lap when he sat down. Once, when the two of them had been in bed with a kids-at-camp case of the giggles, Donna had told Vic she thought Roger's lap had been shot off in Vietnam.

'It looks piss-poor,' Roger admitted. 'It looks so fucking piss-poor you wouldn't believe it, Victor old buddy.'

'You really think making this trip will solve anything?'

'Maybe not,' Roger said, 'but we're going to lose the Sharp account for sure if we don't go. Maybe we can salvage something. Work our way back in.' He bit into his sandwich.

'Closing up for ten days is going to hurt us.'

'You think we're not hurting now?'

'Sure, we're hurting. But we've got those Book Folks spots to shoot down at Kennebunk Beach—'

'Lisa can handle that.'

'I'm not entirely convinced that Lisa can handle her own love-life, let alone the Book Folks spots,' Vic said. 'But even supposing she *can* handle it, the Yor Choice Blueberries series is still hanging fire . . . Casco Bank and Trust . . . and you're supposed to meet with the head honcho from the Main Realtors' Association—'

'Huh-uh, that's yours.'

'Fuck you it's mine,' Vic said. 'I break up every time I think of those red pants and white shoes. I kept wanting to look in the closet to see if I could find the guy a sandwich board.'

'It doesn't matter, and you know it doesn't. None of them bills a tenth of what Sharp bills. What else can I say? You know Sharp and the kid are going to want to talk to both of us. Do I book you a seat or not?'

The thought of ten days, five in Boston and five in New York, gave Vic a mild case of the cold sweats. He and Roger had both worked for the Ellison Agency in New York for six years. Vic now had a home in Castle Rock. Roger and Althea Breakstone lived in neighboring Bridgton, about fifteen miles away.

For Vic, it had been a case of never even wanting to look back. He felt he had never come fully alive, had never really known what he was for, until he and Donna moved to Maine. And now he had a morbid sense that New York had only been waiting these last three years to get him in its clutches again. The plane would skid off the runway coming in and be engulfed in a roaring firecloud of hi-test jet fuel. Or there would be a crash on the Triborough Bridge, their Checker crushed into a bleeding yellow accordion. A mugger would use his gun instead of just waving it. A gas main would explode and he would be decapitated by a manhole cover flying through the air like a deadly ninety-pound Frisbee. Something. If he went back, the city would kill him.

'Rog,' he said, putting down his meatball sandwich after one small bite, 'have you ever thought that it might not be the end of the world if we *did* lose the Sharp account?'

'The world will go on,' Roger said, pouring a Busch down the side of a pilsner glass, 'but will we? Me, I've got seventeen years left on a twenty-year mortgage and twin girls who have their hearts set on Bridgton Academy. You've got your own mortgage, your own kid, plus that old Jag sportster that's going to half-buck you to death.'

'Yes, but the local economy—'

'The local economy *sucks!*' Roger exclaimed violently, and set his pilsner glass down with a bang.

A party of four at the next table, three in UMP tennis shirts and one wearing a faded T-shirt with the legend DARTH VADER IS GAY written across the front, began to applaud.

Roger waved a hand at them impatiently and leaned toward Vic. 'We're not going to make it happen doing campaigns for Yor Choice Blueberries and the Main Realtors, and you know it. If we lose the Sharp account, we're going to go under without a ripple. On the other hand, if we can keep even a piece of Sharp over the next two years, we'll be in line for some of the Department of Tourism budget, maybe even a crack at the state lottery if they don't mismanage it into oblivion by then. Juicy pies, Vic. We can wave so long to Sharp and their crappy cereals and there's happy endings all around. The big bad wolf has to go somewhere else to get his dinner; these little piggies are home free.'

'All contingent on us being able to save something,' Vic said, 'which is about as likely as the Cleveland Indians winning the World Series this fall.'

'I think we better try, buddy.'

Vic sat silent, looking at his congealing sandwich and thinking. It was totally unfair, but he could live with unfairness. What really hurt was the whole situation's crazed absurdity. It had blown up out of a clear sky like a killer tornado that lays a zigzagging trail of destruction and then disappears. He and Roger and Ad Worx itself were apt to be numbered among the fatalities no matter what they did; he could read it on Roger's round face, which had not looked so pallidly serious since he and Althea had lost their boy, Timothy, to the crib-death syndrome when the infant was only nine days old. Three weeks after that happened, Roger had broken down and wept, his hands plastered to his fat face in a kind of terrible hopeless sorrow that had squeezed Vic's heart into his throat. That had been bad. But the incipient panic he saw in Roger's eyes now was bad, too.

Tornadoes blew out of nowhere in the advertising business from time to time. A bit outfit like the Ellison Agency, which billed in the millions, could withstand them. A little one like Ad Worx just couldn't. They had been carrying one basket with a lot of little eggs in it and another basket with one big egg – the Sharp account – and it now remained to be seen whether the big egg had been lost entirely or if it could at least be scrambled. None of it had been their fault, but ad agencies make lovely whipping boys.

Vic and Roger had teamed naturally together ever since their first joint effort at the Ellison Agency, six years ago. Vic, tall and skinny and rather quiet, had formed the perfect yin for Roger Breakstone's fat, happy, and extroverted yang. They had clicked on a personal basis and on a professional one. That first assignment had been a minor one, to submit a magazine ad campaign for United Cerebral Palsy.

They had come up with a stark black-and-white ad that showed a small boy in huge, cruel leg braces standing in foul territory by the first-base line of a Little League ballfield. A New York Mets cap was perched on his head, and his expression – Roger had always maintained that it had been the boy's expression which sold the ad – wasn't sad at all; it was simply dreamy. Almost happy, in fact. The copy read simply: BILLY BELLAMY IS NEVER GOING TO BAT CLEANUP. Beneath: BILLY HAS CEREBRAL PALSY. Beneath that, smaller type: *Give Us a Hand, Huh?*

CP donations had taken a noticeable leap. Good for them, good for Vic and Roger. The team of Trenton and Breakstone had been off and running. Half a dozen successful campaigns had followed, Vic dealing most commonly with broad-scope conception, Roger dealing with actual execution.

For the Sony Corporation, a picture of a man sitting

cross-legged on the median strip of a sixteen-lane super-highway in a business suit, a big Sony radio on his lap, a seraphic smile on his kisser. The copy read: POLICE BAND, THE ROLLING STONES, VIVALDI, MIKE WALLACE, THE KINGSTON TRIO, PAUL HARVEY, PATTI SMITH, JERRY FALWELL. And below that: HELLO, LA!

For the Voit people, makers of swim equipment, an ad that showed a man who was the utter antithesis of the Miami beachboy. Standing arrogantly hipshot on the golden beach of some tropical paradise, the model was a fifty-year-old man with tattoos, a beer belly, slab-muscled arms and legs, and a puckered scar high across one thigh. In his arms this battered soldier of fortune was cradling a pair of Voit swimfins. MISTER, the copy for this one read, I DIVE FOR A LIVING. I DON'T MESS AROUND. There was a lot more underneath, stuff Roger always referred to as the blah-blah, but the copy set in boldface was the real hooker. Vic and Roger had wanted it to read I DON'T SCREW AROUND, but they hadn't been able to sell the Voit people on that. Pity, Vic was fond of saying over drinks. They could have sold a lot more swimfins.

Then there was Sharp.

The Sharp Company of Cleveland had stood twelfth in the Great American Bakestakes when old man Sharp reluctantly came to the Ellison Agency in New York after more than twenty years with a hometown ad agency. Sharp had been bigger than Nabisco before World War II, the old man was fond of pointing out. His son was just as fond of pointing out that World War II had ended thirty years ago.

The account — on a six-month trial basis at first — had been handed over to Vic Trenton and Roger Breakstone.

At the end of the trial period, Sharp had vaulted from twelfth in the cookies-cakes-and-cereals market to ninth. A year later, when Vic and Roger pulled up stakes and moved to Maine to open up their own business, the Sharp Company had climbed to seventh.

Their campaign had been a sweeping one. For Sharp Cookies, Vic and Roger had developed the Cookie Sharpshooter, a bumbling Western peace officer whose six-guns shot cookies instead of bullets, courtesy of the special-effects people – Chocka Chippers in some spots, Ginger Snappies in others, Oh Those Oatmeals in still others. The spots always ended with the Sharpshooter standing sadly in a pile of cookies with his guns out. 'Well, the bad guys got away,' he'd tell millions of Americans every day or so, 'but I got the cookies. Best cookies in the West . . . or anywhere else, I reckon.' The Sharpshooter bites into a cookie. His expression suggests that he is experiencing the gastronomic equivalent of a boy's first orgasm. Fadeout.

For the prepared cakes – sixteen different varieties ranging from pound to crumb to cheese – there was what Vic called the George and Gracie spot. We fade in on George and Gracie leaving a posh dinner party where the buffet table groans with every possible delicacy. We dissolve to a dingy little cold-water flat, starkly lighted. George is sitting at a plain kitchen table with a checked tablecloth. Gracie takes a Sharp Pound Cake (or Cheese Cake or Crumb Cake) from the freezer of their old refrigerator and sets it on the table. They are both still in their evening clothes. They smile into each other's eyes with warmth and love and understanding, two people who are utterly in sync with each other. Fade to these words, on black: SOMETIMES ALL YOU WANT IS A SHARP CAKE. Not a word spoken in the entire spot. That one had won a Clio.

As had the Sharp Cereal Professor, hailed in the trades as 'the most responsible advertisement ever produced for children's programming.' Vic and Roger had considered it their crowning achievement . . . but now it was the Sharp Cereal Professor who had come back to haunt them.

Played by a character actor in late middle age, the Sharp Cereal Professor was a low-key and daringly adult advertisement in a sea of animated kiddie-vid ads selling bubble gum, adventure toys, dolls, action figures . . . and rival cereals.

The ad faded in on a deserted fourth- or fifth-grade classroom, a scene Saturday-morning viewers of *The Bugs Bunny/Roadrunner Hour* and *The Drac Pack* could readily identify with. The Sharp Cereal Professor was wearing a suit, a V-necked sweater, and a shirt open at the collar. Both in looks and in speech he was mildly authoritarian; Vic and Roger had talked to some forty teachers and half a dozen child psychiatrists and had discovered that this was the sort of parental role model that the majority of kids feel most comfortable with, and the sort that so few actually have in their homes.

The Cereal Professor was sitting on a teacher's desk, hinting at some informality – the soul of a real pal hidden somewhere beneath that gray-green tweed, the young viewer might assume – but he spoke slowly and gravely. He did not command. He did not talk down. He did not wheedle. He did not cajole or extol. He spoke to the millions of T-shirted, cereal-slurping, cartoon-watching Saturday-morning viewers as though they were *real people*.

CUJO

'Good morning, children,' the Professor said quietly.
'This is a commercial for cereal. Listen to me carefully,
please. I know a lot about cereals, because I'm the Sharp
Cereal Professor. Sharp Cereals – Twinkles, Cocoa Bears,
Bran-16, and Sharp All-Grain Blend – are the best-tasting
cereals in America. And they're good for you.' A beat of
silence, and then the Sharp Cereal Professor grinned . . .
and when he grinned, you *knew* there was the soul of a
real pal in there. 'Believe me, because I know. Your mom
knows; I just thought you'd like to know too.'

A young man came into the ad at that point, and he
handed the Sharp Cereal Professor a bowl of Twinkles or
Cocoa Bears or whatever. The Sharp Cereal Professor dug
in, then looked straight into every living room in the
country and said: 'Nope, nothing wrong here.'

Old man Sharp hadn't cared for that last line, or
the idea that anything *could* be wrong with one of his
cereals. Eventually Vic and Roger had worn him down,
but not with rational arguments. Making ads was not a
rational business. You often did what felt right, but that
didn't mean you could understand *why* it felt right. Both
Vic and Roger felt that the Professor's final line had a
power which was both simple and enormous. Coming
from the Cereal Professor, it was the final, total comfort,
a complete security blanket. I'll never hurt you, it implied.
In a world where parents get divorced, where older kids
sometimes beat the shit out of you for no rational reason,
where the rival Little League team sometimes racks the
crap out of your pitching, where the good guys don't
always win like they do on TV, where you don't always
get invited to the *good* birthday party, in a world where

35

so *much* goes wrong, there will always be Twinkles and Cocoa Bears and All-Grain Blend, and they'll always taste good. 'Nope, nothing wrong here.'

With a little help from Sharp's son (later on, Roger said, you would have believed the kid thought the ad up and wrote it himself), the Cereal Professor concept was approved and saturated Saturday-morning TV, plus such weekly syndicated programs as *Star Blazers, U.S. of Archie, Hogan's Heroes*, and *Gilligan's Island*. Sharp Cereals surged even more powerfully than the rest of the Sharp line, and the Cereal Professor became an American institution. His tag line, 'Nope, nothing wrong here,' became one of those national catch phrases, meaning roughly the same thing as 'Stay cool' and 'No sweat'.

When Vic and Roger decided to go their own way, they had observed strict protocol and had not gone to any of their previous clients until their connections with the Ellison Agency were formally – and amicably – severed. Their first six months in Portland had been a scary, pressure-cooker time for all of them. Vic and Donna's boy, Tad, was only a year old. Donna, who missed New York badly, was by turns sullen, petulant, and just plain scared. Roger had an old ulcer – a battle scar from his years in the Big Apple advertising wars – and when he and Althea lost the baby the ulcer had flared up again, turning him into a closet Gelusil chugger. Althea bounced back as well as possible under the circumstances, Vic thought; it was Donna who pointed out to him that placid Althea's single weak drink before dinner had turned into two before and three after. The two couples had vacationed in Maine, separately and together, but neither Vic nor Roger had realized how many

36

doors are initially closed to folks who have moved in, as Mainers say, from 'outta state'.

They would indeed have gone under, as Roger pointed out, if Sharp hadn't decided to stay with them. And at the company's Cleveland headquarters, positions had done an ironic flip-flop. Now it was the old man who wanted to stick with Vic and Roger and it was the kid (by this time forty years old) who wanted to jettison them, arguing with some logic that it would be madness to hand their account over to a two-bit ad agency six hundred miles north of the New York pulsebeat. The fact that Ad Worx was affiliated with a New York market-analysis firm cut zero ice with the kid, as it had cut zero ice with the other firms for which they had put together campaigns in the past few years.

'If loyalty was toilet paper,' Roger had said bitterly, 'we'd be hard-pressed to wipe our asses, old buddy.'

But Sharp had come along, providing the margin they had so desperately needed. 'We made do with an ad agency here in town for forty years,' old man Sharp said, 'and if those two boys want to move out of that Christless city, they're just showing good old common sense.'

That was that. The old man had spoken. The kid shut up. And for the last two and a half years, the Cookie Sharpshooter had gone on shooting, George and Gracie had gone on eating Sharp Cakes in their cold-water flat, and the Sharp Cereal Professor had gone on telling kids that there was nothing wrong here. Actual spot production was handled by a small independent studio in Boston, the New York market-analysis firm went on doing its thing competently, and three or four times a year either Vic or

Roger flew to Cleveland to confer with Carroll Sharp and his kid – said kid now going decidedly gray around the temples. All the rest of the client–agency intercourse was handled by the U.S. Post Office and Ma Bell. The process was perhaps strange, certainly cumbersome, but it seemed to work fine.

Then along came Red Razberry Zingers.

Vic and Roger had known about Zingers for some time, of course, although it had only gone on the general market some two months ago, in April of 1980. Most of the Sharp cereals were lightly sweetened or not sweetened at all. All-Grain Blend, Sharp's entry in the 'natural' cereal arena, had been quite successful. Red Razberry Zingers, however, was aimed at a segment of the market with a sweeter tooth: at those prepared-cereal eaters who bought such cereals as Count Chocula, Frankenberry, Lucky Charms, and similar pre-sweetened breakfast foods which were somewhere in the twilight zone between cereal and candy.

In the late summer and early fall of 1979, Zingers had been successfully test-marketed in Boise, Idaho, Scranton, Pennsylvania, and in Roger's adopted Maine hometown of Bridgton. Roger had told Vic with a shudder that he wouldn't let the twins near it with a ten-foot pole (although he had been pleased when Althea told him the kids had clamored for it when they saw it shelved at Gigeure's Market). 'It's got more sugar than whole grain in it, and it looks like the side of a firebarn.'

Vic had nodded and replied innocently enough, with no sense of prophecy, 'The first time I looked in one of those boxes, I thought it was full of blood.'

* * *

38

CUJO

'So what do you think?' Roger repeated. He had made it halfway through his sandwich as Vic reviewed the dismal train of events in his mind. He was becoming more and more sure that in Cleveland old man Sharp and his aging kid were looking again to shoot the messenger for the message.

'Guess we better try.'

Roger clapped him on the shoulder. 'My man,' he said. 'Now eat up.'

But Vic wasn't hungry.

The two of them had been invited to Cleveland to attend an 'emergency meeting' that was to be held three weeks after the Fourth of July – a good many of the Sharp regional sales managers and executives were vacationing, and it would take at least that long to get them all together. One of the items on the agenda had to do directly with Ad Worx: 'an assessment of the association to this point,' the letter had said. Which meant, Vic assumed, that the kid was using the Zingers debacle to dump them at last.

About three weeks after Red Razberry Zingers went national, enthusiastically – if gravely – pitched by the Sharp Cereal Professor ('Nope, nothing wrong here'), the first mother had taken her little one to the hospital, nearly hysterical and sure the child was bleeding internally. The little girl, victim of nothing more serious than a low-grade virus, had thrown up what her mother had first believed to be a huge amount of blood.

Nope, nothing wrong here.

That had been in Iowa City, Iowa. The following day there had been seven more cases. The day after, twenty-four. In all cases the parents of children afflicted with vomiting or diarrhea had rushed the kids to the hospital, believing them to be suffering internal bleeding. After that, the cases had skyrocketed – first into the hundreds, then into the thousands. In none of these cases had the vomiting and/or diarrhea been caused by the cereal, but that was generally overlooked in the growing furor.

Nope, not a single thing wrong here.

The cases had spread west to east. The problem was the food dye that gave Zingers its zingy red color. The dye itself was harmless, but that was also mostly overlooked. Something had gone wrong, and instead of assimilating the red dye, the human body simply passed it along. The goofed-up dye had only gotten into one batch of cereal, but it had been a whopper of a batch. A doctor told Vic that if a child who had just died after ingesting a big bowl of Red Razberry Zingers were the subject of an autopsy, the postmortem would reveal a digestive tract as red as a stop sign. The effect was strictly temporary, but that had been overlooked too.

Roger wanted them to go down with all guns firing, if they were to go down. He had proposed marathon conferences with the Image-Eye people in Boston, who actually did the spots. He wanted to talk with the Sharp Cereal Professor himself, who had gotten so involved with his role that he was mentally and emotionally torn up over what had happened. Then on to New York, to talk to the marketing people. Most important, it would be almost two weeks at Boston's Ritz-Carlton and at New York's UN Plaza, two weeks Vic and Roger would spend mostly in each other's hip pockets, digesting the input and brainstorming as they had in the old days. What Roger hoped would come out of it was a rebound campaign that would blow the socks off both old man Sharp and the kid. Instead of going to Cleveland with their necks shaved for the drop of the guillotine blade, they would show up with battle plans drawn to reverse the effects of the Zingers snafu. That was the theory. In practice, they both realized that their chances were about as good as they were for a pitcher who deliberately sets out to throw a no-hitter.

Vic had other problems. For the last eight months or so, he had sensed that he and his wife were drifting slowly apart. He still loved her, and he damn near idolized Tad, but things had gone from a little uneasy to bad, and he sensed that there were worse things – and worse times – waiting. Just over the horizon, maybe. This trip, a grand tour from Boston to New York to Cleveland, coming at what should have been their at-home season, their doing-things-together season, was maybe not such a hot idea. When he looked at her face lately he saw a stranger lurking just below its planes and angles and curves.

And the question. It played over and over in his mind on nights when he wasn't able to sleep, and such nights had become more common lately. Had she taken a lover? They sure didn't sleep together much any more. Had she done it? He hoped it wasn't so, but what did he think? Really? Tell the truth, Mr Trenton, or you'll be forced to pay the consequences.

He wasn't sure. He didn't want to be sure. He was afraid that if he became sure, the marriage would end. He was still completely gone on her, had never so much as considered an extramarital fling, and he could forgive her much. But not being cuckolded in his own home. You don't want to wear those horns; they grow out of your ears, and kids laugh at the funny man on the street. He –

'What?' Vic said, emerging from his reverie. 'I missed it, Rog.'

'I said, "That goddam red cereal." Unquote. My exact words.'

'Yeah,' Vic said. 'I'll drink to that.'

Roger raised his pilsner glass. 'Do it,' he said.

Vic did.

Gary Pervier sat out on his weedy front lawn at the bottom of Seven Oaks Hill on Town Road No. 3 about a week after Vic and Roger's depressing luncheon meeting at the Yellow Sub, drinking a screwdriver that was 25 percent Bird's Eye frozen orange juice and 75 percent Popov vodka. He sat in the shade of an elm that was in the last stages of rampant Dutch elm disease, his bottom resting against the frayed straps of a Sears, Roebuck mail-order lawn chair that was in the last stages of useful service. He was drinking Popov because Popov was cheap. Gary had purchased a large supply of it in New Hampshire, where booze was cheaper, on his last liquor run. Popov was cheap in Maine, but it was *dirt* cheap in New Hampshire, a state which took its stand for the finer things in life – a fat state lottery, cheap booze, cheap cigarettes, and tourist attractions like Santa's Village and Six-Gun City. New Hampshire was a great old place. The lawn chair had slowly settled into his run-to-riot lawn, digging deep divots. The house behind the lawn had also run to riot; it was a gray, paint-peeling, roof-sagging shambles. Shutters hung. The chimney hooked at the sky like a drunk trying to get up from a tumble. Shingles blown off in the previous winter's last big storm still hung limply from some of the branches of the dying elm. It ain't the Taj Mahal, Gary sometimes said, but who gives a shit?

Gary was, on this swelteringly hot late-June day, as drunk as a coot. This was not an uncommon state of affairs with him. He did not know Roger Breakstone from shit. He did not know Vic Trenton from shit. He didn't know Donna Trenton from shit, and if he had known her, he wouldn't have given a shit if the visiting team was throwing line drives into her catcher's mitt. He did know the Cambers and their dog Cujo; the family lived up the hill, at the end of Town Road No. 3. He and Joe Camber did a good deal of drinking together, and in a rather foggy fashion Gary realized that Joe Camber was already a goodly way down the road to alcoholism. It was a road Gary himself had toured extensively.

'Just a good-for-nothing drunk and I don't give a shit!' Gary told the birds and the shingles in the diseased elm. He tipped his glass. He farted. He swatted a bug. Sunlight and shadow dappled his face. Behind the house, a number of disemboweled cars had almost disappeared in the tall weeds. The ivy which grew on the west side of his house had gone absolutely apeshit, almost covering it. One window peeked out – barely – and on sunny days it glittered like a dirty diamond. Two years ago, in a drunken frenzy, Gary had uprooted a bureau from one of the upstairs rooms and had thrown it out a window – he could not remember why now. He had reglazed the window himself because it had let in one crotch of a draft come winter, but the bureau rested exactly where it had fallen. One drawer was popped out like a tongue.

In 1944, when Gary Pervier had been twenty, he had single-handedly taken a German pillbox in France and, following that exploit, had led the remains of his squad ten miles farther before collapsing with the six bullet wounds he had suffered in his charge of the machine-gun emplacement. For this he had been awarded one of his grateful country's highest honors, the Distinguished Service Cross. In 1968 he had gotten Buddy Torgeson down in Castle Falls to turn the medal into an ashtray. Buddy had been shocked. Gary told Buddy he would have gotten him to make it into a toilet bowl so he could shit in it, but it wasn't big enough. Buddy spread the story, and maybe that had been Gary's intention, or maybe it hadn't.

Either way, it had driven the local hippies crazy with admiration. In the summer of '68 most of these hippies were on vacation in the Lakes Region with their wealthy parents before returning to their colleges in September, where they were apparently studying up on Protest, Pot, and Pussy.

After Gary had his DSC turned into an ashtray by Buddy Torgeson, who did custom welding in his spare time and who worked days down to the Castle Falls Esso (they were all Exxon stations now, and Gary Pervier didn't give a shit), a version of the story found its way into the Castle Rock *Call*. The story was written by a local-yokel reporter who construed the act as an antiwar gesture. That was when the hippies started to show up at Gary's place on Town

Road No. 3. Most of them wanted to tell Gary he was 'far out'. Some of them wanted to tell him he was 'some kind of heavy'. A few wanted to tell him that he was 'too fucking much'.

Gary showed them all the same thing, which was his Winchester .30-.06. He told them to get off his property. As far as he was concerned they were all a bunch of long-haired muff-diving crab-crawling asshole pinko fucksticks. He told them he didn't give a shit if he blew their guts from Castle Rock to Fryeburg. After a while they stopped coming, and that was the end of the DSC affair.

One of those German bullets had taken Gary Pervier's right testicle off; a medic had found most of it splattered across the seat of his GI-issue underwear. Most of the other one survived, and sometimes he could still get a pretty respectable bone-on. Not, he had frequently told Joe Camber, that he gave much of a shit one way or the other. His grateful country had given him the Distinguished Service Cross. A grateful hospital staff in Paris had discharged him in February 1945 with an 80-percent disability pension and a gold-plated monkey on his back. A grateful hometown gave him a parade on the Fourth of July 1945 (by then he was twenty-one instead of twenty, able to vote, his hair graying around the temples, and he felt all of seven hundred, thank you very much). The grateful town selectmen had remanded the property taxes on the Pervier place in perpetuity. That was good, because he would have lost it twenty years ago otherwise. He had replaced the morphine he could no longer obtain with high-tension booze and had then proceeded to get about his life's work, which was killing himself as slowly and as pleasantly as he could.

Now, in 1980, he was fifty-six years old, totally gray, and meaner than a bull with a jackhandle up its ass. About the only three living creatures he could stand were Joe Camber, his boy Brett, and Brett's big Saint Bernard, Cujo.

He tilted back in the decaying lawn chair, almost went over on his back, and used up some more of his screwdriver. The screwdriver was in a glass he had gotten free from a McDonald's restaurant. There was some sort of purple animal on the glass. Something called a Grimace. Gary ate a lot of his meals at the Castle Rock McDonald's, where you could still get a cheap hamburger. Hamburgers were good. But as for the Grimace . . . and Mayor McCheese . . . and Monsieur Ronald Fucking McDonald . . . Gary Pervier didn't give a shit for any of them.

A broad, tawny shape was moving through the high grass to his left, and a moment later Cujo, on one of his rambles, emerged into Gary's tattered front yard. He saw Gary and barked once, politely. Then he came over, wagging his tail.

'Cuje, you old sonofawhore,' Gary said. He put his screwdriver down and began digging methodically through his pockets for dog biscuits. He always kept a few on hand for Cujo, who was one of your old-fashioned, dyed-in-the-wool good dogs.

He found a couple in his shirt pocket and held them up.

'Sit boy. Sit up.'

No matter how low or how mean he was feeling, the sight of that two-hundred-pound dog sitting up like a rabbit never failed to tickle him.

Cujo sat up, and Gary saw a short but ugly-looking

scratch healing on the dog's muzzle. Gary tossed him the biscuits, which were shaped like bones, and Cujo snapped them effortlessly out of the air. He dropped one between his forepaws and began to gnaw the other one.

'Good dog,' Gary said, reaching out to pat Cujo's head. 'Good—'

Cujo began to growl. Deep in his throat. It was a rumbling, almost reflective sound. He looked up at Gary, and there was something cold and speculative in the dog's eyes that gave Gary a chill. He took his hand back to himself quickly. A dog as big as Cujo was nothing to get screwing around with. Not unless you wanted to spend the rest of your life wiping your ass with a hook.

'What's got into you, boy?' Gary asked. He had never heard Cujo growl, not in all the years the Cambers had had him. To tell the truth, he wouldn't have believed ole Cuje had a growl in him.

Cujo wagged his tail a little bit and came over to Gary to be patted, as if ashamed of his momentary lapse.

'Hey, that's more like it,' Gary said, ruffling the big dog's fur. It had been one scorcher of a week, and more coming, according to George Meara, who had heard it from Aunt Evvie Chalmers. He supposed that was it. Dogs felt the heat even more than people did, and he guessed there was no rule against a mutt getting testy once in a while. But it sure had been funny, hearing Cujo growl like that. If Joe Camber had told him, Gary wouldn't have believed it.

'Go get your other biscuit,' Gary said, and pointed.

Cujo turned around, went to the biscuit, picked it up, mouthed it — a long string of saliva depending from his mouth – and then dropped it. He looked at Gary apologetically.

'You, turnin down chow?' Gary said unbelievingly. '*You?*'

Cujo picked up the dog biscuit again and ate it.

'That's better,' Gary said. 'A little heat ain't gonna killya. Ain't gonna kill me either, but it bitches the *shit* outta my hemorrhoids. Well, I don't give a shit if they get as big as fucking golfballs. You know it?' He swatted a mosquito.

Cujo lay down beside Gary's chair as Gary picked up his screwdriver again. It was almost time to go in and freshen it up, as the country-club cunts said.

'Freshen up my ass,' Gary said. He gestured at the roof of his house, and a sticky mixture of orange juice and vodka trickled down his sunburned, scrawny arm. 'Look at that chimbly, Cuje ole guy. Fallin right the fuck down. And you know what? I don't give a shit. The whole place could fall flat and I wouldn't fart sideways to a dime. You know that?'

Cujo thumped his tail a little. He didn't know what this MAN was saying, but the rhythms were familiar and the patterns were soothing. These polemics had gone on a dozen times a week since . . . well, as far as Cujo was concerned, since forever. Cujo liked this MAN, who always had food. Just lately Cujo didn't seem to want food, but if THE MAN wanted him to eat, he would. Then he could lie here – as he was now – and listen to the soothing talk. All in all, Cujo didn't feel very well. He hadn't growled at THE MAN because he was hot but simply because he didn't feel good. For a moment there – just a moment – he had felt like biting THE MAN.

CUJO

'Got your nose in the brambles, looks like,' Gary said. 'What was you after? Woodchuck? Rabbit?'

Cujo thumped his tail a little. Crickets sang in the rampant bushes. Behind the house, honeysuckle grew in a wild drift, calling the somnolent bees of a summer afternoon. Everything in Cujo's life should have been right, but somehow it wasn't. He just didn't feel good at all.

'I don't even give a shit if all that Georgia redneck's teeth fall out, and all of Ray-Gun's teeth too,' Gary said, and stood up unsteadily. The lawn chair fell over and collapsed itself. If you had guessed that Gary Pervier didn't give a shit, you would have been right. 'Scuse me, boy.' He went inside and built himself another screwdriver. The kitchen was buzzing, fly-blown horror of split-open green garbage bags, empty cans, and empty liquor bottles.

When Gary came back out again, fresh drink in hand, Cujo had left.

On the last day of June, Donna Trenton came back from downtown Castle Rock (the locals called it 'downstreet', but at least she hadn't picked up *that* particular Maine-ism yet), where she had dropped Tad off at his afternoon daycamp and picked up a few groceries at the Agway Market. She was hot and tired, and the sight of Steve Kemp's battered Ford Econoline van with the gaudy desert murals painted on the sides suddenly turned her furious.

Anger had simmered all day. Vic had told her about the impending trip at breakfast, and when she had protested being left alone with Tad for what might be ten days or two weeks or God only knew, he made it clear to her exactly what the stakes were. He had thrown a scare into

49

her, and she didn't like to be frightened. Up until this morning she had treated the Red Razberry Zingers affair as a joke – a rather good one at Vic and Roger's expense. She had never dreamed that such an absurd thing could have such serious consequences.

Then Tad had been scratchy about going off to the daycamp, complaining that a bigger boy had pushed him down last Friday. The bigger boy's name was Stanley Dobson, and Tad was afraid that Stanley Dobson might push him down again today. He had cried and clutched onto her when she got him to the American Legion field where the camp was held, and she'd had to pry his fingers loose from her blouse finger by finger, making her feel more like a Nazi than a mom: *You vill go to daykemp, ja? Ja, mein Mamma!* Sometimes Tad seemed so *young* for his age, so vulnerable. Weren't only children supposed to be precocious and resourceful? His fingers had been choco-latey and had left fingerprints on her blouse. They reminded her of the bloodstained handprints you sometimes saw in cheap detective magazines.

To add to the fun, her Pinto had started to act funny on the way home from the market, jerking and hitching, as if it had an automotive case of the hiccups. It had smoothed out after a bit, but what could happen once could happen again, and –

– and, just to put a little icing on the cake, here was Steve Kemp.

'Well, no bullshit,' she muttered, grabbed her bag of groceries, and got out, a pretty, dark-haired woman of twenty-nine, tall, gray-eyed. She somehow managed to look tolerably fresh in spite of the relentless heat, her Tad-printed blouse, and academy-gray shorts that felt pasted to her hips and fanny.

She went up the steps quickly and into the house by the porch door. Steve was sitting in Vic's living-room chair. He was drinking one of Vic's beers. He was smoking a cigarette – presumably one of his own. The TV was on, and the agonies of *General Hospital* played out there, in living color.

'The princess arrives,' Steve said with the lopsided grin she had once found so charming and interestingly dangerous. 'I thought you were never going to—'

'I want you out of here, you son of a bitch,' she said tonelessly, and went through into the kitchen. She put the grocery bag down on the counter and started putting things away. She could not remember when she had last been so angry, so furious that her stomach had tied itself in a gripping, groaning knot. One of the endless arguments with her mother, maybe. One of the real horrorshows before she had gone away to school. When Steve came up behind her and slipped his tanned arms around her bare midriff, she acted with no thought at all; she brought her elbow back into his lower chest. Her temper was not cooled by the obvious fact that he had anticipated her. He played a lot of tennis, and her elbow felt as if it had struck a stone wall coated with a layer of hard rubber.

She turned around and looked into his grinning, bearded face. She stood five-eleven and was an inch taller than Vic when she wore heels, but Steve was nearly six-five.

'Didn't you hear me? I want you *out* of here!'

51

'Now, what for?' he asked. 'The little one is off making beaded loincloths or shooting apples off the heads of counselors with his little bow and arrow . . . or whatever they do . . . and hubby is busting heavies at the office . . . and now is the time for Castle Rock's prettiest *hausfrau* and Castle Rock's resident poet and tennis bum to make all the bells of sexual congress chime in lovely harmony.'

'I see you parked out in the driveway,' Donna said. 'Why not just tape a big sign to the side of your van? I'M FUCKING DONNA TRENTON, or something witty like that?'

'I've got every reason to park in the driveway,' Steve said, still grinning. 'I've got that dresser in the back. Stripped clean. Even as I wish you were yourself, my dear.'

'You can put it on the porch. I'll take care of it. While you're doing that, I'll write you a check.'

His smile faded a little. For the first time since she had come in, the surface charm slipped a little and she could see the real person underneath. It was a person she didn't like at all, a person that dismayed her when she thought of him in connection with herself. She had lied to Vic, gone behind his back, in order to go to bed with Steve Kemp. She wished that what she felt now could be something as simple as rediscovering herself, as after a nasty bout of fever. Or rediscovering herself as Vic's mate. But when you took the bark off it, the simple fact was that Steve Kemp — publishing poet, itinerant furniture stripper and refinisher, chair caner, fair amateur tennis player, excellent afternoon lover — was a turd.

'Be serious,' he said.

'Yeah, no one could reject handsome, sensitive Steven Kemp,' she said. 'It's got to be a joke. Only it's not. So what you do, handsome, sensitive Steven Kemp, is put the dresser on the porch, get your check, and blow.'

'Don't talk to me like that, Donna.' His hand moved to her breast and squeezed. It hurt. She began to feel a little scared as well as angry. [But hadn't she been a little scared all along? Hadn't that been part of the nasty, scuzzy little thrill of it?]

She slapped his hand away.

'Don't you get on my case, Donna.' He wasn't smiling now. 'It's too goddam hot.'

'*Me*? On *your* case? You were here when I came in.' Being frightened of him had made her angrier than ever. He wore a heavy black beard that climbed high on his cheekbones, and it occurred to her suddenly that although she had seen his penis close up – had had it in her mouth – she had never really seen what his face looked like.

'What you mean,' he said, 'is that you had a little itch and now it's scratched, so fuck off. Right? Who gives a crap about how I feel?'

'You're breathing on me,' she said, and pushed him away to take the milk to the refrigerator.

He was not expecting it this time. Her shove caught him off balance, and he actually stumbled back a step. His forehead was suddenly divided by lines, and a dark flush flared high on his cheekbones. She had seen him look this way on the tennis courts behind the Bridgton Academy buildings, sometimes. When he blew an easy point. She had watched him play several times – including two sets during which he had mopped up her panting, puffing husband with ease – and on the few occasions she had seen him lose, his reaction had made her extremely uneasy about what she had gotten into with him. He had published poems in over two dozen little magazines, and a book, *Chasing Sundown*, had been published by an outfit in Baton Rouge called The Press over the Garage. He had graduated from Drew, in New Jersey; he held strong opinions on modern art, the upcoming nuclear referendum question in Maine, the films of Andy Warhol, and he took a double fault the way Tad took the news it was bedtime.

Now he came after her, grabbed her shoulder, and spun her around to face him. The carton of milk fell from her hand and split open on the floor.

'There, look at that,' Donna said. 'Nice going, hotshot.'

'Listen, I'm not going to be pushed around. Do you—'

'*You get out of here!*' she screamed into his face. Her spittle sprayed his cheeks and his forehead. '*What do I have to do to convince you? Do you need a picture? You're not welcome here! Go be God's gift to some other woman!*'

'You cheap, cockteasing little bitch,' he said. His voice was sullen, his face ugly. He didn't let go of her arm.

'And take the bureau with you. Pitch it in the dump.'

She pulled free of him and got the washrag from its place, hung over the sink faucet. Her hands were trembling, her stomach was upset, and she was starting to get a headache. She thought that soon she would vomit.

She got down on her hands and knees and began wiping up the spilt milk.

'Yeah, you think you're something,' he said. 'When did your crotch turn to gold? You loved it. You screamed for more.'

'You've got the right tense, anyway, champ,' she said,

not looking up. Her hair hung in her face and she liked it that way just fine. She didn't want him to see how pale and sick her face was. She felt as if someone had pushed her into a nightmare. She felt that if she looked at herself in a mirror at this moment she would see an ugly, capering witch. 'Get out, Steve. I'm not going to tell you again.'

'And what if I don't? You going to call Sheriff Bannerman? Sure. Just say, "Hi, there George, this is Mr Businessman's wife, and the guy I've been screwing on the side won't leave. Would you please come on up here and roust him?" That what you're going to say?'

The fright went deep now. Before marrying Vic, she had been a librarian in the Westchester school system, and her own private nightmare had always been telling the kids for the third time – in her loudest speaking voice – to quiet down *at once*, please. When she did that, they always had – enough for her to get through the period, at least – but what if they wouldn't? That was her nightmare. What if they absolutely wouldn't? What did that leave? The question scared her. It scared her that such a question should ever have to be asked, even to oneself, in the dark of night. She had been afraid to use her loudest voice, and had done so only when it became absolutely necessary. Because that was where civilization came to an abrupt, screeching halt. That was the place where the tar turned to dirt. If they wouldn't listen when you used your very loudest voice, a scream became your only recourse.

This was the same sort of fear. The only answer to the man's question, of course, was that she would scream if he came near her. But would she?

'Go,' she said in a lower voice. 'Please. It's over.'

'What if I decide it isn't? What if I decide to just rape you there on the floor in that damned spilt milk?'

She looked up at him through the tangle of hair. Her face was still pale, and her eyes were too big, ringed with white flesh. 'Then you'll have a fight on your hands. And if I get a chance to tear your balls off or put one of your eyes out, I won't hesitate.'

For just a moment, before his face closed up, she thought he looked uncertain. He knew she was quick, in pretty good shape. He could beat her at tennis, but she made him sweat to do it. His balls and his eyes were probably safe, but she might very well put some furrows in his face. It was a question of how far he wanted to go. She smelled something thick and unpleasant in the air of her kitchen, some whiff of the jungle, and realized with dismay that it was a mixture of her fear and his rage. It was coming out of their pores.

'I'll take the bureau back to my shop,' he said. 'Why don't you send your handsome hubby down for it, Donna? He and I can have a nice talk. About stripping.'

He left then, pulling the door which communicated between the living room and the porch to behind him almost hard enough to break the glass. A moment later the engine of his van roared, settled into a ragged idle, and then dropped to a working pitch as he threw it in gear. He screeched his tires as he left.

Donna finished wiping the milk up slowly, rising from time to time to wring out her rag in the stainless steel sink. She watched the threads of milk run down the drain. She was trembling all over, partly from reaction, partly from relief. She had barely heard Steve's implied threat to tell

Vic. She could only think, over and over again, about the chain of events that had led to such an ugly scene.

She sincerely believed she had drifted into her affair with Steve Kemp almost inadvertently. It was like an explosion of sewage from a buried pipe. A similar sewer pipe, she believed, ran beneath the neatly tended lawns of almost every marriage in America.

She hadn't wanted to come to Maine and had been appalled when Vic had sprung the idea on her. In spite of vacations there (and the vacations themselves might have reinforced the idea), she had thought of the state as a woodsy wasteland, a place where the snow drifted twenty feet high in the winters and people were virtually cut off. The thought of taking their baby into such an environment terrified her. She had pictured — to herself and aloud to Vic — sudden snowstorms blowing up, stranding him in Portland and her in Castle Rock. She thought and spoke of Tad swallowing pills in such a situation, or burning himself on the stove, or God knew what. And maybe part of her resistance had been a stubborn refusal to give up the excitement and hurry of New York.

Well, face it — the worst hadn't been any of those things. The worst had been a nagging conviction that Ad Worx would fail and they would have to go crawling back with their tails between their legs. That hadn't happened, because Vic and Roger had worked their butts off. But that had also meant that she was left with a growing-up child and too much time on her hands.

She could count her life's close friends on the fingers of one hand. She was confident that the ones she made would be her friends forever, come hell or high water, but she had never made friends quickly or easily. She had toyed with the idea of getting her Maine certification – Maine and New York were reciprocal; it was mostly a matter of filling out some forms. Then she could go see the Superintendent of Schools and get her name put on the sub list for Castle Rock High. It was a ridiculous notion, and she shelved it after running some figures on her pocket calculator. Gasoline and sitters' fees would eat up most of the twenty-eight bucks a day she might have made.

I've become the fabled Great American Housewife, she had thought dismally one day last winter, watching sleet spick and spack down against the porch storm windows. Sitting home, feeding Tab his franks and beans and his toasted cheese sandwiches and Campbell's Soup for lunch, getting my slice of life from Lisa on *As the World Turns* and from Mike on *The Young and the Restless*. Every now and then we jive it up with a *Wheel of Fortune* session. She could go over and see Joanie Welsh, who had a little girl about Tad's age, but Joanie always made her uneasy. She was three years older than Donna and ten pounds heavier. The extra ten pounds did not seem to bother her. She said her husband liked her that way. Joanie was contented with things as they were in Castle Rock.

A little at a time, the shit had started to back up in the pipe. She started to sharpshoot at Vic about little things, sublimating the big things because they were hard to define and even harder to articulate. Things like loss and fear and getting older. Things like being lonely and then getting terrified of being lonely. Things like hearing a song on the radio that you remembered from high school and bursting into tears for no reason. Feeling jealous of Vic because his life was a daily struggle to build something, he was a knight-errant with a family crest embossed on his shield, and her life was back here, getting Tad through the day, jollying him when he was cranky, listening to his raps, fixing his meals and snacks. It was a life lived in the trenches. Too much of it was waiting and listening.

And all along she had thought that things would begin to smooth out when Tad was older; the discovery that it wasn't true brought on a kind of low-level horror. This past year he had been out of the house three mornings a week, at Jack and Jill Nursery School; this summer it had been five afternoons a week at playcamp. When he was gone the house seemed shockingly empty. Doorways leaned and gaped with no Tad to fill them; the staircase yawned with no Tad halfway up, sitting there in his pajama bottoms before his nap, owlishly looking at one of his picture books.

Doors were mouths, stairways throats. Empty rooms became traps.

So she washed floors that didn't need to be washed. She watched the soaps. She thought about Steve Kemp, with whom she'd had a little flirtation since he had rolled into town the previous fall with Virginia license plates on his van and had set up a small stripping and refinishing business. She had caught herself sitting in front of the TV with no idea what was going on because she had been thinking about the way his deep tan contrasted with his tennis whites, or the way his ass pumped when he moved fast. And finally she had done something. And today –

She felt her stomach knot up and she ran for the

bathroom, her hands plastered to her mouth, her eyes wide and starey. She made it, barely, and tossed up everything. She looked at the mess she had made, and with a groan she did it again.

When her stomach felt better (but her legs were all atremble again, something lost, something gained), she looked at herself in the bathroom mirror. Her face was thrown into hard and unflattering relief by the fluorescent bar. Her skin was too white, her eyes red-rimmed. Her hair was plastered to her skull in an unflattering helmet. She saw what she was going to look like when she was old, and the most terrifying thing of all was that right now, if Steve Kemp was here, she thought she would let him make love to her if he would only hold her and kiss her and say that she didn't have to be afraid, that time was a myth and death was a dream, that everything was okay.

A sound came out of her, a screaming sob that could surely not have been born in her chest. It was the sound of a madwoman.

She lowered her head and cried.

Charity Camber sat on the double bed she shared with her husband, Joe, and looked down at something she held in her hands. She had just come back from the store, the same one Donna Trenton patronized. Now her hands and feet and cheeks felt numb and cold, as if she had been out with Joe on the snowmobile for too long. But tomorrow as the first of July; the snowmobile was put neatly away in the back shed with its tarp snugged down.

It can't be. There's been some mistake.

60

But there was no mistake. She had checked half a dozen times, and there was no mistake.

After all, it has to happen to somebody, *doesn't it?*

Yes, of course. To *somebody*. But to *her*?

She could hear Joe pounding on something in his garage, a high, belling sound that beat its way into the hot afternoon like a hammer shaping thin metal. There was a pause, and then, faintly: 'Shit!'

The hammer struck once more and there was a longer pause. Then her husband hollered: '*Brett!*'

She always cringed a little when he raised his voice that way and yelled for their boy. Brett loved his father very much, but Charity had never been sure just how Joe felt about his son. That was a dreadful thing to be thinking, but it was true. Once, about two years ago, she had had a horrible nightmare, one she didn't think she would ever forget. She dreamed that her husband drove a pitchfork directly into Brett's chest. The tines went right through him and poked out the back of Brett's T-shirt, holding it out the way tent poles hold a tent up in the air. *Little sucker didn't come when I hollered him down,* her dream husband said, and she had awakened with a jerk beside her real husband, who had been sleeping the sleep of beer beside her in his boxer shorts. The moonlight had been falling through the window and onto the bed where she now sat, moonlight in a cold and uncaring flood of light, and she had understood just how afraid a person could be, how fear was a monster with yellow teeth, set afoot by an angry God to eat the unwary and the unfit. Joe had used his hands on her a few times in the course of their marriage, and she had learned. She wasn't a genius, maybe, but her mother hadn't raised any *fools*. Now she did what Joe told her and rarely argued. She guessed Brett was that way too. But she feared for the boy sometimes.

She went to the window in time to see Brett run across the yard and into the barn. Cujo trailed at Brett's heels, looking hot and dispirited.

Faintly: 'Hold this for me, Brett.'

More faintly: 'Sure, Daddy.'

The hammering started again, that merciless icepick sound: *Whing! Whing! Whing!* She imagined Brett holding something against something – a coldchisel against a frozen bearing, maybe, or a square spike against a lockbolt. Her husband a Pall Mall jittering in the corner of his thin mouth, his T-shirt sleeves rolled up, swinging a five-pound pony-hammer. And if he was drunk . . . if his aim was a little off . . .

In her mind she could hear Brett's agonized howl as the hammer mashed his hand to a red, splintered pulp, and she crossed her arms over her bosom against the vision.

She looked at the thing in her hand again and wondered if there was a way she could use it. More than anything in the world, she wanted to go to Connecticut to see her sister Holly. It had been six years now, in the summer of 1974 – she remembered well enough, because it had been a bad summer for her except for that one pleasant weekend. 'Seventy-four had been the year Brett's night problems had begun – restlessness, bad dreams, and, more and more frequently, incidents of sleepwalking. It was also the year Joe began drinking heavily. Brett's uneasy nights and his somnambulism had eventually gone away. Joe's drinking had not.

Brett had been four then; he was ten now and didn't even remember his Aunt Holly, who had been married for six years. She had a little boy, named after her husband, and a little girl. Charity had never seen either child, her own niece and nephew, except for the Kodachromes Holly occasionally sent in the mail.

She had gotten scared of asking Joe. He was tired of hearing her talk about it, and if she asked him again he might hit her. It had been almost sixteen months since she'd last asked him if maybe they couldn't take a little vacation down Connecticut way. Not much of a one for traveling was Mrs Camber's son Joe. He liked it just fine in Castle Rock. Once a year he and that old tosspot Gary Pervier and some of their cronies would go up north to Moosehead to shoot deer. Last November he had wanted to take Brett. She had put her foot down and it had *stayed* down, in spite of Joe's sullen mutterings and Brett's wounded eyes. She was not going to have the boy out with that bunch of men for two weeks, listening to a lot of vulgar talk and jokes about sex and seeing what animals men could turn into when they got to drinking nonstop over a period of days and weeks. All of them with loaded guns, walking in the woods. Loaded guns, loaded men, somebody always got hurt sooner or later, fluorescent-orange hats and vests or not. It wasn't going to be Brett. Not her son.

The hammer struck the steel steadily, rhythmically. It stopped. She relaxed a little. Then it started again.

She supposed that sooner or later Brett would go

with them, and that would be the end of him for her. He would join their club, and ever after she would be little more than a kitchen drudge that kept the clubhouse neat. Yes, that day would come, and she knew it, and she grieved for it. But at least she had been able to stave it off for another year.

And this year? Would she be able to keep him home with her this November? Maybe not. Either way, it would be better – not all right but at least better – if she could take Brett down to Connecticut first. Take him down there and show him how some . . .

. . . some . . .

Oh, say it, if only to yourself.

(how some decent people lived)

If Joe would let them go alone . . . but there was no sense thinking of that. Joe could go places alone or with his friends, but she couldn't, not even with Brett in tow. That was one of their marriage's ground rules. Yet she couldn't help thinking about how much better it would be without him – without him sitting in Holly's kitchen, swilling beer, looking Holly's Jim up and down with those insolent brown eyes. It would be better without him being impatient to be gone until Holly and Jim were also impatient for them to be gone . . .

She and Brett.

Just the two of them.

They could go on the bus.

She thought: Last November, he wanted to take Brett hunting with him.

She thought: Could a trade be worked out?

Cold came to her, filling the hollows of her bones

with spun glass. Would she actually *agree* to such a trade? He could take Brett to Moosehead with him in the fall if Joe in his turn would agree to let them go to Stratford on the bus –

There was money enough – now there was – but money alone wouldn't do it. He'd take the money and that would be the last she would see of it. Unless she played her cards just right. Just . . . right.

Her mind began to move faster. The pounding outside stopped. She saw Brett leave the barn, trotting, and was dimly grateful. Some premonitory part of her was convinced that if the boy ever came to serious harm, it would be in that dark place with the sawdust spread over the old grease on the plank floor.

There was a way. There *must* be a way.

If she was willing to gamble.

In her fingers she held a lottery ticket. She turned it over and over in her hand as she stood at the window, thinking.

When Steve Kemp got back to his shop, he was in a kind of furious ecstasy. His shop was on the western outskirts of Castle Rock, on Route 11. He had rented it from a farmer who had holdings in both Castle Rock and in neighboring Bridgton. The farmer was not just a nurd; he was a Super Nurd.

The shop was dominated by Steve's stripping vat, a corrugated iron pot that looked big enough to boil an entire congregation of missionaries at one time. Sitting around it like small satellites around a large planet was his work: bureaus, dressers, china cupboards, bookcases, tables.

The air was aromatic with varnish, stripping compound, linseed oil.

He had a fresh change of clothes in a battered TWA flightbag; he had planned to change after making love to the fancy cunt. Now he hurled the bag across the shop. It bounced off the far wall and landed on top of a dresser. He walked across to it and batted it aside. He drop-kicked it as it came down, and it hit the ceiling before falling on its side like a dead woodchuck. Then he simply stood, breathing hard, inhaling the heavy smells, staring vacantly at three chairs he had promised to cane by the end of the week. His thumbs were jammed into his belt. His fingers were curled into fists. His lower lip was pooched out. He looked like a kid sulking after a bawling-out.

'Cheap-*shit!*' he breathed, and went after the flightbag. He made as if to kick it again, then changed his mind and picked it up. He went through the shed and into the three-room house that adjoined the shop. If anything, it was hotter in the house. Crazy July heat. It got in your head. The kitchen was full of dirty dishes. Flies buzzed around a green plastic Hefty bag filled with Beefaroni and tuna-fish cans. The living room was dominated by a big old Zenith black-and-white TV he had rescued from the Naples dump. A big spayed brindle cat, name of Bernie Carbo, slept on top of it like a dead thing.

The bedroom was where he worked on his writing. The bed itself was a rollaway, not made, the sheets stiff with come. No matter how much he was getting (and over the last two weeks that had been zero), he masturbated a great deal. Masturbation, he believed, was a sign of creativity.

Across from the bed was his desk. A big old-fashioned Underwood sat on top of it. Manuscripts were stacked to both sides. More manuscripts, some in boxes, some secured with rubber bands, were piled up in one corner. He wrote a lot and he moved around a lot and his main luggage was his work – mostly poems, a few stories, a surreal play in which the characters spoke a grand total of nine words, and a novel he had attacked badly from six different angles. It had been five years since he had lived in one place long enough to get completely unpacked.

Last December, while shaving one day, he had discovered the first threads of gray in his beard. The discovery had thrown him into a savage depression, and he had stayed depressed for weeks. He hadn't touched a razor between then and now, as if it was the act of shaving that had somehow caused the gray to show up. He was thirty-eight. He refused to entertain the thought of being that old, but sometimes it crept up on his blind side and surprised him. To be that old – less than seven hundred days shy of forty – terrified him. He had really believed that forty was for other people.

That bitch, he thought over and over again. That *bitch*.

He had left dozens of women since he had first gotten laid by a vague, pretty, softly helpless French substitute when he was a high school junior, but he himself had only been dropped two or three times. He was good at seeing the drop coming and opting out of the relationship first. It was a protective device, like bombing the queen of spades on someone else in a game of Hearts. You had to do it while you could still cover the bitch, or you got screwed. You covered yourself. The way you didn't think about your age. He had known Donna was cooling it, but she had struck him as a woman who could be manipulated with no great difficulty, at least for a while, by a combination of psychological and sexual factors. By fear, if you wanted to be crude. That it hadn't worked that way left him feeling hurt and furious, as if he had been whipped raw.

He got out of his clothes, tossed his wallet and change onto his desk, went into the bathroom, showered. When he came out he felt a little better. He dressed again, pulling jeans and a faded chambray shirt from the flightbag. He picked his change up, put it in a front pocket, and paused, looking speculatively at his Lord Buxton. Some of the business cards had fallen out. They were always doing that, because there were so many of them.

Steve Kemp had a packrat sort of wallet. One of the items he almost always picked up and tucked away were business cards. They made nice bookmarks, and the space on the blank flip side was just right for jotting an address, simple directions, or a phone number. He would sometimes take two or three if he happened to be in a plumbing shop or if an insurance salesman stopped by. Steve would unfailingly ask the nine-to-fiver for his card with a big shiteating grin.

When he and Donna were going at it hot and heavy, he had happened to notice one of her husband's business cards lying on top of the TV. Donna had been taking a shower or something. He had taken the business card. No big reason. Just the packrat thing.

Now he opened his wallet and thumbed through the cards, cards from Prudential agents in Virginia, realtors in

Colorado, a dozen businesses in between. For a moment he thought he had lost Handsome Hubby's card, but it had just slipped down between a couple of dollar bills. He fished it out and looked at it. White card, blue lettering done in modish lower case, Mr Businessman Triumphant. Quiet but impressive. Nothing flashy.

roger breakstone   ad worx   victor trenton
1633 congress street
telex: ADWORX portland, maine 04001 tel (207)555-8600

Steve pulled a sheet of paper from a ream of cheap mimeo stuff and cleared a place in front of him. He looked briefly at his typewriter. No. Each machine's type-script was as individual as a fingerprint. It was his crooked lower-case 'a' that hung the blighter, Inspector. The jury was only out long enough to have tea.

This would not be a police matter, nohow, no way, but caution came without even thinking. Cheap paper, available at any office supply store, no typewriter.

He took a Pilot Razor Point from the coffee can on the corner of the desk and printed in large block letters:

HELLO, VIC.
NICE WIFE YOU'VE GOT THERE.
I ENJOYED FUCKING THE SHIT OUT OF HER.

He paused, tapping the pen against his teeth. He was starting to feel good again. On top. Of course, she was a good-looking woman, and he supposed there was always

69

the possibility that Trenton might discount what he had written so far. Talk was cheap, and you could mail someone a letter for less than the price of a coffee. But there was something . . . always something. What might it be?

He smiled suddenly; when he smiled that way his entire face lit up, and it was easy to see why he had never had much trouble with women since the evening with the vague, pretty French sub.

He wrote:

> WHAT'S THAT MOLE JUST ABOVE HER
> PUBIC HAIR LOOK LIKE TO YOU?
> TO ME IT LOOKS LIKE A QUESTION MARK.
> DO _YOU_ HAVE ANY QUESTIONS?

That was enough; a meal is as good as a feast, his mother had always said. He found an envelope and put the message inside. After a pause, he slipped the business card in, and addressed the envelope, also in block letters, to Vic's office. After a moment's thought, he decided to show the poor slob a little mercy and added PERSONAL below the address.

He propped the letter on the windowsill and leaned back in his chair, feeling totally good again. He would be able to write tonight, he felt sure of it.

Outside, a truck with out-of-state plates pulled into his driveway. A pickup with a great big Hoosier cabinet in the back. Someone had picked up a bargain at a barn sale. Lucky them.

Steve strolled out. He would be glad to take their

money and their Hoosier cabinet, but he really doubted if he would have time to do the work. Once that letter was mailed, a change of air might be in order. But not too big a change, at least not for a while. He felt he owed it to himself to stay in the area long enough to make at least one more visit to Little Miss Highpockets . . . when it could be ascertained that Handsome Hubby was definitely not around, of course. Steve had played tennis with the guy and he was no ball of fire – thin, heavy glasses, spaghetti backhand – but you never knew when a Handsome Hubby was going to go off his gourd and do something antisocial. A good many Handsome Hubbies kept guns around the house. So he would want to check out the scene carefully before popping in. He would allow himself the one single visit and then close this show entirely. He would maybe go to Ohio for a while. Or Pennsylvania. Or Taos, New Mexico. But like a practical joker who had stuffed a load into someone's cigarette, he wanted to stick around (at a prudent distance, of course) and watch it blow up.

The driver of the pickup and his wife were peering into the shop to see if he was there. Steve strolled out, hands in the pockets of his jeans, smiling. The woman smiled back immediately. 'Hi, folks, can I help you?' he asked, and thought that he would mail the letters as soon as he could get rid of them.

That evening, as the sun went down red and round and hot in the west, Vic Trenton, his shirt tied around his waist by the arms, was looking into the engine compartment of his wife's Pinto. Donna was standing beside him, looking young and fresh in a pair of white shorts and a red-checked sleeveless blouse. Her feet were bare. Tad, dressed only in his bathing suit, was driving his trike madly up and down the driveway, playing some sort of mind game that apparently had Ponch and John from *CHiPS* pitted against Darth Vader.

'Drink your iced tea before it melts,' Donna told Vic.

'Uh-huh.' The glass was on the side of the engine compartment. Vic had a couple of swallows, put it back without looking, and it tumbled off – into his wife's hand.

'Hey,' he said. 'Nice catch.'

She smiled. 'I just know you when your mind's somewhere else, that's all. Look. Didn't spill a drop.'

They smiled into each other's eyes for a moment – a *good* moment, Vic thought. Maybe it was just his imagination, or wishful thinking, but lately it seemed there were more of the good small moments. Less of the sharp words. Fewer silences which were cold, or – maybe this was worse – just indifferent. He didn't know what the cause was, but he was grateful.

'Strictly Triple-A farm club,' he said. 'You got a ways to go before you make the bigs, kid.'

'So what's wrong with my car, coach?'

He had the air cleaner off; it was sitting in the driveway. 'Never saw a Frisbee like that before,' Tad had said matter-of-factly a few moments ago, swerving his trike around it. Vic leaned back in and poked aimlessly at the carburetor with the head of his screwdriver.

'It's in the carb. I think the needle valve's sticking.'

'That's bad?'

'Not too bad,' he said, 'but it can stop you cold if it decides to stick shut. The needle valve controls the flow of gas into the carb, and without gas you don't go. It's like a national law, babe.'

'Daddy, will you push me on the swing?'

'Yeah, in a minute.'

'Good! I'll be in the back!'

Tad started round the house toward the swing-and-gym set Vic had built last summer, while lubricating himself well with gin and tonics, working from a set of plans, doing it after supper on week nights and on weekends with the voices of the Boston Red Sox announcers blaring from the transistor radio beside him. Tad, then three, sat solemnly on the cellar bulkhead or on the back steps, chin cupped in his hands, fetching things sometimes, mostly watching silently. Last summer. A good summer, not as beastly hot as this one. It had seemed then that Donna had finally adjusted and was seeing that Maine, Castle Rock, Ad Worx – those things could be good for all of them.

Then the mystifying bad patch, the worst of it being that nagging, almost psychic feeling that things were even more wrong than he wanted to think about. Things in the house began to seem subtly out of place, as if unfamiliar hands had been moving them around. He had gotten the crazy idea – *was* it crazy? – that Donna was changing the sheets too often. They were always clean, and one night that old fairy-tale question had popped into his mind, echoing unpleasantly: *Who's been sleeping in my bed?*

Now things had loosened up, it seemed. If not for the crazy Razberry Zingers business and the rotten trip hanging over his head, he would feel that this could be a pretty good summer too. It might even turn out that way.

You won, sometimes. Not all hopes were vain. He believed that, although his belief had never been seriously tested.

'Tad!' Donna yelled, bringing the boy to a screeching halt. 'Put your trike in the garage.'

'Mom-*mee*!'

'Now, please, monsieur.'

'Monsewer,' Tad said, and laughed into his hands. 'You didn't put your car away, Mom.'

'Daddy is working on my car.'

'Yeah, but—'

'Mind your mom, Tadder,' Vic said, picking up the air cleaner. 'I'll be around shortly.'

Tad mounted his trike and drove it into the garage, accompanying himself with a loud, ululating ambulance wail.

'Why are you putting it back on?' Donna asked. 'Aren't you going to fix it?'

'It's a precision job,' Vic said. 'I don't have the tools. Even if I did, I'd probably make it worse instead of better.'

'Damn,' she said morosely, and kicked a tire. 'These things never happen until after the warranty runs out, do they?' The Pinto had just over 20,000 miles on it, and was still six months from being theirs, free and clear.

'That's like a national law too,' Vic said. He put the air cleaner back on its post and tightened the butterfly nut.

'I guess I can run it over to South Paris while Tad's in his daycamp. I'll have to get a loaner, though, with you being gone. Will it get me to South Paris, Vic?'

'Sure. But you don't have to do that. Take it out to Joe Camber's place. That's only seven miles, and he does good work. Remember when that wheel bearing went on

74

the Jag? He took it out with a chainfall made out of old lengths of telephone pole and charged ten bucks. Man, if I'd gone to that place in Portland, they would have mounted my checkbook like a moosehead.'

'That guy made me nervous,' Donna said. 'Aside from the fact that he was about two and a half sheets to the wind, I mean.'

'How did he make you nervous?'

'Busy eyes.'

Vic laughed. 'Honey, with you, there's a lot to be busy about.'

'Thank you,' she said. 'A woman doesn't necessarily mind being *looked* at. It's being mentally undressed that makes you nervous.' She paused, strangely, he thought, looking away at the grim red light in the west. Then she looked back at him. 'Some men give you the feeling that there's a little movie called *The Rape of the Sabine Women* going on in their heads all the time and you just got the . . . the starring role.'

He had that curious, unpleasant feeling that she was talking about several things at once – again. But he didn't want to get into that tonight, not when he was finally crawling out from under a shitheap of a month.

'Babe, he's probably completely harmless. He's got a wife, a kid—'

'Yes, probably he is.' But she crossed her arms over her breasts and cupped her elbows in her palms, a characteristic gesture of nervousness with her.

'Look,' he said. 'I'll run your Pinto up there this Saturday and leave it if I have to, okay? More likely he'll be able to get right to it. I'll have a couple of beers with him and pat his dog. You remember that Saint Bernard?'

Donna grinned. 'I even remember his name. He practically knocked Tad over licking him. You remember?'

Vic nodded. 'The rest of the afternoon Tad goes around after him saying "*Cooojo . . . heere, Cooojo.*"'

They laughed together.

'I feel so damn stupid sometimes,' Donna said. 'If I could use a standard shift, I could just run the Jag while you're gone.'

'You're just as well off. The Jag's eccentric. You gotta talk to it.' He slammed the hood of the Pinto back down.

'*Ooooh, you DUMMY!*' she moaned. 'Your iced tea glass was in there!'

And he looked so comically surprised that she went off into gales of laughter. After a minute he joined her. Finally it got so bad that they had to hang on to each other like a couple of drunks. Tad came back around the house to see what was going on, his eyes round. At last, convinced that they were mostly all right in spite of the nutty way they were acting, he joined them. This was about the same time that Steve Kemp mailed his letter less than two miles away.

Later, as dusk settled down and the heat slacked off a little and the first fireflies started to stitch seams in the air across the back yard, Vic pushed his son on the swing.

'Higher, Daddy! Higher!'

'If you go any higher, you're gonna loop the loop, kid.'

'Gimme under, then, Dad! Gimme under!'

Vic gave Tad a huge push, propelling the swing toward a sky where the first stars were just beginning to appear, and ran all the way under the swing. Tad screamed joyfully, his head tilted back, his hair blowing.

'That was *good*, Daddy! Gimme under again!'

Vic gave his son under again, from the front this time, and Tad went soaring into the still, hot night. Aunt Evvie Chalmers lived close by, and Tad's shouts of terrified glee were the last sounds she heard as she died; her heart gave out, one of its paper-thin walls breaching suddenly (and almost painlessly) as she sat in her kitchen chair, a cup of coffee by one hand and a straight-eight Herbert Tareyton by the other; she leaned back and her vision darkened and somewhere she heard a child crying, and for a moment it seemed that the cries were joyful, but as she went out, suddenly propelled as if by a hard but not unkind push from behind, it seemed to her that the child was screaming in fear, in agony; then she was gone, and her niece Abby would find her the following day, her coffee as cold as she was, her cigarette a perfect and delicate tube of ash, her lower plate protruding from her wrinkled mouth like a slot filled with teeth.

Just before Tad's bedtime, he and Vic sat on the back stoop. Vic had beer. Tad had milk.

'Daddy?'

'What?'

'I wish you didn't have to go away next week.'

'I'll be back.'

'Yeah, but—'

Tad was looking down, struggling with tears. Vic put a hand on his neck.

'But what, big guy?'

'Who's gonna say the words that keep the monster out of the closet? Mommy doesn't know them! Only you know them!'

Now the tears spilled over and ran down Tad's face.

'Is that all?' Vic asked.

The Monster Words (Vic had originally dubbed them the Monster Catechism, but Tad had trouble with that word, so it had been shortened) had come about in late spring, when Tad began to be afflicted by bad dreams and night fears. There was something in his closet, he said; sometimes at night his closet door would swing open and he would see it in there, something with yellow eyes that wanted to eat him up. Donna had thought it might have been some fallout with Maurice Sendak's book *Where the Wild Things Are*. Vic had wondered aloud to Roger (but not to Donna) if maybe Tad had picked up a garbled account of the mass murders that had taken place in Castle Rock and had decided that the murderer – who had become a kind of town bogeyman – was alive and well in his closet. Roger said he supposed it was possible; with kids, *anything* was possible.

And Donna herself had begun to get a little spooked after a couple of weeks of this; she told Vic one morning in a kind of laughing, nervous way that things in Tad's closet sometimes appeared moved around. Well, Tad did it, Vic had responded. You don't understand, Donna said. He doesn't go back there any more, Vic . . . never. He's scared to. And she had added that sometimes it seemed to her that the closet actually smelled bad after Tad's bouts of nightmare, followed by waking fear. Like an animal had been caged up in there. Disturbed, Vic had gone into the closet and sniffed. In his mind was a half-formed idea that perhaps Tad was sleepwalking; perhaps going into his closet and urinating in there as a part of some odd dream cycle. He had smelled nothing but mothballs. The closet, finished wall on one side and bare lathing on the other, stretched back some eight feet. It was as narrow as a Pullman car. There was no bogeyman back in there, and Vic most certainly did not come out in Narnia. He got a few cobwebs in his hair. That was all.

Donna had suggested first what she called 'good-dream thoughts' to combat Tad's night fears, then prayer. Tad responded to the former by saying that the thing in his closet stole his good-dream thoughts; he responded to the latter by saying that since God didn't believe in monsters, prayers were useless. Her temper had snapped – perhaps partly because she had been spooked by Tad's closet herself. Once, while hanging some of Tad's shirts in there, the door had swung quietly shut behind her and she'd had a bad forty seconds fumbling her way back to the door and getting out. She had smelled something in there that time – something hot and close and violent. A matted smell. It reminded her a little of Steve Kemp's sweat after they finished making love. The upshot was her curt suggestion that since there *were* no such things as monsters, Tad should put the whole thing out of his mind, hug his Teddy, and go to sleep.

Vic either saw more deeply or remembered more clearly about the closet door that turned into an unhinged idiot mouth in the dark of night, a place where strange things sometimes rustled, a place where hanging clothes sometimes turned into hanging men. He remembered vaguely about the shadows the streetlight could throw on the wall in the endless four hours that follow the turn of the day, and the creaking sounds that might have been the house settling or that might – just *might* – be something creeping up.

His solution had been the Monster Catechism, or just the Monster Words if you were four and not into semantics. Either way, it was nothing more (nor less) than a primitive incantation to keep evil at bay. Vic had invented it one day on his lunch hour, and to Donna's mixed relief and chagrin, it worked when her own efforts to use psychology, Parent Effectiveness Training, and, finally, blunt discipline had failed. Vic spoke it over Tad's bed every night like a benediction as Tad lay there naked under a single sheet in the sweltering dark.

'Do you think that's going to do him any good in the long run?' Donna asked. Her voice held both amusement and irritation. This had been in mid-May, when the tensions between them had been running high.

'Admen don't care about the long run,' Vic had answered. 'They care about fast, fast, fast relief. And I'm good at my job.'

'Yeah, nobody to say the Monster Words, that's the matter, that's a *lot* the matter,' Tad answered now, wiping the tears off his cheeks in disgust and embarrassment.

'Well, listen,' Vic said. 'They're written down. That's how I can say them the same every night. I'll print them on a piece of paper and tack them to your wall. And Mommy can read them to you every night I'm gone.'

'Yeah? Will you?'

'Sure. Said I would.'

'You won't forget?'

'No way, man. I'll do it tonight.'

Tad put his arms around his father, and Vic hugged him tight.

That night, after Tad slept, Vic went quietly into the boy's room and tacked a sheet of paper to the wall with a pushpin. He put it right next to Tad's Mighty Marvel Calender, where the kid couldn't miss it. Printed in large, clear letters on this sheet of paper was:

THE MONSTER WORDS

For Tad

Monsters, stay out of this room!
You have no business here.
No monsters under Tad's bed!
You can't fit under there.
No monsters hiding in Tad's closet!
It's too small in there.
No monsters outside of Tad's window!
You can't hold on out there.
No vampires, no werewolves, no things that bite.
You have no business here.
Nothing will touch Tad, or hurt Tad, all this night.
You have no business here.

Vic looked at this for a long time and reminded himself to tell Donna at least twice more before he left to read it to the kid every night. To impress on her how important the Monster Words were to Tad.

On his way out, he saw the closet door was open. Just a crack. He closed the door firmly and left his son's room.

Sometime much later that evening, the door swung open again. Heat lightning flickered sporadically, tattooing crazy shadows in there.

But Tad did not wake.

The next day, at quarter past seven in the morning, Steve Kemp's van backed out onto Route 11. Steve made miles, heading for Route 302. There he would turn left and drive southeast, crossing the state to Portland. He intended to flop at the Portland YMCA for a while.

On the van's dashboard was a neat pile of addressed mail – not printed in block letters this time but typed on his own machine. The typewriter was now in the back of the van, along with the rest of his stuff. It had taken him only an hour and a half to pack in his Castle Rock operation, including Bernie Carbo, who was now snoozing in his box by the rear doors. He and Bernie traveled light.

The typing job on the envelopes was a professional one. Sixteen years of creative writing had turned him into an excellent typist, if nothing else. He pulled over to the same box from which he had posted the anonymous note to Vic Trenton the night before and dropped the letters in. It would not have bothered him in the least to run out owing rent on the shop and the house if he had intended to leave the state, but since he was only going as far as Portland, it seemed prudent to do everything legally. This time he could afford not to cut corners; there was better than six hundred dollars in cash tucked into the small bolt-hole behind the van's glove compartment.

In addition to a check covering the rent he owed, he was returning deposits to several people who had made them on bigger jobs. Accompanying each check was a polite note saying he was very sorry to have caused any inconvenience, but his mother had been taken suddenly and seriously ill (every red-blooded American was a sucker for a momstory). Those for whom he had contracted to do work could pick up their furniture at the shop – the key was on the ledge above the door, just to the right, and would they kindly return the key to the same place after they had made their pickup. Thank you, thank you, blahde-blah, bullshit-bullshit. There would be some inconvenience, but no real hassle.

Steve dropped the letters into the mailbox. There was that satisfied feeling of having his ass well covered. He drove away toward Portland, singing along with the Grateful Dead, who were delivering 'Sugaree.' He pushed the van up to fifty-five, hoping traffic would stay light so he could get to Portland early enough to grab a court at Tennis of Maine. All in all, it looked like a good day. If Mr Businessman hadn't received his little letter bomb yet, he surely would today. Nifty, Steve thought, and burst out laughing.

At half past seven, as Steve Kemp was thinking Tennis and Vic Trenton was reminding himself to call Joe Camber about his wife's balky Pinto, Charity Camber was fixing her son's breakfast. Joe had left for Lewiston half an hour ago, hoping to find a '72 Camaro windshield at one of the city's automobile junkyards or used-parts outfits. This jibed well with Charity's plans, which she had made slowly and carefully.

She put Brett's plate of scrambled eggs and bacon in front of him and then sat down next to the boy. Brett glanced up from the book he was reading in mild surprise. After fixing his breakfast, his mother usually started on her round of morning chores. If you spoke to her too much before she got herself around a second cup of coffee, she was apt to show you the rough side of her tongue.

'Can I talk to you a minute, Brett?'

Mild surprise turned to something like amazement. Looking at her, he saw something utterly foreign to his mother's taciturn nature. She was nervous. He closed his book and said, 'Sure, Mom.'

'Would you like—' She cleared her throat and began again. 'How would you like to go down to Stratford, Connecticut, and see your Aunt Holly and your Uncle Jim? And your cousins?'

Brett grinned. He had only been out of Maine twice in his life, most recently with his father on a trip to Portsmouth, New Hampshire. They had gone to a used-car auction where Joe had picked up a '58 Ford with a hemi engine. 'Sure!' he said. 'When?'

'I was thinking of Monday,' she said. 'After the weekend of the Fourth. We'd be gone a week. Could you do that?'

'I *guess*! Jeez, I thought Dad had a lot of work lined up for next week. He must have—'

'I haven't mentioned this to your father yet.'

Brett's grin fell apart. He picked up a piece of bacon and began to eat it. 'Well, I know he promised Richie

Simms he'd pull the motor on his International Harvester. And Mr Miller from the school was gonna bring over his Ford because the tranny's shot. And—'

'I thought just the two of us would go,' Charity said. 'On the Greyhound from Portland.'

Brett looked doubtful. Outside the back-porch screen, Cujo padded slowly up the steps and collapsed onto the boards in the shade with a grunt. He looked in at THE BOY and THE WOMAN with weary, red-rimmed eyes. He was feeling very bad now, very bad indeed.

'Jeez, Mom, I don't know—'

'Don't say jeez. It's just the same as swearing.'

'Sorry.'

'Would you *like* to go? If your father said it was all right?'

'Yeah, really! Do you really think we could?'

'Maybe.' She was looking out through the window over the sink thoughtfully.

'How far is it to Stratford, Mom?'

'About three hundred and fifty miles, I guess.'

'Jee – I mean, boy, that's a long way. Is it—'

'Brett.'

He looked at her attentively. That curious intense quality was back in her voice and on her face. That nervousness.

'What, Mom?'

'Can you think of anything your father needs out in the shop? Any one thing he's been looking to get?'

The light dawned in Brett's eyes a little. 'Well, he always needs adjustable wrenches . . . and he's been wanting a new set of ball-and-sockets . . . and he could use a new

85

welder's helmet since the old one got a crack in the face-plate—'

'No, I mean anything big. Expensive.'

Brett thought awhile, then smiled. 'Well, what he'd really like to have is a new Jörgen chainfall, I guess. Rip that old motor out of Richie Simms's International just as slick as sh— well, slick.' He blushed and hurried on. 'But you couldn't get him nothing like that, Mom. That's really dear.'

Dear. Joe's word for expensive. She hated it.

'How much?'

'Well, the one in the catalogue says seventeen hundred dollars, but Dad could probably get it from Mr Belasco at Portland Machine for wholesale. Dad says Mr Belasco's scared of him.'

'Do you think there's something smart about that?' she asked sharply.

Brett sat back in his chair, a little frightened by her fierceness. He couldn't remember his mother ever acting quite like this. Even Cujo, out on the porch, pricked his ears a little.

'Well? Do you?'

'No, Mom,' he said, but Charity knew in a despairing way that he was lying. If you could scare somebody into giving you wholesale, you were trading a right smart. She had heard the admiration in Brett's voice, even if the boy himself had not. *Wants to be just like him. Thinks his daddy is just standing tall when he scares someone. Oh my God.*

'There's nothing smart about being able to scare people,' Charity said. 'All it takes is a big voice and a mean disposition. There's no smart to it.' She lowered her voice and flapped a hand at him. 'Go on and eat your eggs. I'm not going to shout at you. I guess it's the heat.'

He ate, but quietly and carefully, looking at her now and then. There were hidden mines around this morning.

'What would wholesale be, I wonder? Thirteen hundred dollars? A thousand?'

'I don't know, Mamma.'

'Would this Belasco deliver? On a big order like that?'

'Ayuh, I guess he would. If we had that kind of money.'

Her hand went to the pocket of her housedress. The lottery ticket was there. The green number on her ticket, 76, and the red number, 434, matched the numbers drawn by the State Lottery Commission two weeks before. She had checked it dozens of times, unable to believe it. She had invested fifty cents that week, as she had done every week since the lottery began in 1975, and this time she had won five thousand dollars. She hadn't cashed the ticket in yet, but neither had she let it out of her sight or her reach since she found out.

'We do have that kind of money,' she said. Brett goggled at her.

At quarter past ten, Vic slipped out of his Ad Worx office and went around to Bentley's for his morning coffee, unable to face the bitch's brew that was available at the office. He had spent the morning writing ads for Decoster Egg Farms. It was hard going. He had hated eggs since his boyhood, when his mother grimly forced one down his throat four days a week. The best he had been able to come up with so far was EGGS SAY LOVE . . . SEAMLESSLY. Not very good.

Seamlessly had given him the idea of a trick photo which would show an egg with a zipper running around it's middle. It was a good image, but where did it lead? Noplace that he had been able to discover. Ought to ask the Tadder, he thought, as the waitress brought him coffee and a blueberry muffin. Tad liked eggs.

It wasn't really the egg ad that was bringing him down, of course. It was having to take off for twelve days. Well, it had to be. Roger had convinced him of that. They would have to get in there and pitch like hell.

Good old garrulous Roger, whom Vic loved almost like a brother. Roger would have been more than glad to cruise down here to Bentley's with him, to have a coffee with him, and to talk his ear off. But this one time, Vic needed to be alone. To think. The two of them would be spending most of two weeks together starting Monday, sweating it out, and that was quite enough, even for soul brothers.

His mind turned toward the Red Razberry Zingers fiasco again, and he let it, knowing that sometimes a no-pressure, almost idle review of a bad situation could – for him, at least – result in some new insight, a fresh angle.

What had happened was bad enough, and Zingers had been withdrawn from the market. Bad enough, but not terrible. It wasn't like that canned mushroom thing; no one had gotten sick or died, and even consumers realized that a company could take a pratfall now and then. Look at that McDonald's glass giveaway a couple-three years ago. The paint on the glasses had been found to contain an unacceptably high lead content. The glasses had been withdrawn quickly, consigned to that promotional limbo inhabited by creatures such as Speedy AlkaSeltzer and Vic's own personal favorite, Big Dick Chewing Gum.

The glasses had been bad for the McDonald's Corporation, but no one had accused Ronald McDonald of trying to poison his pre-teen constituency. And no one had actually accused the Sharp Cereal Professor either, although comedians from Bob Hope to Steve Martin had taken potshots at him, and Johnny Carson had run off an entire monologue – couched in careful double entendre – about the Red Razberry Zingers affair one evening during his opening spot on *The Tonight Show*. Needless to say, the Sharp Cereal Professor ads had been jerked from the tube. Also needless to say, the character actor who played the Professor was wild at the way events had turned on him.

I could imagine a worse situation, Roger had said after the first shock waves had subsided a bit and the thrice-daily long-distance calls between Portland and Cleveland were no longer flying.

What? Vic had asked.

Well, Roger had answered, straight-faced, *we could be working on the Bon Vivant Vichysoisse account.*

'More coffee, sir?'

Vic glanced up at the waitress. He started to say no, then nodded. 'Half a cup, please,' he said.

She poured it and left. Vic stirred it randomly, not drinking it.

There had been a mercifully brief health scare before a number of doctors spoke up on TV and in the papers, all of them saying the coloration was harmless. There had been something like it once before; the stews on a commercial airline had been struck down with weird orange skin discolorations which finally proved to be nothing more serious than a rub-off of the orange dye on the life jackets they demonstrated for their passengers before takeoff. Years before that, the food dye in a certain brand of frankfurters had produced an internal effect similar to that of Red Razberry Zingers.

Old man Sharp's lawyers had lodged a multimillion-dollar damage suit against the dye manufacturer, a case that would probably drag on for three years and then be settled out of court. No matter; the suit provided a forum from which to make the public aware that the fault – the *totally temporary* fault, the *completely harmless* fault – had not been that of the Sharp Company.

Nonetheless, Sharp stock had tumbled sharply on the Big Board. It had since made up less than half the original drop. The cereals themselves had shown a sudden dip in sales but had since made up most of the ground that had been lost after Zingers showed its treacherous red face. Sharp's All-Grain Blend, in fact, was doing better than ever before.

So there was nothing wrong here, right?

Wrong. So wrong.

The Sharp Cereal Professor was what was wrong. The poor guy would never be able to make a comeback. After the scare come the laughs, and the Professor, with his sober mien and his schoolroom surroundings, had been literally laughed to death.

George Carlin, in his nightclub routine: 'Yeah, it's a crazy world. Crazy world.' Carlin bends his head over his mike for a moment, meditating, and then looks up again. 'The Reagan guys are doing their campaign shit on TV, right? Russians are getting ahead of us in the arms race. The Russians are turning out missiles by the thousands, right? So Jimmy gets on TV to do one of *his* spots, and he says, "My fellow Americans, the day the Russians get ahead of us in the arms race will be the day the youth of America shits red."'

Big laugh from the audience.

'So Ronnie gets on the phone to Jimmy, and he says, "Mr President, what did Amy have for breakfast?"'

A gigantic laugh from the audience. Carlin pauses. The *real* punchline is then delivered in a low, insinuating tone:

'Nooope . . . nothing wrong here.'

The audience roars its approval, applauds wildly. Carlin shakes his head sadly. 'Red shit, man. Wow. Dig on it awhile.'

That was the problem. George Carlin was the problem. Bob Hope was the problem. Johnny Carson was the problem. Steve Martin was the problem. Every barbershop wit in America was the problem.

And then, consider this: Sharp stock had gone down nine and had only rebounded four and a quarter. The shareholders were going to be hollering for somebody's head. Let's see . . . whose do we give them? Who had the bright idea of the Sharp Cereal Professor in the first place? How about those guys as the most eligible? Never mind the fact that the Professor had been on for four years before the Zingers debacle. Never mind the fact that when the Sharp Cereal Professor (and his cohorts the Cookie Sharpshooter and George and Gracie) had come on the scene, Sharp stock had been three and a quarter points lower than it was now.

Never mind all that. Mind this instead: Just the *fact*, just the *public announcement* in the trades that Ad Worx had lost the Sharp account — just that would probably cause shares to bob up another point and a half to two points. And when a new ad campaign actually began, investors would take it as a sign that the old woes were finally behind the company, and the stock might creep up another point.

Of course, Vic thought, stirring Sweet 'n Low into his coffee, that was only theory. And even if the theory turned out to be true, both he and Roger believed that a short-run gain for Sharp would be more than offset if a new ad campaign, hastily thrown together by people who didn't know the Sharp Company as he and Roger did, or the competitive cereal market in general, didn't do the job.

And suddenly that new slant, that fresh angle, popped into his mind. It came unbidden and unexpected. His coffee cup paused halfway to his mouth and his eyes widened. In his mind he saw two men — perhaps him and Roger, perhaps old man Sharp and his ageing kid — filling in a grave. Their spades were flying. A lantern flickered fitfully in the windy night. Rain was drizzling down. These corporate sextons threw an occasional furtive glance behind them. It was a burial by night, a covert act performed in the darkness. They were burying the Sharp Cereal Professor in secret, *and that was wrong*.

'Wrong,' he muttered aloud.

Sure it was. Because if they buried him in the dead of night, he could never say what he had to say: that he was sorry.

He took his Pentel pen from his inner coat pocket, took a napkin from the holder, and wrote swiftly across it:

CUJO

The Sharp Cereal Professor needs to apologize.

He looked at it. The letters were getting larger, fuzzing as the ink sank into the napkin. Below that first sentence he added:

Decent burial.

And below that:

DAYLIGHT burial.

He still wasn't sure what it meant; it was more metaphor than sense, but that was how his best ideas came to him. And there was something there. He felt sure of it.

Cujo lay on the floor of the garage, in semi-gloom. It was hot in here but it was even worse outside . . . and the daylight outside was too bright. It never had been before; in fact, he had never even really noticed the quality of the light before. But he was noticing now. Cujo's head hurt. His muscles hurt. The bright light made his eyes hurt. He was hot. And his muzzle still ached where he had been scratched.

Ached and festered.

THE MAN was gone somewhere. Not long after he left, THE BOY and THE WOMAN had gone somewhere, leaving him alone. THE BOY had put a big dish of food out for Cujo, and Cujo had eaten a little bit. The food made him feel worse instead of better, and he left the rest of it alone.

Now there was the growl of a truck turning into the driveway. Cujo got up and went to the barn door, knowing already it was a stranger. He knew the sound of both THE MAN'S truck and the family car. He stood in the doorway, head poking out into the bright glare that hurt his eyes. The truck backed up the driveway and then stopped. Two men got down from the cab and came around to the back. One of them ran up the truck's sliding back door. The rattling, banging noise hurt Cujo's ears. He whined and retreated back into the comforting gloom.

The truck was from Portland Machine. Three hours ago, Charity Camber and her still-dazzled son had gone into Portland Machine's main office on Brighton Avenue and she had written a personal check for a new Jörgen chainfall – wholesale had turned out to be exactly $1,241.71, tax included. Before going to Portland Machine she had gone into the State Liquor Store on Congress Street to fill out a lottery claim form. Brett, forbidden absolutely to come inside with her, stood on the sidewalk with his hands in his pockets.

The clerk told Charity she would get a Lottery Commission check in the mail. How long? Two weeks at the very outside. It would come minus a deduction of roughly eight hundred dollars for taxes. This sum was based on her declaration of Joe's yearly income.

The deduction for taxes before the fact did not anger Charity at all. Up until the moment when the clerk had checked her number against his sheet, she had been holding her breath, still unable to believe this had really happened to her. Then the clerk had nodded, congratulated her. None of that mattered. What mattered was that now she could breathe again, and the ticket was no longer her responsibility. It had returned to the bowels of the Lottery Commission. Her Check Would Be in the Mail – wonderful, mystical, talismanic phrase.

And still she felt a small pang as she watched the

dog-eared ticket, limp with her own nervous perspiration, clipped to the form she had filled out and then stored away. Lady Luck had singled her out. For the first time in her life, maybe for the only time, that heavy muslin drape of the everyday had been twitched a little, showing her a bright and shining world beyond. She was a practical woman, and in her heart she knew that she hated her husband more than a little, and feared him more than a little, but that they would grow old together, and he would die, leaving her with his debts and – this she would not admit for sure even in her secret heart, but now she feared it! – perhaps with his spoilt son.

If her name had been plucked from the big drum in the twice-yearly Super Drawing, if she had won ten times the five thousand dollars she had won, she might have entertained notions of pushing aside that dull muslin curtain, taking her son by the hand, and leading them both out into whatever was beyond Town Road No. 3 and Camber's Garage, Foreign Cars Our Specialty, and Castle Rock. She might have taken Brett to Connecticut with the express purpose of asking her sister how much a small apartment in Stratford would cost.

But it had only been a twitch of the curtain. That was all. She had seen Lady Luck for a bare, brief moment, as wonderful, puzzling, and inexplicable as a bright fairy dancing under mushrooms in the dewy light of dawn . . . seen once, never again. So she felt a pang when the ticket disappeared from her view, even though it had robbed her sleep. She understood that she would buy a lottery ticket a week for the rest of her life and never win more than two dollars all at once.

Never mind. You don't count teeth in a gifthorse. Not if you were smart.

They went out to Portland Machine and she had written the check, reminding herself to stop at the bank on their way home and transfer enough money from savings to checking so that the check wouldn't bounce. She and Joe had a little over four thousand dollars in their savings account after fifteen years. Just about enough to cover three quarters of their outstanding debts, if you excluded the mortgage on the farm. She had no right to exclude that, of course, but she always did. She could not bring herself to think about the mortgage except payment by payment. But they would dent the savings all they wanted to now, and then deposit the Lottery Commission check in that account when it came. All they would be losing was two weeks' interest.

The man from Portland Machine, Lewis Belasco, said he would have the chainfall machine delivered that very afternoon, and he was as good as his word.

Joe Magruder and Ronnie DuBay got the chainfall on the truck's pneumatic Step-Loader, and it whooshed gently down to the dirt driveway on a sigh of air.

'Pretty big order for ole Joe Camber,' Ronnie said.

Magruder nodded. 'Put it in the barn, his wife said. That's his garage. Better get a good hold, Ronnie. This is a heavy whore.'

Joe Magruder got his hold, Ronnie got his, and, puffing and grunting, the two of them half walked it, half carried it into the barn.

'Let's set it down a minute,' Ronnie managed. 'I can't

see where the hell I'm goin. Let's get used to the dark before we go ass over cowcatcher.'

They set the chainfall down with a thump. After the bright afternoon glare outside, Joe was mostly blinded. He could only make out the vague shapes of things – a car up on jacks, a workbench, a sense of beams going up to a loft.

'This thing ought—' Ronnie began, and then stopped abruptly.

Coming out of the darkness from beyond the front end of the jacked-up car was a low, guttural growling. Ronnie felt the sweat he had worked up suddenly turn clammy. The hairs on the back of his neck stirred.

'Holy crow, you hear that?' Magruder whispered. Ronnie could see Joe now. Joe's eyes were big and scared-looking.

'I hear it.'

It was a sound as low as a powerful outboard engine idling. Ronnie knew it took a big dog to make a sound like that. And when a big dog did, it more often than not meant business. He hadn't seen a BEWARE OF DOG sign when they drove up, but sometimes these bumpkins from the boonies didn't bother with one. He knew one thing. He hoped to God that the dog making that sound was chained up.

'Joe? You ever been out here before?'

'Once. It's a Saint Bernard. Big as a fucking house. He didn't do that before.' Joe gulped. Ronnie heard some-thing in his throat click. 'Oh, God. Lookit there, Ronnie.'

Ronnie's eyes had come partway to adjusting, and his half-sight lent what he was seeing a spectral, almost supernatural cast. He knew you never showed a mean dog your fear — they could smell it coming off you — but he began to shudder helplessly anyway. He couldn't help it. The dog was a monster. It was standing deep in the barn, beyond the jacked-up car. It was a Saint Bernard for sure; there was no mistaking the heavy coat, tawny even in the shadows, the breadth of shoulder. Its head was down. Its eyes glared at them with steady, sunken animosity.

It wasn't on a chain.

'Back up slow,' Joe said. 'Don't run, for Christ's sake.'

They began to back up, and as they did, the dog began to walk slowly forward. It was a stiff walk; not really a walk at all, Ronnie thought. It was a *stalk*. That dog wasn't fucking around. Its engine was running and it was ready to go. Its head remained low. That growl never changed pitch. It took a step forward for every step they took back.

For Joe Magruder the worst moment came when they backed into the bright sunlight again. It dazzled him, blinded him. He could no longer see the dog. If it came for him now —

Reaching behind him, he felt the side of the truck. That was enough to break his nerve. He bolted for the cab.

On the other side, Ronnie DuBay did the same. He reached the passenger door and fumbled at the latch for an endless moment. He clawed at it. He could still hear that low growling, so much like an idling Evinrude 80 hp motor. The door wouldn't open. He waited for the dog to pull a chunk of his ass off. At last his thumb found the button, the door opened, and he scrambled into the cab, panting.

He looked in the rearview mirror bolted outside his

window and saw the dog standing in the open barn door, motionless. He looked over at Joe, who was sitting behind the wheel and grinning at him sheepishly. Ronnie offered his own shaky grin in return.

'Just a dog,' Ronnie said.

'Yeah. Bark's worse'n his bite.'

'Right. Let's go back in there and screw around with that chainfall some more.'

'Fuck you,' Joe said.

'And the horse you rode in on.'

They laughed together. Ronnie passed him a smoke. 'What do you say we get going?'

'I'm your guy,' Joe said, and started the truck.

Halfway back to Portland, Ronnie said, almost to himself: 'That dog's going bad.'

Joe was driving with his elbow cocked out the window. He glanced over at Ronnie. 'I was scared, and I don't mind saying so. One of those little dogs gives me shit in a situation like that, with nobody home, I'd just as soon kick it in the balls, you know? I mean, if people don't chain up a dog that bites, they deserve what they get, you know? *That* thing . . . did you see it? I bet that mother-humper went two hundred pounds.'

'Maybe I ought to give Joe Camber a call,' Ronnie said. 'Tell him what happened. Might save him gettin his arm chewed off. What do you think?'

'What's Joe Camber done for you lately?' Joe Magruder asked with a grin.

Ronnie nodded thoughtfully. 'He don't blow me like you do, that's true.'

'Last blowjob I had was from your wife. Wasn't half bad, either.'

'Get bent, you fairy.'

They laughed together. Nobody called Joe Camber. When they got back to Portland Machine, it was near knocking-off time. Screwing-around time. They took fifteen minutes writing the trip up. Belasco came out back and asked them if Camber had been there to take delivery. Ronnie DuBay said sure. Belasco, who was a prick of the highest order, went away. Joe Magruder told Ronnie to have a nice weekend and a happy fucking Fourth. Ronnie said he planned to get in the bag and stay that way until Sunday night. They clocked out.

Neither of them thought about Cujo again until they read about him in the paper.

Vic spent most of that afternoon before the long weekend going over the details of the trip with Roger. Roger was so careful about details that he was almost paranoid. He had made the plane and hotel reservations through an agency. Their flight to Boston would leave Portland Jetport at 7:10 A.M. Monday. Vic said he would pick Roger up in the Jag at 5:30. He thought that was unnecessarily early, but he knew Roger and Roger's little tics. They talked generally about the trip, consciously avoiding specifics. Vic kept his coffee-break ideas to himself and the napkin stowed safely away in his sport-jacket pocket. Roger would be more receptive when they were away.

Vic thought about leaving early and decided to go back and check the afternoon mail first. Lisa, their secretary, had already left for the day, getting a jump on the holiday weekend. Hell, you couldn't get a secretary to stay until the stroke of five any more, holiday weekend or not. As far as Vic was concerned, it was just another sign of the continuing decay of Western Civ. Probably at this very moment Lisa, who was beautiful, just twenty-one, and almost totally breastless, was entering the Interstate flow of traffic, bound south to Old Orchard or the Hamptons, dressed in tight jeans and a nothing halter. Get down, disco Lisa, Vic thought, and grinned a little.

There was a single unopened letter on his desk blotter.

He picked it up curiously, noting first the word PERSONAL printed below the address, and second the fact that his address had been printed in solid caps.

He held it, turning it over in his hands, feeling a vague thread of disquiet slip into what was a general mood of tired well-being. Far back in his mind, hardly even acknowledged, was a sudden urge to rip the letter into halves, fourths, eighths, and then toss the pieces into the waste-basket.

Instead, he tore it open and pulled out a single sheet of paper.

More block letters.

The simple message – six sentences – hit him like a straight shot just below the heart. He did not so much sit in his chair as collapse into it. A little grunt escaped him, the sound of a man who has suddenly lost all his wind. His mind roared with nothing but white noise for a length of time he didn't – couldn't – understand or comprehend. If Roger had come in just then, he likely would have thought Vic was having a heart attack. In a way, he was.

His face was paper-white. His mouth hung open. Bluish half-moons had appeared under his eyes.

He read the message again.

And then again.

At first his eyes were drawn to the first interrogative:

WHAT'S THAT MOLE JUST ABOVE HER PUBIC HAIR LOOK LIKE TO YOU?

It's a mistake, he thought confusedly. *No one knows about that but me . . . well, her mother. And her father.* Then, hurt, he felt the first splinters of jealousy: *Even her bikini covers that . . . her* little *bikini.*

He ran a hand through his hair. He put the letter down and ran both hands through his hair. That punched, gasping feeling was still there in his chest. The feeling that his heart was pumping air instead of blood. He felt fright and pain and confusion. But of the three, the dominant feeling, the overriding emotion, was terrible fright.

The letter glared up at him and shouted:

I ENJOYED FUCKING THE SHIT OUT OF HER .

Now it was this line his eyes fixed upon, not wanting to leave. He could hear the drone of a plane in the sky outside, leaving the Jetport, heading up, heading out, making for points unknown, and he thought, I ENJOYED FUCKING THE SHIT OUT OF HER. *Crude, that's crude.* Yes sir and yes ma'am, yes indeedy. It was the hack of a blunt knife. FUCKING THE SHIT OUT OF HER, what an image that made.

Nothing fancy about it. It was like getting a splash in the eyes from a squirtgun loaded up with battery acid.

He tried hard to think coherently and
(I ENJOYED)
just couldn't
(FUCKING THE SHIT OUT OF HER)
do it.

Now his eyes went to the last line and that was the one he read over and over again, as if trying to cram the sense of it somehow into his brain. That huge feeling of fright kept getting in the way.

DO YOU HAVE ANY QUESTIONS?

Yes. All of a sudden he had all kinds of questions. The only thing was, he didn't seem to want answers to any of them.

A new thought crossed his mind. What if Roger hadn't gone home? Often he poked his head into Vic's office before leaving if there was a light on. He might be even more likely to do so tonight, with the trip pending. The thought made Vic feel panicky, and an absurd memory surfaced: all those times he had spent masturbating in the bathroom as a teenager, unable to help himself but terribly afraid everyone must know exactly what he was up to in there. If Roger came in, he would see something was wrong. He didn't want that. He got up and went to the window, which looked down six stories to the parking lot which served the building. Roger's bright-yellow Honda Civic was gone from its space. He had gone home.

Pulled out of himself, Vic listened. The offices of Ad Worx were totally silent. There was the resonating quiet that seems the sole property of business quarters after hours. There was not even the sound of old Mr Steigmeyer, the custodian, rattling around. He would have to sign out in the lobby. He would have to –

Now there *was* a sound. At first he didn't know what it was. It came to him in a moment. It was whimpering. The sound of an animal with a smashed foot. Still looking out the window, he saw the cars left in the parking lot double, then treble, through a film of tears.

Why couldn't he get mad? Why did he have to be so fucking *scared*?

An absurd, antique word came to mind. *Jilted*, he thought. *I've been jilted.*

The whimpering sounds kept coming. He tried to lock his throat, and it did no good. He lowered his head and gripped the convector grille that ran below the window at waist height. Gripped it until his fingers hurt, until the metal creaked and protested.

How long had it been since he had cried? He had cried the night Tad was born, but that had been relief. He had cried when his dad died after fighting grimly for his life for three days after a massive heart attack struck him, and those tears, shed at seventeen, had been like these, burning, not wanting to come; it was more like bleeding than crying. But at seventeen it was easier to cry, easier to bleed. When you were seventeen you still expected to have to do your share of both.

He stopped whimpering. He thought it was done. And then a low cry came out of him, a harsh, wavering sound, and he thought: *Was that me? God, was it me that made that sound?*

The tears began to slide down his cheeks. There was another harsh sound, then another. He gripped the convector grille and cried.

Forty minutes later he was sitting in Deering Oaks Park. He had called home and told Donna he would be late. She started to ask why, and why he sounded so strange. He told her he would be home before dark. He told her to go ahead and feed Tad. Then he hung up before she could say anything else.

Now he was sitting in the park.

The tears had burned off most of the fear. What was left was an ugly slag of anger. That was the next level in this geological column of knowledge. But anger wasn't the right word. He was enraged. He was infuriated. It was as if he had been stung by something. A part of him had recognized that it would be dangerous for him to go home now . . . dangerous for all three of them.

It would be so pleasurable to hide the wreckage by making more; it would (let's face it) be mindlessly pleasurable to punch her cheating face in.

He was sitting beside the duckpond. On the other side, a spirited Frisbee game was going on. He noticed that all four of the girls playing – and two of the boys – were on roller skates. Roller skates were big this summer. He saw a young girl in a tube top pushing a cart of pretzels, peanuts, and canned soft drinks. Her face was soft and fresh and innocent. One of the guys playing Frisbee flipped her the disk; she caught it deftly and flipped it back. In the sixties, Vic thought, she would have been in a commune, diligently picking bugs off tomato plants. Now she was probably a member in good standing of the Small Business Administration.

He and Roger used to come down here to eat their lunches sometimes. That had been in the first year. Then Roger noticed that, although the pond looked lovely, there was a faint but definite odor of putridity hanging around it . . . and the small house on the rock in the center of the pond was whitewashed not with paint but with gullshit. A few weeks later, Vic had noted a decaying rat floating amid the condoms and gum wrappers at the edge of the pond. He didn't think they had been back since then.

The Frisbee, a bright red, floated across the sky.

The image that had provoked his anger kept recurring. He couldn't keep it away. It was as crude as his anonymous correspondent's choice of words had been, but he couldn't ditch it. He saw them screwing in his and Donna's bedroom. Screwing in their bed. What he saw in this mind-movie was every bit as explicit as one of those grainy X-rated pictures you see at the State Theater on Congress Street. She was groaning, sheened lightly with perspiration, beautiful. Every muscle pulled taut. Her eyes had that hungry look they got when the sex was good, their color darker. He knew the expression, he knew the posture, he knew the sounds. He had thought – *thought* – he was the only one who did. Not even her mother and father would know about that.

Then he would think of the man's penis – his cock – going up inside her. *In the saddle*; that phrase came and clanged in his mind idiotically, refusing to die away. He saw them screwing to a Gene Autry soundtrack: *I'm back in the saddle again, out where a friend is a friend . . .*

It made him feel creepy. It made him feel outraged. It made him feel *infuriated*.

The Frisbee soared and came down. Vic followed its course.

He had suspected something, yes. But suspecting was not like knowing; he knew that now, if nothing else. He could write an essay on the difference between suspecting and knowing. What made it doubly cruel was the fact that he had really begun to believe that the suspicions were groundless. And even if they weren't, what you didn't know couldn't hurt you. Wasn't that right? If a man is crossing a darkened room with a deep, open hole in the middle of it, and if he passes within inches of it, he doesn't need to know he almost fell in. There is no need for fear. Not if the lights are off.

Well, he hadn't fallen in. He had been *pushed*. The question was, What was he going to do about it? The angry part of him, hurt, bruised, and bellowing, was not in the slightest inclined to be 'adult', to acknowledge that there were slips on one or both sides in a great many marriages. Fuck the Penthouse *Forum*, or *Variations*, or whatever they're calling it these days, that's my *wife* we're talking about, she was screwing someone

(out where a friend is a friend)

when my back was turned, when Tad was out of the house –

The images began to unreel again, crumpled sheets, straining bodies, soft sounds. Ugly phrases, terrible terms kept crowding up like a bunch of freaks looking at an accident: *nooky, hair pie, put the boots to her, shot my load, I-don't-fuck-for-fortune-and-I-don't-fuck-for-fame-but-the-way-I-fuck-ya-mamma-is-a-goddam-shame, my turtle in your mud, bang for the gang, stoop for the troops* –

Inside my wife! he thought, agonized, hands clenching. *Inside my wife!*

But the angry, hurt part acknowledged – grudgingly – that he couldn't go home and beat the hell out of Donna. He could, however, take Tad and go. Never mind the explanations. Let her try and stop him, if she had cheek enough to do it. He didn't think she would. Take Tad, go to a motel, get a lawyer. Cut the cord cleanly, and don't look back.

But if he just grabbed Tad and took him to a motel, wouldn't the boy be frightened? Wouldn't he want an explanation? He was only four, but that was old enough to know when something was badly, frighteningly wrong. Then there was the matter of the trip – Boston, New York, Cleveland. Vic didn't give a goddam about the trip, not now; old man Sharp and his kid could take a flying jump at the moon for all he cared. But he wasn't in it alone. He had a partner. The partner had a wife and two kids. Even now, hurting as badly as he was, Vic recognized his responsibility to at least go through the motions of trying to save the account – which was tantamount to trying to save Ad Worx itself.

And although he didn't want to ask it, there was another question: Exactly why did he want to take Tad and go, without even hearing her side of the story? Because her sleeping around was wrecking Tad's morals? He didn't think so. It was because his mind had immediately seized upon the fact that the way to hurt her most surely and most deeply (as deeply as he hurt right now) was through Tad. But did he want to turn his son into the emotional equivalent of a crowbar, or a sledgehammer? He thought not.

Other questions.

The note. Think about the note for a minute. Not just what it said, not just those six lines of battery-acid filth; think about the *fact* of the note. Someone had just killed the goose that had been — pardon the pun — laying the golden eggs. Why had Donna's lover sent that note?

Because the goose was no longer laying, of course. And the shadow man who had sent the note was mad as hell.

Had Donna dumped the guy?

He tried to see it any other way and couldn't. Stripped of its sudden, shocking force, wasn't I ENJOYED FUCKING THE SHIT OUT OF HER the classic dog-in-the-manger ploy? If you can't have it any more, piss on it so no one else will want it either. Illogical, but ah so satisfying. The new, easier atmosphere at home fit into that reading, as well. The almost palpable sense of relief Donna radiated. She had turned the shadow man out, and the shadow man had hit back at her husband with the anonymous note.

Last question: Did it make any difference?

He took the note out of his jacket pocket again and turned it over and over in his hands, not unfolding it. He watched the red Frisbee float across the sky and wondered what the hell he was going to do.

'What the Christ is that?' Joe Camber asked.

Each word came out spaced, almost inflectionless. He

stood in the doorway, looking at his wife. Charity was setting his place. She and Brett had already eaten. Joe had come in with a truckful of odds and ends, had begun to drive into the garage, and had seen what was waiting for him.

'It's a chainfall,' she said. She had sent Brett over to play with his buddy Dave Bergeron for the evening. She didn't want him around if this went badly. 'Brett said you wanted one. A Jörgen chainfall, he said.'

Joe crossed the room. He was a thin man with a scrawny-strong physique, a big blade nose, and a quiet, agile way of walking. Now his green felt hat was tipped back on his head to show his receding hairline. There was a smudge of grease on his forehead. There was beer on his breath. His blue eyes were small and hard. He was a man who didn't like surprises.

'You talk to me, Charity,' he said.

'Sit down. Your supper will get cold.'

His arm shot out like a piston. Hard fingers bit into her arm. 'What the fuck are you up to? Talk to me, I said.'

'Don't curse at me, Joe Camber.' He was hurting her badly, but she wouldn't give him the satisfaction of seeing it in her face or in her eyes. He was like a beast in many ways, and although this had excited her when she was young, it excited her no longer. She had recognized over the course of their years together that she could sometimes gain the upper hand just by seeming brave. Not always, but sometimes.

'You tell me what the fuck you been up to, Charity!'

'Sit down and eat,' she said quietly, 'and I will.'

He sat down and she brought his plate. There was a sirloin steak on it.

'Since when can we afford to eat like the Rockefellers?' he asked. 'You got some pretty tall explaining to do, I'd say.'

She brought his coffee and a split baked potato. 'Can't you use the chainfall?'

'Never said I couldn't use it. But I damn well can't afford it.' He began to eat, his eyes never leaving her. He wouldn't hit her now, she knew. This was her chance, while he was still relatively sober. If he was going to hit her, it would be after he came back from Gary Pervier's, sloshing with vodka and filled with wounded male pride.

Charity sat down across from him and said, 'I won the lottery.'

His jaws halted and then began moving again. He forked steak into his mouth. 'Sure,' he said. 'And tomorrow ole Cujo out there's gonna shit a mess of gold buttons.' He pointed his fork at the dog, who was pacing restlessly up and down the porch. Brett didn't like to take him over to the Bergerons' because they had rabbits in a hutch and they drove Cujo wild.

Charity reached into her apron pocket, took out her copy of the prize claim form that the agent had filled out, and handed it across the table to Joe.

Camber flattened the paper out with one blunt-fingered hand and stared it up and down. His eyes centred on the figure. 'Five—' He began, and then shut his mouth with a snap.

Charity watched him, saying nothing. He didn't smile. He didn't come around the table and kiss her. For a man

111

with his turn of mind, she thought bitterly, good fortune only meant that something was lying in wait.

He looked up at last. 'You won five thousand dollars?'

'Less taxes, ayuh.'

'How long you been playing the lottery?'

'I buy a fifty-center every week . . . and you don't dare dun me about it, either, Joe Camber, with all the beer you buy.'

'Watch your mouth, Charity,' he said. His eyes were unblinking, brilliant blue. 'Just watch your mouth, or it might swell up on you all at once.' He began to eat his steak again, and behind the set mask of her face, she relaxed a little. She had thrust the chair in the tiger's face for the first time, and it hadn't bitten her. At least not yet. 'This money. When do we get it?'

'The check will come in two weeks or a little less. I bought the chainfall out of the money that's in our savings account. That claim form is just as good as gold. That's what the agent said.'

'You went out and bought that thing?'

'I asked Brett what he thought you'd want most. It's a present.'

'Thanks.' He went on eating.

'I got you a present,' she said. 'Now you give me one, Joe. Okay?'

He went on eating and he went on looking at her. He didn't say anything. His eyes were totally expressionless. He was eating with his hat on, still pushed back on his head.

She spoke to him slowly, deliberately, knowing it would be a mistake to rush. 'I want to go away for a week. With Brett. To see Holly and Jim down in Connecticut.'

'No,' he said, and went on eating.

'We could go on the bus. We'd stay with them. It would be cheap. There would be plenty of money left over. That found money. It wouldn't cost a third of what that chainfall cost. I called the bus station and asked them about the round-trip fare.'

'No. I need Brett here to help me.'

She clutched her hands together in a hard, twisting fury under the table, but made her face remain calm and smooth. 'You get along without him in the school year.'

'I said no, Charity,' he said, and she saw with galling, bitter certainty that he was enjoying this. He saw how much she wanted this. How she had planned for it. He was enjoying her pain.

She got up and went to the sink, not because she had anything to do there, but because she needed time to get herself under control. The evening star peeped in at her, high and remote. She ran water. The porcelain was a discolored yellowish color. Like Joe, their water was hard.

Maybe disappointed, feeling that she had given up too easily, Camber elaborated. 'The boy's got to learn some responsibility. Won't hurt him to help me this summer instead of running off to Davy Bergeron's house every day and night.'

She turned off the water. 'I sent him over there.'

'*You* did? Why?'

'Because I thought it might go like this,' she said, turning back to him. 'But I told him you'd say yes, what with the money and the chainfall.'

'If you knew better, you sinned against the boy,' Joe said. 'Next time I guess you'll think before you throw your tongue in gear.' He smiled at her through a mouthfull of food and reached for the bread.

'You could come with us, if you wanted.'

'Sure. I'll just tell Richie Simms to forget getting in his first cutting this summer. Besides, why do I want to go down and see them two? From what I've seen of them and what you tell of them, I got to think they're a couple of first-class snots. Only reason you like them is because you'd like to be a snot like them.' His voice was gradually rising. He began to spray food. When he got like this he frightened her and she gave in. Most times. She would not do that tonight. 'Mostly you'd like the boy to be a snot like them. That's what I think. You'd like to turn him against me, I guess. Am I wrong?'

'Why don't you ever call him by his name?'

'You want to just shut the craphouse door now, Charity,' he said, looking at her hard. A flush had crept up his cheeks and across his forehead. 'Mind me, now.'

'No,' she said. 'That's not the end.'

He dropped his fork, astounded. '*What*? What did you say?'

She walked towards him, allowing herself the luxury of total anger for the first time in her marriage. But it was all inside, burning and sloshing like acid. She could feel it eating. She daren't shout. To shout would be the end for sure. She kept her voice low.

'Yes, you'd think that about my sister and her husband. Sure you would. Look at you, sitting there and eating with your dirty hands and your hat still on. You don't want him down there seeing how other people live. Just the same way I don't want him seeing how you and your friends live when you're off to yourselves. That's why I wouldn't let him go on that hunting trip with you last November.'

She paused and he only sat there, a half-eaten slice of Wonder Bread in one hand, steak juice on his chin. She thought that the only thing keeping him from springing at her was his total amazement that she should be saying these things at all.

'So I'll trade with you,' she said. 'I've got you that chainfall and I'm willing to hand over the rest of the money to you – lots wouldn't – but if you're going to be so ungrateful, I'll go you one more. You let him go down with me to Connecticut, and I'll let him go up to Moosehead with you come deerhunting season.' She felt cold and prickly all over, as if she had just offered to strike a bargain with the devil.

'I ought to strap you,' he said wonderingly. He spoke to her as if she were a child who had misunderstood some very simple case of cause and effect. 'I'll take him hunting with me if I want, when I want. Don't you know that? He's my *son*. God's sake. *If* I want, *when* I want.' He smiled a little, pleased with the sound it made. 'Now – you got that?'

She locked her eyes with his. 'No,' she said. 'You won't.'

He got up in a hurry then. His chair fell over.

'I'll put a stop to it,' she said. She wanted to step back from him, but that would end it too. One false move, one sign of giving, and he would be on her.

He was unbuckling his belt. 'I'm going to strap you, Charity,' he said regretfully.

'I'll put a stop to it any way I can. I'll go up to the

school and report him truant. Go to Sheriff Bannerman and report him kidnapped. But most of all . . . I'll see to it that Brett doesn't want to go.'

He pulled his belt from the loops of his pants and held it with the buckle end penduluming back and forth by the floor.

'The only way you'll get him up there with the rest of those drunks and animals before he's fifteen is if I let him go,' she said. 'You sling your belt on me if you want, Joe Camber. Nothing is going to change that.'

'Is that so?'

'I'm standing here and telling you it is.'

But suddenly he didn't seem to be in the room with her any more. His eyes had gone far away, musing. She had seen him do this other times. Something had just crossed his mind, a new fact to be laboriously added into the equation. She prayed that whatever it was would be on her side of the equals sign. She had never gone so much against him before, and she was scared.

Camber suddenly smiled. 'Regular little spitfire, ain't you?'

She said nothing.

He began to slip his belt back into the loops of his pants again. He was still smiling, his eyes still far away. 'You suppose you can screw like one of those spitfires? Like one of those little Mexican spitfires?'

She still said nothing, wary.

'If I say you and him can go, what about then? You suppose we could shoot for the moon?'

'What do you mean?'

'It means okay,' he said. 'You and him.'

He crossed the room in his quick, agile way, and it made her cold to think of how quick he could have crossed it a minute before, how quick he could have had his belt on her. And who would there have been to stop him? What a man did with − or to − his wife, that was their own affair. She could have done nothing, said nothing. Because of Brett. Because of her pride.

He put his hand on her shoulder. He dropped it to one of her breasts. He squeezed it, 'Come on,' he said. 'I'm horny.'

'Brett—'

'He won't be in until nine. Come on. Told you, you can go. You can at least say thanks, can't you?'

A kind of cosmic absurdity rose to her lips and had passed through them before she could stop it: 'Take off your hat.'

He sailed it heedlessly across the kitchen. He was smiling. His teeth were quite yellow. The two top ones in front were dentures. 'If we had the money now, we could screw on a bedful of greenbacks,' he said. 'I saw that in a movie once.'

He took her upstairs and she kept expecting him to turn vicious, but he didn't. His lovemaking was as it usually was, quick and hard, but he was not vicious. He did not hurt her intentionally, and tonight, for perhaps the tenth or eleventh time since they had been married, she had a climax. She let herself go to him, eyes closed, feeling the shelf of his chin dig into the top of her head. She stifled the cry that rose to her lips. It would have made him suspicious if she had cried out. She was not sure he really knew that what always happened at the end for men sometimes happened for women too.

Not long after (and still an hour before Brett came home from the Bergerons) he left her, not telling her where he was going. She surmised it was down to Gary Pervier's, where the drinking would start. She lay in bed and wondered if what she had done and what she had promised could ever be worth it. Tears tried to come and she drove them back. She lay hot-eyed and straight in bed, and just before Brett came in, his arrival announced by Cujo's barks and the slam of the back-door screen, the moon rose in all its silvery, detached glory. *Moon doesn't care*, Charity thought, but the thought brought her no comfort.

'What is it?' Donna asked.

Her voice was dull, almost defeated. The two of them were sitting in the living room. Vic had not gotten home until nearly Tad's bedtime, and that was now half an hour past. He was sleeping in his room upstairs, the Monster Words tacked up by his bed, the closet door firmly shut.

Vic got up and crossed to the window, which now looked out only on darkness. *She knows*, he thought glumly. *Not the fine tuning, maybe, but she's getting a pretty clear picture.* All the way home he had tried to decide if he should confront her with it, lance the boil, try living with the laudable pus . . . or if he should just deep-six it. After leaving Deering Oaks he had torn the letter up, and on his way home up 302 he had fed the scraps out the window. *Litterbug Trenton*, he thought. And now the choice had been taken out of his hands. He could see her pale reflection in the dark glass, her face a white circle in yellow lamplight.

118

He turned toward her, having absolutely no idea what he was going to say.

He knows, Donna was thinking.

It was not a new thought, not by now, because the last three hours had been the longest three of her whole life. She had heard the knowledge in his voice when he called to say he would be home late. At first there had been panic – the raw, fluttering panic of a bird trapped in a garage. The thought had been in italics followed by comic-book exclamation points: *He knows! He knows! He KNOWS!!* She had gotten Tad his supper in a fog of fear, trying to see what might logically happen next, but she was unable. I'll wash the dishes next, she thought. Then dry them. Then put them away. Then read Tad some stories. Then I'll just sail off the edge of the world.

Panic had been superseded by guilt. Terror had followed the guilt. Then a kind of fatalistic apathy had settled in as certain emotional circuits quietly shut themselves down. The apathy was even tinged by a certain relief. The secret was out. She wondered if Steve had done it, or if Vic had guessed on his own. She rather thought it had been Steve, but it didn't really matter. There was also relief that Tad was in bed, safely asleep. But she wondered what sort of morning he would wake up to. And that thought brought her full circle to her original panicky fear again. She felt sick, lost.

He turned toward her from the window and said, 'I got a letter today. An unsigned letter.'

He couldn't finish. He crossed the room again, restlessly, and she found herself thinking what a handsome man he was, and that it was too bad he was going gray so early. It looked good on some young men, but on Vic it was just going to make him look prematurely old and —

— and what was she thinking about his *hair* for? It wasn't his *hair* she had to worry about, was it?

Very softly, still hearing the shake in her voice, she said everything that was salient, spitting it out like some horrible medicine too bitter to swallow. 'Steve Kemp. The man who refinished your desk in the den. Five times. Never in our bed, Vic. Never.'

Vic put out his hand for the pack of Winstons on the endtable by the sofa and knocked it onto the floor. He picked it up, got one out, and lit it. His hands were shaking badly. They weren't looking at each other. *That's bad*, Donna thought. *We should be looking at each other.* But she couldn't be the one to start. She was scared and ashamed. He was only scared.

'Why?'

'Does it matter?'

'It matters to me. It means a lot. Unless you want to cut loose. If you do, I guess it doesn't matter. I'm mad as hell, Donna. I'm trying not to let that . . . that part get on top, because if we never talk straight again, we have to do it now. Do you want to cut loose?'

'Look at me, Vic.'

With a great effort, he did. Maybe he was as mad as he said he was, but she could see only species of miserable fright. Suddenly, like the thud of a boxing glove on her mouth, she saw how close to the edge of everything he was. The agency was tottering, that was bad enough, and now, on top of that, like a grisly dessert following a putrid main course, his marriage was tottering too. She felt a rush of warmth for him, for this man she had sometimes hated and had, for the last three hours, at least, feared. A kind of epiphany filled her. Most of all, she hoped he would always think he had been as mad as hell, and not . . . not the way his face said he felt.

'I don't want to cut loose,' she said. 'I love you. These last few weeks I think I've just found that out again.'

He looked relieved for a moment. He went back to the window, then returned to the couch. He dropped down there and looked at her.

'Why, then?'

The epiphany was lost in low-key, exasperated anger. *Why*, it was a man's question. Its origin lay far down in whatever the concept of masculinity was in an intelligent late-twentieth-century Western man. *I have to know why you did it.* As if she were a car with a stuck needle valve that had caused the machine to start hitching and sputtering or a robot that had gotten its servotapes scrambled so that it was serving meatloaf in the morning and scrambled eggs for dinner. What drove women crazy, she thought suddenly, wasn't really sexism at all, maybe. It was this mad, masculine quest for efficiency.

'I don't know if I can explain. I'm afraid it will sound stupid and petty and trivial.'

'Try. Was it . . .' He cleared his throat, seemed to mentally spit on his hands (that cursed *efficiency* thing again) and then fairly wrenched the thing out. 'Haven't I been satisfying you? Was that it?'

'No,' she said.

'Then what?' he said helplessly. 'For Christ's sake, *what*?'

Okay . . . you asked for it.

'Fear,' she said. 'Mostly, I think it was fear.'

'Fear?'

'When Tad went to school, there was nothing to keep me from being afraid. Tad was like . . . what do they call it? . . . white noise. The sound the TV makes when it isn't tuned to a station that comes in.'

'He wasn't in real school,' Vic said quickly, and she knew he was getting ready to be angry, getting ready to accuse her of trying to lay it off on Tad, and once he was angry things would come out between them that shouldn't be spoken, at least not yet. There were things, being the woman she was, that she would have to rise to. The situation would escalate. Something that was now very fragile was being tossed from his hands to hers and back again. It could easily be dropped.

'That was part of it,' she said. 'He wasn't in real school. I still had him most of the time, and the time when he was gone . . . there was a contrast . . .' She looked at him. 'The quiet seemed very loud by comparison. That was when I started to get scared. Kindergarten next year, I'd think. Half a day every day instead of half a day three times a week. The year after that, all day five days a week. And there would still be all those hours to fill up. And I just got scared.'

'So you thought you'd fill up a little of that time by fucking someone?' he asked bitterly.

That stung her, but she continued on grimly, tracing it out as best she could, not raising her voice. He had asked. She would tell him.

'I didn't want to be on the Library Committee and I didn't want to be on the Hospital Committee and run the bake sales or be in charge of getting the starter change or making sure that not everybody is making the same Hamburger Helper casserole for the Saturday-night supper. I didn't want to see those same depressing faces over and over again and listen to the same gossipy stories about who is doing what in this town. I didn't want to sharpen my claws on anyone else's reputation.'

The words were gushing out of her now. She couldn't have stopped them if she wanted to.

'I didn't want to sell Tupperware and I didn't want to sell Amway and I didn't want to give Stanley parties and I don't need to join Weight Watchers. You—'

She paused for the tiniest second, grasping it, feeling the weight of the idea.

'You don't know about emptiness, Vic. Don't think you do. You're a man, and men *grapple*. Men grapple, and women dust. You dust the empty rooms and you listen to the wind blowing outside sometimes. Only sometimes it seems like the wind's inside, you know? So you put on a record, Bob Seger or J. J. Cale or someone, and you can *still* hear the wind, and thoughts come to you, ideas, nothing good, but they come. So you clean both toilets and you do the sink and one day you're down in one of the antique shops looking at little pottery knickknacks, and you think about how your mother had a shelf of knickknacks like that, and your *aunts* all had shelves of them, and your *grand-mother* had them as well.'

He was looking at her closely, and his expression was so honestly perplexed that she felt a wave of her own despair.

'It's *feelings*, I'm talking about, not facts!'

'Yes, but why—'

'I'm *telling* you why!' I'm telling you that I got so I was spending enough time in front of the mirror to see how my face was changing, how no one was ever going to mistake me for a teenager again or ask to see my driver's license when I ordered a drink in a bar. I started to be afraid because I grew up after all. Tad's going to preschool and that means he's going to go to *school*, then *high school*—'

'Are you saying you took a lover because you felt *old*?' He was looking at her, surprised, and she loved him for that, because she supposed that *was* a part of it; Steve Kemp had found her attractive and of course that was flattering, that was what had made the flirtation fun in the first place. But it was in no way the greatest part of it.

She took his hands and spoke earnestly into his face, thinking – *knowing* – that she might never speak so earnestly (or honestly) to any man again. 'It's more. It's knowing you can't wait any longer to be a grownup, or wait any longer to make your peace with what you have. It's knowing that your choices are being narrowed almost daily. For a woman – no, for *me* – that's a brutal thing to have to face. Wife, that's fine. But you're gone at work, even when you're home you're gone at work so much. Mother, that's fine, too. But there's a little less of it every year, because every year the world gets another little slice of him.

'Men . . . they know what they are. They have an image of what they are. They never live up to the ideal, and it breaks them, and maybe that's why so many men die unhappy and before their time, but they *know* what being a grownup is supposed to mean. They have some kind of handle on thirty, forty, fifty. They don't hear that wind, or if they do, they find a lance and tilt at it, thinking it must be a windmill or some fucking thing that needs knocking down.

'And what a woman does – what *I* did – was to run from becoming. I got scared of the way the house sounded when Tad was gone. Once, do you know – this is crazy – I was in his room, changing the sheets, and I got thinking about these girlfriends I had in high school. Wondering what happened to them, where they went. I was almost in a daze. And Tad's closet door swung open and . . . I screamed and ran out of the room. I don't know why . . . except I guess I do. I thought for just a second there that Joan Brady would come out of Tad's closet, and her head would be gone and there would be blood all over her clothes and she would say, "I died in a car crash when I was nineteen coming back from Sammy's Pizza and I don't give a damn."'

'Christ, Donna,' Vic said.

'I got scared, that's all. I got scared when I'd start looking at knickknacks or thinking about taking a pottery course or yoga or something like that. And the only place to run from the future is into the past. So . . . so I started flirting with him.'

She looked down and then suddenly buried her face in her hands. Her words were muffled but still understandable.

'It was fun. It was like being in college again. It was like a dream. A stupid dream. It was like he was white noise. He blotted out that wind sound. The flirting part was fun. The sex . . . it was no good. I had orgasms, but it was no good. I can't explain why not, except that I still loved you through all of it, and understood that I was running away . . .' She looked up at him again, crying now. 'He's running too. He's made a career of it. He's a poet . . . at least that's what he calls himself. I couldn't make head or tail of the things he showed me. He's a roadrunner, dreaming he's still in college and protesting the war in Vietnam. That's why it was him, I guess. And now I think you know everything I can tell you. An ugly little tale, but mine own.'

'I'd like to beat him up,' Vic said. 'If I could make his nose bleed, I guess that would make me feel better.'

She smiled wanly. 'He's gone. Tad and I went for a Dairy Queen after we finished supper and you still weren't home. There's a FOR RENT sign in the window of his shop. I told you he was a roadrunner.'

'There was no poetry in that note,' Vic said. He looked at her briefly, then down again. She touched his face and he winced back a little. That hurt more than anything else, hurt more than she would have believed. The guilt and fear came again, in a glassy, crushing wave. But she wasn't crying any more. She thought there would be no more tears for a very long time. The wound and the attendant shock trauma were too great.

'Vic,' she said. 'I'm sorry. You're hurt and I'm sorry.'

'When did you break it off?'

She told him about the day she had come back and found him there, omitting the fear she'd had that Steve might actually rape her.

'Then the note was his way of getting back at you.'

She brushed hair away from her forehead and nodded.

Her face was pale and wan. There were purplish patches of skin under her eyes. 'I guess so.'

'Let's go upstairs,' he said. 'It's late. We're both tired.'

'Will you make love to me?'

He shook his head slowly. 'Not tonight.'

'All right.'

They went to the stairs together. At the foot of them, Donna asked, 'So what comes next, Vic?'

He shook his head. 'I just don't know.'

'Do I write "I promise never to do it again" five hundred times on the blackboard and miss recess? Do we get a divorce? Do we never mention it again? What?' She didn't *feel* hysterical, only tired, but her voice was rising in a way she didn't like and hadn't intended. The shame was the worst, the shame of being found out and seeing how it had punched his face in. And she hated him as well as herself for making her feel so badly ashamed, because she didn't believe she was responsible for the factors leading up to the final decision – if there really had been a decision.

'We ought to be able to get it together,' he said, but she did not mistake him; he wasn't talking to her. 'This thing—' He looked at her pleadingly. 'He was the only one, wasn't he?'

It was the one unforgivable question, the one he had no right to ask. She left him, almost ran up the stairs, before everything could spill out, the stupid recriminations and accusations that would not solve anything but only muddy up whatever poor honesty they had been able to manage.

There was little sleep for either of them that night.

And the fact that he had forgotten to call Joe Camber and ask him if he could work on his wife's ailing Pinto Runabout was the furthest thing from Vic's mind.

As for Joe Camber himself, he was sitting with Gary Pervier in one of the decaying lawn chairs which dotted Gary's run-to-riot side yard. They were drinking vodka martinis out of McDonald's glasses under the stars. Lightning bugs flickered across the dark, and the masses of honeysuckle clinging to Gary's fence filled the hot night with its cloying, heavy scent.

Cujo would ordinarily have been chasing after the fireflies, sometimes barking, and tickling both men no end. But tonight he only lay between them with his nose on his paws. They thought he was sleeping, but he wasn't. He simply lay there, feeling the aches that filled his bones and buzzed back and forth in his head. It had gotten hard for him to think what came next in his simple dog's life; something had gotten in the way of ordinary instinct. When he slept, he had dreams of uncommon, unpleasant vividity. In one of these he had savaged THE BOY, had ripped his throat open and then pulled his guts out of his body in steaming bundles. He had awakened from this dream twitching and whining.

He was continually thirsty, but he had already begun to shy away from his water dish some of the time, and when he did drink, the water tasted like steel shavings. The water made his teeth ache. The water sent bolts of pain through his eyes. And now he lay on the grass, not caring about the lightning bugs or anything else. The voices of THE MEN were unimportant rumbles coming from somewhere above him. They meant little to him compared to his own growing misery.

'Boston!' Gary Pervier said, and cackled. '*Boston*! What the hell are you going to do in Boston, and what makes you think I could afford to tag along? I don't think I got enough to go down to the Norge until I get my check cashed.'

'Fuck you, you're rolling in it,' Joe replied. He was getting pretty drunk. 'You might have to dig into what's in your mattress a little, that's all.'

'Nothing in there but bedbugs,' Gary said, and cackled again. 'Place is crawlin with em, and I don't give a shit. You ready for another blast?'

Joe held out his glass. Gary had the makings right beside his chair. He mixed in the dark with the practiced, steady, and heavy hand of the chronic drinker.

'Boston!' He said again, handing Joe his drink. He said slyly, 'Kickin up your heels a little, Joey, I guess.' Gary was the only man in Castle Rock – perhaps in the world – who could have gotten away with calling him Joey. 'Kicking up some whoopee, I guess. Never known you to go further than Portsmouth before.'

'I been to Boston once or twice,' Joe said. 'You better look out, Pervert, or I'll sic my dog on you.'

'You couldn't sic that dog on a yellin nigger with a straight razor in each hand,' Gary said. He reached down and ruffled Cujo's fur briefly. 'What's your wife say about it?'

'She don't know we're goin. She don't have to know.'
'Oh, yeah?'
'She's takin the boy down to Connecticut to see

her sister 'n' that freak she's married to. They're gonna be gone a week. She won some money in the lottery. Might as well tell you that right out. They use all the names on the radio, anyway. It's all in the prize form she had to sign.'

'Won some money in the lottery, did she?'

'Five thousand dollars.'

Gary whistled. Cujo flicked his ears uncomfortably at the sound.

Joe told Gary what Charity had told him at supper, leaving out the argument and making it appear a straight trade that had been his idea: The boy could go down to Connecticut for a week with her, and up to Moosehead for a week with him in the fall.

'And you're gonna go down to Boston and spend some of that dividend yourself, you dirty dog,' Gary said. He clapped Joe on the shoulder and laughed. 'Oh, you're a one, all right.'

'Why shouldn't I? You know when the last time was I had a day off? I don't. Can't remember. I ain't got much on this week. I'd planned to take most of a day and a half pulling the motor on Richie's International, doing a valve job and all, but with that chainfall it won't take four hours. I'll get him to bring it in tomorrow and I can do it tomorrow afternoon. I got a transmission job, but that's just a teacher. From the grammar school. I can put that back. A few other things the same way. I'll just call em up and tell em I'm having a little holiday.'

'What you gonna do down in Beantown?'

'Well, maybe see the Dead Sox play a couple at Fenway. Go down there to Washington Street—'

'The combat zone! Hot damn, I knew it!' Gary snorted laughter and slapped his leg. 'See some of those dirty shows and try to catch the clap!'

'Wouldn't be much fun alone.'

'Well, I guess I could tag along with you if you was willin to put some of that money my way until I get my check cashed.'

'I'd do that,' Joe said. Gary was a drunkard, but he took a debt seriously.

'I ain't been with a woman for about four years, I guess,' Gary said reminiscently. 'Lost most of the old sperm factory over there in France. What's left, sometimes it works, sometimes it don't. Might be fun to find out if I still got any ram left in my ramrod.'

'Ayuh,' Joe said. He was slurring now, and his ears were buzzing. 'And don't forget the baseball. You know when the last time was I went to Fenway?'

'No.'

'Nine-teen-six-ty-eight,' Joe said, leaning forward and tapping out each syllable on Gary's arm for emphasis. He spilled most of his new drink in the process. 'Before my kid was born. They played the Tigers and lost six to four, those suckers. Norm Cash hit a homer in the top of the eighth.'

'When you thinking of going?'

'Monday afternoon around three, I thought. The wife and the boy will want to go out that morning, I guess. I'll take them in to the Greyhound station in Portland. That gives me the rest of the morning and half the afternoon to catch up whatever I have to catch up.'

'You takin the car or the truck?'

'Car.'

Gary's eyes went soft and dreamy in the dark. 'Booze, baseball, and broads,' he said. He sat up straighter. 'I don't give a shit if I do.'

'You want to go?'

'Ayuh.'

Joe let out a little whoop and they both got laughing. Neither noticed that Cujo's head had come off his paws at the sound and that he was growling very softly.

Monday morning dawned in shades of pearl and dark gray; the fog was so thick that Brett Camber couldn't see the oak in the side yard from his window, and that oak wasn't but thirty yards away.

The house still slept around him, but there was no more sleep left in him. He was going on a trip, and every part of his being vibrated with the news. Just he and his mother. It would be a good trip, he felt that, and deep down inside, beyond any conscious thought, he was glad his father wasn't coming. He would be free to be himself; he would not have to try to live up to some mysterious ideal of masculinity that he knew his father had achieved but which he himself couldn't yet even begin to comprehend. He felt good – incredibly good and incredibly alive. He felt sorry for anyone in the world who was not going on a trip this fine, foggy morning, which would be another scorcher as soon as the fog burned off. He planned to sit in a window seat of the bus and watch every mile of the journey from the Greyhound terminal on Spring Street all the way to Stratford. It had been a long time before he had been able to get to sleep last night and here it was, not yet five o'clock . . . but if he stayed in bed any longer, he would explode, or something.

Moving as quietly as he could, he put on jeans and his Castle Rock Cougars T-shirt, a pair of white athletic socks, and his Keds. He went downstairs and fixed himself a bowl of Cocoa Bears. He tried to eat quietly but was sure that the crunch of the cereal that he heard in his head must be audible all over the house. Upstairs he heard his dad grunt and turn over in the double bed he and his mom shared. The springs rasped. Brett's jaws froze. After a moment's debate he took his second bowl of Cocoa Bears out on the back porch, being careful not to let the screen door slam.

The summer smells of everything were greatly clarified in the heavy fog, and the air was already warm. In the east, just above the faint fuzz that marked a belt of pines at the end of the east pasture, he could see the sun. It was as small and silver-bright as the full moon when it has risen well up in the sky. Even now the humidity was a dense thing, heavy and quiet. The fog would be gone by eight or nine, but the humidity would remain.

But for now what Brett saw was a white, secret world, and he was filled with the secret joys of it: the husky smell of hay that would be ready for its first cutting in a week, of manure, of his mother's roses. He could even faintly make out the aroma of Gary Pervier's triumphant honeysuckle which was slowly burying the fence which marked the edge of his property – burying it in a drift of cloying, grasping vines.

He put his cereal bowl aside and walked toward where he knew the barn to be. Halfway across the dooryard he looked over his shoulder and saw that the house had receded to nothing but a misty outline. A few steps farther and it was swallowed. He was alone in the white with only the tiny silver sun looking down on him. He could smell dust, damp, honeysuckle, roses.

And then the growling began.

His heart leaped into his throat and he fell back a step, all his muscles tensing into bundles of wire. His first panicky thought, like a child who has suddenly tumbled into a fairy tale, was *wolf*, and he looked around wildly. There was nothing to see but white.

Cujo came out of the fog.

Brett began to make a whining noise in his throat. The dog he had grown up with, the dog who had pulled a yelling, gleeful five-year-old Brett patiently around and around the dooryard on his Flexible Flyer, buckled into a harness Joe had made in the shop, the dog who had been waiting calmly by the mailbox every afternoon during school for the bus, come shine or shower . . . that dog bore only the slightest resemblance to the muddy, matted apparition slowly materializing from the morning mist. The Saint Bernard's big, sad eyes were now reddish and stupid and lowering: more pig's eyes than dog's eyes. His coat was plated with brownish-green-mud, as if he had been rolling around in the boggy place at the bottom of the meadow. His muzzle was wrinkled back in a terrible mock grin that froze Brett with horror. Brett felt his heart slugging away in his throat.

Thick white foam dripped slowly from between Cujo's teeth.

'Cujo?' Brett whispered. 'Cuje?'

★   ★   ★

Cujo looked at THE BOY, not recognizing him any more, not his looks, not the shadings of his clothes (he could not precisely see colors, at least as human beings understand them), not his scent. What he saw was a monster on two legs. Cujo was sick, and all things appeared monstrous to him now. His head clanged dully with murder. He wanted to bite and rip and tear. Part of him saw a cloudy image of him springing at THE BOY, bringing him down, parting flesh with bone, drinking blood as it still pulsed, driven by a dying heart.

Then the monstrous figure spoke, and Cujo recognized the voice. It was THE BOY, THE BOY, and THE BOY had never done him any harm. Once he had loved THE BOY and would have died for him, had that been called for. There was enough of that feeling left to hold the image of murder at bay until it grew as murky as the fog around them. It broke up and rejoined the buzzing, clamorous river of his sickness.

'Cujo? What's wrong, boy?'

The last of the dog that had been before the bat scratched its nose turned away, and the sick and dangerous dog, subverted for the last time, was forced to turn with it. Cujo stumbled away and moved deeper into the fog. Foam splattered from his muzzle onto the dirt. He broke into a lumbering run, hoping to outrun the sickness, but it ran with him, buzzing and yammering, making him ache with hatred and murder. He began to roll over and over in the high timothy grass, snapping at it, his eyes rolling.

The world was a crazy sea of smells. He would track each to its source and dismember it.

Cujo began to growl again. He found his feet. He

slipped deeper into the fog that was even now beginning to thin, a big dog who weighed just under two hundred pounds.

Brett stood in the dooryard for more than fifteen minutes after Cujo had melted back into the fog, not knowing what to do. Cujo had been sick. He might have eaten a poison bait or something. Brett knew about rabies, and if he had ever seen a woodchuck or a fox or a porcupine exhibiting the same symptons, he would have guessed rabies. But it never crossed his mind that his dog could have that awful disease of the brain and the nervous system. A poison bait, that seemed the most likely.

He should tell his father. His father could call the vet. Or maybe Dad could do something himself, like that time two years ago, when he had pulled the porcupine needles out of Cujo's muzzle with his pliers, working each quill first up, then down, then out, being careful not to break them off because they would fester in there. Yes, he would have to tell Dad. Dad would do something, like that time Cuje got into it with Mr Porky Pine.

But what about the trip?

He didn't need to be told that his mother had won them the trip through some desperate stratagem, or luck, or a combination of the two. Like most children, he could sense the vibrations between his parents, and he knew the way the emotional currents ran from one day to the next the way a veteran guide knows the twists and turns of an upcountry river. It had been a near thing, and even though his dad had agreed, Brett sensed that this agreement had been grudging and unpleasant. The trip was not on for sure until he had dropped them off and driven away. If he told Dad Cujo was sick, might he not seize on that as an excuse to keep them home?

He stood motionless in the dooryard. He was, for the first time in his life, in a total mental and emotional quandary. After a little while he began to hunt for Cujo behind the barn. He called him in a low voice. His parents were still sleeping, and he knew how sound carried in the morning fog. He didn't find Cujo anywhere . . . which was just as well for him.

The alarm burred Vic awake at quarter to five. He got up, shut it off, and blundered down to the bathroom, mentally cursing Roger Breakstone, who could never get to the Portland Jetport twenty minutes before check-in like any normal air traveler. Not Roger. Roger was a contingency man. There might always be a flat tire or a roadblock or a wash out or an earthquake. Aliens from outer space might decide to touch down on runway 22.

He showered, shaved, gobbled vitamins, and went back to the bedroom to dress. The big double bed was empty and he sighed a little. The weekend he and Donna had just passed hadn't been very pleasant . . . in fact, he could honestly say he never wanted to go through such a weekend again in his life. They had kept their normal, pleasant faces on – for Tad – but Vic had felt like a participant at a masquerade ball. He didn't like to be aware of the muscles in his face at work when he smiled.

They had slept in the same bed together, but for the first time the king-sized double seemed too small to Vic. They slept each on one side, the space between them a crisply sheeted no-man's-land. He had lain awake both Friday and Saturday nights, morbidly aware of each shift in Donna's weight as she moved, the sound of her night-dress against her body. He found himself wondering if she was awake, too, on her side of the emptiness that lay between them.

Last night, Sunday night, they had tried to do some-thing about that empty space in the middle of the bed. The sex part had been moderately successful, if a little tentative (at least neither of them had cried when it was over; for some reason he had been morbidly sure that one of them would do that). But Vic was not sure you could call what they had done making love.

He dressed in his summerweight gray suit – as gray as the early light outside – and picked up his two suit-cases. One of them was much heavier than the other. That one contained most of the Sharp Cereals file. Roger had all the graphic layouts.

Donna was making waffles in the kitchen. The teapot was on, just beginning to huff and puff. She was wearing his old blue flannel robe. Her face was puffy, as if instead of resting her, sleep had punched her unconscious.

'Will the planes fly when it's like that?' she asked.

'It's going to burn off. You can see the sun already.' He pointed at it and then kissed her lightly on the nape of the neck. 'You shouldn't have gotten up.'

'No problem.' She lifted the waffle iron's lid and deftly turned a waffle out on a plate. She handed it to him. 'I wish you weren't going away.' Her voice was low. 'Not now. After last night.'

'It wasn't that bad, was it?'

'Not like before,' Donna said. A bitter, almost secret smile touched her lips and was gone. She beat the waffle mixture with a wire whisk and then poured a ladleful into the waffle iron and dropped its heavy lid. Sssss. She poured boiling water over a couple of Red Rose bags and took the cups – one said VIC, the other DONNA – over to the table. 'Eat your waffle. There's strawberry preserves, if you want them.'

He got the preserves and sat down. He spread some oleo across the top of the waffle and watched it melt into the little squares, just as he had when he was a child. The preserves were Smucker's. He liked Smucker's preserves. He spread the waffle liberally with them. It looked great. But he wasn't hungry.

'Will you get laid in Boston or New York?' she asked, turning her back on him. 'Even it out? Tit for tat?'

He jumped a little – perhaps even flushed. He was glad her back was turned because he felt that at that precise moment there was more of him on his face than he wanted her to see. Not that he was angry; the thought of giving the bellman a ten instead of the usual buck and then asking the fellow a few questions had certainly crossed his mind. He knew that Roger had done it on occasion.

'I'm going to be too busy for anything like that.'

'What does the ad say? There's Always Room for Jell-O.'

'Are you trying to make me mad, Donna? Or what?'

'No. Go on and eat. You got to feed the machine.'

She sat down with a waffle of her own. No oleo for her. A dash of Vermont Maid Syrup, that was all. How well we know each other, he thought.

'What time are you picking Roger up?' she asked him.

'After some hot negotiations, we've settled on six.'

She smiled again, but this time the smile was warm and fond. 'He really took that early-bird business to heart at some point, didn't he?'

'Yeah. I'm surprised he hasn't called yet to make sure I'm up.'

The phone rang.

They looked at each other across the table, and after a silent considering pause they both burst out laughing. It was a rare moment, certainly more rare than the careful lovemaking in the dark the night before. He saw how fine her eyes were, how lucent. They were as gray as the morning mist outside.

'Get it quick before it wakes the Tadder up,' she said.

He did. It was Roger. He assured Roger that he was up, dressed, and in a fighting frame of mind. He would pick Roger up on the dot of six. He hung up wondering if he would end up telling Roger about Donna and Steve Kemp. Probably not. Not because Roger's advice would be bad; it wouldn't be. But, even though Roger would promise not to tell Althea, he most certainly would. And he had a suspicion that Althea would find it difficult to resist sharing out such a juicy bit of bridge-table gossip. Such careful consideration of the question made him feel depressed all over again. It was as if, by trying to work out the problem between them, he and Donna were burying their own body by moonlight.

'Good old Roger,' he said, sitting down again. He tried on a smile but it felt wrong. The moment of spontaneity was gone.

'Will you be able to get all of your stuff and all of Roger's into the Jag?'

'Sure,' he said. 'We'll have to. Althea needs their car, and you've got— oh, *shit*, I completely forgot to call Joe Camber about your Pinto.'

'You had a few other things on your mind,' she said. There was faint irony in her voice. 'That's all right. I'm not going to send Tad to the playground today. He has the sniffles. I may keep him home the rest of the summer, if that suits you. I get into trouble when he's gone.'

There were tears choking her voice, squeezing it and blurring it, and he didn't know what to say or how to respond. He watched helplessly as she found a Kleenex, blew her nose, wiped her eyes.

'Whatever,' he said, shaken. 'Whatever seems best.' He rushed on: 'Just give Camber a call. He's always there, and I don't think it would take him twenty minutes to fix it. Even if he has to put in another carb—'

'Will you think about it while you're gone?' she asked. 'About what we're going to do? The two of us?'

'Yes,' he said.

'Good. I will too. Another waffle?'

'No, thanks.' The whole conversation was turning surreal. Suddenly he wanted to be out and gone. Suddenly the trip felt very necessary and very attractive. The idea of getting away from the whole mess. Putting miles between him and it. He felt a sudden jab of anticipation. In his mind he could see the Delta jet cutting through the unraveling fog and into the blue.

'Can I have a waffle?'

They both looked around, startled. It was Tad, standing

in the hallway in his yellow footy pajamas, his stuffed coyote grasped by one ear, his red blanket wrapped around his shoulders. He looked like a small, sleepy Indian.

'I guess I could rustle one up,' Donna said, surprised. Tad was not a notably early riser.

'Was it the phone, Tad?' Vic asked.

Tad shook his head. 'I made myself wake up early so I could say good-bye to you, Daddy. Do you really have to go?'

'It's just for a while.'

'It's too long,' Tad said blackly. 'I put a circle around the day you're coming home on my calendar. Mom showed me which one. I'm going to mark off every day, and she said she'd tell me the Monster Words every night.'

'Well, that's okay, isn't it?'

'Will you call?'

'Every other night,' Vic said.

'Every night,' Tad insisted. He crawled up into Vic's lap and set his coyote next to Vic's plate. Tad began to crunch up a piece of toast. 'Every *night*, Daddy.'

'I can't every night,' Vic said, thinking of the backbreaking schedule Roger had laid out on Friday, before the letter had come.

'Why not?'

'Because—'

'Because your Uncle Roger is a hard taskmaster,' Donna said, putting Tad's waffle on the table. 'Come on over here and eat. Bring your coyote. Daddy will call us tomorrow night from Boston and tell us everything that happened to him.'

Tad took his place at the end of the table. He had a

large plastic placemat that said TAD. 'Will you bring me a toy?'

'Maybe. If you're good. And maybe I'll call tonight so you'll know I got to Boston in one piece.'

'Good deal.' Vic watched, fascinated, as Tad poured a small ocean of syrup over his waffle. 'What kind of toy?'

'We'll see,' Vic said. He watched Tad eat his waffle. It suddenly occurred to him that Tad liked eggs. Scrambled, fried, poached, or hard-boiled, Tad gobbled them up. 'Tad?'

'What, Daddy?'

'If you wanted people to buy eggs, what would you tell them?'

Tad considered. 'I'd tell em eggs taste good,' he said.

Vic met his wife's eyes again, and they had a second moment like the one that had occurred when the phone rang. This time they laughed telepathically.

Their good-byes were light. Only Tad, with his imperfect grasp of how short the future really was, cried.

'You'll think about it?' Donna asked him again as he climbed into the Jag.

'Yes.'

But driving into Bridgton to get Roger, what he thought about were those two moments of near-perfect communication. Two in one morning, not bad. All it took was eight or nine years together, roughly a quarter of all the years so far spent on the face of the earth. He got thinking about how ridiculous the whole concept of human communication was – what monstrous, absurd overkill was necessary to achieve even a little. When you'd invested the time and made it good, you had to be careful. Yes, he'd think about it. It had been good between them, and although some of the channels were now closed, filled with God knew how much muck (and some of that muck might still be squirming), plenty of the others seemed open and in reasonably good working order.

There had to be some careful thought – but perhaps not too much at once. Things had a way of magnifying themselves.

He turned the radio up and began to think about the poor old Sharp Cereal Professor.

Joe Camber pulled up in front of the Greyhound terminal in Portland at ten minutes to eight. The fog had burned off and the digital clock atop the Casco Bank and Trust read 73 degrees already.

He drove with his hat planted squarely on his head, ready to be angry at anyone who pulled out or cut in front of him. He hated to drive in the city. When he and Gary got to Boston he intended to park the car and leave it until they were ready to come home. They could take the subways if they could puzzle them out, walk if they couldn't.

Charity was dressed in her best pants suit – it was a quiet green – and a white cotton blouse with a ruffle at the neck. She was wearing earrings, and this had filled Brett with a mild sense of amazement. He couldn't remember his mother wearing earrings at all, except to church.

Brett had caught her alone when she went upstairs to dress after getting Dad his breakfast oatmeal. Joe had been mostly silent, grunting answers to questions in mono-syllables, then shutting off conversation entirely by tuning the radio to WCSH for the ball scores. They were both afraid that the silence might presage a ruinous outburst and a sudden change of mind on their trip.

Charity had the slacks of her pants suit on and was slipping into her blouse. Brett noted she was wearing a peach-colored bra, and that had also amazed him. He hadn't known his mother had underclothes in any color other than white.

'Ma,' he said urgently.

She turned to him – it seemed almost that she was turning *on* him. 'Did he say something to you?'

'No . . . no. It's Cujo.'

'Cujo? What about Cujo?'

'He's sick.'

'What do you mean, sick?'

Brett told her about having his second bowl of Cocoa Bears out on the back steps, about walking into the fog, and how Cujo had suddenly appeared, his eyes red and wild, his muzzle dripping foam.

'And he wasn't walking right,' Brett finished. 'He was kind of, you know, staggering. I think I better tell Daddy.'

'No,' his mother said fiercely, and grasped him by the shoulders hard enough to hurt. 'You do no such a thing!'

He looked at her, surprised and frightened. She relaxed her grip a little and spoke more quietly.

'He just scared you, coming out of the fog like that. There's probably nothing wrong with him at all. Right?'

Brett groped for the right words to make her understand how terrible Cujo had looked, and how for a moment he had thought the dog was going to turn on him. He couldn't find the words. Maybe he didn't want to find them.

'If there is something wrong,' Charity continued, 'it's probably just some little thing. He might have gotten a dose of skunk –'

'I didn't smell any sk—'

'– or he might have been running a woodchuck or a rabbit. Might even have jumped a moose down there in that bog. Or he might have eaten some nettles.'

'I guess he could have,' Brett said doubtfully.

'Your father would just jump on something like that,' she said. 'I can hear him now. "Sick, is he? Well, he's your dog, Brett. You see to him. I got too much work to do to be messing around with your mutt."'

Brett nodded unhappily. It was his own thought exactly, magnified by the brooding way his father had been eating breakfast while the sports blared around the kitchen.

'If you just leave him, he'll come mooching around your dad, and your dad will take care of him,' Charity said. 'He loves Cujo almost as much as you do, although he'd never say it. If he sees something's wrong, he'll fetch him over to the vet's in South Paris.'

'Yeah, I guess he would.' His mother's words rang true to him, but he was still unhappy about it.

She bent and kissed his cheek. 'I'll tell you! We can call your father tonight, if you want. How would that be? And when you talk to him, you just say, sort of casually, "You feeding my dog, Daddy?" And then you'll know.'

'Yeah,' Brett said. He smiled gratefully at his mother, and she smiled back, relieved, the trouble averted. But, perversely, it had given them something else to worry about during the seemingly interminable period before Joe backed the car up to the porch steps and silently began to load their four pieces of luggage into the wagon (into one of them Charity had surreptitiously placed all six of her snapshot albums). This new worry was that Cujo would lurch into the yard before they could drive away and stick Joe Camber with the problem.

But Cujo hadn't shown up.

Now Joe lowered the tailgate of the Country Squire, handed Brett the two small bags, and took the two large ones for himself.

'Woman, you got so much luggage I wonder if you ain't leavin on one of those Reno divorce cruises instead of going down to Connecticut.'

Charity and Brett smiled uneasily. It sounded like an attempt at humor, but with Joe Camber you were never really sure.

'That would be a day,' she said.

'I guess I'd just have to chase you down and drag you back with my new chainfall,' he said, unsmiling. His green hat was cocked squarely on the back of his head. 'Boy, you gonna take care of your mom?'

Brett nodded.

'Yeah, you better.' He measured the boy. 'You're getting pretty damn big. Probably you ain't got a kiss to give your old man.'

'I guess I do, Daddy,' Brett said. He hugged his father tight and kissed his stubbly cheek, smelling sour sweat and a phantom of last night's vodka. He was surprised and overwhelmed by his love for his father, a feeling that sometimes still came, always when it was least expected (but less and less often over the last two or three years, something his mother did not know and would not have believed if told).

It was a love that had nothing to do with Joe Camber's day-to-day behavior toward him or his mother; it was a brute, biological thing that he would never be free of, a phenomenon with many illusory referents of the sort which haunt for a lifetime: the smell of cigarette smoke, the look of a double-edged razor reflected in a mirror, pants hung over a chair, certain curse words.

His father hugged him back and then turned to Charity. He put a finger under her chin and turned her face up a little. From the loading bays behind the squat brick building they heard a bus warming up. Its engine was a low and guttural diesel rumble. 'Have a good time,' he said.

Her eyes filled with tears and she wiped them away quickly. The gesture was nearly one of anger. 'Okay,' she said.

Abruptly the tight, closed, noncommittal expression descended over his face. It came down like the clap of a knight's visor. He was the perfect country man again. 'Let's get these cases in, boy! Feels like there's lead in this one . . . Jesus-please-us!'

He stayed with them until all four bags had been checked, looking closely at each tag, oblivious of the baggage handler's condescending expression of amusement. He watched the handler trundle the bags out on a dolly and load them into the guts of the bus. Then he turned to Brett again.

'Come on out on the sidewalk with me,' he said.

Charity watched them go. She sat down on one of the hard benches, opened her purse, took out a handkerchief, and began fretting at it. It would just be like him to wish her a good time and then try to talk the boy into going back to the home place with him.

On the sidewalk, Joe said: 'Lemme give you two pieces of advice, boy. You probably won't take neither of them, boys seldom do, but I guess that never stopped a father giving em. First piece of advice is this: That fella you're going to see, that Jim, he's nothing but a piece of shit. One of the reasons I'm letting you go on this jaunt is that you're ten now, and ten's old enough to tell the difference between a turd and a tearose. You watch him and you'll see. He don't do nothing but sit in an office and push papers. People like him is half the trouble with this world, because their brains have got unplugged from their hands.' Thin, hectic color had risen in Joe's cheeks. 'He's a piece of shit. You watch him and see if you don't agree.'

'All right,' Brett said. His voice was low but composed.

Joe Camber smiled a little. 'The second piece of advice is to keep your hand on your pocketbook.'

'I haven't got any mon—'

Camber held out a rumpled five-dollar bill. 'Yeah, you got this. Don't spend it all in one place. The fool and his money soon parted.'

'All right. Thank you!'

'So long,' Camber said. He didn't ask for another kiss.

'Good-bye, Daddy.' Brett stood on the sidewalk and watched his father climb into the car and drive away. He never saw his father alive again.

At quarter past eight that morning, Gary Pervier staggered out of his house in his pee-stained underwear shorts and urinated into the honeysuckle. In a perverse sort of way he hoped that someday his piss would become so rancid with booze that it would blight the honeysuckle. That day hadn't come yet.

'*Arrrouggh, my head!*' he screamed, holding it with his free hand as he watered the honeysuckle which had buried his fence. His eyes were threaded with bright snaps of scarlet. His heart clattered and roared like an old water pump that was drawing more air than water just lately. A terrible stomach cramp seized him as he finished voiding himself – they had been getting more common lately – and as he doubled up a large and foul-smelling flatulence purred out from between his skinny shanks.

He turned to go back in, and that was when he heard the growling begin. It was a low, powerful sound coming from just beyond the point where his overgrown side yard merged with the hayfield beyond it.

He turned toward the sound quickly, his headache forgotten, the clatter and roar of his heart forgotten, the cramp forgotten. It had been a long time since he'd had a flashback to his war in France, but he had one now. Suddenly his mind was screaming, *Germans! Germans! Squad down!*

But it wasn't the Germans. When the grass parted it was Cujo who appeared.

'Hey, boy, what are you growling f—' Gary said, and then faltered.

It had been twenty years since he had seen a rabid dog, but you didn't forget the look. He had been in an Amoco station east of Machias, headed back from a camping trip down Eastport way. He had been driving the old Indian motorcycle he'd had for a while in the mid-fifties. A panting, slat-sided yellow dog had drifted by outside that Amoco station like a ghost. Its sides had been moving in and out in rapid, shallow springs of respiration. Foam was dripping from its mouth in a steady watery stream. It's eyes were rolling wildly. Its hindquarters were caked with shit. It had been reeling rather than walking, as if some unkind soul had opened its jaws an hour before and filled it full of cheap whiskey.

'Hot damn, there he is,' the pump jockey said. He had dropped the adjustable wrench he was holding and had rushed into the cluttered, dingy little office which adjoined the station's garage bay. He had come out with a .30-.30 clutched in his greasy, big-knuckled hands. He went out onto the tarmac, dropped to one knee, and started shooting. His first shot had been low, shearing away one of the dog's back legs in a cloud of blood. That yellow dog never even moved, Gary remembered as he stared at Cujo now. Just looked around blankly as if he didn't have the slightest idea what was happening to it. The pump jockey's second try had cut the dog almost in half. Guts hit the station's one pump in a black and red splash. A moment later three more guys had pulled in, three of Washington County's finest crammed shoulder to shoulder in the cab of a 1940 Dodge pickup. They were all armed. They piled out and pumped another eight or nine rounds into the dead dog. An hour after that, as the pump jockey was finishing up putting a new headlamp on the front of Gary's Indian cycle, the County Dog Officer arrived in a Studebaker with no door on the passenger side. She donned long rubber gloves and cut off what was left of the yellow dog's head to send to State Health and Welfare.

Cujo looked a hell of a lot spryer than that long-ago

yellow dog, but the other symptoms were exactly the same. *Not too far gone*, he thought. *More dangerous. Holy Jesus, got to get my gun* –

He started to back away. 'Hi, Cujo . . . nice dog, nice boy, nice doggy––' Cujo stood at the edge of the lawn, his great head lowered, his eyes reddish and filmy, growling.

'Nice boy––'

To Cujo, the words coming from THE MAN meant nothing. They were meaningless sounds, like the wind. What mattered was the *smell* coming from THE MAN. It was hot, rank, and pungent. It was the smell of fear. It was maddening and unbearable. He suddenly understood THE MAN had made him sick. He lunged forward, the growl in his chest mounting into a heavy roar of rage.

Gary saw the dog coming for him. He turned and ran. One bite, one scratch, could mean death. He ran for the porch and the safety of the house beyond the porch. But there had been too many drinks, too many long winter days by the stove, and too many long summer nights in the lawn chair. He could hear Cujo closing in behind him, and then there was the terrible split second when he could hear nothing and understood that Cujo had leaped.

As he reached the first splintery step of his porch, two hundred pounds of Saint Bernard hit him like a loco-motive, knocking him flat and driving the wind from him. The dog went for the back of his neck. Gary tried to scramble up. The dog was over him, the thick fur of its underbelly nearly suffocating him, and it knocked him back down easily. Gary screamed.

Cujo bit him high on the shoulder, his powerful jaws closing and crunching through the bare skin, pulling tendons like wires. He continued to growl. Blood flew. Gary felt it running warmly down his skinny upper arm. He turned over and battered at the dog with his fists. It gave back a little and Gary was able to scramble up three more steps on his feet and hands. Then Cujo came again.

Gary kicked at the dog. Cujo feinted the other way and then came boring in, snapping and growling. Foam flew from his jaws, and Gary could smell his breath. It smelled rotten – rank and yellow. Gary balled his right fist and swung in a roundhouse, connecting with the bony shelf of Cujo's lower jaw. It was mostly luck. The jolt of the impact ran all the way up to his shoulder, which was on fire from the deep bite.

Cujo backed off again.

Gary looked at the dog, his thin, hairless chest moving rapidly up and down. His face was ashy gray. The laceration on his shoulder welled blood that splattered on the peeling porch steps. 'Come for me, you sonofawhore,' he said. 'Come on, come on, I don't give a shit.' He screamed, '*You hear me? I don't give a shit!*'

But Cujo backed off another pace.

The words still had no meaning, but the smell of fear had left THE MAN. Cujo was no longer sure if he wanted to attack or not. He hurt, he hurt so miserably, and the world was a crazyquilt of sense and impression –

Gary got shakily to his feet. He backed up the last two steps of the porch. He backed across the porch's width and felt behind him for the handle of the screen door. His shoulder felt as if raw gasoline had been poured under the skin. His mind raved at him, *Rabies! I got the rabies!*

Never mind. One thing at a time. His shotgun was in the hall closet. Thank Christ Charity and Brett Camber were gone from up on the hill. That was God's mercy at work.

He found the screen door's handle and pulled the door open. He kept his eyes locked on Cujo's until he had backed in and pulled the screen door shut behind him. Then a great relief swept through him. His legs went rubbery. For a moment the world swam away, and he pulled himself back by sticking his tongue out and biting down on it. This was no time to swoon like a girl. He could do that after the dog was dead, if he wanted. Christ, but it had been close out there; he had thought he was going to punch out for sure.

He turned and headed down the darkened hallway to the closet, and that was when Cujo smashed through the lower half of the screen door, muzzle wrinkled back from his teeth in a kind of sneer, a dry volley of barking sounds coming from his chest.

Gary screamed again and whirled just in time to catch Cujo in both arms as the dog leaped again, driving him back down the hall, bouncing from side to side and trying to keep his feet. For a moment they almost seemed to waltz. Then Gary, who was fifty pounds lighter, went down. He was dimly aware of Cujo's muzzle burrowing in under his chin, was dimly aware that Cujo's nose was almost sickeningly hot and dry. He tried getting his hands up and was thinking that he would have to go for Cujo's eyes with his thumbs when Cujo seized his throat and tore it open. Gary screamed and the dog savaged him again. Gary felt warm blood sheet across his face and thought, *Dear God, that's mine!* His hands beat weakly and ineffectually at Cujo's upper body, doing no damage. At last they fell away.

Faintly, sick and cloying, he smelled honeysuckle.

'What do you see out there?'

Brett turned a little toward the sound of his mother's voice. Not all the way – he did not want to lose sight of the steadily unrolling view even for a little while. The bus had been on the road for almost an hour. They had crossed the Million Dollar Bridge into South Portland (Brett had stared with fascinated, wondering eyes at the two scum-caked, rustbucket freighters in the harbor), joined the Turnpike going south, and were now approaching the New Hampshire border.

'Everything,' Brett said. 'What do you see, Mom?'

She thought: *Your reflection in the glass – very faint. That's what I see.*

Instead she answered, 'Why, the world, I guess. I see the world unrolling in front of us.'

'Mom? I wish we could ride all the way to California on this bus. See everything there is in the geography books at school.'

She laughed and ruffled his hair. 'You'd get damn tired of scenery, Brett.'

'No. No, I wouldn't.'

And he probably wouldn't, she thought. Suddenly she felt both sad and old. When she had called Holly Saturday morning to ask her if they could come, Holly had been delighted, and her delight had made Charity feel young. It was strange that her own son's delight, his almost palpable euphoria, would make her feel old. Nevertheless . . .

What exactly is there going to be for him? she asked herself, studying his ghostlike face, which was superimposed over the moving scenery like a camera trick. He was bright, brighter than she was and much brighter than Joe. He ought to go to college, but she knew that when he got to high school Joe would press him to sign up for the shop and automotive maintenance courses so he could be more help around the place. Ten years ago he wouldn't have been able to get away with it, the guidance counselors wouldn't have *allowed* a bright boy like Brett to opt for all manual trades courses, but in these days of phase electives and do your own thing, she was terribly afraid it might happen.

It made her afraid. Once she had been able to tell herself that school was far away, so very far away – high school, *real* school. Grammar school was nothing but play to a boy who slipped through his lessons as easily as Brett did. But in high school the business of irrevocable choices began. Doors slipped shut with a faint locking click that was only heard clearly in the dreams of later years.

She gripped her elbows and shivered, not even kidding herself that it was because the Hound's air conditioning was turned up too high.

For Brett, high school was now just four years away.

She shivered again and suddenly found herself wishing viciously that she had never won the money, or that she had lost the ticket. They had only been away from Joe for an hour, but it was the first time she had really been separated from him since they had married in late 1966. She hadn't realized that perspective would be so sudden, so dizzying, and so bitter. Picture this: Woman and boy are let free from brooding castle keep . . . but there's a catch. Stapled to their backs are large hooks, and slipped over the ends of the hooks are heavy-duty invisible rubber hands. And before you can get too far, presto-whizzo! You're snapped back inside for another fourteen years!

She made a little croaking sound in her throat.

'Did you say something, Mom?'

'No. Just clearing my throat.'

She shivered a third time, and this time her arms broke out in gooseflesh. She had recalled a line of poetry from one of her own high school English classes (she had wanted to take the college courses, but her father had been furious at the idea – did she think they were *rich*? – and her mother had laughed the idea to death gently and pity-ingly). It was from a poem by Dylan Thomas, and she couldn't remember the whole thing, but it had been some-thing about moving through dooms of love.

That line had seemed funny and perplexing to her then, but she thought she understood it now. What else did you call that heavy-duty invisible rubber hand, if not love? Was she going to kid herself and say that she did not, even now, in some way love the man she had married? That she stayed with him only out of duty, or for the sake of the child (*that* was a bitter laugh; if she ever left him it would be for the sake of the child)? That he had never pleasured her in bed? That he could not, sometimes at the most unexpected moments (like the one back at the bus station), be tender?

And yet . . . and yet . . .

Brett was looking out the window, enrapt. Without turning from the view, he said, 'You think Cujo's all right, Mom?'

'I'm sure he's fine,' she said absently.

For the first time she found herself thinking about divorce in a concrete way – what she could do to support herself and her son, how they would get along in such an unthinkable (*almost* unthinkable) situation. If she and Brett didn't come home from this trip, would he come after them, as he had vaguely threatened back in Portland? Would he decide to let Charity go to the bad but try to get Brett back by fair means . . . or foul?

She began to tick the various possibilities over in her mind, weighing them, suddenly thinking that maybe a little perspective wasn't such a bad thing after all. Painful, maybe. Maybe useful, too.

The Greyhound slipped across the state line into New Hampshire and rolled on south.

The Delta 727 rose steeply, buttonhooked over Castle Rock – Vic always looked for his house near Castle Lake and 117, always fruitlessly – and then headed back toward the coast. It was a twenty-minute run to Logan Airport.

Donna was down there, some eighteen thousand feet below. And the Tadder. He felt a sudden depression mixed with a black premonition that it wasn't going to work, that they were crazy to even think it might. When your house blew down, you had to build a new house. You couldn't put the old one back together again with Elmer's Glue.

The stewardess came by. He and Roger were riding in

first class ('Might as well enjoy it while we can, buddy,' Roger had said last Wednesday when he made the reservations; 'not everyone can go to the poorfarm in such impeccable style'), and there were only four or five other passengers, most of them reading the morning paper — as was Roger.

'Can I get you anything?' she asked Roger with that professional twinkly smile that seemed to say she had been overjoyed to get up this morning at five thirty to make the upsy-downsy run from Bangor to Portland to Boston to New York to Atlanta.

Roger shook his head absently, and she turned that unearthly smile on Vic. 'Anything for you, sir? Sweet roll? Orange juice?'

'Could you rustle up a screwdriver?' Vic asked, and Roger's head came out of his paper with a snap.

The stew's smile didn't falter; a request for a drink before nine in the morning was no news to her. 'I can rustle one up,' she said, 'but you'll have to hustle to get it all down. It's really only a hop to Boston.'

'I'll hustle,' Vic promised solemnly, and she passed on her way back up to the galley, resplendent in her powder-blue slacks uniform and her smile.

'What's with you?' Roger asked.

'What do you mean, what's with me?'

'You know what I mean. I never even saw you drink a beer before noon before. Usually not before five.'

'I'm launching the boat,' Vic said.

'What boat?'

'The R.M.S. *Titanic*,' Vic said.

Roger frowned. 'That's sort of poor taste, don't you think?'

He did, as a matter of fact. Roger deserved something better, but this morning, with the depression still on him like a foul-smelling blanket, he just couldn't think of anything better. He managed a rather bleak smile instead. But Roger went on frowning at him.

'Look,' Vic said, 'I've got an idea on this Zingers thing. It's going to be a bitch convincing old man Sharp and the kid, but it might work.'

Roger looked relieved. It was the way it had always worked with them; Vic was the raw idea man, Roger the shaper and implementer. They had always worked as a team when it came to translating the ideas into media, and in the matter of presentation.

'What is it?'

'Give me a little while,' Vic said. 'Until tonight, maybe. Then we'll run it up the flagpole —'

'— and see who drops their pants,' Roger finished with a grin. He shook his paper open to the financial page again. 'Okay. As long as I get it by tonight. Sharp stock went up another eighth last week. Were you aware of that?'

'Dandy,' Vic murmured, and looked out the window again. No fog now; the day was as clear as a bell. The beaches at Kennebunk and Ogunquit and York formed a panoramic picture postcard — cobalt blue sea, khaki sand, and then the Maine landscape of low hills, open fields, and thick bands of fir stretching west and out of sight. Beautiful. And it made his depression even worse.

If I have to cry, I'm damn well going into the crapper to do it, he thought grimly. Six sentences on a sheet of cheap paper had done this to him. It was a goddam fragile world, as fragile as one of those Easter eggs that were all pretty colors on the outside but hollow on the inside. Only last week he had been thinking of just taking Tad and moving out. Now he wondered if Tad and Donna would still be there when he and Roger got back. Was it possible that Donna might just take the kid and decamp, maybe to her mother's place in the Poconos?

Sure it was possible. She might decide that ten days apart wasn't enough, not for him, not for her. Maybe a six months' separation would be better. And she had Tad now. Possession was nine points of the law, wasn't it?

And maybe, a crawling, insinuating voice inside spoke up, *maybe she knows where Kemp is. Maybe she'll decide to go to him. Try it with him for a while. They can search for their happy pasts together.* Now *there's* a nice crazy Monday-morning thought, he told himself uneasily.

But the thought wouldn't go away. Almost, but not quite.

He managed to finish every drop of his screwdriver before the plane touched down at Logan. It gave him acid indigestion that he knew would last all morning long — like the thought of Donna and Steve Kemp together, it would come creeping back even if he gobbled a whole roll of Tums — but the depression lifted a little and so maybe it was worth it.

Maybe.

Joe Camber looked at the patch of garage floor below his big vise clamp with something like wonder. He pushed his green felt hat back on his forehead, stared at what was there awhile longer, then put his fingers between his teeth and whistled piercingly.

'Cujo! Hey, boy! Come, Cujo!'

He whistled again and then leaned over, hands on his knees. The dog would come, he had no doubt of that. Cujo never went far. But how was he going to handle this?

The dog had shat on the garage floor. He had never known Cujo to do such a thing, not even as a pup. He had piddled around a few times, as puppies will, and he had torn the bejesus out of a chair cushion or two, but there had never been anything like this. He wondered briefly if maybe some other dog had done it, and then dismissed the thought. Cujo was the biggest dog in Castle Rock, so far as he knew. Big dogs ate big, and big dogs crapped big. No poodle or beagle or Heinz Fifty-seven Varieties had done this mess. Joe wondered if the dog could have sensed that Charity and Brett were going away for a spell. If so, maybe this was his way of showing just how that idea set with him. Joe had heard of such things.

He had taken the dog in payment for a job he had done in 1975. The customer had been a one-eyed fellow named Ray Crowell from up Fryeburg way. This Crowell spent most of his time working in the woods, although it was acknowledged that he had a fine touch with dogs – he was good at breeding them and good at training them. He could have made a decent living doing what New England country people sometimes called 'dog farming', but his temper was not good, and he drove many customers away with his sullenness.

'I need a new engine in my truck,' Crowell had told Joe that spring.

'Ayuh,' Joe had said.

'I got the motor, but I can't pay you nothing. I'm tapped out.'

They had been standing just inside Joe's garage, chewing on stems of grass. Brett, then five, had been goofing around in the dooryard while Charity hung out clothes.

'Well, that's too bad, Ray,' Joe said, 'but I don't work for free. This ain't no charitable organization.'

'Mrs Beasley just had herself a litter,' Ray said. Mrs Beasley was a prime bitch Saint Bernard. 'Purebreds. You do the work and I'll give you the pick of the litter. What do you say? You'd be coming out ahead, but I can't cut no pulp if I don't have a truck to haul it in.'

'Don't need a dog,' Joe said. 'Especially a big one like that. Goddam Saint Bernards ain't nothing but eatin machines.'

'*You* don't need a dog,' Ray said, casting an eye out at Brett, who was now just sitting on the grass and watching his mother, 'but your boy might appreciate one.'

Joe opened his mouth and then closed it again. He and Charity didn't use any protection, but there had been no more kids since Brett, and Brett himself had been a long while coming. Sometimes, looking at him, a vague question would form itself in Joe's head: Was the boy lonely? Perhaps he was. And perhaps Ray Crowell was right. Brett's birthday was coming up. He could give him the pup then.

'I'll think about it,' he said.

'Well, don't think too long,' Ray said, bridling. 'I can go see Vin Callahan over in North Conway. He's just as handy as you are, Camber. Handier, maybe.'

'Maybe,' Joe said, unperturbed. Ray Crowell's temper did not scare him in the least.

Later that week, the manager of the Shop 'n Save drove his Thunderbird up to Joe's to get the transmission looked at. It was a minor problem, but the manager, whose name was Donovan, fussed around the car like a worried mother while Joe drained the transmission fluid well, refilled it, and tightened the bands. The car was a piece of work, all right, a 1960 T-Bird in cherry condition. And as he finished the job, listening to Donovan talk about how his wife wanted him to sell the car, Joe had had an idea.

'I'm thinking about getting my boy a dog,' he told this Donovan as he let the T-Bird down off the jacks.

'Oh, yes?' Donovan asked politely.

'Ayuh. Saint Bernard. It's just a pup now, but it's gonna eat big when it grows. Now I was just thinking that we might make a little deal, you and me. If you was to guarantee me a discount on that dry dog food, Gaines Meal, Ralston-Purina, whatever you sell, I'd guarantee you to work on your Bird here every once in a while. No labor charges.'

Donovan had been delighted and the two of them had shaken on it. Joe had called Ray Crowell and said he'd decided to take the pup if Crowell was still agreeable. Crowell was, and when his son's birthday rolled around that year, Joe had astounded both Brett and Charity by putting the squirming, wriggling puppy into the boy's arms.

'Thank you, Daddy, thank you, thank you!' Brett had cried, hugging his father and covering his cheeks with kisses.

'Sure,' Joe said. 'But you take care of him, Brett. He's your dog, not mine. I guess if he does any piddling or crapping around, I'll take him out in back of the barn and shoot him for a stranger.'

CUJO

'I will, Daddy . . . I promise!'

He had kept his promise, pretty much, and on the few occasions he forgot, either Charity or Joe himself had cleaned up after the dog with no comment. And Joe had discovered it was impossible to stand aloof from Cujo; as he grew (and he grew damned fast, developing into exactly the sort of eating machine Joe had foreseen), he simply took his place in the Camber family. He was one of your bona fide good dogs.

He had house-trained quickly and completely . . . and now this. Joe turned around, hands stuffed in his pockets, frowning. No sign of Cuje anywhere.

He stepped outside and whistled again. Damn dog was maybe down in the creek, cooling off. Joe wouldn't blame him. It felt like eighty-five in the shade already. But the dog would come back soon, and when he did, Joe would rub his nose in that mess. He would be sorry to do it if Cujo had made it because he was missing his people, but you couldn't let a dog get away with –

A new thought came. Joe slapped the flat of his hand against his forehead. Who was going to feed Cujo while he and Gary were gone?

He supposed he could fill up that old pig trough behind the barn with Gaines Meal – they had just about a long ton of the stuff stored downstairs in the cellar – but it would get soggy if it rained. And if he left it in the house or the barn, Cujo might just decide to up and crap on the floor again. Also, when it came to food, Cujo was a big cheerful glutton. He would eat half the first day, half the second day, and then walk around hungry until Joe came back.

165

'Shit,' he muttered.

The dog wasn't coming. Knew Joe would have found his mess and ashamed of it, probably. Cujo was a bright dog, as dogs went, and knowing (or guessing) such a thing was by no means out of his mental reach.

Joe got a shovel and cleaned up the mess. He spilled a capful of the industrial cleaner he kept handy on the spot, mopped it, and rinsed it off with a bucket of water from the faucet at the back of the garage.

That done, he got out the small spiral notebook in which he kept his work schedule and looked it over. Richie's International Harvester was taken care of – that chainfall surely did take the ouch out of pulling a motor. He had pushed the transmission job back with no trouble; the teacher had been every bit as easygoing as Joe had expected. He had another half a dozen jobs lined up, all of them minor.

He went into the house (he had never bothered to have a phone installed in his garage; they charged you dear for that extra line, he had told Charity) and began to call people and tell them he would be out of town for a few days on business. He would get to most of them before they got around to taking their problems somewhere else. And if one or two couldn't wait to get their new fanbelt or radiator hose, piss on em.

The calls made, he went back out to the barn. The last item before he was free was an oil change and a ring job. The owner had promised to come by and pick up his car by noon. Joe got to work, thinking how quiet the home place seemed with Charity and Brett gone . . . and with Cujo gone. Usually the big Saint Bernard would lie in the patch of shade by the big sliding garage door, panting, watching Joe as he worked. Sometimes Joe would talk to him, and Cujo always looked as if he was listening carefully.

Been deserted, he thought semi-resentfully. Been deserted by all three. He glanced at the spot where Cujo had messed and shook his head again in a puzzled sort of disgust. The question of what he was going to do about feeding the dog recurred to him and he came up empty again. Well, later on he would give the old Pervert a call. Maybe he would be able to think of someone – some kid – who would be willing to come up and give Cujo his chow for a couple-three days.

He nodded his head and turned the radio on to WOXO in Norway, turning it up loud. He didn't really hear it unless the news or the ball scores were on, but it was company. Especially with everyone gone. He got to work. And when the phone in the house rang a dozen or so times, he never heard it.

Tad Trenton was in his room at midmorning, playing with his trucks. He had accumulated better than thirty of them in his four years on the earth, an extensive collection which ranged from the seventy-nine-cent plastic jobs that his dad sometimes bought him at the Bridgton Pharmacy where he always got *Time* magazine on Wednesday evenings (you had to play carefully with the seventy-nine-cent trucks because they were MADE IN TAIWAN and had a tendency to fall apart) to the flagship of his line, a great yellow Tonka bulldozer that came up to his knees when he was standing.

He had various 'men' to stick into the cabs of his

trucks. Some of them were round-headed guys scrounged from his PlaySkool toys. Others were soldiers. Not a few were what he called 'Star Wars Guys'. These included Luke, Han Solo, the Imperial Creep (aka Darth Vader), a Bespin Warrior, and Tad's absolute favorite, Greedo. Greedo always got to drive the Tonka dozer.

Sometimes he played *Dukes of Hazzard* with his trucks, sometimes *B. J. and the Bear*, sometimes Cops and Moonshiners (his dad and mom had taken him to see *White Lightning* and *White Line Fever* on a double bill at the Norway Drive-In and Tad had been *very* impressed), sometimes a game he had made up himself. That one was called Ten-Truck Wipe-Out.

But the game he played most often – and the one he was playing now – had no name. It consisted of digging the trucks and the 'men' out of his two playchests and lining the trucks up one by one in diagonal parallels, the men inside, as if they were all slant-parked on a street that only Tad could see. Then he would run them to the other side of the room one by one, very slowly, and line them up on that side bumper-to-bumper. Sometimes he would repeat this cycle ten or fifteen times, for an hour or more, without tiring.

Both Vic and Donna had been struck by this game. It was a little disturbing to watch Tad set up this constantly repeating, almost ritualistic pattern. They had both asked him on occasion what the attraction was, but Tad did not have the vocabulary to explain. *Dukes of Hazzard*, Cops and Moonshiners, and Ten-Truck Wipe-Out were simple crash-and-bash games. The no-name game was quiet, peaceful, tranquil, ordered. If his vocabulary *had* been big enough, he might have told his parents it was his way of saying Om and thereby opening the doors to contemplation and reflection.

Now as he played it, he was thinking something was wrong.

His eyes went automatically — unconsciously — to the door of his closet, but the problem wasn't there. The door was firmly latched, and since the Monster Words, it never came open. No, the something wrong was something else.

He didn't know exactly what it was, and wasn't sure he even wanted to know. But, like Brett Camber, he was already adept at reading the currents of the parental river upon which he floated. Just lately he had gotten the feeling that there were black eddies, sandbars, maybe deadfalls hidden just below the surface. There could be rapids. A waterfall. Anything.

Things weren't right between his mother and father.

It was in the way they looked at each other. The way they talked to each other. It was on their faces and behind their faces. In their thoughts.

He finished changing a slant-parked row of trucks on one side of the room to bumper-to-bumper traffic on the other side and got up and went to the window. His knees hurt a little because he had been playing the no-name game for quite a while. Down below in the back yard his mother was hanging out clothes. Half an hour earlier she had tried to call the man who could fix the Pinto, but the man wasn't home. She waited a long time for someone to say hello and then slammed the phone down, mad. And his mom hardly ever got mad at little things like that.

As he watched, she finished hanging the last two sheets. She looked at them . . . and her shoulders kind of sagged. She went to stand by the apple tree beyond the double clothesline, and Tad knew from her posture – her legs spread, her head down, her shoulders in slight motion – that she was crying. He watched her for a little while and then crept back to his trucks. There was a hollow place in the pit of his stomach. He missed his father already, missed him badly, but this was worse.

He ran the trucks slowly back across the room, one by one, returning them to their slant-parked row. He paused once when the screen door slammed. He thought she would call to him, but she didn't. There was the sound of her steps crossing the kitchen, then the creak of her special chair in the living room as she sat down. But the TV didn't go on. He thought of her just sitting down there, just . . . *sitting* . . . and dismissed the thought, quickly from his mind.

He finished the row of trucks. There was Greedo, his best, sitting in the can of the dozer, looking blankly out of his round black eyes at the door of Tad's closet. His eyes were wide, as if he had seen something there, something so scary it had shocked his eyes wide, something really gooshy, something *horrible*, something that was coming –

Tad glanced nervously at the closet door. It was firmly latched.

Still, he was tired of the game. He put the trucks back in his playchest, clanking them loudly on purpose so she would know he was getting ready to come down and watch *Gunsmoke* on Channel 8. He started for the door and then paused, looking at the Monster Words, fascinated.

> *Monsters, stay out of this room!*
> *You have no business here.*

He knew them by heart. He liked to look at them, read them by rote, look at his daddy's printing.

> *Nothing will touch Tad, or hurt Tad, all this night.*
> *You have no business here.*

On a sudden, powerful impulse, he pulled out the pushpin that held the paper to the wall. He took the Monster Words carefully — almost reverently — down. He folded the sheet of paper up and put it carefully into the back pocket of his jeans. Then, feeling better than he had all day, he ran down the stairs to watch Marshal Dillon and Festus.

That last fellow had come and picked up his car at ten minutes of twelve. He had paid cash, which Joe had tucked away into his old greasy wallet, reminding himself to go down to the Norway Savings and pick up another five hundred before he and Gary took off.

Thinking of taking off made him remember Cujo, and the problem of who was going to feed him. He got into his Ford wagon and drove down to Gary Pervier's at the foot of the hill. He parked in Gary's driveway. He started up the porch steps, and the hail that had been rising in his throat died there. He went back down and bent over the steps.

There was blood there.

Joe touched it with his fingers. It was tacky but not completely dry. He stood up again, a little worried but not yet unduly so. Gary might have been drunk and stumbled with a glass in his hand. He wasn't really worried until he saw the way the rusty bottom panel of the screen door was crashed in.

'Gary?'

There was no answer. He found himself wondering if someone with a grudge had maybe come hunting ole Gary. Or maybe some tourist had come asking directions and Gary had picked the wrong day to tell someone he could take a flying fuck at the moon.

He climbed the steps. There were more splatters of blood on the boards of the porch.

'Gary?' he called again, and suddenly wished for the weight of his shotgun cradled over his right arm. But if someone had punched Gary out, bloodied his nose, or maybe popped out a few of the old Pervert's remaining teeth, that person was gone now, because the only car in the yard other than Joe's rusty Ford LTD wagon was Gary's white '66 Chrysler hardtop. And you just didn't walk out to Town Road No. 3. Gary Pervier's was seven miles from town, two miles off the Maple Sugar Road that led back to Route 117.

More likely he just cut himself, Joe thought. But Christ, I hope it was just his hand he cut and not his throat.

Joe opened the screen door. It squealed on its hinges. 'Gary?'

Still no answer. There was a sickish-sweet smell in here that he didn't like, but at first he thought it was the

172

honeysuckle. The stairs to the second floor went up on his left. Straight ahead was the hall to the kitchen, the living room doorway opening off the hall about halfway down on the right.

There was something on the hall floor, but it was too dark for Joe to make it out. Looked like an endtable that had been knocked over, or something like that . . . but so far as Joe knew, there wasn't now and never had been any furniture in Gary's front hall. He leaned his lawn chairs in here when it rained, but there hadn't been any rain for two weeks. Besides, the chairs had been out by Gary's Chrysler in their accustomed places. By the honeysuckle.

Only that smell wasn't honeysuckle. It was blood. A whole lot of blood. And that was no tipped-over endtable.

Joe hurried down to the shape, his heart hammering in his ears. He knelt by it, and a sound like a squeak escaped his throat. Suddenly the air in the hall seemed too hot and close. It seemed to be strangling him. He turned away from Gary, one hand cupped over his mouth. Someone had murdered Gary. Someone had –

He forced himself to look back. Gary lay in a pool of his own blood. His eyes glared sightlessly up at the hallway ceiling. His throat had been opened. Not just opened, dear God, it looked as if it had been *chewed* open.

This time there was no struggle with his gorge. This time he simply let everything come up in a series of hopeless choking sounds. Crazily, the back of his mind had turned to Charity with childish resentment. Charity had gotten *her* trip, but he wasn't going to get his. He wasn't going to get his because some crazy bastard had done a Jack the Ripper act on poor old Gary Pervier and –

– and he had to call the police. Never mind all the rest of it. Never mind the way the ole Pervert's eyes were glaring up at the ceiling in the shadows, the way the sheared-copper smell of his blood mingled with the sickish-sweet aroma of the honeysuckle.

He got to his feet and staggered down toward the kitchen. He was moaning deep in his throat but was hardly aware of it. The phone was on the wall in the kitchen. He had to call the State Police, Sheriff Bannerman, someone –

He stopped in the doorway. His eyes widened until they actually seemed to be bulging from his head. There was a pile of dog droppings in the doorway of the kitchen . . . and he knew from the size of the pile whose dog had been here.

'Cujo,' he whispered. 'Oh my God, Cujo's gone rabid!'

He thought he heard a sound behind him and he whirled around, hair freezing up from the back of his neck. The hallway was empty except for Gary, Gary who had said the other night that Joe couldn't sic Cujo on a yelling nigger, Gary with his throat laid open all the way to the knob of his backbone.

There was no sense in taking chances. He bolted back down the hallway, skidding momentarily in Gary's blood, leaving an elongated footmark behind him. He moaned again, but when he had shut the heavy inner door he felt a little better.

He went back to the kitchen, shying his way around Gary's body, and looked in, ready to pull the kitchen-hallway door shut quickly if Cujo was in there. Again he wished distractedly for the comforting weight of his shotgun over his arm.

The kitchen was empty. Nothing moved except the curtains, stirring in a sluggish breeze which whispered through the open windows. There was a smell of dead vodka bottles. It was sour, but better than that . . . that other smell. Sunlight lay on the faded hilly linoleum in orderly patterns. The phone, its once-white plastic case now dulled with the grease of many bachelor meals and cracked in some long-ago drunken stumble, hung on the wall as always.

Joe went in and closed the door firmly behind him. He crossed to the two open windows and saw nothing in the tangle of the back yard except the rusting corpses of the two cars that had predated Gary's Chrysler. He closed the windows anyway.

He went to the telephone, pouring sweat in the explosively hot kitchen. The book was hanging beside the phone on a hank of hayrope. Gary had made the hole through the book where the hayrope was threaded with Joe's drillpunch about a year ago, drunk as a lord and proclaiming that he didn't give a shit.

Joe picked the book up and then dropped it. The book thudded against the wall. His hands felt too heavy. His mouth was slimy with the taste of vomit. He got hold of the book again and opened it with a jerk that nearly tore off the cover. He could have dialed O, or 555-1212, but in his shock he never thought of it.

The sound of his rapid, shallow breathing, his racing heart, and the riffle of the thin phonebook pages masked a faint noise from behind him: the low creak of the cellar door as Cujo nosed it open.

He had gone down cellar after killing Gary Pervier. The light in the kitchen had been too bright, too dazzling.

It sent white-hot shards of agony into his decomposing brain. The cellar door had been ajar and he had padded jerkily down the stairs into the blessedly cool dark. He had fallen asleep next to Gary's old Army footlocker, and the breeze from the open windows had swung the cellar door most of the way closed. The breeze had not been quite strong enough to latch the door.

The moans, the sound of Joe retching, the thumpings and slammings as Joe ran down the hall to close the front door – these things had awakened him to his pain again. His pain and his dull, ceaseless fury. Now he stood behind Joe in the dark doorway. His head was lowered. His eyes were nearly scarlet. His thick, tawny fur was matted with gore and drying mud. Foam drizzled from his mouth in a lather, and his teeth showed constantly because his tongue was beginning to swell.

Joe had found the Castle Rock section of the book. He got the C's and ran a shaking finger down to CASTLE ROCK MUNICIPAL SERVICES in a boxed-off section halfway down one column. There was the number for the sheriff's office. He reached up a finger to begin dialing, and that was when Cujo began to growl deep in his chest.

All the nerves seemed to run out of Joe Camber's body. The telephone book slithered from his fingers and thudded against the wall again. He turned slowly toward that growling sound. He saw Cujo standing in the cellar doorway.

'Nice doggy,' he whispered huskily, and spit ran down his chin.

He made helpless water in his pants, and the sharp, ammoniac reek of it struck Cujo's nose like a keen slap.

He sprang. Joe lurched to one side on legs that felt like stilts and the dog struck the wall hard enough to punch through the wallpaper and knock out plaster dust in a white, gritty puff. Now the dog wasn't growling; a series of heavy, grinding sounds escaped him, sounds more savage than any barks.

Joe backed toward the rear door. His feet tangled in one of the kitchen chairs. He pinwheeled his arms madly for balance, and might have gotten it back, but before that could happen Cujo bore down on him, a bloodstreaked killing machine with strings of foam flying backward from his jaws. There was a green, swampy stench about him.

'*Oh m'God lay off'n me!*' Joe Camber shrieked.

He remembered Gary. He covered his throat with one hand and tried to grapple with Cujo with the other. Cujo backed off momentarily, snapping, his muzzle wrinkled back in a great humorless grin that showed teeth like a row of slightly yellowed fence spikes. Then he came again.

And this time he came for Joe Camber's balls.

'Hey kiddo, you want to come grocery shopping with me? And have lunch at Mario's?'

Tad got up. 'Yeah! Good!'

'Come on, then.'

She had her bag over her shoulder and she was wearing jeans and a faded blue shirt. Tad thought she was looking very pretty. He was relieved to see there was no sign of her tears, because when she cried, *he* cried. He knew it was a baby thing to do, but he couldn't help it.

He was halfway to the car and she was slipping behind

the wheel when he remembered that her Pinto was all screwed up.

'Mommy?'

'What? Get in.'

But he hung back a little, afraid. 'What if the car goes kerflooey?'

'Ker—?' She was looking at him, puzzled, and then he saw by her exasperated expression that she had forgotten all about the car being screwed up. He had reminded her, and now she was unhappy again. Was it the Pinto's fault, or was it his? He didn't know, but the guilty feeling inside said it was his. Then her face smoothed out and she gave him a crooked little smile that he knew well enough to feel it was his special smile, the one she saved just for him. He felt better.

'We're just going into town, Tadder. If Mom's ole blue Pinto packs it in, we'll just have to blow two bucks on Castle Rock's one and only taxi getting back home. Right?'

'Oh, Okay.' He got in and managed to pull the door shut. She watched him closely, ready to move at an instant, and Tad supposed she was thinking about last Christmas, when he had shut the door on his foot and had to wear an Ace bandage for about a month. But he had been just a baby then, and now he was four years old. Now he was a big boy. He knew that was true because his dad had told him. He smiled at his mother to show her the door had been no problem, and she smiled back.

'Did it latch tight?'

'Tight,' Tad agreed, so she opened it and slammed it again, because moms didn't believe you unless you told them something bad, like you spilled the bag of sugar reaching for the peanut butter or broke a window while trying to throw a rock all the way over the garage roof.

'Hook your belt,' she said, getting in herself again. 'When that needle valve or whatever it is messes up, the car jerks a lot.'

A little apprehensively, Tad buckled his seat belt and harness. He sure hoped they weren't going to have an accident, like in Ten-Truck Wipe-Out. Even more than that, he hoped Mom wouldn't cry.

'Flaps down?' she asked, adjusting invisible goggles.

'Flaps down,' he agreed, grinning. It was just a game they played.

'Runway clear?'

'Clear.'

'Then here we go.' She keyed the ignition and backed down the driveway. A moment later they were headed for town.

After about a mile they both relaxed. Up to that point Donna had been sitting bolt upright behind the wheel and Tad had been doing the same in the passenger bucket. But the Pinto ran so smoothly that it might have popped off the assembly line only yesterday.

They went to the Agway Market and Donna bought forty dollars' worth of groceries, enough to keep them the ten days that Vic would be gone. Tad insisted on a fresh box of Twinkles, and would have added Cocoa Bears if Donna had let him. They got shipments of the Sharp cereals regularly, but they were currently out. It was a busy trip, but she still had time for bitter reflection as she waited in the checkout lane (Tad sat in the cart's child seat, swinging his legs nonchalantly) on how much three lousy bags of groceries went for these days. It wasn't just depressing; it was scary. That thought led her to the frightening possibility – *probability*, her mind whispered – that Vic and Roger might actually lose the Sharp account and, as a result of that, the agency itself. What price groceries then?

She watched a fat woman with a lumpy behind packed into avocado-colored slacks pull a food-stamp booklet out of her purse, saw the checkout girl roll her eyes at the girl running the next register, and felt sharp rat-teeth of panic gnawing at her belly. It couldn't come to that, could it? *Could it?* No, of course not. Of course not. They would go back to New York first, they would –

She didn't like the way her thoughts were speeding up, and she pushed the whole mess resolutely away before it could grow to avalanche size and bury her in another deep depression. Next time she wouldn't have to buy coffee, and that would knock three bucks off the bill.

She trundled Tad and the groceries out to the Pinto and put the bags into the hatchback and Tad into the passenger bucket, standing there and listening to make sure the door latched, wanting to close the door herself but understanding it was something he felt he had to do. It was a big-boy thing. She had almost had a heart attack last December when Tad shut his foot in the door. How he had *screamed*! She had nearly fainted . . . and then Vic had been there, charging out of the house in his bathrobe, splashing out fans of driveway slush with his bare feet. And she had let him take over and be competent, which she hardly ever was in emergencies; she usually just turned to mush. He had checked to make sure the foot wasn't broken,

180

then had changed quickly and driven them to the emergency room at the Bridgton hospital.

Groceries stowed, likewise Tad, she got behind the wheel and started the Pinto. *Now* it'll fuck up, she thought, but the Pinto took them docilely up the street to Mario's, which purveyed delicious pizza stuffed with enough calories to put a spare tire on a lumberjack. She did a passable job of parallel parking, ending up only eighteen inches or so from the curb, and took Tad in, feeling better than she had all day. Maybe Vic had been wrong; maybe it had been bad gas or dirt in the fuel line and it had finally worked its way out of the car's system. She hadn't looked forward to going out to Joe Camber's Garage. It was too far out in the boonies (what Vic always referred to with high good humor as East Galoshes Corners – but of course he could afford high good humor, he was a *man*), and she had been a little scared of Camber the one time she had met him. He was the quintessential back-country Yankee, grunting instead of talking, sullen-faced. And the dog . . . what was his name? Something that sounded Spanish. Cujo, that was it. The same name William Wolfe of the SLA had taken, although Donna found it impossible to believe that Joe Camber had named his Saint Bernard after a radical robber of banks and kidnapper of rich young heiresses. She doubted if Joe Camber had ever heard of the Symbionese Liberation Army. The dog had seemed friendly enough, but it had made her nervous to see Tad patting that monster – the way it made her nervous to stand and watch him close the car door himself. Cujo looked big enough to swallow the likes of Tad in two bites.

She ordered Tad a hot pastrami sandwich because he

didn't care much for pizza – kid sure didn't get that from *my* side of the family, she thought – and a pepperoni and onion pizza with double cheese for herself. They ate at one of the tables overlooking the road. My breath will be fit to knock over a horse, she thought, and then realised it didn't matter. She had managed to alienate both her husband and the guy who came to visit in the course of the last six weeks or so.

That brought depression cruising her way again, and once again she forced it back . . . but her arms were getting a little tired.

They were almost home and Springsteen was on the radio when the Pinto started doing it again.

At first there was a small jerk. That was followed by a bigger one. She began to pump the accelerator gently; sometimes that helped.

'Mommy?' Tad asked, alarmed.

'It's all right, Tad,' she said, but it wasn't. The Pinto began to jerk hard, throwing them both against their seatbelts with enough force to lock the harness clasps. The engine chopped and roared. A bag fell over in the hatchback compartment, spilling cans and bottles. She heard something break.

'*You goddamned shitting thing!*' she cried in an exasperated fury. She could see their house just below the brow of the hill, mockingly close, but she didn't think the Pinto was going to get them there.

Frightened as much by her shout as by the car's spasms, Tad began to cry, adding to her confusion and upset and anger.

'*Shut up!*' she yelled at him. '*Oh Christ, just shut up, Tad!*'

He began to cry harder, and his hand went to the bulge in his back pocket, where the Monster Words, folded up to packet size, were stowed away. Touching them made him feel a little bit better. Not much, but a little.

Donna decided she was going to have to pull over and stop; there was nothing else for it. She began to steer toward the shoulder, using the last of her forward motion to get there. They could use Tad's wagon to pull the groceries up to the house and then decide what to do about the Pinto. Maybe —

Just as the Pinto's offside wheels crunched over the sandy gravel at the edge of the road, the engine backfired twice and then the jerks smoothed out as they had done on previous occasions. A moment later she was scooting up to the driveway of the house and turning in. She drove uphill, shifted to park, pulled the emergency brake, turned off the motor, leaned over the wheel, and cried.

'Mommy?' Tad said miserably. *Don't cry no more*, he tried to add, but he had no voice and he could only mouth the words soundlessly, as if struck dumb by laryngitis. He looked at her only, wanting to comfort, not knowing just how it was done. Comforting her was his daddy's job, not his, and suddenly he hated his father for being somewhere else. The depth of his emotion both shocked and frightened him, and for no reason at all he suddenly saw his closet door coming open and spilling out a darkness that stank of something low and bitter.

At last she looked up, her face puffy. She found a handkerchief in her purse and wiped her eyes. 'I'm sorry, honey. I wasn't really shouting at you. I was shouting at this . . . this *thing*.' She struck the steering wheel with her hand, hard. 'Ow!' She put the edge of her hand in her mouth and then laughed a little. It wasn't a happy laugh.

'Guess it's still kerflooey,' Tad said glumly.

'I guess it is,' she agreed, almost unbearably lonesome for Vic. 'Well, let's get the things in. We got the supplies anyway, Cisco.'

'Right, Pancho,' he said. 'I'll get my wagon.'

He brought his Redball Flyer down and Donna loaded the three bags into it, after repacking the bag that had fallen over. It had been a ketchup bottle that had shattered. You'd figure it, wouldn't you? Half a bottle of Heinz had puddled out on the powder-blue pile carpeting of the hatchback. It looked as if someone had committed hara-kiri back there. She supposed she could sop up the worst of it with a sponge, but the stain would still show. Even if she used a rug shampoo she was afraid it would show.

She tugged the wagon up to the kitchen door at the side of the house while Tad pushed. She lugged the groceries in and was debating whether to put them away or clean up the ketchup before it could set when the phone rang. Tad was off for it like a sprinter at the sound of a gun. He had gotten very good at answering the phone.

'Yes, who is it please?'

He listened, grinned, then held out the phone to her.

Figures, she thought. Someone who'll want to talk for two hours about nothing. To Tad she said, 'Do you know who it is, hon?'

'Sure,' he said. 'It's Dad.'

Her heart began to beat more rapidly. She took the phone from Tad and said, 'Hello? Vic?'

'Hi, Donna.' It was his voice all right, but so

reserved . . . so *careful*. It gave her a deep sinking feeling that she didn't need on top of everything else.

'Are you all right?' she asked.

'Sure.'

'I just thought you'd call later. If at all.

'Well, we went right over to Image-Eye. They did all the Sharp Cereal Professor spots, and what do you think? They can't find the frigging kinescopes. Roger's ripping his hair out by the roots.'

'Yes,' she said, nodding. 'He hates to be off schedule, doesn't he?'

'That's an understatement.' He sighed deeply. 'So I just thought, while they were looking . . .'

He trailed off vaguely, and her feelings of depression – her feelings of *sinking* – feelings that were so unpleasant and yet so childishly passive, turned to a more active sense of fear. Vic *never* trailed off like that, not even if he was being distracted by stuff going on at his end of the wire. She thought of the way he had looked on Thursday night, so ragged and close to the edge.

'Vic, *are* you all right?' She could hear the alarm in her voice and knew he must hear it too; even Tad looked up from the coloring book with which he had sprawled out on the hall floor, his eyes bright, a tight little frown on his small forehead.

'Yeah,' he said. 'I just started to say that I thought I'd call now, while they're rummaging around. Won't have a chance later tonight, I guess. How's Tad?'

'Tad's fine.'

She smiled at Tad and then tipped him a wink. Tad smiled back, the lines on his forehead smoothed out, and he went back to his coloring. *He sounds tired and I'm not going to lay all that shit about the car on him*, she thought, and then found herself going right ahead and doing it anyway.

She heard the familiar whine of self-pity creeping into her voice and struggled to keep it out. Why was she even telling him all of this, for heaven's sake? He sounded like he was falling apart, and she was prattling on about her Pinto's carburetor and a spilled bottle of ketchup.

'Yeah, it sounds like the needle valve, okay,' Vic said. He actually sounded a little better now. A little less down. Maybe because it was a problem which mattered so little in the greater perspective of things which they had now been forced to deal with. 'Couldn't Joe Camber get you in today?'

'I tried him but he wasn't home.'

'He probably was, though,' Vic said. 'There's no phone in his garage. Usually his wife or his kid runs his messages out to him. Probably they were out someplace.'

'Well, he still might be gone—'

'Sure,' Vic said. 'But I really doubt it, babe. If a human being could actually put down roots, Joe Camber's the guy that would do it.'

'Should I just take a chance and drive out there?' Donna asked doubtfully. She was thinking of the empty miles along 117 and the Maple Sugar Road . . . and all that was *before* you got to Camber's road, which was so far out it didn't even have a name. And if that needle valve chose a stretch of that desolation in which to pack up for good, it would just make another hassle.

'No, I guess you better not,' Vic said. 'He's probably

there . . . unless you really need him. In which case he'd
be gone. Catch-22.' He sounded depressed.

'Then what should I do?'

'Call the Ford dealership and tell them you want a
tow.'

'But—'

'No, you have to. If you try to drive twenty-two miles
over to South Paris, it'll pack up on you for sure. And if
you explain the situation in advance, they might be able
to get you a loaner. Barring that, they'll lease you a car.'

'Lease . . . Vic, isn't that expensive?'

'Yeah,' he said.

She thought again that it was wrong of her to be
dumping all this on him. He was probably thinking that
she wasn't capable of anything . . . except maybe screwing
the local furniture refinisher. She was fine at that. Hot salt
tears, partly anger, partly self-pity, stung her eyes again. 'I'll
take care of it,' she said, striving desperately to keep her
voice normal, light. Her elbow was propped on the wall
and one hand was over her eyes. 'Not to worry.'

'Well, I— oh, shit, there's Roger. He's dust up to his
neck, but they got the kinescopes. Put Tad on for a second,
would you?'

Frantic questions backed up in her throat. Was it all
right? Did he think it could be all right? Could they get
back to go and start again? Too late. No time. She had
spent the time gabbing about the car. Dumb broad, stupid
quiff.

'Sure,' she said. 'He'll say good-bye for both of us.
And . . . Vic?'

'What?' He sounded impatient now, pressed for time.

'I love you,' she said, and then before he could reply, she added: 'Here's Tad.' She gave the phone to Tad quickly, almost conking him on the head with it, and went through the house to the front porch, stumbling over a hassock and sending it spinning, seeing everything through a prism of tears.

She stood on the porch looking out at 117, clutching her elbows, struggling to get herself under control – control, dammit, *control* – and it was amazing, wasn't it, how bad you could hurt when there was nothing physically wrong.

Behind her she could hear the soft murmur of Tad's voice, telling Vic they had eaten at Mario's, that Mommy had her favorite Fat Pizza and the Pinto had been okay until they were almost home. Then he was telling Vic that he loved him. Then there was the soft sound of the phone being hung up. Contact broken.

Control.

At last she felt as if she had some. She went back into the kitchen and began putting away the groceries.

Charity Camber stepped down from the Greyhound bus at quarter past three that afternoon. Brett was right at her heels. She was clutching the strap of her purse spasmodically. She was suddenly, irrationally afraid that she would not recognize Holly. Her sister's face, held in her mind like a photograph all these years (The Younger Sister Who Had Married Well), had gone suddenly and mysteriously out of her mind, leaving only a fogged blank where the picture should have been.

'You see her?' Brett asked as they alighted. He looked around at the Stratford bus depot with bright interest and no more. There was certainly no fear in his face.

188

'Give me a chance to look around!' Charity said sharply. 'Probably she's in the coffee shop or—'

'Charity?'

She turned and there was Holly. The picture held in her memory came flooding back, but it was now a transparency overlying the real face of the woman standing by the Space Invaders game. Charity's first thought was that Holly was wearing *glasses* – how funny! Her second, shocked, was that Holly had wrinkles – not many, but there could be no question about what they were. Her third thought was not precisely a thought at all. It was an image, as clear, true, and heartbreaking as a sepia-toned photograph: Holly leaping into old man Seltzer's cowpond in her underpants, pigtails standing up against the sky, thumb and forefinger of left hand pinching her nostrils closed for comic effect. *No glasses then*, Charity thought, and pain came to her then, and it squeezed her heart.

Standing at Holly's sides, looking shyly at her and Brett, were a boy of about five and a girl who was perhaps two and a half. The little girl's bulgy pants spoke of diapers beneath. Her stroller stood off to one side.

'Hi, Holly,' Charity said, and her voice was so thin she could hardly hear it.

The wrinkles were small. They turned upward, the way their mother had always said the good ones did. Her dress was dark blue, moderately expensive. The pendant she wore was either a very good piece of costume jewelry or a very small emerald.

There was a moment then. Some space of time. In it, Charity felt her heart fill with a joy so fierce and complete that she knew there could never be any real question about what this trip had or had not cost her. For now she was *free*, her son was free. This was her sister and those children were her kin, not pictures but real.

Laughing and crying a little, the two women stepped toward each other, hesitantly at first, then quickly. They embraced. Brett stood where he was. The little girl, maybe scared, went to her mother and wrapped a hand firmly around the hem of her dress, perhaps to keep her mother and this strange lady from flying off together.

The little boy stared at Brett, then advanced. He was wearing Tuffskin jeans and a T-shirt with the words HERE COMES TROUBLE printed on it.

'You're my cousin Brett,' the kid said.

'Yeah.'

'My name's Jim. Just like my dad.'

'Yeah.'

'You're from Maine,' Jim said. Behind him, Charity and Holly were talking rapidly, interrupting each other and laughing at their hurry to tell everything right here in this grimy bus station south of Milford and north of Bridgeport.

'Yeah, I'm from Maine,' Brett said.

'You're ten.'

'Right.'

'I'm five.'

'Oh yeah?'

'Yeah. But I can beat you up, *Ka-whud*!' He hit Brett in the belly, doubling him up.

Brett uttered a large and surprised 'Oof!' Both women gasped.

'*Jimmy!*' Holly cried in a kind of resigned horror.

Brett straightened up slowly and saw his mother watching him, her face in a kind of suspension.

'Yeah, you can beat me up anytime,' Brett said, and smiled.

And it was all right. He saw from his mother's face that it was all right, and he was glad.

By three thirty Donna had decided to leave Tad with a baby-sitter and try taking the Pinto up to Camber's. She had tried the number again and there had still been no response, but she had reasoned that even if Camber wasn't in his garage, he would be back soon, maybe even by the time she arrived there . . . always assuming she *did* arrive there. Vic told her last week that Camber would probably have some old junker to loan her if it looked like her Pinto was going to be an overnight job. That had really been the deciding factor. But she thought that taking Tad would be wrong. If the Pinto seized up on that back road and she had to take a hike, well, okay. But Tad shouldn't have to do it.

Tad, however, had other ideas.

Shortly after talking to his dad, he had gone up to his room and had stretched out on his bed with a stack of Little Golden Books. Fifteen minutes later he had dozed off, and a dream had come to him, a dream which seemed utterly ordinary but which had a strange, nearly terrifying power. In his dream he saw a big boy throwing a friction-taped baseball up and trying to hit it. He missed twice, three times, four. On the fifth swing he hit the ball . . . and the bat, which had also been taped, shattered at the handle. The boy held the handle for a moment (black tape flapped

191

from it), then bent and picked up the fat of the bat. He looked at it for a moment, shook his head disgustedly, and tossed it into the high grass at the side of the driveway. Then he turned, and Tad saw with a sudden shock that was half dread, half delight, that the boy was himself at ten or eleven. Yes, it was him. He was sure of it.

Then the boy was gone, and there was a grayness. In it he could hear two sounds: creaking swing chains . . . and the faint quacking of ducks. With these sounds and the grayness came a sudden scary feeling that he could not breathe, he was suffocating. *And a man was walking out of the mist . . . a man who wore a black shiny raincoat and held a stop sign on a stick in one hand. He grinned, and his eyes were shiny silver coins. He raised one hand to point at Tad, and he saw with horror it wasn't a hand at all, it was* bones, *and the face inside the shiny vinyl hood of the raincoat wasn't a face at all. It was a skull. It was —*

He jerked awake, his body bathed in sweat that was only in part due to the room's almost explosive heat. He sat up, propped on his elbows, breathing in harsh gasps.

Snick.

The closet door was swinging open. And as it swung open he saw something inside, only for a second and then he was flying for the door which gave on the hall as fast as he could. He saw it only for a second, long enough to tell it wasn't the man in the shiny black raincoat, Frank Dodd, the man who had killed the ladies. Not him. Something else. Something with red eyes like bloody sunsets.

But he could not speak of these things to his mother. So he concentrated on Debbie, the sitter, instead.

He didn't *want* to be left with Debbie, Debbie was mean to him, she always played the record player loud, et cetera, et cetera. When none of this had much effect on his mother, Tad suggested ominously that Debbie might shoot him. When Donna made the mistake of giggling helplessly at the thought of fifteen-year-old myopic Debbie Gehringer shooting anyone, Tad burst into miserable tears and ran into the living room. He needed to tell her that Debbie Gehringer might not be strong enough to keep the monster in his closet – that if dark fell and his mother was not back, it might come out. It might be the man in the black raincoat, or it might be the beast.

Donna followed him, sorry for her laughter, wondering how she could have been so insensitive. The boy's father was gone, and that was upsetting enough. He didn't want to lose sight of his mother for even an hour. And –

And isn't it possible he senses some of what's gone on between Vic and me? Perhaps even heard . . . ?

No, she didn't think that. She *couldn't* think that. It was just the upset in his routine.

The door to the living room was shut. She reached for the knob, hesitated, then knocked softly instead. There was no answer. She knocked again and when there was still no answer, she went in quietly. Tad was lying face down on the couch with one of the back cushions pulled firmly down over his head. It was behavior reserved only for major upsets.

'Tad?'

No answer.

'I'm sorry I laughed.'

His face looked out at her from beneath one edge of the puffy, dove-gray sofa cushion. There were fresh tears on his face. 'Please can't I come?' he asked. 'Don't make me stay here with Debbie, Mom.' Great histrionics, she thought. Great histrionics and blatant coercion. She recognized it (or felt she did) and at the same time found it impossible to be tough . . . partly because her own tears were threatening again. Lately it seemed that there was always a cloudburst just over the horizon.

'Honey, you know the way the Pinto was when we came back from town. It could break down in the middle of East Galoshes Corners and we'd have to walk to a house and use the telephone, maybe a long way—'

'So? I'm a good walker!'

'I know, but you might get scared.'

Thinking of the thing in the closet, Tad suddenly cried out with all his force, *'I will not get scared!'* His hand had gone automatically to the bulge in his hip pocket of his jeans, where the Monster Words were stowed away.

'Don't raise your voice that way, please. It sounds ugly.'

He lowered his voice. 'I won't get scared. I just want to go with you.'

She looked at him helplessly, knowing that she really ought to call Debby Gehringer, feeling that she was being shamelessly manipulated by her four-year-old son. And if she gave in it would be for all the wrong reasons. She thought helplessly, *It's like a chain reaction that doesn't stop anyplace and it's gumming up works I didn't even know existed. O God I wish I was in Tahiti.*

She opened her mouth to tell him, quite firmly and

once and for all, that she was going to call Debbie and they could make popcorn together if he was good and that he would have to go to bed right after supper if he was bad and that was the *end* of it. Instead, what came out was, 'All right, you can come. But our Pinto might not make it, and if it doesn't we'll have to walk to a house and have the Town Taxi come and pick us up. And if we *do* have to walk, I don't want to have to listen to you crabbing at me, Tad Trenton.

'No, I won't—'

'Let me finish. I don't want you crabbing at me or asking me to carry you, because I won't do it. Do we have an understanding?'

'Yeah! Yeah, sure!' Tad hopped off the sofa, all grief forgotten. 'Are we going now?'

'Yes, I guess so. Or . . . I know what. Why don't I make us a snack first? A snack and we'll put some milk in the Thermos bottles, too.'

'In case we have to camp out all *night*?' Tad looked suddenly doubtful again.

'No, honey.' She smiled and gave him a little hug. 'But I still haven't been able to get Mr Camber on the telephone. Your daddy says it's probably just because he doesn't have a phone in his garage so he doesn't know I'm calling. And his wife and his little boy might be someplace, so —'

'He should have a phone in his garage,' Tad said. 'That's *dumb*.'

'Just don't you tell him that,' Donna said quickly, and Tad shook his head that he wouldn't. 'Anyway, if nobody's there, I thought you and I could have a little snack in the car or maybe on his steps and wait for him.'

Ted clapped his hands. 'Great! Great! Can I take my Snoopy lunchbox?'

'Sure,' Donna said, giving in completely.

She found a box of Keebler figbars and a couple of Slim Jims (Donna thought they were hideous things, but they were Tad's all-time favorite snack). She wrapped some green olives and cucumber slices in foil. She filled Tad's Thermos with milk and half-filled Vic's big Thermos, the one he took on camping trips.

For some reason, looking at the food made her uneasy.

She looked at the phone and thought about trying Joe Camber's number again. Then she decided there was no sense in it, since they would be going out there either way. Then she thought of asking Tad again if he wouldn't rather she called Debbie Gehringer, and then wondered what was wrong with her – Tad had made himself perfectly clear on *that* point.

It was just that suddenly she didn't feel good. Not good at all. It was nothing she could put her finger on. She looked around the kitchen as if expecting the source of her unease to announce itself. It didn't.

'We going, Mom?'

'Yes,' she said absently. There was a noteminder on the wall by the fridge, and on this she scrawled: *Tad & I have gone out to J. Camber's garage w/Pinto. Back soon.*

'Ready, Tad?'

'Sure.' He grinned. 'Who's the note for, Mom?'

'Oh, Joanie might drop by with those raspberries,' she said vaguely. 'Or maybe Alison MacKenzie. She was going to show me some Amway and Avon stuff.'

'Oh.'

196

Donna ruffled his hair and they went out together. The heat hit them like a hammer wrapped in pillows. Buggardly car probably won't even start, she thought.

But it did.

It was 3:45 P.M.

They drove southeast along Route 117 toward the Maple Sugar Road, which was about five miles out of town. The Pinto behaved in exemplary fashion, and if it hadn't been for the bout of snaps and jerks coming home from the shopping trip, Donna would have wondered what she had bothered making such a fuss about. But there *had* been that bout of the shakes, and so she drove sitting bolt upright again, going no faster than forty, pulling as far to the right as she could when a car came up behind her. And there was a lot of traffic on the road. The summer influx of tourists and vacationers had begun. The Pinto had no air conditioning, so they rode with both windows open.

A Continental with New York plates towing a gigantic trailer with two mopeds on the back swung around them on a blind curve, the driver bleating his horn. The driver's wife, a fat woman wearing mirror sunglasses, looked at Donna and Tad with imperious contempt.

'Get stuffed!' Donna yelled, and popped her middle finger up at the fat lady. The fat lady turned away quickly. Tad was looking at his mother just a little nervously, and Donna smiled at him. 'No hassle, big guy. We're going good. Just out-of-state fools.'

'Oh,' Tad said cautiously.

Listen to me, she thought. *The big Yankee. Vic would be proud.*

She had to grin to herself, because everyone in Maine understood that if you moved here from another place, you would be an out-of-stater until you were sent to your grave. And on your tombstone they would write something like HARRY JONES, CASTLE CORNERS, MAINE *(Originally from Omaha, Nebraska)*.

Most of the tourists were headed toward 302, where they would turn east to Naples or west toward Bridgton, Fryeburg, and North Conway, New Hampshire, with its alpine slides, cut-rate amusement parks, and tax-free restaurants. Donna and Tad were not going up to the 302 junction.

Although their home overlooked downtown Castle Rock and its picturebook Town Common, woods had closed in on both sides of the road before they were five miles from their own front door. These woods drew back occasionally – a little – to show a lot with with a house or a trailer on it, and as they went farther out, the houses were more often of the type that her father had called 'shanty Irish'. The sun still shone brightly down and there was a good four hours of daylight left, but the emptiness made her feel uneasy again. It was not so bad here, on 117, but once they left the main road –

Their turnoff was marked with a sign saying MAPLE SUGAR ROAD in faded, almost unreadable letters. It had been splintered considerably by kids banging away with .22s and birdshot. This road was two-lane blacktop, bumpy and frost-heaved. It wound past two or three nice houses, two or three not-so-nice houses, and one old and shabby RoadKing trailer sitting on a crumbling concrete foundation. There was a yardful of weeds in front of the trailer.

Donna could see cheap-looking plastic toys in the weeds. A sign nailed askew to a tree at the head of the driveway read FREE KITTEN'S. A potbellied kid of maybe two stood in the driveway, his sopping Pamper hanging below his tiny penis. His mouth hung open and he was picking his nose with one finger and his navel with another. Looking at him, Donna felt a helpless chill of gooseflesh.

Stop it! For Christ's sake, what's wrong with you?

The woods closed in around them again. An old '68 Ford Fairlane with a lot of rusty-red primer paint on the hood and around the headlights passed them going the other way. A young kid with a lot of hair was slouched nonchalantly behind the wheel. He wasn't wearing a shirt. The Fairlane was doing maybe eighty. Donna winced. It was the only traffic they saw.

The Maple Sugar Road climbed steadily, and when they passed the occasional field or large garden they were afforded a stunning view of western Maine toward Bridgton and Fryeburg. Long Lake glittered in the farthest distance like the sapphire pendant of a fabulously rich woman.

They were climbing another long slope up one of these eroded hills (as advertised, the sides of the road were now lined with dusty, heat-drooping maples) when the Pinto began to buck and jolt again. Donna's breath clogged in her throat and she thought, *Oh come on, oh come on, come on, you cruddy little car, come* on!

Tad shifted uneasily in the passenger bucket and held onto his Snoopy lunchbox a little tighter.

She began to tap the accelerator lightly, her mind repeating the same words over and over like an inarticulate prayer: come *on*, come *on*, come *on*.

'Mommy? Is it—'

'Hush, Tad.'

The jerking grew worse. She pressed the gas pedal harder in frustration – and the Pinto squirted ahead, the engine smoothing out once more.

'Yay!' Tad said, so suddenly and loudly that she jumped.

'We're not there yet, Tadder.'

A mile farther along they came to an intersection marked with another wooden sign, this one reading TOWN ROAD NO. 3. Donna turned in, feeling triumphant. As well as she remembered, Camber's place was less than a mile and a half from here. If the Pinto gave up the ghost now, she and Tad could ankle it.

They passed a ramshackle house with a station wagon and a big old rusty white car in the driveway. In her rearview mirror, Donna noticed that the honeysuckle had really gone crazy on the side of the house that would catch most of the sun. A field opened up on their left after they passed the house, and the Pinto began to climb a long, steep hill.

Halfway up, the little car began to labor again. This time it was jerking harder than it ever had before.

'Will it get up, Mommy?'

'Yes,' she said grimly.

The Pinto's speedometer needle dropped from forty to thirty. She dropped the transmission selector lever from drive into the lower range, thinking vaguely that it might help compression or something. Instead, the Pinto began to buck worse than ever. A fusillade of backfires roared through the exhaust pipe, making Tad cry out. Now they were down to fast running speed, but she could see the Camber house and the red barn that served as his garage.

Flooring the accelerator had helped before. She tried again, and for a moment the engine smoothed out. The speedometer needle crept up from fifteen to twenty. Then it began to shake and shudder once more. Donna tried flooring the gas yet again, but this time, instead of smoothing out, the engine began to fail. The AMP idiot light on the dashboard began to flicker dully, signaling the fact that the Pinto was now on the edge of a stall.

But it didn't matter because the Pinto was now laboring past the Camber mailbox. They were here. There was a package hung over the mailbox lid, and she saw the return address clearly as they passed it: J. C. Whitney & Co.

The information went directly to the back of her mind without stopping. Her immediate attention was focused on getting the car into the driveway. *Let it stall then*, she thought. *He'll have to fix it before he can get in or out.*

The driveway was a little beyond the house. If it had been an uphill driveway all the way, as the Trentons' own was, the Pinto would not have made it. But after a small initial rise, the Cambers' driveway ran either dead level or slightly downhill toward the big converted barn.

Donna shifted into neutral and let what was left of the Pinto's forward motion carry them toward the big barn doors, which stood half open on their tracks. As soon as her foot left the accelerator pedal to tap the brake and stop them, the motor began to hitch again . . . but feebly this time. The AMP light pulsed like a slow heartbeat, then brightened. The Pinto stalled.

Tad looked at Donna.

She grinned at him. 'Tad, ole buddy,' she said, 'we have arrived.'

'Yeah,' he said. 'But is anybody home?'

There was a dark green pickup truck parked beside the barn. That was Camber's truck, all right, not someone else's waiting to be fixed. She remembered it from last time. But the lights were off inside. She craned her neck to the left and saw they were off in the house too. And there had been a package hung over the mailbox lid.

The return address on the package had been J. C. Whitney & Co. She knew what that was; her brother had gotten their catalogue in the mail when he was a teenager. They sold auto parts, accessories, customizing equipment. A package for Joe Camber from J. C. Whitney was the most natural thing in the world. But if he was here, he surely would have gotten his mail by now.

Nobody home, she thought dispiritedly, and felt a weary sort of anger at Vic. *He's always home, sure he is, the guy would put down roots in his garage if he could, sure he would, except when I need him.*

'Well, let's go see, anyhow,' she said, opening her door.

'I can't get my seatbelt unhooked,' Tad said, scratching futilely at the buckle release.

'Okay, don't have a hemorrhage, Tad. I'll come around and let you out.'

She got out, slammed her door, and took two steps toward the front of the car, intending to cross in front of the hood to the passenger side and let Tad out of his harness. It would give Camber a chance to come out and see who his company was, if he was here. She somehow didn't relish poking her head in on him unannounced. It was probably

foolish, but since that ugly and frightening scene with Steve
Kemp in her kitchen, she had become more aware of what
it was to be an unprotected woman than she had since she
was sixteen and her mother and father had let her begin
dating.

The quiet struck her at once. It was hot and so quiet
that it was somehow unnerving. There were sounds, of
course, but even after several years in Castle Rock, the
most she could say about her ears was that they had slowly
adapted from 'city ears' to 'town ears'. They were by no
means 'country ears' . . . and this was the real country.

She heard birdsong, and the harsher music of a crow
somewhere in the long field which stretched down the
flank of the hill they had just climbed. There was the sigh
of a light breeze, and the oaks that lined the driveway made
moving patterns of shadow around her feet. But she could
not hear a single car engine, not even the faraway burp of
a tractor or a baling machine. City ears and town ears are
most closely attuned to man-made sounds; those that nature
makes tend to fall outside the tightly drawn net of selec-
tive perception. A total lack of such sounds makes for
unease.

I'd hear him if he was working in the barn, Donna thought.
But the only sounds that registered were her own crunching
footfalls on the crushed gravel of the driveway and a low
humming sound, barely audible – with no real conscious
thought at all, her mind placed it as the hum of a power
transformer on one of the poles back by the road.

She reached the front of the hood and started to cross
in front of the Pinto, and that was when she heard a new
sound. A low, thick growling.

She stopped, her head coming up at once, trying to pinpoint the source of that sound. For a moment she couldn't and she was suddenly terrified, not by the sound itself but by its seeming directionlessness. It was nowhere. It was everywhere. And then some internal radar – survival equipment, perhaps – turned on all the way, and she understood that the growling was coming from inside the garage.

'Mommy?' Tad poked his head out his open window as far as the seatbelt harness would allow. 'I can't get this damn old—'

'*Shhhh!*'

(growling)

She took a tentative step backward, her right hand resting lightly on the Pinto's low hood, her nerves on trip-wires as thin as filaments, not panicked but in a state of heightened alertness, thinking: *It didn't growl before.*

Cujo came out of Joe Camber's garage. Donna stared at him, feeling her breath come to a painless and yet complete stop in her throat. It was the same dog. It was Cujo. But –

But oh my

(oh my God)

The dog's eyes settled on hers. They were red and rheumy. They were leaking some viscous substance. The dog seemed to be weeping gummy tears. His tawny coat was caked and matted with mud and –

Blood, is that

(it is it's blood Christ Christ)

She couldn't seem to move. No breath. Dead low tide in her lungs. She had heard about being paralyzed with fear but had never realized it could happen with such totality. There was no contact between her brain and her legs. That twisted gray filament running down the core of her spine had shut off the signals. Her hands were stupid blocks of flesh south of her wrists with no feeling in them. Her urine went. She was unaware of it save for some vague sensation of distant warmth.

And the dog seemed to know. His terrible, thought-less eyes never left Donna Trenton's wide blue ones. He paced forward slowly, almost languidly. Now he was standing on the barnboards at the mouth of the garage. Now he was on the crushed gravel twenty-five feet away. He never stopped growling. It was a low, purring sound, soothing in its menace. Foam dropped from Cujo's snout. And she couldn't move, not at all.

Then Tad saw the dog, recognized the blood which streaked its fur, and shrieked – a high piercing sound that made Cujo shift his eyes. And that was what seemed to free her.

She turned in a great shambling drunk's pivot, slam-ming her lower leg against the Pinto's fender and sending a steely bolt of pain up to her hip. She ran back around the hood of the car. Cujo's growl rose to a shattering roar of rage and he charged at her. Her feet almost skidded out from under her in the loose gravel, and she was only able to recover by slamming her arm down on the Pinto's hood. She hit her crazybone and uttered a thin shriek of pain.

The car door was shut. She had shut it herself, auto-matically, after getting out. The chromed button below the handle suddenly seemed dazzlingly bright, winking arrows of sun into her eyes. *I'll never be able to get that door open and get in and get it shut*, she thought, and the choking realization that she might be about to die rose up in her. *Not enough time. No way.*

She raked the door open. She could hear her breath sobbing in and out of her throat. Tad screamed again, a shrill, breaking sound.

She sat down, almost falling into the driver's seat. She got a glimpse of Cujo coming at her, hindquarters tensing down for the leap that would bring all two hundred pounds of him right into her lap.

She yanked the Pinto's door shut with both hands, reaching over the steering wheel with her right arm, honking the horn with her shoulder. She was just in time. A split second after the door slammed closed there was a heavy, solid thud, as if someone had swung a chunk of stovewood against the side of the car. The dog's barking roars of rage were cut off cleanly, and there was silence.

Knocked himself out, she thought hysterically. *Thank God, thank God for that —*

And a moment later Cujo's foam-covered, twisted face popped up outside her window, only inches away, like a horror-movie monster that has decided to give the audience the ultimate thrill by coming right out of the screen. She could see his huge, heavy teeth. And again there was that swooning, terrible feeling that the dog was looking at *her*, not at a woman who just happened to be trapped in her car with her little boy, but at *Donna Trenton*, as if he had just been hanging around, waiting for her to show up.

Cujo began to bark again, the sound incredibly loud even through the Saf-T-Glas. And suddenly it occurred to her that if she had not automatically rolled her window up as she brought the Pinto to a stop (something her father had insisted on: stop the car, roll up the windows, set the brake, take the keys, lock the car), she would now be minus her throat. Her blood would be on the wheel, the dash, the windshield. That one action, so automatic she could not even really remember performing it.

She screamed.

The dog's terrible face dropped from view.

She remembered Tad and looked around. When she saw him, a new fear invaded her, drilling like a hot needle. He had not fainted, but he was not really conscious, either. He had fallen back against the seat, his eyes dazed and blank. His face was white. His lips had gone bluish at the corners.

'Tad!' She snapped her fingers under his nose, and he blinked sluggishly at the dry sound. 'Tad!'

'Mommy,' he said thickly. 'How did the monster in my closet get out? Is it a dream? Is it my nap?'

'It's going to be all right,' she said, chilled by what he had said about his closet nonetheless. 'It's –'

She saw the dog's tail and the top of its broad back over the hood of the Pinto. It was going around to Tad's side of the car –

And Tad's window wasn't shut.

She jackknifed across Tad's lap, moving with such a hard muscular spasm that she cracked her fingers on the window crank. She turned it as fast as she could, panting, feeling Tad squirming beneath her.

It was three quarters of the way up when Cujo leaped at the window. His muzzle shot in through the closing gap and was forced upward toward the ceiling by the closing window. The sound of his snarling barks filled the small

207

car. Tad shrieked again and wrapped his arms around his head, his forearms crossed over his eyes. He tried to dig his face into Donna's belly, reducing her leverage on the window crank in his blind efforts to get away.

'Momma! Momma! Momma! *Make it stop! Make it go away!*'

Something warm was running across the backs of her hands. She saw with mouting horror that it was mixed slime and blood running from the dog's mouth. Using everything that she had, she managed to force the window crank through another quarter turn . . . and then Cujo pulled back. She caught just a glimpse of the Saint Bernard's features, twisted and crazy, a mad caricature of a friendly Saint Bernard's face. Then it dropped back to all fours and she could only see its back.

Now the crank turned easily. She shut the window, then wiped the backs of her hands on her jeans, uttering small cries of revulsion.

(oh Christ oh Mary Mother of God)

Tad had gone back to that dazed state of semiconsciousness again. This time when she snapped her fingers in front of his face there was no reaction.

He's going to have some complexes out of this, oh God yes. Oh sweet Tad, if only I'd left you with Debbie.

She took him by the shoulders and began to shake him gently back and forth.

'Is it my nap?' he asked again.

'No,' she said. He moaned – a low, painful sound that tore at her heart. 'No, but it's all right. Tad? It's okay. That dog can't get in. The windows are shut now. It can't come in. It can't get us.'

That got through and Tad's eyes cleared a little. 'Then let's go home, Mommy. I don't want to be here.'

'Yes. Yes, we'll—'

Like a great tawny projectile, Cujo leaped onto the hood of the Pinto and charged at the windshield, barking. Tad uttered another scream, his eyes bulging, his small hands digging at his cheeks, leaving angry red welts there.

'It can't get us!' Donna shouted at him. 'Do you hear me? It can't get in, Tad!'

Cujo struck the windshield with a muffled thud, bounced back, and scrabbled for purchase on the hood. He left a series of new scratches on the paint. Then he came again.

'*I want to go home!*' Tad screamed.

'Hug me tight, Tadder, and don't worry.'

How insane that sounded . . . but what else was there to say?

Tad buried his face against her breasts just as Cujo struck the windshield again. Foam smeared against the glass as he tried to bite his way through. Those muddled, bleary eyes stared into Donna's. I'm going to pull you to pieces, they said. You and the boy both. Just as soon as I find a way to get into this tin can, I'll eat you alive; I'll be swallowing pieces of you while you're still screaming.

Rabid, she thought. *That dog is rabid.*

With steadily mounting fear, she looked past the dog on the hood and at Joe Camber's parked truck. Had the dog bitten him?

She found the horn buttons and pressed them. The Pinto's horn blared and the dog skittered back, again almost losing its balance. 'Don't like that much, do you?' she shrieked triumphantly at it. 'Hurts your ears, doesn't it?' She jammed the horn down again.

Cujo leaped off the hood.

'Mommy, *pleeease* let's go home.'

She turned the key in the ignition. The motor cranked and cranked and cranked . . . but the Pinto did not start. At last she turned the key off again.

'Honey, we can't go just yet. The car—'

'Yes! Yes! Now! *Right now!*'

Her head began to thud. Big, whacking pains that were in perfect sync with her heartbeat.

'Tad. Listen to me. The car doesn't want to start. It's that needle valve thing. We've got to wait until the engine cools off. It'll go then, I think. We can leave.'

All we have to do is get back out of the driveway and get pointed down the hill. Then it won't matter even if it does stall, because we can coast. If I don't chicken out and hit the brake, I should be able to make it most of the way back to the Maple Sugar Road even with the engine shut down . . . or . . .

She thought of the house at the bottom of the hill, the one with the honeysuckle running wild all over the east side. There were people there. She had seen cars.

People!

She began to use the horn again. Three short blasts, three long blasts, three shorts, over and over, the only Morse she remembered from her two years in the Girl Scouts. They would hear. Even if they didn't understand the message, they would come up to see who was raising hell at Joe Camber's – and why.

Where was the dog? She couldn't see him any more.

But it didn't matter. The dog couldn't get in and help would be here shortly.

'Everything's going to be fine,' she told Tad. 'Wait and see.'

A dirty brick building in Cambridge housed the offices of Image-Eye Studios. The business offices were on the fourth floor, a suite of two studios were on the fifth, and a poorly air-conditioned screening room only big enough to hold sixteen seats in rows of four was on the sixth and top floor.

On that early Monday evening Vic Trenton and Roger Breakstone sat in the third row of the screening room, jackets off, ties pulled down. They had watched the kinescopes of the Sharp Cereal Professor commercials five times each. There were exactly twenty of them. Of the twenty, three were the infamous Red Razberry Zingers spots.

The last reel of six spots had finished half an hour ago, and the projectionist had called good night and gone to his evening job, which was running films at the Orson Welles Cinema. Fifteen minutes later Rob Martin, the president of Image-Eye, had bade them a glum good night, adding that his door would be open to them all day tomorrow and Wednesday, if they needed him. He avoided what was in all three of their minds: The door'll be open if you think of something worth talking about.

Rob had every right to look glum. He was a Vietnam vet who had lost a leg in the Tet offensive. He had opened I-E Studios in late 1970 with his disability money and a lot of help from his in-laws. The studio had gasped and struggled along since then, mostly catching crumbs from that well-stocked media table at which the larger Boston studios banqueted. Vic and Roger had been taken with him because he reminded them of themselves, in a way – struggling to make a go of it, to get up to that fabled corner and turn it. And, of course, Boston was good because it was an easier commute than New York.

In the last sixteen months, Image-Eye had taken off. Rob had been able to use the fact that his studio was doing the Sharp spots to land other business, and for the first time things had looked solid. In May, just before the cereal had hit the fan, he sent Vic and Roger a postcard showing a Boston T-bus going away. On the back were four lovely ladies, bent over to show their fannies, which were encased in designer jeans. Written on the back of the card, tabloid style, was this message: IMAGE-EYE LANDS CONTRACT TO DO BUTTS FOR BOSTON BUSES; BILLS BIG BUCKS. Funny then. Not such a hoot now. Since the Zingers fiasco, two clients (including Cannes-Look Jeans) had canceled their arrangements with I-E, and if Ad Worx lost the Sharp account, Rob would lose other accounts in addition to Sharp. It had left him feeling angry and scared . . . emotions Vic understood perfectly.

They had been sitting and smoking in silence for almost five minutes when Roger said in a low voice, 'It just makes me want to puke, Vic. I see that guy sitting on his desk and looking out at me like butter wouldn't melt in his mouth, taking a big bite of that cereal with the runny dye in it and saying, "Nope, nothing wrong here," and I get sick to my stomach. Physically sick to my stomach. I'm glad the projectionist had to go. If I watched them one more time, I'd have to do it with an airsick bag in my lap.'

He stubbed out his cigarette in the ashtray set into

the arm of his chair. He *did* look ill; his face had a yellowish sheen that Vic didn't like at all. Call it shell-shock, combat fatigue, whatever you wanted, but what you meant was scared shitless, backed into a rathole. It was looking into the dark and seeing something that was going to eat you up.

'I kept telling myself,' Roger said, reaching for another cigarette, 'that I'd see something. You know? *Something.* I couldn't believe it was as bad as it seemed. But the cumulative effect of those spots . . . it's like watching Jimmy Carter saying, "I'll never lie to you".' He took a drag from the new cigarette, grimaced, and stuffed it into the ashtray. 'No wonder George Carlin and Steve Martin and fucking *Saturday Night Live* had a field day. That guy just looks so *sanctimonious* to me now . . .' His voice had developed a sudden watery tremble. He shut his mouth with a snap.

'I've got an idea,' Vic said quietly.

'Yeah, you said something on the plane.' Roger looked at him, but without much hope. 'If you got one, let's hear it.'

'I think the Sharp Cereal Professor has to make one more spot,' Vic said. 'I think we have to convince old man Sharp of that. Not the kid. The old man.'

'What's the old prof gonna sell this time?' Roger asked, twisting open another button on his shirt. 'Rat poison or Agent Orange?'

'Come on, Roger. No one got poisoned.'

'Might as well have,' Roger said, and laughed shrilly. 'Sometimes I wonder if you understand what advertising really is. It's holding a wolf by the tail. Well, we lost our grip on this particular wolf and he's just about to come back on us and eat us whole.'

'Roger—'

'This is the country where it's front-page news when some consumer group weighed the McDonald's Quarter Pounder and found out it weighed a little shy of a quarter pound. Some obscure California magazine publishes a report that a rear-end collision can cause a gas-tank explosion in Pintos, and the Ford Motor Company shakes in its shoes—'

'Don't get on that,' Vic said, laughing a little. 'My wife's got a Pinto. I got problems enough.'

'All I'm saying is that getting the Sharp Cereal Professor to do another spot seems about as shrewd to me as having Richard Nixon do an encore State of the Union address. He's *compromised*, Vic, he's totally blown!' He paused, looking at Vic. Vic looked back at him gravely. 'What do you want him to say?'

'That he's sorry.'

Roger blinked at him glassily for a moment. Then he threw back his head and cackled. 'That he's sorry. *Sorry?* Oh, dear, that's wonderful. Was that your great idea?

'Hold on, Rog. You're not even giving me a chance. That's not like you.'

'No,' Roger said. 'I guess it's not. Tell me what you mean. But I can't believe you're—'

'Serious? I'm serious, all right. You took the courses. What's the basis of all successful advertising? Why bother to advertise at all?'

'The basis of all successful advertising is that people want to believe. That people sell themselves.'

'Yeah. When the Maytag Repairman says he's the

loneliest guy in town, people want to believe that there really is such a guy someplace, not doing anything but listening to the radio and maybe jacking off once in a while. People want to believe that their Maytags will *never* need repairs. When Joe DiMaggio comes on and says Mr Coffee saves coffee, saves money, people want to believe *that*. If—'

'But isn't that why we've got our asses in a crack? They wanted to believe the Sharp Cereal Professor and he let them down. Just like they wanted to believe in Nixon, and *he*—'

'Nixon, Nixon, Nixon!' Vic said, surprised by his own angry vehemence. 'You're getting blinded by that particular comparison, I've heard you make it two hundred times since this thing blew, and it *doesn't fit!*'

Roger was looking at him, stunned.

'Nixon was a crook, he knew he was a crook, and he said he wasn't a crook. The Sharp Cereal Professor said there was nothing wrong with Red Razberry Zingers and there *was* something wrong, but he didn't know it.' Vic leaned forward and pushed his finger gently against Roger's arm, emphasizing. 'There was no breach of faith. He has to say that, Rog. He has to get up in front of the American people and tell them there was no breach of faith. What there was, there was a mistake made by a company which manufactures food dye. The mistake was *not* made by the Sharp Company. He has to say that. And most important of all, he has to say he's sorry that mistake happened and that, although no one was *hurt*, he's sorry people were frightened.'

Roger nodded, then shrugged. 'Yes, I see the thrust

of it. But neither the old man or the kid will go for it, Vic. They want to bury the b—'

'Yes, yes, *yes!*' Vic cried, actually making Roger flinch. He jumped to his feet and began to walk jerkily up and down the screening room's short aisle. 'Sure they do, and they're right, he's dead and he has to be buried, the Sharp Cereal Professor has to be buried, Zingers has *already* been buried. But the thing we've got to make them see is that it can't be a *midnight* burial. That's the exact point! Their impulse is to go at this thing like a Mafia button man . . . or a scared relative burying a cholera victim.'

He leaned over Roger, so close that their noses were almost touching.

'Our job is to make them understand that the Cereal Professor will never rest easy unless he's interred in broad daylight. And I'd like to make the whole country mourners at his burial.'

'You're cr—' Roger began . . . then closed his mouth with a snap.

At long last Vic saw that scared, vague expression go out of his partner's eyes. A sudden sharpening happened in Roger's face, and the scared expression was replaced by a slightly mad one. Roger began to grin. Vic was so relieved to see that grin that he forgot about Donna and what had happened with her for the first time since he had gotten Kemp's note. The job took over completely, and it was only later that he would wonder, slightly dumbfounded, how long it had been since he had felt that pure, trippy, wonderful feeling of being fully involved with something he was good at.

'On the surface, we just want him to repeat the things

Sharp has been saying since it happened,' Vic went on. 'But when the Cereal Professor *himself* says them—'

'It comes full circle,' Roger murmured. He lit another cigarette.

'Sure, right. We can maybe pitch it to the old man as the final scene in the Red Razberry Zingers farce. Coming clean. Getting it behind us—'

'Taking the bitter medicine. Sure, that'd appeal to the old goat. Public penance . . . scourging himself with whips . . .'

'And instead of going out like a dignified guy that took a pratfall in a mudpuddle, everyone laughing at him, he goes out like Douglas MacArthur, saying old soldiers never die, they just fade away. That's the surface of the thing. But underneath, we're looking for a *tone . . . a feeling . . .*' He was crossing the border into Roger's country now. If he could only delineate the shape of what he meant, the idea that had come to him over coffee at Bentley's, Roger would take it from there.

'MacArthur,' Roger said softly. 'But that's it, isn't it? The tone is farewell. The feeling is regret. Give people the feeling that he's been unjustly treated, but it's too late now. And –' He looked at Vic, almost startled.

'What?'

'Prime time,' Roger said.

'Huh?'

'The spots. We run em in prime time. These ads are for the parents, not the kids. Right?'

'Yeah, yeah.'

'If we ever get the damned things made.'

Vic grinned. 'We'll get them made.' And using one

of Roger's terms for good ad copy: 'It's a tank, Roger. We'll drive it right to fuck over them if we have to. As long as we can get something concrete down before we go to Cleveland . . .'

They sat and talked it over in the tiny screening room for another hour, and when they left to go back to the hotel, both of them sweaty and exhausted, it was full dark.

'Can we go home now, Mommy?' Tad asked apathetically.

'Pretty soon, honey.'

She looked at the key in the ignition switch. Three other keys on the ring: house key, garage key, and the key that opened the Pinto's hatchback. There was a piece of leather attached to the ring with a mushroom branded on it. She had bought the keyring in Swanson's, a Bridgton department store, back in April. Back in April when she had been so disillusioned and scared, never knowing what real fear was, real fear was trying to crank your kid's window shut while a rabid dog drooled on the backs of your hands.

She reached out. She touched the leather tab. She pulled her hand back again.

The truth was this: She was afraid to try.

It was quarter past seven. The day was still bright, although the Pinto's shadow trailed out long, almost to the garage door. Although she did not know it, her husband and his partner were still watching kinescopes of the Sharp Cereal Professor at Image-Eye in Cambridge. She didn't know why no one had answered the SOS she had been beeping out. In a book, someone would have come. It was the heroine's reward for having thought up such a clever idea. But no one had come.

Surely the sound had carried down to the ramshackle house at the foot of the hill. Maybe they were drunk down there. Or maybe the owners of the two cars in the driveway (*dooryard*, her mind corrected automatically, *up here they call it a dooryard*) had both gone off somewhere in a third car. She wished she could see that house from here, but it was out of sight beyond the descending flank of the hill.

Finally she had given the SOS up. She was afraid that if she kept tooting the horn it would drain the Pinto's battery, which had been in since they got the car. She still believed the Pinto would start when the engine was cool enough. It always had before.

But you're afraid to try, because if it doesn't start what then?

She was reaching for the ignition again when the dog stumbled back into view. It had been lying out of sight in front of the Pinto. Now it moved slowly toward the barn, its head down and its tail drooping. It was staggering and weaving like a drunk near the bitter end of a long toot. Without looking back, Cujo slipped into the shadows of the building and disappeared.

She drew her hand away from the key again.

'Mommy? Aren't we going?'

'Let me think, hon,' she said.

She looked to her left, out the driver's side window. Eight running steps would take her to the back door of the Camber house. In high school she had been the star of her high school's girls' track team, and she still jogged regularly. She could beat the dog to the door and inside, she was sure of that. There would be a telephone. One call to Sheriff Bannerman's office and this horror would end.

STEPHEN KING

On the other hand, if she tried cranking the engine again, it might not start . . . but it would bring the dog on the run. She knew hardly anything about rabies, but she seemed to remember reading at some time or other that rabid animals were almost supernaturally sensitive to sounds. Loud noises could drive them into a frenzy.

'Mommy?'

'Shhh, Tad. Shhh!'

Eight running steps. Dig it.

Even if Cujo was lurking and watching inside the garage just out of sight, she felt sure – she *knew* – she could win a footrace to the back door. The telephone, yes. And . . . a man like Joe Camber surely kept a gun. Maybe a whole rack of them. What pleasure it would give her to blow that fucking dog's head to so much oatmeal and strawberry jam!

Eight running steps.

Sure. Dig on it awhile.

And what if that door giving on the porch was locked? *Worth the risk?*

Her heart thudded heavily in her breast as she weighed the chances. If she had been alone, that would have been one thing. But suppose the door was locked? She could beat the dog to the door, but not to the door and then back to the car. Not if it came running, not if it charged her as it had done before. And what would Tad do? What if Tad saw his mother being savaged by a two-hundred-pound mad dog, being ripped and bitten, being pulled open –

No. They were safe here.

Try the engine again!

She reached for the ignition, and part of her mind

clamored that it would be safer to wait longer, until the engine was perfectly cool –

Perfectly cool? They had been here three hours or more already.

She grasped the key and turned it.

The engine cranked briefly once, twice, three times – and then caught with a roar.

'Oh, thank God!' she cried.

'Mommy?' Tad asked shrilly. 'Are we going? Are we going?'

'We're going,' she said grimly, and threw the transmission into reverse. Cujo lunged out of the barn . . . and then just stood there, watching. *'Fuck you dog!'* she yelled at it triumphantly.

She touched the gas pedal. The Pinto rolled back perhaps two feet – and stalled.

'No!' she screamed as the red idiot lights came on again. Cujo had taken another two steps when the engine cut out, but now he only stood there silent, his head down. *Watching* me, the thought occurred again. His shadow trailed out behind him, as clear as a silhouette cut out of black crepe paper.

Donna fumbled for the ignition switch and turned it from ON to START. The motor began to turn over again, but this time it didn't catch. She could hear a harsh panting sound in her own ears and didn't realize for several seconds that she was making the sound herself – in some vague way she had the idea that it must be the dog. She ground the starter, grimacing horribly, swearing at it, oblivious of Tad, using words she had hardly known she knew. And all the time Cujo stood there, trailing his shadow from his heels like some surreal funeral drape, watching.

At last he lay down in the driveway, as if deciding there was no chance for them to escape. She hated it more than she had when it had tried to force its way in through Tad's window.

'Mommy . . . Mommy . . . Mommy!'

From far away. Unimportant. What was important now was this goddamned sonofabitching little car. It was going to start. She was going to *make* it start by *pure . . . force . . . of will!*

She had no idea how long, in real time, she sat hunched over the wheel with her hair hanging in her eyes, futilely grinding the starter. What at last broke through to her was not Tad's cries – they had trailed off to whimpers – but the sound of the engine. It would crank briskly for five seconds, then lag off, then crank briskly for another five, then lag off again. A longer lag each time, it seemed.

She was killing the battery.

She stopped.

She came out of it a little at a time, like a woman coming out of a faint. She remembered a bout of gastroenteritis she'd had in college – everything inside her had either come up by the elevator or dropped down the chute – and near the end of it she had grayed out in one of the dorm toilet stalls. Coming back had been like this, as if you were the same but some invisible painter was adding color to the world, bringing it first up to full and then to overfull. Colors shrieked at you. Everything looked plastic and phony, like a display in a department store window – SWING INTO SPRING, perhaps, or READY FOR THE FIRST KICKOFF.

Tad was cringing away from her, his eyes squeezed

shut, the thumb of one hand in his mouth. The other hand was pressed against his hip pocket, where the Monster Words were. His respiration was shallow and rapid.

'Tad,' she said. 'Honey, don't worry.'

'Mommy, are you all right?' His voice was little more than a husky whisper.

'Yeah. So are you. At least we're safe. This old car will go. Just wait and see.'

'I thought you were mad at me.'

She took him in her arms and hugged him tight. She could smell sweat in his hair and the lingering undertone of Johnson's No More Tears shampoo. She thought of that bottle sitting safely and sanely on the second shelf of the medicine cabinet in the upstairs bathroom. If only she could touch it! But all that was here was that faint, dying perfume.

'No, honey, not at you,' she said. 'Never at you.'

Tad hugged her back. 'He can't get us in here, can he?'

'No.'

'He can't . . . he can't eat his way in, can he?'

'No.'

'I hate him,' Tad said reflectively. 'I wish he'd die.'

'Yes. Me too.'

She looked out the window and saw that the sun was getting ready to go down. A superstitious dread settled into her at the thought. She remembered the childhood games of hide-and-seek that had always ended when the shadows joined each other and grew into purple lagoons, that mystic call drifting through the suburban streets of her childhood, talismanic and distant, the high voice of a child announcing suppers that were ready, doors ready to be shut against the night:

'Alleee-alleee-infree! Alleee-alleee-infree!'

The dog was watching her. It was crazy, but she could no longer doubt it. Its mad, senseless eyes were fixed unhesitatingly on hers.

No, you're imagining it. It's only a dog, and a sick dog at that. Things are bad enough without you seeing something in that dog's eyes that can't be there.

She told herself that. A few minutes later she told herself that Cujo's eyes were like the eyes of some portraits which seem to follow you wherever you move in the room where they are hung.

But the dog was looking at her. And . . . and there was something familiar about it.

No, she told herself, and tried to dismiss the thought, but it was too late.

You've seen him before, haven't you? The morning after Tad had the first of his bad dreams, the morning that the blankets and sheets were back on the chair, his Teddy on top of them, and for a moment when you opened the closet door you only saw a slumped shape with red eyes, something in Tad's closet ready to spring, it was him, it was Cujo, Tad was right all along, only the monster wasn't in his closet . . . it was out here. It was

(stop it)

out here just waiting to

(! YOU STOP IT DONNA!)

She stared at the dog and imagined she could hear its thoughts. Simple thoughts. The same simple pattern, repeated over and over in spite of the whirling boil of its sickness and delirium.

Kill THE WOMAN. *Kill* THE BOY. *Kill* THE WOMAN. *Kill* —

Stop it, she commanded herself roughly. *It doesn't think and it's not some goddamned bogeyman out of a child's closet. It's a sick dog and that's all it is. Next you'll believe the dog is God's punishment for committing —*

Cujo suddenly got up — almost as if she had called him — and disappeared into the barn again.

(almost as if I called it)

She uttered a shaky, semi-hysterical laugh.

Tad looked up. 'Mommy?'

'Nothing, hon.'

She looked at the dark maw of the garage-barn, then at the back door of the house. *Locked? Unlocked? Locked? Unlocked?* She thought of a coin rising in the air, flipping over and over. She thought of whirling the chamber drum of a pistol, five holes empty, one full. *Locked? Unlocked?*

The sun went down, and what was left of the day was a white line painted on the western horizon. It looked no thicker than the white stripe painted down the center of the highway. That would be gone soon enough. Crickets sang in the high grass to the right of the driveway, making a mindlessly cheerful *rickety-rickety* sound.

Cujo was still in the barn. Sleeping? she wondered. Eating?

That made her remember that she had packed them some food. She crawled between the two front buckets and got the Snoopy lunchbox and her own brown bag. Her Thermos had rolled all the way to the back, probably when the car had started to buck and jerk coming up the road. She had to stretch, her blouse coming untucked, before she could hook it with her fingers. Tad, who had been in a half doze, stirred awake. His voice was immediately filled with a sharp fright that made her hate the damned dog even more.

'Mommy? *Mommy?* What are you—'

'Just getting the food,' she soothed him. 'And my Thermos – see?'

'Okay.' He settled back into his seat and put his thumb in his mouth again.

She shook the big Thermos gently beside her ear, listening for the grating sound of broken glass. She only heard milk swishing around inside. That was something, anyhow.

'Tad? You want to eat?'

'I want to take a nap,' he said around his thumb, not opening his eyes.

'You gotta feed the machine, chum,' she said.

He didn't even smile. 'Not hungry. Sleepy.'

She looked at him, troubled, and decided it would be wrong to force the issue any further. Sleep was Tad's natural weapon – maybe his only one – and it was already half an hour past his regular bedtime. Of course, if they had been home, he would have had a glass of milk and a couple of cookies before brushing his teeth . . . and a story, one of his Mercer Mayer books, maybe . . . and . . .

She felt the hot sting of tears and tried to push all those thoughts away. She opened her Thermos with shaky hands and poured herself half a cup of milk. She set it on the dashboard and took one of the figbars. After one bite she realized she was absolutely ravenous. She ate three more figbars, drank some milk, popped four or five of the green olives, then drained her cup. She burped gently . . . and then looked more sharply at the barn.

CUJO

There was a darker shadow in front of it now. Except it wasn't just a shadow. It was the dog. It was Cujo.

He's standing watch over us.

No, she didn't believe that. Nor did she believe she had seen a vision of Cujo in a pile of blankets stacked in her son's closet. She didn't . . . except . . . except part of her did. But that part wasn't in her mind.

She glanced up into the rearview mirror at where the road was. It was too dark now to see it, but she knew it was there, just as she knew that nobody was going to go by. When they had come out that other time with Vic's Jag, all three of them (*the dog was nice then*, her brain muttered, *the Tadder patted him and laughed, remember?*), laughing it up and having a great old time, Vic had told her that until five years ago the Castle Rock Dump had been out at the end of Town Road No. 3. Then the new waste treatment plant had gone into operation on the other side of town, and now, a quarter of a mile beyond the Camber place, the road simply ended at a place where a heavy chain was strung across it. The sign which hung from the chain read NO TRESPASSING DUMP CLOSED. Beyond Cambers', there was just no place to go.

Donna wondered if maybe some people in search of a really private place to go parking might not ride by, but she couldn't imagine that even the horniest of local kids would want to neck at the old town dump. At any rate, no one had passed yet.

The white line on the western horizon had faded to a bare afterglow now . . . and she was afraid that even that was mostly wishful thinking. There was no moon.

Incredibly, she felt drowsy herself. Maybe sleep was

her natural weapon, too. And what else was there to do? The dog was still out there (at least she thought it was; the darkness had gotten just deep enough to make it hard to tell if that was a real shape or just a shadow). The battery had to rest. Then she could try again. So why not sleep?

The package on his mailbox. That package from J. C. Whitney.

She sat up a little straighter, a puzzled frown creasing her brow. She turned her head, but from here the front corner of the house blocked her view of the mailbox. But she had seen the package, hung from the front of the box. Why had she thought of that? Did it have some significance?

She was still holding the Tupperware dish with the olives and slices of cucumbers inside, each wrapped neatly in Saran Wrap. Instead of eating anything else, she carefully put the white plastic cover on the Tupperware dish and stowed it back in Tad's lunchbox. She did not let herself think much about why she was being so careful of the food. She settled back in the bucket seat and found the lever that tipped it back. She meant to think about the package hooked over the mailbox – there was something there, she was almost sure of it – but soon her mind had slipped away to another idea, one that took on the bright tones of reality as she began to doze off.

The Cambers had gone to visit relatives. The relatives were in some town that was two, maybe three hours' drive away. Kennebunk, maybe. Or Hollis. Or Augusta. It was a family reunion.

Her beginning-to-dream mind saw a gathering of fifty people or more on a green lawn of TV-commercial size and beauty. There was a fieldstone barbecue pit with a shimmer of heat over it. At a long trestle table there were at least four dozen people, passing platters of corn on the cob and dishes of home-baked beans – pea beans, soldier beans, red kidney beans. There were plates of barbecued franks (Donna's stomach made a low goinging sound at this vision). On the table was a homely checked tablecloth. All this was being presided over by a lovely old woman with pure white hair that had been rolled into a bun at the nape of her neck. Fully inserted into the capsule of her dream now, Donna saw with no surprise at all that this woman was her mother.

The Cambers were there, but they weren't really the Cambers at all. Joe Camber looked like Vic in a clean Sears work coverall, and Mrs Camber was wearing Donna's green watered-silk dress. Their boy looked the way Tad was going to look when he was in the fifth grade . . .

'Mommy?'

The picture wavered, started to break up. She tried to hold on to it because it was peaceful and lovely: the archetype of a family life she had never had, the type she and Vic would never have with their one planned child and their carefully programmed lives. With sudden rising sadness, she wondered why she had never thought of things in that light before.

'Mommy?'

The picture wavered again and began to darken. That voice from outside, piercing the vision the way a needle may pierce the shell of an egg. Never mind. The Cambers were at their family reunion and they would pull in later, around ten, happy and full of barbecue. Everything would be all right. The Joe Camber with Vic's face would take care of everything. Everything would be all right again. There were some things that God never allowed. It would –

'*Mommy!*'

She came out of the doze, sitting up, surprised to find herself behind the wheel of the Pinto instead of at home in bed . . . but only for a second. Already the lovely, surreal image of the relatives gathered around the trestle picnic table were beginning to dissolve, and in fifteen minutes she would not even remember that she had dreamed.

'Huh? What?'

Suddenly, shockingly, the phone inside the Cambers' house began to ring. The dog rose to its feet, moving shadows that resolved themselves into its large and ungainly form.

'Mommy, I have to go to the bathroom.'

Cujo began to roar at the sound of the telephone. He was not barking; he was *roaring*. Suddenly he charged at the house. He struck the back door hard enough to shake it in its frame.

No, she thought sickly, *oh no, stop, please, stop* –

'Mommy, I have to –'

The dog was snarling, biting at the wood of the door. She could hear the sick splintering sounds its teeth made.

'– go weewee.'

The phone rang six times. Eight times. Ten. Then it stopped.

She realized she had been holding her breath. She let it out through her teeth in a low, hot sigh.

Cujo stood at the door, his back paws on the ground,

230

his forepaws on the top step. He continued to growl low in his chest – a hateful, nightmarish sound. At last he turned and looked at the Pinto for a time – Donna could see the dried foam caked on his muzzle and chest – then he padded back into the shadows and grew indistinct. It was impossible to tell exactly where he went. In the garage, maybe. Or maybe down the side of the barn.

Tad was tugging desperately at the sleeve of her shirt. 'Mommy, I have to go *bad*!'

She looked at him helplessly.

Brett Camber put the phone down slowly. 'No one answered. He's not home, I guess.'

Charity nodded, not terribly surprised. She was glad that Jim had suggested they make the call from his office, which was downstairs and off the 'family room'. The family room was soundproofed. There were shelves of board games in there, a Panasonic large-screen TV with a video recorder and an Atari video-games setup attached to it. And standing in one corner was a lovely old Wurlitzer jukebox that really worked.

'Down at Gary's, I guess,' Brett added disconsolately.

'Yes, I imagine he's with Gary,' she agreed, which wasn't exactly the same as saying they were together at Gary's house. She had seen the faraway look that had come into Joe's eyes when she had finally struck the deal with him, the deal that had gotten her and her son down here. She hoped Brett wouldn't think of calling directory assistance for Gary Pervier's number, because she doubted if there would be any answer there either. She suspected that there were two old dogs out somewhere tonight howling at the moon.

'Do you think Cuje is okay, Mom?'

'Why, I don't think your father would go off and leave him if he wasn't, she said, and that was true – she didn't believe he would. 'Why don't we leave it for tonight and you call him in the morning? You ought to be getting to bed anyway. It's past ten. You've had a big day.'

'I'm not tired.'

'Well, it's not good to go too long on nervous excitement. I put your toothbrush out, and your Aunt Holly put out a washcloth and a towel for you. Do you remember which bedroom—?'

'Yeah, sure. You going to bed, Mom?'

'Soon. I'm going to sit up with Holly for a while. We've got a lot of history to catch up on, she and I.'

Shyly, Brett said, 'She looks like you. Y'know that?'

Charity looked at him, surprised. 'Does she? Yes, I suppose she does. A little.'

'And that little kid, Jimmy. He's got a real right hook. Pow!' Brett burst out laughing.

'Did he hurt your stomach?'

'Heck, no.' Brett was looking around Jim's study carefully, noting the Underwood typewriter on the desk, the Rolodex, the neat open file of folders with the names on the tabs in alphabetical order. There was a careful, measuring look in his eyes that she couldn't understand or evaluate. He seemed to come back from far away. 'Nah, he didn't hurt me. He's just a little kid.' He cocked his head at her. 'My cousin, right?'

'Right.'

'Blood relation.' He seemed to muse over it.

'Brett, do you like your Uncle Jim and Aunt Holly?'

'I like her. I can't tell about him yet. That jukebox. That's really neat. But . . .' He shook his head in a kind of impatience.

'What about it, Brett?'

'He takes so much *pride* in it!' Brett said. 'It was the first thing he showed me, like a kid with a toy, isn't this neat, you know—'

'Well, he's only had it for a little while,' Charity said. An unformed dread had begun to swirl around inside of her, connected somehow with Joe – what had he told Brett when he took him out on the sidewalk? 'Anyone's partial to something new. Holly wrote me when they finally got it, said Jim had wanted one of those things since he was a young man. People . . . honey, different people buy different things to . . . to show themselves that they're successful, I suppose. There's no accounting for it. But usually it's something they couldn't have when they were poor.'

'Was Uncle Jim poor?'

'I really don't know,' she said. 'But they're not poor now.'

'All I meant was that he didn't have anything to *do* with it. You get what I mean?' He looked at her closely. 'He bought it with money and hired some people to fix it and hired some *more* people to bring it here, and he says it's his, but he didn't . . . you know, he didn't . . . aw, I don't know.'

'He didn't make it with his own hands?' Although her fear was greater now, more coalesced, her voice was gentle.

'Yeah! That's right! He bought it with money, but he didn't really have nothing to do—'

'*Anything*—'

'Okay, yeah, *anything* to do with it, but now he's, like, takin credit for it—'

'He said a jukebox is a delicate, complicated machine—'

'Dad could have gotten it running,' Brett said flatly, and Charity thought she heard a door bang shut suddenly, closing with a loud, toneless, frightening bang. It wasn't in the house. It was in her heart. 'Dad would have tinkered it up and it would have been *his*.'

'Brett,' she said (and her voice sounded weak and justifying to her own ears), 'not everybody is good at tinkering and fixing like your father is.'

'I know that,' he said, still looking around the office. 'Yeah. But Uncle Jim shouldn't take credit for it just because he had the money. See? It's him taking the credit that I don't li— that bothers me.'

She was suddenly furious with him. She wanted to take him by the shoulders and shake him back and forth; to raise her voice until it was loud enough to shout the truth into his brain. That money did not come by accident; that it almost always resulted from some sustained act of will, and that will was the core of character. She would tell him that while his father was perfecting his skills as a tinkerer and swilling down Black Label with the rest of the boys in the back of Emerson's Sunoco, sitting in piles of dead bald tires and telling frenchman jokes, Jim Brooks had been in law school, knocking his brains out to make grades, because when you made the grades you got the diploma, and the diploma was your ticket, you got to ride the merry-go-round. Getting on didn't mean you'd

catch the brass ring, no, but it guaranteed you the chance
to at least *try*.

'You go on up now and get ready for bed,' she said
quietly. 'What you think of your Uncle Jim is between you
and you. But . . . give him a chance, Brett. Don't just judge
him on that.' They had gone through into the family room
now, and she jerked a thumb at the jukebox.

'No, I won't,' he said.

She followed him up into the kitchen, where Holly
was making cocoa for the four of them. Jim Junior and
Gretchen had gone to bed long before.

'You get your man?' Holly asked.

'No, he's probably down chewing the fat with that
friend of his,' Charity said. 'We'll try tomorrow.'

'Want some cocoa, Brett?' Holly asked.

'Yes, please.'

Charity watched him sit down at the table. She saw
him put his elbow on it and then take it off again quickly,
remembering that it was impolite. Her heart was so full of
love and hope and fear that it seemed to stagger in her
chest.

Time, she thought. *Time and perspective. Give him that.
If you force him, you'll lose him for sure.*

But how much time was there? Only a week, and
then he would be back under Joe's influence. And even as
she sat down next to her son and thanked Holly for her
cup of hot cocoa, her thoughts had turned speculatively
to the idea of divorce again.

In her dream, Vic had come.

He simply walked down the driveway to the Pinto

and opened her door. He was dressed in his best suit, the three-piece charcoal-gray one (when he put it on she always teased him that he looked like Jerry Ford with hair). *Come on, you two*, he said, and that quirky little grin was on his face. *Time to go home before the vampires come out.*

She tried to warn him, to tell him the dog was rabid, but no words came. And suddenly Cujo was advancing out of the dark, his head down, a steady low growl rumbling in his chest. *Watch out!* she tried to cry. *His bite is death!* But no sound came out.

But just before Cujo launched himself at Vic, he turned and pointed his finger at the dog. Cujo's fur went dead white instantly. His red, rheumy eyes dropped back into his head like marbles into a cup. His muzzle fell off and shattered against the crushed gravel of the driveway like black glass. A moment later all that was left in front of the garage was a blowing fur coat.

Don't you worry, Vic said in a dream. *Don't you worry about that old dog, it's nothing but a fur coat. Did you get the mail yet? Never mind the dog, the mail's coming. The mail's the important thing. Right? The mail —*

His voice was disappearing down a long tunnel, growing echoey and faint. And suddenly it was not a dream of Vic's voice but a memory of a dream — she was awake and her cheeks were wet with tears. She had cried in her sleep. She looked at her watch and could just make out the time: quarter past one. She looked over at Tad and saw he was sleeping soundly, his thumb hooked into his mouth.

Never mind the dog, the mail's coming. The mail's the important thing.

And suddenly the significance of the package hung

236

over the mailbox door came to her, hit her like an arrow fired up from her subconscious mind, an idea she had not quite been able to get hold of before. Perhaps because it was so big, so simple, so elementary-my-dear-Watson. Yesterday was Monday and the mail had come. The J. C. Whitney package for Joe Camber was ample proof of that.

Today was Tuesday and the mail would come again.

Tears of relief began to roll down her not-yet-dry cheeks. She actually had to restrain herself from shaking Tad awake and telling him it was going to be all right, that by two o'clock this afternoon at the lastest – and more probably by ten or eleven in the morning, if the mail delivery out here was as prompt as it was most other places in town – this nightmare would end.

The mailman would come even if he had no mail for the Cambers, that was the beauty of it. It would be his job to see if the flag was up, signifying outgoing mail. He would have to come up here, to his last stop on Town Road No. 3, to check that out, and today he was going to be greeted by a woman who was semi-hysterical with relief.

She eyed Tad's lunchbox and thought of the food inside. She thought of herself carefully saving some of it aside, in case . . . well, in case. Now it didn't matter so much, although Tad was likely to be hungry in the morning. She ate the rest of the cucumber slices. Tad didn't care for cucumbers much anyway. It would be an odd breakfast for him, she thought, smiling. Figbars, olives, and a Slim Jim or two.

Munching the last two or three cucumber slices, she realized it was the coincidences that had scared her the most. That series of coincidences, utterly random but mimicking a kind of sentient fate, had been what seemed to make the dog so horribly purposeful, so . . . so out to get her personally. Vic being gone for ten days, that was coincidence number one. Vic calling early today, that was coincidence number two. If he hadn't got them then, he would have tried later, kept trying, and begun to wonder where they were. The fact that all three of the Cambers were gone, at least for overnight, the way it looked now. That was number three. Mother, son, and father. All gone. But they had left their dog. Oh yes. They had —

A sudden horrible thought occurred to her, freezing her jaws on the last bite of cucumber. She tried to thrust it away, but it came back. It wouldn't go away because it had its own gargoyle-like logic.

What if they were all dead in the barn?

The image rose behind her eyes in an instant. It had the unhealthy vividness of those waking visions which sometimes come in the morning's small hours. The three bodies tumbled about like badly made toys on the floor in there, the sawdust around them stained red, their dusty eyes staring up into the blackness where barnswallows cooed and fluttered, their clothing ripped and chewed, parts of them —

Oh that's crazy, that's —

Maybe he had gotten the boy first. The other two are in the kitchen, or maybe upstairs having a quickie, they hear screams, they rush out —

(stop it won't you stop it)

— they rush out but the boy is already dead, the dog has torn his throat out, and while they're still stunned by the death of their son, the Saint Bernard comes lurching out of the shadows, old and terrible engine of destruction, yes, the old monster comes from the shadows, rabid and snarling. He goes for the woman first and the man tries to save her –

(no, he would have gotten his gun or brained it with a wrench or something and where's the car? There was a car here before they all went off on a family trip – do you hear me FAMILY TRIP – took the car left the truck)

Then why had no one come to feed the dog?

That was the logic of the thing, part of what frightened her. Why hadn't anyone come to feed the dog? Because if you were going to be away for a day or for a couple of days, you made an arrangement with somebody. They fed your dog for you, and then when they were gone, you fed their cat for them, or their fish, or their parakeet, or whatever. So where –

And the dog kept going back into the barn.

Was it eating in there?

That's the answer, her mind told her, relieved. *He didn't have anyone to feed the dog, so he poured it a tray of food. Gaines Meal, or something.*

But then she stuck upon what Joe Camber himself had stuck upon earlier on that long, long day. A big dog would gobble it all at once and then go hungry. Surely it would be better to get a friend to feed the dog if you were going to be gone. On the other hand, maybe they had been held up. Maybe there really had been a family reunion, and Camber had gotten drunk and passed out. Maybe this, maybe that, maybe anything.

Is the dog eating in the barn?

(what *is it eating in there? Gaines Meal? or people?*)

She spat the last of the cucumber into her cupped hand and felt her stomach roll, wanting to send up what she had already eaten. She set her will upon keeping it down, and because she could be very determined when she wanted to, she did keep it down. They had left the dog some food and had gone off in the car. You didn't have to be Sherlock Holmes to deduce that. The rest of it was nothing but a bad case of the willies.

But that image of death kept trying to creep back in. The dominant image was the bloody sawdust, sawdust which had gone the dark color of natural-casing franks.

Stop. Think about the mail, if you have to think about anything. Think about tomorrow. Think about being safe.

There was a soft, scuffling, scratching noise on her side of the car.

She didn't want to look but was helpless to stop herself. Her head began to turn as if forced by invisible yet powerful hands. She could hear the low creak of the tendons in her neck. Cujo was there, looking in at her. His face was less than six inches from her own. Only the Saf-T-Glas of the driver's side window separated them. Those red, bleary eyes stared into hers. The dog's muzzle looked as if it had been badly lathered with shaving cream that had been left to dry.

Cujo was grinning at her.

She felt a scream building in her chest, coming up in her throat like iron, because she could feel the dog thinking at her, telling her *I'm going to get you, babe. I'm going to get you, kiddo. Think about the mailman all you want to. I'll kill him too if I have to, the way I killed all three of the*

Cambers, the way I'm going to kill you and your son. You might as well get used to the idea. You might as well —

The scream, coming up her throat. It was a live thing struggling to get out, and everything was coming on her at once: Tad having to pee, she had unrolled his window four inches and held him up so he could do it out the window, watching all the time for the dog, and for a long time he hadn't been able to go and her arms had begun to ache; then the dream, then the images of death, and now this —

The dog was grinning in at her; he was grinning in at her, Cujo was his name, and his bite was death.

The scream had to come

(but Tad's)

or she would go mad.

(sleeping)

She locked her jaws against the scream the way she had locked her throat against the urge to vomit a few moments ago. She struggled with it, she fought it. And at last her heart began to slow down and she knew she had it licked.

She smiled at the dog and raised both of her middle fingers from closed fists. She held them against the glass, which was now slightly fogged on the outside with Cujo's breath. 'Go get fucked,' she whispered.

After what seemed an endless time, the dog put its forepaws down and went back into the barn. Her mind turned down the same dark track again

(what's it eating in there?)

and then she slammed a door shut somewhere in her mind.

But there would be no more sleep, not for a long

time, and it was so long until dawn. She sat upright behind the wheel, trembling, telling herself over and over again that it was ridiculous, really ridiculous, to feel that the dog was some kind of a hideous revenant which had escaped from Tad's closet, or that it knew more about the situation than she did.

Vic jerked awake in total darkness, rapid breath as dry as salt in his throat. His heart was triphammering in his chest, and he was totally disoriented – so disoriented that for a moment he thought he was falling, and reached out to clutch the bed.

He closed his eyes for a moment, forcibly holding himself together, making himself coalesce.

(you are in)

He opened his eyes and saw a window, a bedstand, a lamp.

(the Ritz-Carlton Hotel in Boston Massachusetts)

He relaxed. That reference point given, everything came together with a reassuring *click*, making him wonder how he could have been so lost and totally apart, even momentarily. It was being in a strange place, he supposed. That, and the nightmare.

Nightmare! Jesus, it had been a beaut. He couldn't remember having such a bad one since the falling dreams that had plagued him off and on during early puberty. He reached for the Travel-Ette clock on the nightstand, gripped it in both hands, and brought it close to his face. It was twenty minutes of two. Roger was snoring lightly in the other bed, and now that his eyes had adjusted to the dark he could see him, sleeping flat on his back. He had kicked the sheet over the end of the bed. He was wearing an absurd pair of pajamas covered with small yellow college pennants.

Vic swung his legs out of bed, went quietly into the bathroom, and closed the door. Roger's cigarettes were on the washstand and he helped himself to one. He needed it. He sat on the toilet and smoked, tapping ashes into the sink.

An anxiety dream, Donna would have said, and God knew he had enough to be anxious about. Yet he had gone to bed around ten thirty in better spirits than he had been in for the last week. After arriving back at the hotel, he and Roger had spent half an hour in the Ritz-Carlton's bar, kicking the apology idea around, and then, from the bowels of the huge old wallet he hauled around, Roger produced the home number of Yancey Harrington. Harrington was the actor who played the Sharp Cereal Professor.

'Might as well see if he'll do it before we go any further,' Roger said. He had picked up the phone and dialed Harrington, who lived in Westport, Connecticut. Vic hadn't known just what to expect. If pressed for his best guess, he would have said that probably Harrington would have to be stroked a little – he had been just miserable over the Zingers affair and what he considered it had done to his image.

Both of them had been in for a happy surprise. Harrington had agreed instantly. He recognized the realities of the situation and knew the Professor was pretty well finished ('Poor old guy's a gone goose,' Harrington had said glumly). But he thought the final ad might be just the thing to get the company over the affair. Put it back on the rails, so to speak.

'Bullshit,' Roger said, grinning, after he had hung up. 'He just likes the idea of one final curtain call. Not many actors in advertising get a chance like that. He'd buy his own plane ticket to Boston if we asked him to.'

So Vic had gone to bed happy and had fallen asleep almost instantly. Then, the dream. He was standing in front of Tad's closet door in the dream and telling Tad that there was nothing in there, nothing at all. *I'll show you once and for all*, he told Tad. He opened the closet door and saw that Tad's clothes and toys were gone. There was a forest growing in Tad's closet – old pines and spruces, ancient hardwoods. The closet floor was covered with fragrant needles and leafy mulch. He had scraped at it, wanting to see if the floor of painted boards was beneath. It wasn't; his foot scraped up rich black forest earth instead.

He stepped into the closet and the door closed behind him. That was all right. There was enough light to see by. He found a trail and began to hike along it. All at once he realized there was a pack on his back and a canteen slung over one shoulder. He could hear the mysterious sound of the wind, soughing through the firs, and faint birdsong. Seven years ago, long before Ad Worx, they had all gone hiking on part of the Appalachian Trail during one of their vacations, and that land had looked a good deal like the geography of his dream. They had done it only that once, sticking to the seacoast after that. Vic, Donna, and Roger had had a wonderful time, but Althea Breakstone loathed hiking and had come down with a good, itchy case of poison oak on top of that.

The first part of the dream had been rather pleasant. The thought that all this had been right inside Tad's closet was, in its own strange way, wonderful. Then he had come into a clearing and he had seen . . . but it was already beginning to tatter, the way dreams do when they are exposed to waking thought.

The other side of the clearing had been a sheer gray wall rising maybe a thousand feet into the sky. About twenty feet up there was a cave – no, not really deep enough to be a cave. It was more of a niche, just a depression in the rock that happened to have a flat floor. Donna and Tad were cowering inside. Cowering from some sort of monster that was trying to reach up, trying to reach up and then reach in. Get them. Eat them.

It had been like that scene in the original *King Kong* after the great ape has shaken Fay Wray's would-be rescuers from the log and is trying to get the lone survivor. But the guy has gotten into a hole, and Kong isn't quite able to get him.

The monster in his dream hadn't been a giant ape, though. It had been a . . . what? Dragon? No, nothing like that. Not a dragon, not a dinosaur, not a troll. He couldn't get it. Whatever it was, it couldn't quite get in and get Donna and Tad, so it was merely waiting outside their bolt-hole, like a cat waiting with dreadful patience for a mouse.

He began to run, but no matter how fast he went, he never got any closer to the other side of the clearing. He could hear Donna screaming for help, but when he called back his words seemed to die two feet out of his mouth. It was Tad who had finally spotted him.

'*They don't work!*' Tad had screamed in a hopeless,

despairing voice that had hollowed out Vic's guts with fear. *'Daddy, the Monster Words don't work! Oh, Daddy, they don't work, they never worked! You lied, Daddy! You lied!'*

He ran on, but it was as if he were on a treadmill. And he had looked at the base of that high gray wall and had seen a heaped drift of old bones and grinning skulls, some of them furred with green moss.

That was when he woke up.

What had the monster been, anyway?

He just couldn't remember. Already the dream seemed like a scene observed through the wrong end of a telescope. He dropped the cigarette into the john, flushed it, and ran water into the sink as well to swirl the ashes down the drain.

He urinated, shut off the light, and went back to bed. As he lay down he glanced at the telephone and felt a sudden irrational urge to call home. Irrational? That was putting it mildly. It was ten minutes of two in the morning. He would not only wake her up, he would probably scare the living hell out of her in the bargain. You didn't interpret dreams literally; everyone knew that. When both your marriage and your business seemed in danger of running off the rails at the same time, it wasn't really surprising that your mind pulled a few unsettling head games, was it?

Still, just to hear her voice and know she's okay –

He turned away from the telephone, punched up the pillow, and resolutely shut his eyes.

Call her in the morning, if that'll make you feel better. Call her right after breakfast.

That eased his mind, and very shortly he drifted off to sleep again. This time he did not dream – or if he did, these dreams never imprinted themselves on his conscious mind. And when the wake-up call came on Tuesday, he had forgotten all about the dream of the beast in the clearing. He had only the vaguest recollection of having gotten up in the night at all. Vic did not call home that day.

Charity Camber awoke that Tuesday morning on the dot of five and went through her own brief period of disorientation – yellow wallpaper instead of wood walls, colorful green print curtains instead of white chintz, a narrow single bed instead of the double that had begun to sag in the middle.

Then she saw where she was – Stratford, Connecticut – and felt a burst of pleased anticipation. She would have the whole day to talk to her sister, to hash over old times, to find out what she had been doing the last few years. And Holly had talked about going into Bridgeport to do some shopping.

She had awakened an hour and a half before her usual time, probably two hours or more before things began to stir in this household. But a person never slept well in a strange bed until the third night – that had been one of her mother's sayings, and it was a true one.

The silence began to give up its little sounds as she lay awake and listening, looking at the thin five-o'clock light that fell between the half-drawn curtains . . . dawn's early light, always so white and clear and fine. She heard the creak of a single board. A bluejay having its morning tantrum. The day's first commuter train, bound for Westport, Greenwich, and New York City.

The board creaked again.

And again.

It wasn't just the house settling. It was footsteps.

Charity sat up in bed, the blanket and sheet pooling around the waist of her sensible pink nightgown. Now the steps were going slowly downstairs. It was a light tread: bare feet or sock feet. It was Brett. When you lived with people, you got to know the sound of their walk. It was one of those mysterious things that just happen over a course of years, like the shape of a leaf sinking into a rock.

She pushed the covers back, got up, and went to the door. Her room opened on the upstairs hall, and she just saw the top of Brett's head disappearing, his cowlick sticking up for a moment and then gone.

She went after him.

When Charity reached the top of the stairs, Brett was just disappearing down the hallway that ran the width of the house, from the front door to the kitchen. She opened her mouth to call him . . . and then shut it again. She was intimidated by the sleeping house that wasn't her house.

Something about the way he had been walking . . . the set of his body . . . but it had been years since –

She descended the stairs quickly and quietly in her bare feet. She followed Brett into the kitchen. He was dressed only in light blue pajama bottoms, their white cotton drawstring hanging down to below the neat fork of his crotch. Although it was barely midsummer he was already very brown – he was naturally dark, like his father, and tanned easily.

Standing in the doorway she saw him in profile, that same fine, clear morning light pouring over his body as he hunted along the line of cupboards above the stove and the counter and the sink. Her heart was full of wonder and fear. *He's beautiful,* she thought. *Everything that's beautiful, or ever was, in us, is in him.* It was a moment she never forgot – she saw her son clad only in his pajama bottoms and for a moment dimly comprehended the mystery of his boyhood, so soon to be left behind. Her mother's eyes loved the slim curves of his muscles, the line of his buttocks, the clean soles of his feet. He seemed . . . utterly perfect.

She saw it clearly because Brett wasn't awake. As a child there had been episodes of sleepwalking; about two dozen of them in all, between the ages of four and eight. She had finally gotten worried enough – scared enough – to consult with Dr Gresham (without Joe's knowledge). She wasn't afraid that Brett was losing his mind – anyone who was around him could see he was bright and normal – but she was afraid that he might hurt himself while he was in that strange state. Dr Gresham had told her that was very unlikely, and that most of the funny ideas people had about somnambulism came from cheap, badly researched movies.

'We only know a little about sleepwalking,' he had told her, 'but we do know that it is more common in children than it is in adults. There's a constantly growing, constantly maturing interaction between the mind and body, Mrs Camber, and a lot of people who have done research in this field believe that sleepwalking may be a symptom of a temporary and not terribly significant imbalance between the two.'

'Like growing pains?' she had asked doubtfully.

'Very much like that,' Gresham had said with a grin.

He drew a bell curve on his office pad, suggesting that Brett's somnambulism would reach a peak, hold for a while, then begin to taper off. Eventually it would disappear.

She had gone away a little reassured by the doctor's conviction that Brett would not go sleepwalking out a window or down the middle of a highway, but without being much enlightened. A week later she had brought Brett in. He had been just a month or two past his sixth birthday then. Gresham had given him a complete physical and had pronounced him normal in every way. And indeed, Gresham had appeared to be right. The last of what Charity thought of as his 'nightwalks' had occurred more than two years ago.

The last, that was, until now.

Brett opened the cupboards one by one, closing each neatly before going on to the next, disclosing Holly's casserole dishes, the extra elements to her Jenn-Aire range, her dishtowels neatly folded, her coffee-and-tea creamer, her as-yet-incomplete set of Depression glassware. His eyes were wide and blank, and she felt a cool certainty that he was seeing the contents of other cabinets, in another place.

She felt the old, helpless terror that she had almost completely forgotten as parents do the alarms and the excursions of their children's early years: the teething, the vaccination that brought the frighteningly high fever as a little extra added attraction, the croup, the ear infection, the hand or leg that suddenly began to spray irrational blood. *What's he thinking?* she wondered. *Where is he? And why now, after two quiet years?* Was it being in a strange place? He hadn't seemed duly upset . . . at least, not until now.

He opened the last cupboard and took down a pink

250

gravy boat. He put it on the counter. He picked up empty air and mimed pouring something into the gravy boat. Her arms suddenly broke out in gooseflesh as she realized where he was and what this dumbshow was all about. It was a routine he went through each day at home. He was feeding Cujo.

She took an involuntary step toward him and then stopped. She didn't believe those wives' tales about what might happen if you woke a sleepwalker – that the soul would be forever shut out of the body, that madness might result, or sudden death – and she hadn't needed Dr Gresham to reassure her on that score. She had gotten a book on special loan from the Portland City Library . . . but she hadn't really needed that, either. Her own good common sense told her what happened when you woke up a sleepwalker was that they woke up – no more and no less than just that. There might be tears, even mild hysteria, but that sort of reaction would be provoked by simple disorientation.

Still, she had never wakened Brett during one of his nightwalks, and she didn't dare to do so now. Good common sense was one thing. Her unreasoning fear was another, and she was suddenly very afraid, and unable to think why. What could be so dreadful in Brett's acted-out dream of feeding his dog? It was perfectly natural, as worried as he had been about Cujo.

He was bent over now, holding the gravy boat out, the drawstring of his pajama trousers making a right-angled white line to the horizontal plane of the red and black linoleum floor. His face went through a slow-motion pantomime of sorrow. He spoke then, muttering the words as sleepers so often do, gutturally, rapidly, almost unintelligibly. And with no emotion in the words themselves, that was all inside, held in the cocoon of whatever dream had been vivid enough to make him nightwalk again, after two quiet years. There was nothing inherently melodramatic about the words, spoken all of a rush in a quick sleeping sigh, but Charity's hand went to her throat anyway. The flesh there was cold, cold.

'Cujo's not hungry no more,' Brett said, the words riding out on that sigh. He stood up again, now holding the gravy boat cradled to his chest. 'Not no more, not no more.'

He stood immobile for a short time by the counter, and Charity did likewise by the kitchen door. A single tear had slipped down his face. He put the gravy boat on the counter and headed for the door. His eyes were open but they slipped indifferently and unseeingly over his mother. He stopped, looking back.

'Look in the weeds,' he said to someone who was not there.

Then be began to walk toward her again. She stood aside, her hand still pressed against her throat. He passed her quickly and noiselessly on his bare feet and was gone up the hall toward the stairs.

She turned to follow him and remembered the gravy boat. It stood by itself on the bare, ready-for-the-day counter like the focal point in a weird painting. She picked it up and it slipped through her fingers – she hadn't realized that her fingers were slick with sweat. She juggled it briefly, imagining the crash in the still, sleeping hours. Then she had it cradled safely in both hands. She put it back on the shelf and closed the cupboard door and could only stand there for a moment, listening to the heavy thud of her heart, feeling her strangeness in this kitchen. She was an intruder in this kitchen. Then she followed her son.

She got to the doorway of his room just in time to see him climb into bed. He pulled the sheet up and rolled over on his left side, his usual sleeping position. Although she knew it was over now, Charity stood there yet awhile longer.

Somebody down the hall coughed, reminding her again that this was someone else's house. She felt a strong wave of homesickness; for a few moments it was as if her stomach were full of some numbing gas, the kind of stuff dentists use. In this fine still morning light, her thoughts of divorce seemed as immature and without regard for the realities as the thoughts of a child. It was easy for her to think of such things here. It wasn't her house, not her place.

Why had his pantomime of feeding Cujo, and those rapid, sighing words, frightened her so much? *Cujo's not hungry no more, not no more.*

She went back to her own room and lay there in bed as the sun came up and brightened the room. At breakfast, Brett seemed no different than ever. He did not mention Cujo, and he had apparently forgotten about calling home, at least for the time being. After some interior debate, Charity decided to let the matter rest there.

It was hot.

Donna uncranked her window a little farther – about a quarter of the way, as far as she dared – and then leaned across Tad's lap to unroll his too. That was when she noticed the creased yellow sheet of paper in his lap.

'What's that, Tad?'

He looked up at her. There were smudged brown circles under his eyes. 'The Monster Words,' he said.

'Can I see?'

He held them tightly for a moment and then let her take the paper. There was a watchful, almost proprietary expression on his face, and she felt an instant's jealousy. It was brief but very strong. So far she had managed to keep him alive and unhurt, but it was Vic's hocus-pocus he cared about. Then the feeling dissipated into bewilderment, sadness, and self-disgust. It was she who had put him in this situation in the first place. If she hadn't given in to him about the baby-sitter . . .

'I put them in my pocket yesterday,' he said, 'before we went shopping. Mommy, is the monster going to eat us?'

'It's not a monster, Tad, it's just a *dog*, and no, it isn't going to eat us!' She spoke more sharply than she had intended. 'I told you, when the mailman comes, we can go home.' *And I told him the car would start in just a little while, and I told him someone would come, that the Cambers would be home soon –*

But what was the use of thinking that?

'May I have my Monster Words back?' he asked.

For a moment she felt a totally insane urge to tear the sweat-stained, creased sheet of yellow legal paper to bits and toss them out of her window, so much fluttering confetti. Then she handed the paper back to Tad and ran both hands through her hair, ashamed and scared. What was happening to her, for Christ's sake? A sadistic thought like that. Why would she want to make it worse for him? Was it Vic? Herself? What?

It was so hot – too hot to think. Sweat was streaming down her face and she could see it trickling down Tad's cheeks as well. His hair was plastered against his skull in unlovely chunks, and it looked two shades darker than its usual medium-blond. *He needs his hair washed*, she thought randomly, and that made her think of the bottle of Johnson's No More Tears again, sitting safely and sanely on the bathroom shelf, waiting for someone to take it down and pour a capful or two into one cupped palm.

(don't lose control of yourself)

No, of course not. She had no *reason* to lose control of herself. Everything was going to be all right, wasn't it? Of course it was. The dog wasn't even in sight, hadn't been for more than an hour. And the mailman. It was almost ten o'clock now. The mailman would be along soon, and then it wouldn't matter that it was so hot in the car. 'The greenhouse effect', they called it. She had seen that on an SPCA handout somewhere, explaining why you shouldn't shut your dog up in your car for any length of time when it was hot like this. The greenhouse effect. The pamphlet had said that the temperature in a car that was parked in the sun could go as high as 140 degrees Fahrenheit if the windows were rolled up, so it was cruel and dangerous to lock up a pet while you did your shopping or went to see a movie. Donna uttered a short, cracked-sounding chuckle. The shoe certainly was on the other foot here, wasn't it? It was the dog that had the people locked up.

Well, the mailman was coming. The mailman was coming and that would end it. It wouldn't matter that they had only a quarter of a Thermos of milk left, or that early this morning she had to go to the bathroom and she had used Tad's smaller Thermos – or had tried to – and it had overflowed and now the Pinto smelled of urine, an unpleasant smell that only seemed to grow stronger with the heat. She had capped the Thermos and thrown it out the window. She had heard it shatter as it hit the gravel. Then she had cried.

But none of it mattered. It was humiliating and demeaning to have to try and pee into a Thermos bottle, sure it was, but it didn't matter because the mailman was coming – even now he would be loading his small blue-and-white truck at the ivy-covered brick post office on Carbine Street . . . or maybe he had already begun his route, working his way out Route 117 toward the Maple Sugar Road. Soon it would end. She would take Tad home, and they would go upstairs. They would strip and shower together, but before she got into the tub with him and under the shower, she would take the bottle of shampoo from the shelf and put the cap neatly on the edge of the sink, and she would wash first Tad's hair and then her own.

Tad was reading the yellow paper again, his lips moving soundlessly. Not real reading, not the way he would be reading in a couple of years (*if we get out of this*, her traitorous mind insisted on adding senselessly but instantly), but the kind that came from rote memorization. The way driving schools prepared functional illiterates for the written part of the driver's exam. She had read that somewhere too, or maybe seen it on a TV news story, and wasn't it amazing, the amount of crud the human mind was capable of storing up? And wasn't it amazing how easily it all came spewing out when there was nothing else to engage it? Like a subconscious garbage disposal running in reverse.

That made her think of something that had happened in her parents' house, back when it had still been her house too. Less than two hours before one of her mother's Famous Cocktail Parties (that was how Donna's father always referred to them, with a satirical tone that automatically conferred the capital letters – the same satirical tone that could sometimes drive Samantha into a frenzy), the disposal in the kitchen sink had somehow backed up into the bar sink, and when her mother turned the gadget on again in an effort to get rid of everything, green goo had exploded all over the ceiling. Donna had been about fourteen at the time, and she remembered that her mother's utter, hysterical rage had both frightened and sickened her. She had been sickened because her mother was throwing a tantrum in front of the people who loved and needed her most over the opinion of a group of casual acquaintances who were coming over to drink free booze and munch up a lot of free canapés. She had been frightened because she could see no *logic* in her mother's tantrum . . . and because of the expression she had seen in her father's eyes. It had been a kind of resigned disgust. That had been the first time she had really believed – believed in her gut – that she was going to grow up and become a woman, a woman with at least a fighting chance to be a *better* woman than her own mother, who could get into such a frightening state over what was really such a little thing . . .

She closed her eyes and tried to dismiss the whole train of thought, uneasy at the vivid emotions that memory called up. SPCA, greenhouse effect, garbage disposals, what next? How I Lost My Virginity? Six Well-Loved Vacations?

The *mailman*, that was the thing to think about, the goddam *mailman*.

'Mommy, maybe the car will start now.'

'Honey, I'm scared to try it because the battery is so low.'

'But we're just *sitting* here,' he said, sounding petulant and tired and cross. 'What does it matter if the battery's low or not if we're just *sitting* here? Try it!'

'Don't you go giving me orders, kiddo, or I'll whack your ass for you!'

He cringed away from her hoarse, angry voice and she cursed herself again. He was scratchy . . . so, who could blame him? Besides, he was right. That was what had really made her angry. But Tad didn't understand, the real reason she didn't want to try the engine again was because she was afraid it would bring the dog. She was afraid it would bring Cujo, and more than anything else she didn't want that.

Grimly, she turned the key in the ignition. The Pinto's engine cranked very slowly now, with a draggy, protesting sound. It coughed twice but did not fire. She turned the key off and tapped the horn. It gave a foggy, low honk that probably didn't carry fifty yards, let alone to that house at the bottom of the hill.

'There,' she said briskly and cruelly. 'Are you happy? Good.'

Tad began to cry. He began the way she always remembered it beginning when he was a baby: his mouth drawing into a trembling bow, the tears spilling down his cheeks even before the first sobs came. She pulled him to her then, saying she was sorry, saying she didn't mean to be mean, it was just that she was upset too, telling him that it would be over as soon as the mailman got there, that she would take him home and wash his hair. And thought: *A fighting chance to be a better woman than your mother. Sure. Sure, kid. You're just like her. That's just the kind of thing she would have said in a situation like this. When you're feeling bad, what you do is spread the misery, share the wealth. Well, like mother like daughter, right? And maybe when Tad grows up, he'll feel the same way about you as you feel about —*

'Why is it so hot, Mommy?' Tad asked dully.

'The greenhouse effect,' she answered, without even thinking about it. She wasn't up to this, and she knew it now. If this was, in any sense, a final examination on motherhood – or on adulthood itself – then she was flagging the test. How long had they been stuck in this driveway? Fifteen hours at the very most. And she was cracking up, falling apart.

'Can I have a Dr Pepper when we get home, Mommy?' The Monster Words, sweaty and wrinkled, lay limply on his lap.

'All you can drink,' she said, and hugged him tight. But the feel of his body was frighteningly wooden. *I shouldn't have shouted at him,* she thought distractedly. *If only I hadn't shouted.*

But she would do better, she promised herself. Because the mailman would be along soon.

'I think the muh – I think the doggy's going to eat us,' Tad said.

She started to reply and then didn't. Cujo still wasn't around. The sound of the Pinto's engine turning over hadn't brought him. Maybe he was asleep. Maybe he had had a convulsion and died. That would be wonderful . . . especially if it had been a *slow* convulsion. A painful one. She looked at the back door again. It was so temptingly near. It was locked. She was sure of that now. When people went away, they locked up. It would be foolhardy to try for the door, especially with the mailman due so soon. Play it as though it were real, Vic sometimes said. She would have to, because it *was* real. Better to assume the dog was still alive, and lying just inside those half-open garage doors. Lying in the shade.

The thought of shade made her mouth water.

It was almost eleven o'clock then. It was about forty-five minutes later when she spotted something in the grass beyond the edge of Tad's side of the car. Another fifteen minutes of examination convinced her that it was an old baseball bat with a friction-taped handle, half obscured by witch grass and timothy.

A few minutes after that, just before noon, Cujo stumbled out of the barn, blinking his red, rheumy eyes stupidly in the hot sun.

> *When they come to take you down,*
> *When they bring that wagon 'round,*
> *When they come to call on you*
> *And drag your poor body down . . .*

Jerry Garcia's voice, easy but somehow weary, came floating down the hall, magnified and distorted by someone's transistor radio until it sounded as if the vocal were floating down a long steel tube. Closer by, someone was moaning.

That morning, when he went down to the smelly industrial bathroom to shave and shower, there had been a puddle of vomit in one of the urinals and a large quantity of dried blood in one of the washbasins.

'Shake it, shake it, Sugaree,' Jerry Garcia sang, *'just don't tell 'em you know me.'*

Steve Kemp stood at the window of his room on the fifth floor of the Portland YMCA, looking down at Spring Street, feeling bad and not knowing why. His head was bad. He kept thinking about Donna Trenton and how he had fucked her over – fucked her over and then hung around. Hung around for what? What the fuck had happened?

He wished he were in Idaho. Idaho had been much on his mind lately. So why didn't he stop honking his donk and just go? He didn't know. He didn't like not knowing. He didn't like all these questions screwing up his head. Questions were counterproductive to a state of serenity, and serenity was necessary to the development of the artist. He had looked at himself this morning in one of the toothpaste-spotted mirrors and had thought he looked old. Really old. When he came back to his room he had seen a cockroach zigzagging busily across the floor. The omens were bad.

She didn't give me the brush because I'm old, he thought. *I'm not old. She did it because her itch was scratched, because she's a bitch, and because I gave her a spoonful of her own medicine. How did Handsome Hubby like his little love note, Donna? Did Handsome Hubby dig it?*

Did hubby *get* his little love note?

Steve crushed his cigarette out in the jar top that served the room as an ashtray. That was really the central question, wasn't it? With that one answered, the answers to the other questions would drop into place. The hateful hold she had gotten over him by telling him to get lost before he was ready to end the affair (she had *humiliated* him, goddammit), for one thing – for one very *big* thing.

Suddenly he knew what to do, and his heart began to thud heavily with anticipation. He put a hand into his pocket and jingled the change there. He went out. It was just past noon, and in Castle Rock, the mailman for whom Donna hoped had begun that part of his rounds which covered the Maple Sugar Road and Town Road No. 3.

Vic, Roger, and Rob Martin spent Tuesday morning at Image-Eye and then went out for beers and burgers. A few burgers and a great many beers later, Vic suddenly realized that he was drunker than he had ever been at a business luncheon in his life. Usually he had a single cocktail or a glass of white wine; he had seen too many good New York admen drown themselves slowly in those dark places just off Madison Avenue, talking to their friends about campaigns they would never mount . . . or, if they became drunk enough, to the barmen in those places about novels which they would assuredly never write.

It was a strange occasion, half victory celebration, half wake. Rob had greeted their idea of a final Sharp Cereal Professor ad with tempered enthusiasm, saying that he could knock it a mile . . . always assuming he was given the chance. That was the wake half. Without the approval of old man Sharp and his fabled kid, the greatest spot in the world would do them no good. They would all be out on their asses.

Under the circumstances, Vic supposed it was all right to get loaded.

Now, as the main rush of the restaurant's lunchtime clientele came in, the three of them sat in their shirtsleeves at a corner booth, the remains of their burgers on waxed paper, beer bottles scattered around the table, the ashtray overflowing. Vic was reminded of the day he and Roger had sat in the Yellow Sub back in Portland, discussing this little safari. Back when everything that had been wrong had been wrong with the business. Incredibly, he felt a wave of nostalgia for that day and wondered what Tad and Donna were doing. *Got to call them tonight*, he thought. *If I can stay sober enough to remember, that is.*

'So what now?' Rob asked. 'You hangin out in Boston or going on to New York? I can get you guys tickets to the Boston–Kansas City series, if you want them. Might cheer you up to watch George Brett knock a few holes in the left-field wall.'

Vic looked at Roger, who shrugged and said, 'On to New York, I guess. Thanks are in order, Rob, but I don't think either of us are in the mood for baseball.'

'There's nothing more we can do here,' Vic agreed. 'We had a lot of time scheduled on this trip for brainstorming, but I guess we're all agreed to go with the final spot idea.'

'There's still plenty of rough edges,' Rob said. 'Don't get too proud.'

'We can mill off the rough edges,' Roger said. 'One day with the marketing people ought to do it, I think. You agree, Vic?'

'It might take two,' Vic said. 'Still, there's no reason why we can't tie things up a lot earlier than we'd expected.'

'Then what?'

Vic grinned bleakly. 'Then we call old man Sharp and make an appointment to see him. I imagine we'll end up going straight on to Cleveland from New York. The Magical Mystery Tour.'

'See Cleveland and die,' Roger said gloomily, and poured the remainder of his beer into his glass. 'I just can't wait to see that old fart.'

'Don't forget the young fart,' Vic said, grinning a little.

'How could I forget that little prick?' Roger replied. 'Gentlemen, I propose another round.'

Rob looked at his watch. 'I really ought to—'

'One last round,' Roger insisted. 'Auld Lang Syne, if you want.'

Rob shrugged. 'Okay. But I still got a business to run, don't forget that. Although without Sharp Cereals, there's going to be space for a lot of long lunches.' He raised his glass in the air and waggled it until a waiter saw him and nodded back.

'Tell me what you really think,' Vic said to Rob. 'No bullshit. You think it's a bust?'

Rob looked at him, seemed about to speak, then shook his head.

Roger said, 'No, go ahead. We all set out to sea in the same pea-green boat. Or Red Razberry Zingers carton, or whatever. You think it's no go, don't you?'

'I don't think there's a chance in hell,' Rob said. 'You'll work up a good presentation – you always do. You'll get your background work done in New York, and I have a feeling that everything the market-research boys can tell you on such short notice is all going to be in your favor. And Yancey Harrington . . . I think he'll emote his fucking heart out. His big deathbed scene. He'll be so good he'll make Bette Davis in *Dark Victory* look like Ali MacGraw in *Love Story*.'

'Oh, but it's not like that at all—' Roger began.

Rob shrugged. 'Yeah, maybe that's a little unfair. Okay. Call it his curtain call, then. Whatever you want to call it, I've been in this business long enough to believe that there wouldn't be a dry eye in the house after that commercial was shown over a three- or four-week period. It would knock *everybody* on their asses. But—'

The beers came. The waiter said to Rob, 'Mr Johnson asked me to tell you that he has several parties of three waiting, Mr Martin.'

'Well, you run back and tell Mr Johnson that the boys are on their last round and to keep his undies dry. Okay, Rocky?'

The waiter smiled, emptied the ashtray, and nodded.

He left. Rob turned back to Vic and Roger. 'So what's the bottom line? You're bright boys. You don't need a one-legged cameraman with a snootful of beer to tell you where the bear shat in the buckwheat.'

'Sharp just won't apologize,' Vic said. 'That's what you think, isn't it?' Rob saluted him with his bottle of beer. 'Go to the head of the class.'

'It's not an apology,' Roger said plaintively. 'It's a fucking *explanation*.'

'You see it that way,' Rob answered, 'but will he? Ask yourself that. I've met that old geezer a couple of times.

He'd see it in terms of the captain deserting the sinking ship ahead of the women and children, giving up the Alamo, every stereotype you can think of. No, I'll tell you what I think is going to happen, my friends.' He raised his glass and drank slowly. 'I think a valuable and all too short relationship is going to come to an end very soon now. Old man Sharp is going to listen to your proposal, he's going to shake his head, he's going to usher you out. Permanently. And the next PR firm will be chosen by his son, who will make his pick based on which one he believes will give him the freest rein to indulge his crackpot ideas.'

'Maybe,' Roger said. 'But maybe he'll—'

'Maybe doesn't matter *shit* one way or the other,' Vic said vehemently. 'The only difference between a good advertising man and a good snake-oil salesman is that a good advertising man does the best job he can with the materials at hand . . . without stepping outside the bounds of honesty. That's what this commercial is about. If he turns it down, he's turning down the best we can do. And that's the end. Toot-finny.' He snuffed his cigarette and almost knocked over Roger's half-full bottle of beer. His hands were shaking.

Rob nodded. 'I'll drink to that.' He raised his glass. 'A toast, gentlemen.'

Vic and Roger raised their own glasses.

Rob thought for a moment and then said: 'May things turn out all right, even against the odds.'

'Amen,' Roger said.

They clinked their glasses together and drank. As he downed the rest of his beer, Vic found himself thinking about Donna and Tad again.

* * *

CUJO

George Meara, the mailman, lifted one leg clad in blue-gray Post Office issue and farted. Just lately he farted a great deal. He was mildly worried about it. It didn't seem to matter what he had been eating. Last night he and the wife had had creamed cod on toast and he had farted. This morning, Kellog's Product 19 with a banana cut up in it – and he had farted. This noon, down at the Mellow Tiger in town, two cheeseburgers with mayonnaise . . . ditto farts.

He had looked up the symptom in *The Home Medical Encyclopedia*, an invaluable tome in twelve volumes which his wife had gotten a volume at a time by saving her checkout slips from the Shop 'n Save in South Paris. What George Meara had discovered under the EXCESSIVE FLAT-ULENCE heading had not been particularly encouraging. It could be a symptom of gastric upset. It could mean he had a nice little ulcer incubating in there. It could be a bowel problem. It could even mean the big C. If it kept up he supposed he would go and see old Dr Quentin. Dr Quentin would tell him he was farting a lot because he was getting older and that was it.

Aunt Evvie Chalmers's death that late spring had hit George hard – harder than he ever would have believed – and just lately he didn't like to think about getting older. He preferred to think about the Golden Years of Retirement, years that he and Cathy would spend together. No more getting up at six thirty. No more heaving around sacks of mail and listening to that asshole Michael Fournier, who was the Castle Rock postmaster. No more freezing his balls off in the winter and going crazy with all the summer people who wanted delivery to their camps and cottages when the warm weather came. Instead, there would

267

be a Winnebago for 'Scenic Trips Through New England'. There would be 'Puttering in the Garden'. There would be 'All Sorts of New Hobbies'. Most of all, there would be 'Rest and Relaxation'. And somehow, the thought of farting his way through his late sixties and early seventies like a defective rocket just didn't jibe with his fond picture of the Golden Years of Retirement.

He turned the small blue-and-white mail truck onto Town Road No. 3, wincing as the glare of sunlight shifted briefly across the windshield. The summer had turned out every bit as hot as Aunt Evvie had prophesied – all of that, and then some. He could hear crickets singing sleepily in the high summer grass and had a brief vision out of the Golden Years of Retirement, a scene entitled 'George Relaxes in the Back Yard Hammock'.

He stopped at the Millikens' and pushed a Zayre's advertising circular and a CMP power bill into the box. This was the day all the power bills went out, but he hoped the CMP folks wouldn't hold their breath until the Millikens' check came in. The Millikens were poor white trash, like that Gary Pervier just up the road. It was nothing but a scandal to see what was happening to Pervier, a man who had once won a DSC. And old Joe Camber wasn't a hell of a lot better. They were going to the dogs, the both of them.

John Milliken was out in the side yard, repairing what looked like a harrow. George gave him a wave, and Milliken flicked one finger curtly in return before going back to his work.

Here's one for you, you welfare chiseler, George Meara thought. He lifted his leg and blew his trombone. It was a hell of a thing, this farting. You had to be pretty damn careful when you were out in company.

He drove on up the road to Gary Pervier's, produced another Zayre's circular, another power bill, and added a VFW newsletter. He tucked them into the box and then turned around in Gary's driveway, because he didn't have to drive all the way up to Camber's place today. Joe had called the post office yesterday morning around ten and had asked them to hold his mail for a few days. Mike Fournier, the big talker who was in charge of things at the Castle Rock P.O., had routinely filled out a HOLD MAIL UNTIL NOTIFIED card and flipped it over to George's station.

Fournier told Joe Camber he had called just about fifteen minutes too late to stop the Monday delivery of mail, if that had been his intention.

'Don't matter,' Joe had said. 'I guess I'll be around to get today's.'

When George put Gary Pervier's mail into his box, he noticed that Gary's Monday delivery – a *Popular Mechanix* and a charity begging letter from the Rural Scholarship Fund – had not been removed. Now, turning around, he noticed that Gary's big old Chrysler was in the dooryard and Joe Camber's rusting-around-the-edges station wagon was parked right behind it.

'Gone off together,' he muttered aloud. 'Two fools off hooting somewhere.'

He lifted his leg and farted again.

George's conclusion was that the two of them were probably off drinking and whoring, wheeling around in Joe Camber's pickup truck. It didn't occur to him to wonder why they would have taken Joe's truck when there were two much more comfortable vehicles near at hand, and he didn't notice the blood on the porch steps or the fact that there was a large hole in the lower panel of Gary's screen door.

'Two fools off hooting,' he repeated. 'At least Joe Camber remembered to cancel his mail.'

He drove off the way he had come, back towards Castle Rock, lifting his leg every now and then to blow his trombone.

Steve Kemp drove out to the Dairy Queen by the Westbrook Shopping Mall for a couple of cheeseburgers and a Dilly Bar. He sat in his van, eating and looking out at Brighton Avenue, not really seeing the road or tasting the food.

He had called Handsome Hubby's office. He gave his name as Adam Swallow when the secretary asked. Said he was the marketing director for House of Lights, Inc., and would like to talk to Mr Trenton. He had been drymouthed with excitement. And when Trenton got on the old hooter, they could find more interesting things than marketing to talk about. Like the little woman's birthmark, and what it might look like. Like how she had bitten him once when she came, hard enough to draw blood. Like how things were going for the Bitch Goddess since Handsome Hubby discovered she had a little taste for what she was on the other side of the sheets.

But things hadn't turned out that way. The secretary had said, 'I'm sorry, but both Mr Trenton and Mr Breakstone are out of the office this week. They'll probably be out most of the next week, as well. If I could help you –?' Her voice had a rising, hopeful inflection. She really did want to help. It was her big chance to land an account while the bosses were taking care of business in Boston or maybe New York – surely no place as exotic as LA, not a little dipshit agency like Ad Worx. So get out there and tapdance until your shoes smoke, kid.

He thanked her and told her he would ring back toward the end of the month. He hung up before she could ask for his number, since the office of the House of Lights, Inc., was in a Congress Street phone booth across from Joe's Smoke Shop.

Now here he was, eating cheeseburgers and wondering what to do next. *As if you didn't know,* an interior voice whispered.

He started the van up and headed for Castle Rock. By the time he finished his lunch (the Dilly Bar was practically running down the stick in the heat), he was in North Windham. He threw his trash on the floor of the van, where it joined a drift of like stuff – plastic drink containers, Big Mac boxes, returnable beer and soda bottles, empty cigarette packs. Littering was an antisocial, anti-environmentalist act, and he didn't do it.

Steve got to the Trenton house at just half past three on that hot, glaring afternoon. Acting with almost subliminal caution, he drove past the house without slowing and parked around the corner on a side street about a quarter of a mile away. He walked back.

The driveway was empty, and he felt a pang of frustrated disappointment. He would not admit to himself – especially now that it looked like she was out – that he had intended to give her a taste of what she had been so eager to have during the spring. Nevertheless, he had driven all the way from Westbrook to Castle Rock with a semi-erection that only now collapsed completely.

She was gone.

No; the *car* was gone. One thing didn't necessarily prove the other, did it?

Steve looked around himself.

What we have here, ladies and gents, is a peaceful suburban street on a summer's day, most of the kiddies in for naps, most of the little wifies either doing likewise or glued to their TVs, checking out Love of Life *or* Search for Tomorrow. *All the Handsome Hubbies are busy earning their way into higher tax brackets and very possibly a bed in the Intensive Care ward at the Eastern Maine Medical Center.* Two little kids were playing hopscotch on a blurred chalk grid; they were wearing bathing suits and sweating heavily. An old balding lady was trundling a wire shopping caddy back from town as if both she and it were made of the finest bone china. She gave the kids playing hopscotch a wide berth.

In short, not much happening. The street was dozing in the heat.

Steve walked up the sloping driveway as if he had every right to be there. First he looked in the tiny one-car garage. He had never known Donna to use it, because the doorway was so narrow. If she put a dent in the car, Handsome Hubby would give her hell – no, excuse me; he would give her *heck*.

The garage was empty. No Pinto, no elderly Jag – Donna's Handsome Hubby was into what was known as sports car menopause. She hadn't liked him saying that, but Steve had never seen a more obvious case.

Steve left the garage and went up the three steps to the back stoop. Tried the door. Found it unlocked. He went inside without knocking after another casual glance around to make sure no one was in sight.

He closed the door on the silence of the house. Once more his heart was knocking heavily in his chest, seeming to shake his whole ribcage. And once again he was not admitting things. He didn't *have* to admit them. They were there just the same.

'Hi? Anybody home?' His voice was loud, honest, pleasant, inquiring.

'Hi?' He was halfway down the hall now.

Obviously no one home. The house had a silent, hot, waiting feel. An empty house full of furniture was somehow creepy when it wasn't your house. You felt watched.

'Hello? Anybody home?' One last time.

Give her something to remember you by, then. And split.

He went into the living room and stood looking around. His shirtsleeves were rolled up, his forearms lightly slicked with sweat. Now things could be admitted. How he had wanted to kill her when she called him a son of a bitch, her spittle spraying on his face. How he had wanted to kill her for making him feel old and scared and not able to keep on top of the situation any more. The letter had been something, but the letter hadn't been enough.

To his right, knickknacks stood on a series of glass shelves. He turned and gave the bottom shelf a sudden hard kick. It disintegrated. The frame tottered and then fell over, spraying glass, spraying little china figurines of cats and shepherds and all that happy bourgeois horseshit. A pulse throbbed in the center of his forehead. He was grimacing, unaware of the fact. He walked carefully over the unbroken figurines, crushing them into powder. He pulled a family portrait from the wall, looked curiously at the smiling face of Vic Trenton for a moment (Tad was sitting on his lap, and his arm was around Donna's waist), and then he dropped the picture to the floor and stamped down hard on the glass.

He looked around, breathing hard, as if he had just run a race. And suddenly he went after the room as if it were something alive, something that had hurt him badly and needed to be punished, as if it were the room that had caused his pain. He pushed over Vic's La-Z-Boy recliner. He upended the couch. It stood on end for a moment, rocking uneasily, and then went down with a crash, breaking the back of the coffee table which had stood in front of it. He pulled all the books out of the bookcases, cursing the shitty taste of the people who had bought them under his breath as he did it. He picked up the magazine stand and threw it overhand at the mirror over the mantelpiece, shattering it. Big pieces of black-backed mirror fell onto the floor like chunks of a jigsaw puzzle. He was snorting now, like a bull in heat. His thin cheeks were almost purple with color.

He went into the kitchen by way of the small dining room. As he walked past the dining-room table Donna's parents had bought them as a housewarming present, he extended his arm straight out and swept everything off onto the floor – the lazy Susan with its complement of spices, the cut-glass vase Donna had gotten for a dollar and a quarter at the Emporium Galorium in Bridgton the summer previous, Vic's graduation beer stein. The ceramic salt and pepper shakers shattered like bombs. His erection was back now, raging. Thoughts of caution, of possible discovery, had departed his mind. He was somewhere inside. He was down a dark hole.

In the kitchen he yanked the bottom drawer of the stove out to its stop and threw pots and pans everywhere. They made a dreadful clatter, but there was no satisfaction in mere clatter. A rank of cupboards ran around three of the room's four sides. He pulled them open one after the other. He grabbed plates by the double handful and threw them on the floor. Crockery jingled musically. He swept the glasses out and grunted as they broke. Among them was a set of eight delicate long-stemmed wine glasses that Donna had had since she was twelve years old. She had read about 'hope chests' in some magazine or other and had determined to have such a chest of her own. As it turned out, the wine glasses were the only thing she had actually put in hers before losing interest (her original grand intention had been to lay by enough to completely furnish her bridal house or flat), but she had had them for more than half her life, and they were treasured.

The gravy boat went. The big serving platter. The Sears radio/tape player went on the floor with a heavy crunch. Steve Kemp danced on it; he boogied on it. His penis, hard as stone, throbbed inside his pants. The vein in the center of his forehead throbbed in counterpoint. He discovered booze under the small chromium sink in the corner. He yanked out half- and three-quarters-full bottles by the armload and then flung them at the closed door of the kitchen closet one by one, throwing them overhand as hard as he could; the next day his right arm would be so stiff and sore he would barely be able to lift it to shoulder level. Soon the blue closet door was running with Gilbey's gin, Jack Daniel's, J & B whisky, sticky green crème de menthe, the amaretto that had been a Christmas present from Roger and Althea Breakstone. Glass twinkled benignly in the hot afternoon sunlight pouring through the windows over the sink.

Steve tore into the laundry room, where he found boxes of bleach, Spic 'n Span, Downy fabric softener in a large blue plastic bottle, Lestoil, Top Job, and three kinds of powdered detergent. He ran back and forth pouring these cleaning potions everywhere.

He had just emptied the last carton — when he saw the message scrawled on the noteminder in Donna's unmistakable spiky handwriting: *Tad & I have gone out to J. Camber's garage w/Pinto. Back soon.*

That brought him back to the realities of the situation with a bang. He had already been here half an hour at least, maybe longer. The time had passed in a red blur, and it was hard to peg it any more closely than that. How long had she been gone when he came in? Who had the note been left for? Anybody who might pop in, or someone specific? He had to get out of here . . . but there was one other thing he had to do first.

He erased the message on the noteminder with one swipe of his sleeve and wrote in large block letters:

I LEFT SOMETHING UPSTAIRS FOR YOU, BABY.

He took the stairs two by two and came into their bedroom, which was to the left of the second-floor landing.

He felt terribly pressed now, almost positive that the doorbell was going to ring or someone – another happy housewife, most likely – would poke her head in the back door and call (as he had), 'Hi! Anybody home?'

But, perversely, that added the final spice of excitement to this mad happening. He unbuckled his belt, jerked his fly down, and let his jeans drop down around his knees. He wasn't wearing underpants; he rarely did. His cock stood out stiffly from a mass of reddish-gold pubic hair. It didn't take long; he was too excited. Two or three quick jerks through his closed fist and orgasm came, immediate and savage. He spat semen onto the bedspread in a convulsion.

He yanked his jeans back up, raked the zipper closed (almost catching the head of his penis in the zipper's small gold teeth – *that* would have been a laugh, all right), and ran for the door, buckling his belt again. He would meet someone as he was going out. Yes. He felt positive of it, as if it were preordained. Some happy housewife who would take one look at his flushed face, his bulging eyes, his tented jeans, and scream her head off.

He tried to prepare himself for it as he opened the back door and went out. In retrospect it seemed that he had made enough noise to wake the dead . . . those pans! Why had he thrown those fucking pans around? What had he been thinking of? Everyone in the neighborhood must have heard.

But there was no one in the yard or in the driveway. The peace of the afternoon was undisturbed. Across the street, a lawn sprinkler twirled unconcernedly. A kid went by on roller skates. Straight ahead was a high hedge which separated the Trentons' house lot from the next one over.

Looking to the left from the back stoop was a view of the town nestled at the bottom of the hill. Steve could see the intersection of Route 117 and High Street quite clearly, the Town Common nestled in one of the angles made by the crossing of the two roads. He stood there on the stoop, trying to get his shit back together. His breath slowed a little at a time back into a more normal inhale-exhale pattern. He found a pleasant afternoon face and put it on. All this happened in the length of time it took for the traffic light on the corner to cycle from red to amber to green and back to red again.

What if she pulls into the driveway right now?

That got him going again. He'd left his calling card; he didn't need any hassle from her on top of it. There was no way she could do a thing anyway, unless she called the cops, and he didn't think she'd do that. There were too many things he could tell: The Sex Life of the Great American Happy Housewife in Its Natural Habitat. It had been a crazy scene, though. Best to put miles between himself and Castle Rock. Maybe later he would give her a call. Ask her how she had liked his work. That might be sort of fun.

He walked down the driveway, turned left, and went back to his van. He wasn't stopped. Nobody took any undue notice of him. A kid on roller skates zipped past him and shouted 'Hi!' Steve hi'd him right back.

He got in the van and started it up. He drove up 117 to 302 and followed that road to its intersection with Interstate 95 in Portland. He took an Interstate time-and-toll ticket and rolled south. He had begun having uneasy thoughts about what he had done – the red rage of destruction he had gone into when he saw that no one was home. Had the retribution been too heavy for the offense? So she didn't want to make it with him any more, so what? He had trashed most of the goddamn house. Did that, maybe, say something unpleasant about where his head was at?

He began to work on these questions a little at a time, the way most people do, running an objective set of facts through a bath of various chemicals which, when taken together, make up the complex human perceptual mechanism known as subjectivity. Like a schoolchild who works carefully first with the pencil, then with the eraser, then with the pencil again, he tore down what had happened and then carefully rebuilt it — redrew it in his mind — until both the facts and his perception of the facts jibed in a way he could live with.

When he reached Route 495, he turned west toward New York and the country that sprawled beyond, all the way to the silent reaches of Idaho, the place that Papa Hemingway had gone to when he was old and mortally hurt. He felt the familiar lift in his feelings that came with cutting old ties and moving on — that magical thing that Huck had called 'lighting out for the territory.' At such times he felt almost newborn, felt strongly that he was in possession of the greatest freedom of all, the freedom to recreate himself. He would have been unable to understand the significance if someone had pointed out the fact that, whether in Maine or in Idaho, he would still be apt to throw his racket down in angry frustration if he lost a game of tennis; that he would refuse to shake the hand of his opponent over the net, as he always had when he lost. He only shook over the net when he won.

He stopped for the night in a small town called Twickenham. His sleep was easy. He had convinced himself that trashing the Trentons' house had not been an act of half-mad jealous pique but a piece of revolutionary anarchy – offing a couple of fat middle-class pigs, the sort who made it easy for the fascist overlords to remain in power by blindly paying their taxes and their telephone bills. It had been an act of courage and of clean, justified fury. It was his way of saying 'power to the people', an idea he tried to incorporate in all his poems.

Still, he mused, as he turned toward sleep in the narrow motel bed, he wondered what Donna had thought of it when she and the kid got home. That sent him to sleep with a slight smile on his lips.

By three thirty that Tuesday afternoon, Donna had given up on the mailman.

She sat with one arm lightly around Tad, who was in a dazed half sleep, his lips cruelly puffed from the heat, his face hectic and flushed. There was a tiny bit of milk left, and soon she would give it to him. During the last three and a half hours – since what would have been lunchtime at home – the sun had been monstrous and unremitting. Even with her window and Tad's window open a quarter of the way, the temperature inside must have reached 100 degrees, maybe more. It was the way your car got when you left it in the sun, that was all. Except, under normal circumstances, what you did when your car got like that was you unrolled all the windows, pulled the knobs that opened the air-ducts, and got rolling. *Let's get rolling* – what a sweet sound those words had!

She licked her lips.

For short periods she had unrolled the windows all the way, creating a mild draft, but she was afraid to leave them that way. She might doze off. The heat scared her — it scared her for herself and even more for Tad, what it might be taking out of him — but it didn't scare her as badly as the face of that dog, slavering foam and staring at her with its sullen red eyes.

The last time she had unrolled the windows all the way was when Cujo had disappeared into the shadows of the barn-garage. But now Cujo was back.

He sat in the lengthening shadow of the big barn, his head lowered, staring at the blue Pinto. The ground between his front paws was muddy from his slaver. Every now and then he would growl and snap at empty air, as if he might be hallucinating.

How long? How long before he dies?

She was a rational woman. She did not believe in monsters from closets; she believed in things she could see and touch. There was nothing supernatural about the slobbering wreck of a Saint Bernard sitting in the shade of a barn; he was merely a sick animal that had been bitten by a rabid fox or skunk or something. He wasn't out to get her personally. He wasn't the Reverend Dimmesdale or Moby Dog. He was not four-footed Fate.

But . . . she had just about decided to make a run for the back door of the enclosed Camber porch when Cujo had come rolling and staggering out of the darkness of the barn.

Tad. Tad was the thing. She had to get him out of this. No more fucking around. He wasn't answering very coherently any more. He seemed to be in touch only with the peaks of reality. The glazed way his eyes rolled toward her when she spoke to him, like the eyes of a fighter who has been struck and struck and struck, a fighter who has lost his coherence along with his mouthguard and is waiting only for the final flurry of punches to drop him insensible to the canvas — those things terrified her and roused all her motherhood. Tad was the thing. If she had been alone, she would have gone for that door long ago. It was Tad who had held her back, because her mind kept circling back to the thought of the dog pulling her down, and of Tad in the car alone.

Still, until Cujo had returned fifteen minutes ago, she had been preparing herself to go for the door. She played it over and over in her mind like a home movie, did it until it seemed to one part of her mind as if it had already happened. She would shake Tad fully awake, slap him awake if she had to. Tell him he was not to leave the car and follow her — *under no circumstances, no matter what happens*. She would run from the car to the porch door. Try the knob. If it was unlocked, well and fine. But she was prepared for the very real possibility that it was locked. She had taken off her shirt and now sat behind the wheel in her white cotton bra, the shirt in her lap. When she went, she would go with the shirt wrapped around her hand. Far from perfect protection, but better than none at all. She would smash in the pane of glass nearest the doorknob, reach through, and let herself onto the little back porch. And if the inner door was locked, she would cope with that too. Somehow.

But Cujo had come back out, and that took away her edge.

Never mind. He'll go back in. He has before.

But will he? her mind chattered. *It's all too perfect, isn't it? The Cambers are gone, and they remembered to shut off their mail like good citizens; Vic is gone, and the chances are slim that he'll call before tomorrow night, because we just can't afford long distance every night. And if he does call, he'll call early. When he doesn't get any answer he'll assume we went out to catch some chow at Mario's or maybe a couple of ice creams at the Tastee Freeze. And he won't call later because he'll think we're asleep. He'll call tomorrow instead. Considerate Vic. Yes, it's all just too perfect. Wasn't there a dog in the front of the boat in that story about the boatman on the River Charon? The boatman's dog. Just call me Cujo. All out for the Valley of Death.*

Go in, she silently willed the dog. *Go back in the barn, damn you.*

Cujo didn't move.

She licked her lips, which felt almost as puffy as Tad's looked.

She brushed his hair off his forehead and said softly, 'How you going, Tadder?'

'Shhh,' Tad muttered distractedly. 'The ducks . . .'

She gave him a shake. 'Tad? Honey? You okay? Talk to me!'

His eyes opened a little at a time. He looked around, a small boy who was puzzled and hot and dreadfully tired. 'Mommy? Can't we go home? I'm so *hot . . .*'

'We'll go home,' she soothed.

'When, Mom? *When?*' He began to cry helplessly.

Oh Tad, save your moisture, she thought. *You may need it.* Crazy thing to have to be thinking. But the entire situation was ridiculous to the point of lunacy, wasn't it? The idea of a small boy dying of dehydration

(stop it he is NOT dying)

less than seven miles from the nearest good-sized town was crazy.

But the situation is what it is, she reminded herself roughly. And don't you think anything else, sister. It's like a war on a miniaturized scale, so everything that looked small before looks big now. The smallest puff of air through the quarter-open windows was a zephyr. The distance to the back porch was half a mile across no-man's-land. And if you want to believe the dog is Fate, or the Ghost of Sins Remembered, or even the reincarnation of Elvis Presley, then believe it. In this curiously scaled-down situation – this life-or-death situation – even having to go to the bathroom became a skirmish.

We're going to get out of it. No dog is going to do this to my son.

'When, Mommy?' He looked up at her, his eyes wet, his face as pale as cheese.

'Soon,' she said grimly. 'Very soon.' She brushed his hair back and held him against her. She looked out Tad's window and again her eyes fixed on that thing lying in the high grass, that old friction-taped baseball bat.

I'd like to bash your head in with it.

Inside the house, the phone began to ring.

She jerked her head around, suddenly wild with hope.

'Is it for us, Mommy? Is the phone for us?'

She didn't answer him. She didn't know who it was for. But if they were lucky – and their luck was due to change soon, wasn't it? – it would be from someone with cause to be suspicious that no one was answering the phone at the Cambers'. Someone who would come out and check around.

Cujo's head had come up. His head cocked to one side, and for a moment he bore an insane resemblance to Nipper, the RCA dog with his ear to the gramophone horn. He got shakily to his feet and started toward the house and the sound of the ringing telephone.

'Maybe the doggy's going to answer the telephone,' Tad said. 'Maybe—'

With a speed and agility that was terrifying, the big dog changed direction and came at the car. The awkward stagger was gone now, as if it had been nothing but a sly act all along. It was roaring and bellowing rather than barking. Its red eyes burned. It struck the car with a hard, dull crunch and rebounded — with stunned eyes, Donna saw that the side of her door was actually bowed in a bit. *It must be dead*, she thought hysterically, *bashed its sick brains in spinal fusion deep concussion must have — must have MUST HAVE —*

Cujo got back up. His muzzle was bloody. His eyes seemed wandering, vacuous again. Inside the house the phone rang on and on. The dog made as if to walk away, suddenly snapped viciously at its own flank as if stung, whirled, and sprang at Donna's window. It struck right in front of Donna's face with another tremendous dull thud. Blood sprayed across the glass, and a long silver crack appeared. Tad shrieked and clapped his hands to his face, pulling his cheeks down, harrowing them with his fingernails.

The dog leaped again. Ropes of foam runnered back from his bleeding muzzle. She could see his teeth, heavy as old yellow ivory. His claws clicked on the glass. A cut between his eyes was streaming blood. His eyes were fixed on hers; dumb, dull eyes, but not without – she would have sworn it – not without some knowledge. Some malign knowledge.

'*Get out of here!*' she screamed at it.

Cujo threw himself against the side of the car below her window again. And again. And again. Now her door was badly dented inward. Each time the dog's two-hundred-pound bulk struck the Pinto, it rocked on its springs. Each time she heard that heavy, toneless thud, she felt sure it must have killed itself, at least knocked itself unconscious. And each time it trotted back toward the house, whirled and charged the car again. Cujo's face was a mask of blood and matted fur from which his eyes, once a kind, mild brown, peered with stupid fury.

She looked at Tad and saw that he had gone into a shock reaction, curling himself up into a tight, fetal ball in his bucket seat, his hands laced together at the nape of his neck, his chest hitching.

Maybe that's best. Maybe –

Inside the house the phone stopped ringing. Cujo, in the act of whirling around for another charge, paused. He cocked his head again in that curious, evocative gesture. Donna held her breath. The silence seemed very big. Cujo sat down, raised his horribly mangled nose toward the sky, and howled once – such a dark and lonesome sound and she shivered, no longer hot but as cold as a crypt. In that instant she knew – she did not feel or just think – she *knew* that the dog was something more than just a dog.

The moment passed. Cujo got to his feet, very slowly

286

and wearily, and walked around to the front of the Pinto.
She supposed he had lain down there – she could no longer
see his tail. Nevertheless she held herself tensed for a few
moments longer, mentally ready in case the dog should
spring up onto the hood as it had done before. It hadn't.
There was nothing but silence.

She gathered Tad into her arms and began to croon
to him.

When Brett had at last given up and come out of the telephone booth, Charity took his hand and led him into
Caldor's coffee shop. They had come to Caldor's to look
at matching tablecloths and curtains.

Holly was waiting for them, sipping the last of an
ice-cream soda. 'Nothing wrong, is there?' she asked.

'Nothing too serious,' Charity said, and ruffled his
hair. 'He's worried about his dog. Aren't you, Brett?'

Brett shrugged – nodded miserably.

'You go on ahead, if you want,' Charity said to her.
'We'll catch up.'

'All right. I'll be downstairs.'

Holly finished her soda and said, 'I bet your pooch
is just fine, Brett.'

Brett smiled at her as best he could but didn't reply.
They watched Holly walk away, smart in her dark burgundy
dress and cork-soled sandals, smart in a way Charity knew
she would never be able to duplicate. Maybe once, but not
now. Holly had left her two with a sitter, and they had
come into Bridgeport around noon. Holly had bought
them a nice lunch – paying with a Diners Club card –
and since then they had been shopping. But Brett had been

quiet and withdrawn, worrying about Cujo. Charity didn't feel much like shopping herself; it was hot, and she was still a little unnerved by Brett's sleepwalking that morning. Finally she had suggested that he try calling home from one of the booths around the corner from the snack bar . . . but the results had been precisely those of which she had been afraid.

The waitress came. Charity ordered coffee, milk, and two Danish pastries.

'Brett,' she said, 'when I told your father I wanted us to go on this trip, he was against it –'

'Yeah, I figured that.'

'– and then he changed his mind. He changed it all at once. I think that maybe . . . maybe he saw it as a chance for a little vacation of his own. Sometimes men like to go off by themselves, you know, and do things –'

'Like hunting?'

(and whoring and drinking and God alone knows what else or why)

'Yes, like that.'

'And movies,' Brett said. Their snacks came, and he began munching his Danish.

(yes the X-rated kind on Washington Street they call it the Combat Zone)

'Could be. Anyway, your father might have taken a couple of days to go to Boston—'

'Oh, I don't think so,' Brett said earnestly. 'He had a lot of work. A *lot* of work. He told me so.'

'There might not have been as much as he thought,' she said, hoping that the cynicism she felt hadn't rubbed through into her voice. 'Anyway, that's what I think he did, and that's why he didn't answer the phone yesterday or today. Drink your milk, Brett. It builds up your bones.'

He drank half his milk and grew an old man's mustache. He set the glass down. 'Maybe he did. He could have got Gary to go with him, maybe. He likes Gary a lot.'

'Yes, maybe he did get Gary to go with him,' Charity said. She spoke as if this idea had never occurred to her, but in fact she had called Gary's house this morning while Brett had been out in the back yard, playing with Jim Junior. There had been no answer. She hadn't a doubt in the world that they were together, wherever they were. 'You haven't eaten much of that Danish.'

He picked it up, took a token bite, and put it down again. 'Mom, I think Cujo was sick. He looked sick when I saw him yesterday morning. Honest to God.'

'Brett—'

'He *did*, Mom. You didn't see him. He looked . . . well, gross.'

'If you knew Cujo was all right, would it set your mind at rest?'

Brett nodded.

'Then we'll call Alva Thornton down on the Maple Sugar tonight,' she said. 'Have him go up and check, okay? My guess is your father already called him and asked him to feed Cujo while he's gone.'

'Do you really think so?'

'Yes, I do.' Alva or someone like Alva; not really Joe's friends, because to the best of her knowledge Gary was the only real friend Joe had, but men who would do a favor for a favor in return at some future time.

Brett's expression cleared magically. Once again the grownup had produced the right answer, like a rabbit from a hat. Instead of cheering her, it turned her momentarily glum. What was she going to tell him if she called Alva and he said he hadn't seen Joe since mud season? Well, she would cross that bridge if she came to it, but she continued to believe that Joe wouldn't have just left Cujo to shift for himself. It wasn't like him.

'Want to go and find your aunt now?'

'Sure. Just lemme finish this.'

She watched, half amused and half appalled, as he gobbled the rest of the Danish in three great bites and chased it with the rest of the milk. Then he pushed his chair back.

Charity paid the check and they went out to the down escalator.

'Jeez, this sure is a big store,' Brett said wonderingly. 'It's a big city, isn't it, Mom?'

'New York makes this look like Castle Rock,' she said. 'And don't say jeez, Brett, it's the same as swearing.'

'Okay.' He held the moving railing, looking around. To the right of them was a maze of twittering chirruping parakeets. To the left was the housewares department, with chrome glittering everywhere and a dishwasher that had a front made entirely of glass so you could check out its sudsing action. He looked up at his mother as they got off the escalator. 'You two grew up together, huh?'

'Hope to tell you,' Charity said, smiling.

'She's real nice,' Brett said.

'Well, I'm glad you think so. I was always partial to her myself.'

'How did she get so rich?'

Charity stopped. 'Is that what you think Holly and Jim are? *Rich?*'

'That house they live in didn't come cheap,' he said, and again she could see his father peeking around the corners of his unformed face, Joe Camber with his shapeless green hat tipped far back on his head, his eyes, too wise, shifted off to one side. 'And that jukebox. That was dear, too. She's got a whole wallet of those credit cards and all we've got is the Texaco—'

She rounded on him. 'You think it's smart to go peeking into people's wallets when they've just bought you a nice lunch?'

His face looked hurt and surprised, then it closed up and became smooth. That was a Joe Camber trick too. 'I just noticed. Would have been hard not to, the way she was showing them off—'

'She was *not* showing them off!' Charity said, shocked. She stopped again. They had reached the edge of the drapery department.

'Yeah, she was,' Brett said. 'If they'd been an accordion, she would have been playing "Lady of Spain."'

She was suddenly furious with him – partly because she suspected he might be right.

'She wanted you to see all of them,' Brett said. 'That's what *I* think.'

'I'm not particularly interested in what you think on the subject, Brett Camber.' Her face felt hot. Her hands itched to strike him. A few moments ago, in the cafeteria, she had been loving him . . . just as important, she had felt like his friend. Where had those good feelings gone?

'I just wondered how she got so much dough.'

'That's sort of a crude word to use for it, don't you think?'

He shrugged, openly antagonistic now, provoking her purposely, she suspected. It went back to his perception of what had happened at lunch, but it went further back than that. He was contrasting his own way of life and his father's way of life with another one. Had she thought he would automatically embrace the way that her sister and her husband lived, just because Charity wanted him to embrace it — a life-style that she herself had been denied, either by bad luck, her own stupidity, or both? Had he no right to criticize . . . or analyze?

Yes, she acknowledged that he did, but she hadn't expected that his observation would be so unsettlingly (if intuitively) sophisticated, so accurate, or so depressingly negative.

'I suppose it was Jim who made the money,' she said. 'You know what he does—'

'Yeah, he's a pencil-pusher.'

But this time she refused to be drawn.

'If you want to see it that way. Holly married him when he was in college at the University of Maine in Portland, studying pre-law. While he was in law school in Denver, she worked a lot of crummy jobs to see that he got through. It's often done that way. Wives work so their husbands can go to school and learn some special skill . . .'

She was searching for Holly with her eyes, and finally thought she saw the top of her younger sister's head several aisles to the left.

'Anyway, when Jim finally got out of school, he and

Holly came back east and he went to work in Bridgeport with a big firm of lawyers. He didn't make much money then. They lived in a third-floor apartment with no air conditioning in the summer and not much heat in the winter. But he's worked his way up, and now he's what's called a junior partner. And I suppose he does make a lot of money, by our standards.'

'Maybe she shows her credit cards around because sometimes she still feels poor inside,' Brett said.

She was struck by the almost eerie perceptiveness of that, as well. She ruffled his hair gently, no longer angry at him. 'You did say you liked her.'

'Yeah, I do. There she is, right over there.'

'I see her.'

They went over and joined Holly, who already had an armload of curtains and was now prospecting for table-cloths.

The sun had finally gone down behind the house.

Little by little, the oven that was inside the Trentons' Pinto began to cool off. A more-or-less steady breeze sprang up, and Tad turned his face into it gratefully. He felt better, at least for the time being, than he had all day. In fact, all the rest of the day before now seemed like a terribly bad dream, one he could only partly remember. At times he had gone away; had simply left the car and gone away. He could remember that. He had gone on a horse. He and the horse had ridden down a long field, and there were rabbits playing there, just like in that cartoon his mommy and daddy had taken him to see at the Magic Lantern Theater in Bridgton. There was a pond at the end of the field, and ducks in the pond. The ducks were friendly. Tad played with them. It was better there than with Mommy, because the monster was where Mommy was, the monster that had gotten out of his closet. The monster was not in the place where the ducks were. Tad liked it there, although he knew in a vague way that if he stayed in that place too long, he might forget how to get back to the car.

Then the sun had gone behind the house. There were cool shadows, almost thick enough to have a texture, like velvet. The monster had stopped trying to get them. The mailman hadn't come, but at least now he was able to rest comfortably. The worst thing was being so thirsty. Never in his life had he wanted a drink so much. That was what made the place where the ducks were so nice – it was a wet, green place.

'What did you say, honey?' Mommy's face bending down over him.

'Thirsty,' he said in a frog's croak. 'I'm so thirsty, Mommy.' He remembered that he used to say 'firsty' instead of 'thirsty.' But some of the kids at daycamp had laughed at him and called him a baby, the same way they laughed at Randy Hofnager for saying 'brefkust' when he meant 'breakfast'. So he began to say it right, scolding himself fiercely inside whenever he forgot.

'Yes, I know. Mommy's thirsty too.'

'I bet there's water in that house.'

'Honey, we can't go into the house. Not just yet. The bad dog's in front of the car.'

'Where?' Tad got up on his knees and was surprised at the lightness that ran lazily through his head, like a slow-breaking wave. He put a hand on the dashboard to support himself, and the hand seemed on the end of an arm that was a mile long. 'I don't see him.' Even his voice was distant, echoey.

'Sit back down, Tad. You're . . .'

She was still talking, and he could feel her sitting him back into the seat, but it was all distant. The words were coming to him over a long gray distance; it was foggy between him and her, as it had been foggy this morning . . . or yesterday morning . . . or on whatever morning it had been when his daddy left to go on his trip. But there was a bright place up ahead, so he left his mother to go to it. It was the duck place. Ducks and a pool and lilypads. Mommy's voice became a faraway drone. Her beautiful face, so large, always there, so calm, so like the moon that sometimes looked in his window when he awoke late at night having to go peepee . . . that face became gray and lost definition. It melted into the gray mist. Her voice became the lazy sound of bees which were far too nice to sting, and lapping water.

Tad played with the ducks.

Donna dozed off, and when she woke up again all the shadows had blended with one another and the last of the light in the Camber driveway was the color of ashes. It was dusk. Somehow it had gotten around to dusk again and they were – unbelievably – still here. The sun sat on the horizon, round and scarlet-orange. It looked to her like a basketball that had been dipped in blood. She moved her tongue around in her mouth. Saliva that had clotted into a thick gum broke apart reluctantly and became more or less ordinary spit again. Her throat felt like a flannel. She thought how wonderful it would be to lie under the garden faucet at home, turn the spigot on full, open her mouth, and just let the icy water cascade in. The image was powerful enough to make her shiver and break out in a skitter of gooseflesh, powerful enough to make her head ache.

Was the dog still in front of the car?

She looked, but of course there was no real way of telling. All she could see for sure was that it wasn't in front of the barn.

She tapped the horn, but it only produced a rusty hoot and nothing changed. He could be anywhere. She ran her finger along the silver crack in her window and wondered what would happen if the dog hit the glass a few more times. Could it break through? She wouldn't have believed so twenty-four hours before, but now she wasn't so sure.

She looked at the door leading to Cambers' porch again. It seemed father away than it had before. That made her think of a concept they had discussed in a college psychology course. *Idée fixe*, the instructor, a prissy little man with a toothbrush mustache, had called it. *If you get on a down escalator that isn't moving, you'll suddenly find it very hard to walk.* That had amused her so much that she had eventually found a down escalator in Bloomingdale's that was marked OUT OF ORDER and had walked down it. She had found to her further amusement that the prissy little associate professor was right – your legs just didn't want to move. That had led her to try and imagine what would happen to your head if the stairs in your house suddenly started to move as you were walking down them. The very idea had made her laugh out loud.

But it wasn't so funny now. As a matter of fact, it wasn't funny at all.

That porch door definitely looked farther away.

The dog's psyching me out.

She tried to reject the thought as soon as it occurred to her, and then stopped trying. Things had become too desperate now to indulge in the luxury of lying to herself. Knowingly or unknowingly, Cujo was psyching her out. Using, perhaps, her own *idée fixe* of how the world was supposed to be. But things had changed. The smooth escalator ride was over. She could not just continue to stand on the still steps with her son and wait for somebody to start the motor again. The fact was, she and Tad were under siege by dog.

Tad was sleeping. If the dog was in the barn, she could make it now.

But if it's still in front of the car? Or under it?

She remembered something her father used to say sometimes when he was watching the pro football games on TV. Her dad almost always got tanked for these occasions, and usually ate a large plate of cold beans left over from Saturday-night supper. As a result, the TV room was uninhabitable for normal earth life by the fourth quarter; even the dog would slink out, an uneasy deserter's grin on its face.

This saying of her father's was reserved for particularly fine tackles and intercepted passes. 'He laid back in the tall bushes on that one!' her father would cry. It drove her mother crazy . . . but by the time Donna was a teenager, almost everything about her father drove her mother crazy.

She now had a vision of Cujo in front of the Pinto,

not sleeping at all but crouched on the gravel with his back legs coiled under him, his blood shot eyes fixed intently on the spot where she would first appear if she left the car on the driver's side. He was waiting for her, hoping she would be foolish enough to get out. He was laying back in the tall bushes for her.

She rubbed both hands over her face in a quick and nervous washing gesture. Overhead, Venus now peeked out of the darkening blue. The sun had made its exit, leaving a still but somehow crazed yellow light over the fields. Somewhere a bird sang, stopped, then sang again.

It came to her that she was nowhere near as anxious to leave the car and run for the door as she had been that afternoon. Part of it was having dozed off and then wakened not knowing exactly where the dog was. Part of it was the simple fact that the heat was drawing back – the tormenting heat and what it was doing to Tad had been the biggest thing goading her to make a move. It was quite comfortable in the car now, and Tad's half-lidded, half-swooning state had become a real sleep. He was resting comfortably, at least for the time being.

But she was afraid those things were secondary to the main reason she was still here – that, little by little, some psychological point of readiness had been reached and passed. She remembered from her childhood diving lessons at Camp Tapawingo that there came an instant, that first time on the high board, when you either had to try it or retreat ignominiously to let the girl behind you have her crack at it. There came a day during the learning-to-drive experience when you finally had to leave the empty country roads behind and try it in the city. There came a time. Always there came a time. A time to dive, a time to drive, a time to try for the back door.

Sooner or later the dog would show itself. The situation was bad, granted, but not yet desperate. The right time came around in cycles – that was not anything she had been taught in a psychology class; it was something she knew instinctively. If you chickened down from the high board on Monday, there was no law that said you couldn't go right back again on Tuesday. You could –

Reluctantly, her mind told her that was a deadly-false bit of reasoning.

She was not as strong tonight as she had been last night. She would be even weaker and more dehydrated tomorrow morning. And that was not the worst of it. She had been sitting almost all the time for – how long? – it didn't seem possible, but it was now some twenty-eight hours. What if she was too stiff to do it? What if she got halfway to the porch only to be doubled up and then dropped flopping to the ground by charley horses in the big muscles of her thighs?

In matters of life and death, her mind told her implacably, *the right time only comes around once – once and then it's gone.*

Her breathing and heart rate had speeded up. Her body was aware she was going to make the try before her mind was. Then she was wrapping her shirt more firmly about her right hand, her left hand was settling on the doorhandle, and she knew. There had been no conscious decision she was aware of; suddenly she was simply going. She was going now, while Tad slept deeply and there was no danger he would bolt out after her.

She pulled the doorhandle up, her hand sweat-slick.

She was holding her breath, listening for any change in the world.

The bird sang again. That was all.

If he's bashed the door too far out of shape it won't even open, she thought. That would be a kind of bitter relief. She could sit back then, rethink her options, see if there was anything she had left out of her calculations . . . and get a little thirstier . . . a little weaker . . . a little slower . . .

She brought pressure to bear against the door, slugging her left shoulder against it, gradually settling more and more of her weight upon it. Her right hand was sweating inside the cotton shirt. Her fist was so tightly clenched that the fingers ached. Dimly, she could feel the crescents of her nails biting into her palm. Over and over in her mind's eye she saw herself punching through the glass beside the knob of the porch door, heard the tinkle of the shards striking the boards inside, saw herself reaching for the handle . . .

But the car door wasn't opening. She shoved as hard as she could, straining, the cords in her neck standing out. But it wasn't opening. It —

Then it did open, all of a sudden. It swung wide with a terrible clunking sound, almost spilling her out on all fours. She grabbed for the doorhandle, missed, and grabbed again. She held the handle, and suddenly a panicky certainty stole into her mind. It was as cold and numbing as a doctor's verdict of inoperable cancer. She had gotten the door open, but it wouldn't close again. The dog was going to leap in and kill them both. Tad would have perhaps one confused moment of waking, one last merciful instant in which to believe it was a dream, before Cujo's teeth ripped his throat open.

Her breath rattled in and out, quick and quick. It felt like hot straw. It seemed that she could see each and every piece of gravel in the driveway, but it was hard to think. Her thoughts tumbled wildly. Scenes out of her past zipped through the foreground of her mind like a film of a parade which had been speeded up until the marching bands and horseback riders and baton twirlers seemed to be fleeing the scene of some weird crime.

The garbage disposal regurgitating a nasty green mess all over the kitchen ceiling, backing up through the bar sink.

Falling off the back porch when she was five and breaking her wrist.

Looking down at herself during period 2 – algebra – one day when she was a high school freshman and seeing to her utter shame and horror that there were spots of blood on her light blue linen skirt, she had started her period, how was she ever going to get up from her seat when the bell rang without everybody seeing, without everyone knowing that Donna-Rose was having her period?

The first boy she had ever kissed with her mouth open. Dwight Sampson.

Holding Tad in her arms, newborn, then the nurse taking him away; she wanted to tell the nurse not to do that – *Give him back, I'm not done with him*, those were the words that had come to mind – but she was too weak to talk and then the horrible, squelching, gutty sound of the afterbirth coming out of her; she remembered thinking *I'm puking up his life-support systems*, and then she had passed out.

Her father, crying at her wedding and then getting drunk at the reception.

Faces. Voices. Rooms. Scenes. Books. The terror of this moment, thinking *I AM GOING TO DIE* –

With a tremendous effort, she got herself under some kind of control. She got the Pinto's doorhandle in both hands and gave it a tremendous yank. The door flew shut. There was that clunk again as the hinge Cujo had knocked out of true protested. There was a hefty bang when the door slammed closed that made Tad jump and then mutter a bit in his sleep.

Donna leaned back in the seat, shaking helplessly all over, and cried silently. Hot tears slipped out from under her lids and ran back on a slant toward her ears. She had never in her life been so afraid of anything, not even in her room at night when she was little and it had seemed to her that there were spiders everywhere. She couldn't go now, she assured herself. It was unthinkable. She was totally done up. Her nerves were shot. Better to wait, wait for a better chance . . .

But she didn't dare let that *idée* become *fixe*.

There wasn't going to be a better chance than this one. Tad was out of it, and the dog was out of it too. It had to be true; all logic declared it to be true. That first loud clunk, then another one when she pulled the door to, and the slam of the door actually shutting again. It would have brought him on the run if he had been in front of the car. He might be in the barn, but she believed he would have heard the noise in there, as well. He had almost surely gone wandering off somewhere. There was never going to be a better chance than right now, and if she was too scared to do it for herself, she musn't be too scared to do it for Tad.

All suitably noble. But what finally persuaded her was a vision of letting herself into the Cambers' darkened house, the reassuring feel of the telephone in her hand. She could hear herself talking to one of Sheriff Bannerman's deputies, quite calmly and rationally, and then putting the phone down. Then going into the kitchen for a cold glass of water.

She opened the door again, prepared for the clunking sound this time but still wincing when it came. She cursed the dog in her heart, hoping it was already lying someplace dead of a convulsion, and fly-blown.

She swung her legs out, wincing at the stiffness and the pain. She put her tennis shoes on the gravel. And little by little she stood up under the darkling sky.

The bird sang somewhere nearby: it sang three notes and was still.

Cujo heard the door open again, as instinct had told him it would. The first time it opened he had almost come around from the front of the car where he had been lying in a semi-stupor. He had almost come around to get THE WOMAN who had caused this dreadful pain in his head and in his body. He had almost come around, but that instinct had commanded him to lie still instead. THE WOMAN was only trying to draw him out, the instinct counseled, and this had proved to be true.

As the sickness had tightened down on him, sinking into his nervous system like a ravenous grassfire, all dove-gray smoke and low rose-colored flame, as it continued to go about its work of destroying his established patterns of thought and behaviour, it had somehow deepened his cunning. He was sure to get THE WOMAN and THE BOY.

They had caused his pain – both the agony in his body and the terrible hurt in his head which had come from leaping against the car again and again.

Twice today he had forgotten about THE WOMAN and THE BOY, leaving the barn by the dog bolthole that Joe Camber had cut in the door of the back room where he kept his accounts. He had gone down to the marsh at the back of the Camber property, both times passing quite close to the overgrown entrance to the limestone cave where the bats roosted. There was water in the marsh and he was horribly thirsty, but the actual sight of the water had driven him into a frenzy both times. He wanted to drink the water; kill the water; bathe in the water; piss and shit in the water; cover it over with dirt; savage it; make it bleed. Both times this terrible confusion of feelings had driven him away, whining and trembling. THE WOMAN and THE BOY had made all this happen. And he would leave them no more. No human who had ever lived would have found a dog more faithful or more set in his purpose. He would wait until he could get at them. If necessary he would wait until the world ended. He would wait. He would stand a watch.

It was THE WOMAN most of all. The way she looked at him, as if to say, *Yes, yes, I did it, I made you sick, I made you hurt, I devised this agony just for you and it will be with you always now.*

Oh kill her, kill her!

A sound came. It was a soft sound, but it did not escape Cujo; his ears were preternaturally attuned to all sounds now. The entire spectrum of the aural world was his. He heard the chimes of heaven and the hoarse screams which uprose from hell. In his madness he heard the real and the unreal.

It was the soft sound of small stones slipping and grinding against each other.

Cujo screwed his hindquarters down against the ground and waited for her. Urine, warm and painful, ran out of him unheeded. He waited for THE WOMAN to show herself. When she did, he would kill her.

In the downstairs wreckage of the Trenton house, the telephone began to ring.

It burred six times, eight times, ten. Then it was silent. Shortly after, the Trentons' copy of the Castle Rock *Call* thumped against the front door and Billy Freeman pedaled on up the street on his Raleigh with his canvas sack over his shoulder, whistling.

In Tad's room, the closet door stood open, and an unspeakable dry smell, lionlike and savage, hung in the air.

In Boston, an operator asked Vic Trenton if he would like her to keep trying. 'No, that's okay, operator,' he said, and hung up.

Roger had found the Red Sox playing Kansas City on Channel 38 and was sitting on the sofa in his skivvies with a room-service sandwich and a glass of milk, watching the warm-ups.

'Of all your habits,' Vic said, 'most of which range from the actively offensive to the mildly disgusting, I think that eating in your underpants is probably the worst.'

'Listen to this guy,' Roger said mildly to the empty

room at large. 'He's thirty-two years old and he still calls underwear shorts underpants.'

'What's wrong with that?'

'Nothing . . . if you're still one of the Owl Tent at summer camp.'

'I'm going to cut your throat tonight, Rog,' Vic said, smiling happily. 'You'll wake up strangling in your own blood. You'll be sorry, but it will be . . . *too late!*' He picked up half of Roger's hot pastrami sandwich and wounded it grievously.

'That's pretty fucking unsanitary,' Roger said, brushing crumbs from his bare, hairy chest. 'Donna wasn't home, huh?'

'Uh-uh. She and Tad probably went down to the Tastee Freeze to catch a couple of burgers or something. I wish to God I was there instead of Boston.'

'Oh, just think,' Roger said, grinning maliciously, 'we'll be in the Apple tomorrow night. Having cocktails under the clock at the Biltmore . . .'

'Fuck the Biltmore and fuck the clock,' Vic said. 'Anyone who spends a week away from Maine on business in Boston and New York – and during the summertime – has got to be crazy.'

'Yeah, I'll buy that,' Roger said. On the TV screen, Bob Stanley popped a good curve over the outside corner to start the game. 'It is rawtha shitteh.'

'That's a pretty good sandwich, Roger,' Vic said, smiling winningly at his partner.

Roger grabbed up the plate and held it to his chest. 'Call down for your own, you damn mooch.'

'What's the number?'

'Six-eight-one, I think. It's on the dial there.'

'Don't you want some beer with that?' Vic asked, going to the phone again.

Roger shook his head. 'I had too much at lunch. My head's bad, my stomach's bad, and by tomorrow morning I'll probably have the Hershey-squirts. I'm rapidly discovering the truth, goodbuddy. I'm no kid any more.'

Vic called down for a hot pastrami on rye and two bottles of Tuborg. When he hung up and looked back at Roger, Roger was sitting with his eyes fixed on the TV. His sandwich plate was balanced on his considerable belly and he was crying. At first Vic thought he hadn't seen right; it was some sort of optical illusion. But no, those were tears. The color TV reflected off them in prisms of light.

For a moment Vic stood there, unable to decide if he should go over to Roger or go over the other side of the room and pick up the newspaper, pretending he hadn't seen. Then Roger looked over at him, his face working and utterly naked, as defenseless and as vulnerable as Tad's face when he fell off the swing and scraped his knees or took a tumble on the sidewalk.

'What am I going to do, Vic?' he asked hoarsely.

'Rog, what are you talk—'

'You know what I'm talking about,' he said. The crowd at Fenway cheered as Boston turned a double play to end the top of the first.

'Take it easy, Roger. You—'

'This is going to fall through and we both know it,' Roger said. 'It smells as bad as a carton of eggs that's been sitting all week in the sun. This is some nice little game we're playing. We've got Rob Martin on our side. We've got that refugee from the Home for Old Actors on our side. Undoubtedly we'll have Summers Marketing & Research on our side, since they bill us. How wonderful. We've got everybody on our side but the people who matter.'

'Nothing's decided, Rog. Not yet.'

'Althea doesn't really understand how much is at stake,' Roger said. 'My fault; okay, so I'm a chicken, cluck-cluck. But she loves it in Bridgton, Vic. She *loves* it there. And the girls, they've got their school friends . . . and the lake in the summer . . . they don't know what the fuck's coming down *at all*.'

'Yeah, it's scary. I'm not trying to talk you out of that, Rog.'

'Does Donna know how bad it is?'

'I think she just thought it was an awfully good joke on us at first. But she's getting the drift of it now.'

'But she never took to Maine the way the rest of us did.'

'Not at first, maybe. I think she'd raise her hands in horror at the idea of taking Tad back to New York now.'

'What am I going to do?' Roger asked again. 'I'm no kid any more. You're thirty-two, but Vic, I'm going to be forty-one next month. What am I supposed to do? Start taking my résumé around? Is J. Walter Thompson going to welcome me in with open arms? "Hi, Rog-baby, I've been holding your old spot for you. You start at thirty-five-five." Is that what he's going to say?'

Vic only shook his head, but a part of him was a little irritated with Roger.

'I used to be just mad. Well, I'm still mad, but now

I'm more scared than anything else. I lie in bed at night and try to imagine how it's going to be – after. *What* it's going to be. I can't imagine it. You look at me and you say to yourself, "Roger's dramatizing." You—'

'I never thought any such thing,' Vic said, hoping he didn't sound guilty.

'I won't say you're lying,' Roger said, 'but I've been working with you long enough to have a pretty good idea of how you think. Better than you might know. Anyway I wouldn't blame you for the thought – but there's a big difference between thirty-two and forty-one, Vic. They kick a lot of the guts out of you in between thirty-two and forty-one.'

'Look, I still think we've got a fighting chance with this proposal—'

'What I'd like to do is bring about two dozen boxes of Red Razberry Zingers along with us to Cleveland,' Roger said, 'and then get them to bend over after they tie the can to our tails. I'd have a place for all that cereal, you know it?'

Vic clapped Roger on the shoulder. 'Yeah, I get you.'

'What *are* you going to do if they pull the account?' Roger asked.

Vic had thought about that. He had been around it from every possible angle. It would have been fair to say that he had gotten to the problem quite a while before Roger had been able to make himself approach it.

'If they pull out, I'm going to work harder than I ever have in my life,' Vic said. 'Thirty hours a day, if I have to. If I have to rope in sixty small New England accounts to make up for what Sharp billed, then I'll do it.'

'We'll kill ourselves for nothing.'

'Maybe,' Vic said. 'But we'll go down with all guns firing. Right?'

'I figure,' Roger said unsteadily, 'that if Althea goes to work, we can hold on to the house for about a year. That ought to be just about enough time to sell it, the way interest rates are.'

Suddenly Vic felt it trembling right behind his lips: the whole shitty black mess that Donna had managed to get herself into because of her need to keep pretending that she was still nineteen-going-on-twenty. He felt a certain dull anger at Roger, Roger who had been happily and unquestioningly married for fifteen years, Roger who had pretty, unassuming Althea to warm his bed (if Althea Breakstone had so much as contemplated infidelity, Vic would have been surprised), Roger who had absolutely no idea of how many things could go wrong at once.

'Listen,' he said. 'Thursday I got a note in the late mail—'

There was a sharp rap on the door.

'That'll be room service,' Roger said. He picked up his shirt and wiped his face with it . . . and with the tears gone, it was suddenly unthinkable to Vic that he should tell Roger. Maybe because Roger was right after all, and the one big difference was the nine years lying between thirty-two and forty-one.

Vic went to the door and got his beers and his sandwich. He didn't finish what he had been about to say when the room-service waiter knocked, and Roger didn't ask him. He was back in the ballgame and his own problems.

Vic sat down to eat his sandwich, not entirely surprised

to find that most of his appetite was gone. His eyes fell on the telephone, and, still munching, he tried home again. He let it ring a dozen times before hanging up. He was frowning slightly. It was five past eight, five minutes past Tad's usual bedtime. Perhaps Donna had met someone, or maybe they had gotten feeling dragged down by the empty house and gone visiting. After all, there was no law that said the Tadder had to be in bed on the stroke of eight, especially when it stayed light so late and it was so damned hot. Sure, that was likely. They had maybe gone down to the Common to goof around until it got cool enough to make sleep possible. Right.

(or maybe she's with Kemp)

That was crazy. She had said it was over and he believed it. He really did believe it. Donna didn't lie.

(and she doesn't play around, either, right, champ?)

He tried to dismiss it, but it was no good. The rat was loose and it was going to be busy gnawing at him for some time now. What would she have done with Tad if she had suddenly taken it into her head to go off with Kemp? Were the three of them maybe in some motel right now, some motel between Castle Rock and Baltimore? Don't be a chump, Trenton. They might –

The band concert, that was it, of course. There was a concert at the Common bandstand every Tuesday night. Some Tuesdays the high school band played, sometimes a chamber music group, sometimes a local ragtime group that called themselves the Ragged Edge. That's where they were, of course – enjoying the cool and listening to the Ragged Edge belt their way through John Hurt's 'Candy Man' or maybe 'Beulah Land'.

(unless she's with Kemp)
He drained his beer and started on another.

Donna just stood outside the car for thirty seconds, moving her feet slightly on the gravel to get the pins and needles out of her legs. She watched the front of the garage, still feeling that if Cujo came, he would come from that way – maybe out of the mouth of the barn, maybe from around one of the sides, or perhaps from behind the farm truck, which looked rather canine itself by starlight – a big dusty black mongrel that was fast asleep.

She stood there, not quite ready to commit herself to it yet. The night breathed at her, small fragrances that reminded her of how it had been to be small, and to smell these fragrances in all their intensity almost as a matter of routine. Clover and hay from the house at the bottom of the hill, the sweet smell of honeysuckle.

And she heard something: music. It was very faint, almost not there, but her ears, almost eerily attuned to the night now, picked it up. *Someone's radio*, she thought at first, and then realized with a dawning wonder that it was the band concert on the Common. That was Dixieland jazz she was hearing. She could even identify the tune; it was 'Shuffle Off to Buffalo.' *Seven miles*, she thought. *I never would have believed it – how still the night must be! How calm!*

She felt very alive.

Her heart was a small, powerful machine flexing in her chest. Her blood was up. Her eyes seemed to move effortlessly and perfectly in their bed of moisture. Her kidneys were heavy but not unpleasantly so. This was it; this was for keeps. The thought that it was her *life* she was putting on the line, her very own *real life*, had a heavy, silent fascination, like a great weight which has reached the outermost degree of its angle of repose. She swung the car door shut – *clunk*.

She waited, scenting the air like an animal. There was nothing. The maw of Joe Camber's barn-garage was dark and silent. The chrome of the Pinto's front bumper twinkled dimly. Faintly, the Dixieland music played on, fast and brassy and cheerful. She bent down, expecting her knees to pop, but they didn't. She picked up a handful of the loose gravel. One by one she began to toss the stones over the Pinto's hood at the place she couldn't see.

The first small stone landed in front of Cujo's nose, clicked off more stones, and then lay still. Cujo twitched a little. His tongue hung out. He seemed to be grinning. The second stone struck beyond him. The third struck his shoulder. He didn't move. THE WOMAN was still trying to draw him out.

Donna stood by the car, frowning. She had heard the first stone click off the gravel, also the second. But the third . . . it was as if it had never come down. There had been no minor click. What did that mean?

Suddenly she didn't want to run for the porch door until she could see that there was nothing lurking in front of the car. Then, yes. Okay. But . . . just to make sure.

She took one step. Two. Three.

Cujo got ready. His eyes glowed in the darkness.

★   ★   ★

Four steps from the door of the car. Her heart was a drum in her chest.

Now Cujo could see THE WOMAN'S hip and thigh. In a moment she would see him. Good. He wanted her to see him.

Five steps from the door.

Donna turned her head. Her neck creaked like the spring on an old screen door. She felt a premonition, a sense of low sureness. She turned her head, looking for Cujo. Cujo was there. He had been there all the time, crouched low, hiding from her, waiting for her, laying back in the tall bushes.

Their eyes locked for a moment – Donna's wide blue ones, Cujo's muddy red ones. For a moment she was looking out of his eyes, seeing herself, seeing THE WOMAN – was he seeing himself through hers?

Then he sprang at her.

There was no paralysis this time. She threw herself backward, fumbling behind her for the doorhandle. He was snarling and grinning, and the drool ran out between his teeth in thick strings. He landed where she had been and skidded stiff-legged in the gravel, giving her a precious extra second.

Her thumb found the door button below the handle and depressed it. She pulled. The door was stuck. The door wouldn't open. Cujo leaped at her.

It was as if someone had slung a medicine ball right into the soft, vulnerable flesh of her breasts. She could feel them push out toward her ribs – it *hurt* – and then she had the dog by the throat, her fingers sinking into its heavy, rough fur, trying to hold it away from her. She could hear the quickening sob of her respiration. Starlight ran across Cujo's mad eyes in dull semicircles. His teeth were snapping only inches from her face and she could smell a dead world on his breath, terminal sickness, senseless murder. She thought crazily of the drain backing up just before her mother's party, spurting green goo all over the ceiling.

Somehow, using all her strength, she was able to fling him away when his back feet left the ground in another lunge at her throat. She beat helplessly behind her for the door button. She found it, but before she could even push it in, Cujo came again. She kicked out at him, and the sole of her sandal struck his muzzle, already badly lacerated in his earlier kamikaze charges at the door. The dog sprawled back on his haunches, howling out his pain and his fury.

She found the button set in the doorhandle again, knowing perfectly well that it was her last chance, Tad's last chance. She pushed it in and pulled with all her might as the dog came again, some creature from hell that would come and come and come until she was dead or it was. It was the wrong angle for her arm; her muscles were working at cross-purposes, and she felt an agonizing flare of pain in her back above her right shoulderblade as something sprained. But the door opened. She had just time to fall back into the bucket seat, and then the dog was on her again.

Tad woke up. He saw his mother being driven back toward the Pinto's center console; there was something in his mother's lap, some terrible, hairy thing with red eyes

315

and he knew what it was, oh yes, it was the thing from his closet, the thing that had promised to come a little closer and a little closer until it finally arrived *right by your bed, Tad*, and yes, here it was, all right, here it was. The Monster Words had failed; the monster was here, now, and it was murdering his mommy. He began to scream, his hands clapped over his eyes.

Its snapping jaws were inches from the bare flesh of her midriff. She held it off as best she could, only faintly aware of her son's screams behind her. Cujo's eyes were locked on her. Incredibly, his tail was wagging. His back legs worked at the gravel, trying to get a footing solid enough to allow him to jump right in, but the gravel kept splurting out from under his driving rear paws.

He lunged forward, her hands slipped, and suddenly he was *biting* her, biting her bare stomach just below the white cotton cups of her bra, digging for her entrails —

Donna uttered a low, feral cry of pain and shoved with both hands as hard as she could. Now she was sitting up again, blood trickling down to the waistband of her pants. She held Cujo with her left hand. Her right hand groped for the Pinto's doorhandle and found it. She began to slam the door against the dog. Each time she swept it forward into Cujo's ribs, there was a heavy *whopping* sound, like a heavy rug beater striking a carpet hung over a clothesline. Each time the door hit him, Cujo would grunt, snorting his warm, foggy breath over her.

He drew back a little to spring. She timed it and brought the door toward her again, using all of her failing strength. This time the door closed on his neck and head, and she heard a crunching sound. Cujo howled his pain

CUJO

and she thought, *He must draw back now, he must, he MUST,* but Cujo drove forward instead and his jaws closed on her lower thigh, just above her knee, and with one quick ripping motion he pulled a chunk out of her. Donna shrieked.

She slammed the door on Cujo's head again and again, her screams melting into Tad's, melting into a gray shockworld as Cujo worked on her leg, turning it into something else, something that was red and muddy and churned up. The dog's head was plastered with thick, sticky blood, as black as insect blood in the chancey starlight. Little by little he was forcing his way in again; her strength was on the ebb now.

She pulled the door to one final time, her head thrown back, her mouth drawn open in a quivering circle, her face a livid, moving blur in the darkness. It really was the last time; there was just no more left.

But suddenly Cujo had had enough.

He drew back, whining, staggered away, and suddenly fell over on the gravel, trembling, legs scratching weakly at nothing. He began to dig at his wounded head with his right forepaw.

Donna slammed the door shut and lay back, sobbing weakly.

'Mommy – Mommy – Mommy –'

'Tad . . . okay . . .'

'Mommy!'

'. . . Okay . . .'

Hands: his on her, fluttering and birdlike; hers on Tad's face, touching, trying to reassure, then falling back.

'Mommy . . . home . . . please . . . Daddy and home . . . Daddy and home . . .'

317

'Sure, Tad we will . . . we will, honest to God, I'll get you there . . . we will . . .'

No sense in the words. It was all right. She could feel herself fading back, fading into that gray shockworld, those mists in herself which she had never suspected until now. Tad's words took on a deep chaining sound, words in an echo chamber. But it was all right. It was –

No. It wasn't all right.

Because the dog had bitten her –

– and the dog was rabid.

Holly told her sister not to be foolish, to just dial her call direct, but Charity insisted on calling the operator and having it billed to her home number. Taking handouts, even a little thing like an after-six long-distance call, wasn't her way.

The operator got her directory assistance for Maine and Charity asked for Alva Thornton's number in Castle Rock. A few moments later, Alva's phone was ringing.

'Hello, Thornton's Egg Farms.'

'Hi, Bessie?'

'Ayuh, 'tis.'

'This is Charity Camber. I'm calling from Connecticut. Is Alva right around handy?'

Brett sat on the sofa, pretending to read a book.

'Gee, Charity, he ain't. He's got his bowling league t'night. They're all over to the Pondicherry Lanes in Bridgton. Somethin wrong?'

Charity had carefully and consciously decided what she was going to say. The situation was a bit delicate. Like almost every other married woman in Castle Rock (and that was not to necessarily let out the single ones), Bessie loved to talk, and if she found out that Joe Camber had gone shooting off somewhere without his wife's knowledge as soon as Charity and Brett had left to visit her sister in Connecticut . . . why, that would be something to talk about on the party line, wouldn't it?

'No, except that Brett and I got a little worried about the dog.'

'Your Saint Bernard?'

'Ayuh, Cujo. Brett and I are down here visiting my sister while Joe's in Portsmouth on business.' This was a barefaced lie, but a safe one; Joe did occasionally go to Portsmouth to buy parts (there was no sales tax) and to the car auctions. 'I just wanted to make sure he got someone to feed the dog. You know how men are.'

'Well, Joe was over here yesterday or the day before, I think,' Bessie said doubtfully. Actually, it had been the previous Thursday. Bessie Thornton was not a terribly bright woman (her great-aunt, the late Evvie Chalmers, had been fond of screaming to anyone who would listen that Bessie 'wouldn't never pass none of those IQ tests, but she's good-hearted'), her life on Alva's chicken farm was a hard one, and she lived most fully during her 'stories' – *As the World Turns, The Doctors*, and *All My Children* (she had tried *The Young and the Restless* but considered it 'too racy by half'). She tended to be fuzzy on those parts of the real world that did not bear on feeding and watering the chickens, adjusting their piped-in music, candling and sorting eggs, washing floors and clothes, doing dishes, selling eggs, tending the garden. And in the winter, of course, she could have told a questioner the exact date of the next meeting of the Castle Rock SnoDevils, the snowmobile club she and Alva belonged to.

Joe had come over on that day with a tractor tire he had repaired for Alva. Joe had done the job free of charge since the Cambers got all their eggs from the Thorntons at half price. Alva also harrowed Joe's small patch of garden each April, and so Joe was glad to patch the tire. It was the way country people got along.

Charity knew perfectly well that Joe had gone over to the Thorntons' with the repaired tire the previous Thursday. She also knew that Bessie was apt to get her days mixed up. All of which left her in a pretty dilemma. She could ask Bessie if Joe had had a tractor tire with him when he came up 'yesterday or the day before,' and if Bessie said why yes, now that you mention it, he did, that would mean that Joe hadn't been up to see Alva since last Thursday, which would mean that Joe hadn't asked Alva to feed Cujo, which would *also* mean that Alva wouldn't have any information about Cujo's health and well-being.

Or she could just leave well enough alone and ease Brett's mind. They could enjoy the rest of their visit without thoughts of home intruding constantly. And . . . well, she was a little jealous of Cujo right about now. Tell the truth and shame the devil. Cujo was distracting Brett's attention from what could be the most important trip he ever took. She wanted the boy to see a whole new life, a whole new set of *possibilities*, so that when the time came, a few years from now, for him to decide which doors he wanted to step through and which ones he would allow to swing closed, he could make those decisions with a bit of perspective. Perhaps she had been wrong to believe she could steer him, but let him at least have enough experience to make up his mind for himself.

Was it fair to let his worries about the damned dog stand in the way of that?

'Charity? You there? I said I thought—'

'Ayuh, I heard you, Bessie. He probably did ask Alva to feed him, then.'

'Well, I'll ask him when he gets home, Charity. And I'll let you know, too.'

'You do that. Thanks ever so much, Bessie.'

'Don't even mention it.'

'Fine. Good-bye.' And Charity hung up, realizing that Bessie had forgotten to ask for Jim and Holly's phone number. Which was fine. She turned toward Brett, composing her face. She would say nothing that was a lie. She would not lie to her son.

'Bessie said your dad was over to see Alva Sunday night,' Charity said. 'Must have asked him to take care of Cujo then.'

'Oh.' Brett was looking at her in a speculative way that made her a little uneasy. 'But you didn't talk to Alva himself.'

'No, he was out bowling. But Bessie said she'd let us know if—'

'She doesn't have our number down here.' Was Brett's tone now faintly accusatory? Or was that her own conscience talking?

'Well, I'll call her back in the morning, then,' Charity said, hoping to close the conversation and applying some salve to her conscience at the same time.

'Daddy took a tractor tire over last week,' Brett said

thoughtfully. 'Maybe Mrs Thornton got mixed up on which day Daddy was there.'

'I think Bessie Thornton can keep her days straighter in her head than that,' Charity said, not thinking so at all. 'Besides, she didn't mention anything to me about a tractor tire.'

'Yeah, but you didn't ask her.'

'Go ahead and call her back, then!' Charity flashed at him. A sudden helpless fury swept her, the same ugly feeling that had come when Brett had offered his wickedly exact observation about Holly and her deck of credit cards. When he had done that his father's intonation, even his father's pattern of speech, had crept into his voice, and it had seemed to her, then and now, that the only thing this trip was doing was to show her once and for all who Brett really belonged to – lock, stock, and barrel.

'Mom—'

'No, go ahead, call her back, the number's right here on the scratchpad. Just tell the operator to charge it to our phone so it won't go on Holly's bill. Ask Bessie all your questions. I only did the best I could.'

There, she thought with sad and bitter amusement. *Just five minutes ago I wasn't going to lie to him.*

That afternoon her anger had sparked anger in him. Tonight he only said quietly, 'Naw, that's okay.'

'If you want, we'll call somebody else and have them go up and check,' Charity said. She was already sorry for her outburst.

'Who would we call?' Brett asked.

'Well, what about one of the Milliken brothers?'

Brett only looked at her.

'Maybe that's not such a good idea,' Charity agreed. Late last winter, Joe Camber and John Milliken had had a bitter argument over the charge on some repair work Joe had done on the Milliken brothers' old Chevy Bel Air. Since then, the Cambers and the Millikens hadn't been talking much. The last time Charity had gone to play Beano down at the Grange, she had tried to pass a friendly word with Kim Milliken, Freddy's daughter, but Kim wouldn't say a word to her; just walked away with her head up as if she hadn't been acting the slut with half the boys in Castle Rock High School.

It occurred to her now how really isolated they were, up at the end of Town Road No.3. It made her feel lonely and a little chilled. She could think of no one she could reasonably ask to go up to their place with a flashlight and hunt up Cujo and make sure he was okay.

'Never mind,' Brett said listlessly. 'Probably stupid, anyway. He probably just ate some burdocks or something.'

'Listen,' Charity said, putting an arm around him. 'One thing you aren't is stupid, Brett. I'll call Alva himself in the morning and ask him to go up. I'll do it as soon as we get up. Okay?'

'Would you, Mom?'

'Yes.'

'That'd be great. I'm sorry to bug you about it, but I can't seem to get it off my mind.'

Jim popped his head in. 'I got out the Scrabble board. Anyone want to play?'

'I will,' Brett said, getting up, 'if you show me how.'

'What about you, Charity?'

Charity smiled. 'Not just now, I guess. I'll be in for some of the popcorn.'

Brett went out with his uncle. She sat on the sofa and looked at the telephone and thought of Brett night-walking, feeding a phantom dog phantom dogfood in her sister's modern kitchen.

Cujo's not hungry no more, not no more.

Her arms suddenly tightened, and she shivered. We're going to take care of this business tomorrow morning, she promised herself. One way or the other. Either that or go back and take care of it ourselves. That's a promise, Brett.

Vic tried home again at ten o'clock. There was no answer. He tried again at eleven o'clock and there was still no answer, although he let the phone ring two dozen times. At ten he was beginning to get scared. At eleven he was good and scared – of what, he was not precisely sure.

Roger was sleeping. Vic dialed the number in the dark, listened to it ring in the dark, hung up in the dark. He felt alone, childlike, lost. He didn't know what to do or what to think. Over and over his mind played a simple litany: *She's gone off with Kemp, gone off with Kemp, gone off with Kemp.*

All reason and logic was against it. He played over everything he and Donna had said to each other – he played it over again and again, listening to the words and to the nuances of tone in his mind. She and Kemp had had a falling out. She had told him to go peddle his papers somewhere else. And that had prompted Kemp's vengeful little *billet doux*. It did not seem the rosy scenery into which two mad lovers might decide to elope.

A falling out doesn't preclude a later rapprochement, his mind retorted with a kind of grave and implacable calm.

But what about Tad? She wouldn't have taken Tad with her, would she? From her description, Kemp sounded like some sort of wildman, and although Donna hadn't said so, Vic had gotten the feeling that something damned violent had almost happened on the day she told him to fuck off.

People in love do strange things.

That strange and jealous part of his mind – he hadn't even been aware of that part in him until that afternoon in Deering Oaks – had an answer for everything, and in the dark it didn't seem to matter that most of the answers were irrational.

He was doing a slow dance back and forth between two sharpened points: Kemp on one (DO YOU HAVE ANY QUESTIONS?); a vision of the telephone ringing on and on in their empty Castle Rock house on the other. She could have had an accident. She and Tad could be in hospital. Someone could have broken in. They could be lying murdered in their bedrooms. Of course if she'd had an accident, someone official would have been in touch – the office as well as Donna knew in which Boston hotel he and Roger were staying – but in the dark that thought, which should have been a comfort since no one *had* been in touch, only inclined his thoughts more toward murder.

Robbery and murder, his mind whispered as he lay awake in the dark. Then it danced slowly across to the other sharpened point and took up its original litany: *Gone off with Kemp*.

In between these points, his mind saw a more reasonable explanation, one that made him feel helplessly angry.

Perhaps she and Tad had decided to spend the night with someone and had simply forgotten to call and tell him. Now it was too late to just start calling around and asking people without alarming them. He supposed he could call the sheriff's office and ask them to send someone up and check. But wouldn't that be overreacting?

No, his mind said.

Yes, his mind said, *definitely*.

She and Tad are both dead with knives stuck in their throats, his mind said. *You read about it in the papers all the time. It even happened in Castle Rock just before we came to town. That crazy cop. That Frank Dodd.*

Gone off with Kemp, his mind said.

At midnight he tried again, and this time the constant ringing of the phone with no one to pick it up froze him into a deadly certainty of trouble. Kemp, robbers, murderers, something. Trouble. Trouble at home.

He dropped the phone back into its cradle and turned on the bed lamp. 'Roger,' he said. 'Wake up.'

'Huh. Wuh. Hzzzzzz . . .' Roger had his arm over his eyes, trying to block out the light. He was in his pajamas with the little yellow college pennants.

'Roger. Roger!'

Roger opened his eyes, blinked, looked at the Travel-Ette clock.

'Hey, Vic, it's the middle of the night.'

'Roger . . .' He swallowed and something clicked in his throat. 'Roger, it's midnight and Tad and Donna still aren't home. I'm scared.'

Roger sat up and brought the clock close to his face to verify what Vic had said. It was now four past the hour.

326

'Well, they probably got freaked out staying there by themselves, Vic. Sometimes Althea takes the girls and goes over to Sally Petrie's when I'm gone. She gets nervous when the wind blows off the lake at night, she says.'

'She would have called.' With the light on, with Roger sitting up and talking to him, the idea that Donna might have just run off with Steve Kemp seemed absurd – he couldn't believe he had even indulged it. Forget logic. She had told him it was over, and he had believed her. He believed her now.

'Called?' Roger said. He was still having trouble tracking things.

'She knows I call home almost every night when I'm away. She would have called the hotel and left a message if she was going to be gone overnight. Wouldn't Althea?'

Roger nodded. 'Yeah. She would.'

'She'd call and leave a message so you wouldn't worry. Like I'm worrying now.'

'Yeah. But she might have just forgotten, Vic.' Still, Roger's brown eyes were troubled.

'Sure,' Vic said. 'On the other hand, maybe something's happened.'

'She carries ID, doesn't she? If she and Tad were in an accident, God forbid, the cops would try home first and then the office. The answering service would—'

'I wasn't thinking about an accident,' Vic said. 'I was thinking about . . .' His voice began to tremble. 'I was thinking about her and Tadder being there alone, and . . . shit, I don't know . . . I just got scared, that's all.'

'Call the sheriff's office,' Roger said promptly.

'Yeah, but—'

'Yeah, but nothing. You aren't going to scare Donna, that's for sure. She's not there. But what the hell, set your mind at rest. It doesn't have to be sirens and flashing lights. Just ask if they can send a cop by to check and make sure that everything looks normal. There must be a thousand places she could be. Hell, maybe she just tied into a really good Tupperware party.'

'Donna hates Tupperware parties.'

'So maybe the girls got playing penny-ante poker and lost track of the time and Tad's asleep in someone's spare room.'

Vic remembered her telling him how she had steered clear of any deep involvement with 'the girls' – *I don't want to be one of those faces you see at the bake sales*, she had said. But he didn't want to tell Roger that; it was too close to the subject of Kemp.

'Yeah, maybe something like that,' Vic said.

'Have you got an extra key to the place tucked away somewhere?'

'There's one on a hook under the eave of the front porch.'

'Tell the cops. Someone can go in and have a good look around . . . unless you've got pot or coke or something you'd just as soon they didn't stumble over.'

'Nothing like that.'

'Then do it,' Roger said earnestly. 'She'll probably call here while they're out checking and you'll feel like a fool, but sometimes it's *good* to feel like a fool. You know what I mean?'

'Yeah,' Vic said, grinning a little. 'Yeah, I do.'

He picked the telephone up again, hesitated, then

tried home again first. No answer. Some of the comfort he had gotten from Roger evaporated. He got directory assistance for Maine and jotted down the number of the Castle County Sheriff's Department. It was now nearly fifteen minutes past twelve on Wednesday morning.

Donna Trenton was sitting with her hands resting lightly on the steering wheel of the Pinto. Tad had finally fallen asleep again, but his sleep was not restful; he twisted, turned, sometimes moaned. She was afraid he was reliving in his dreams what had happened earlier.

She felt his forehead; he muttered something and pulled away from her touch. His eyelids fluttered and then slipped closed again. He felt feverish – almost surely a result of the constant tension and fear. She felt feverish herself, and she was in severe pain. Her belly hurt, but those wounds were superficial, little more than scratches. She had been lucky there. Cujo had damaged her left leg more. The wounds there (the *bites*, her mind insisted, as if relishing the horror of it) were deep and ugly. They had bled a lot before clotting, and she hadn't tried to apply a bandage right away, although there was a first-aid kit in the Pinto's glovebox. Vaguely she supposed she had hoped that the flowing blood would wash the wound clean . . . did that really happen, or was it just an old wives' tale? She didn't know. There was so much she didn't know, so goddam much.

By the time the lacerated punctures had finally clotted, her thigh and the driver's bucket seat were both tacky with her blood. She needed three gauze pads from the first-aid kit to cover the wound. They were the last three in the kit. *Have to replace those*, she thought, and that brought on a short, hysterical fit of the giggles.

In the faint light, the flesh just above her knee had looked like dark plowed earth. There was a steady throbbing ache there that had not changed since the dog bit her. She had dry-swallowed a couple of aspirin from the kit, but they didn't make a dent in the pain. Her head ached badly too, as if a bundle of wires were slowly being twisted tighter and tighter inside each temple.

Flexing the leg brought the quality of the pain up from a throbbing ache to a sharp, glassy beat. She had no idea if she could even walk on the leg now, let alone run for the porch door. And did it really matter? The dog was sitting on the gravel between her car door and the door which gave on the porch, its hideously mangled head drooping . . . but with its eyes fixed unfailingly on the car. On *her*.

Somehow she didn't think Cujo was going to move again, at least not tonight. Tomorrow the sun might drive him into the barn, if it was as hot as it had been yesterday.

'It wants me,' she whispered through her blistered lips. It was true. Somehow it was true. For reasons decreed by Fate, or for its own unknowable ones, the dog wanted her.

When it had fallen on the gravel, she had been sure it was dying. No living thing could have taken the pounding she had given it with the door. Even its thick fur hadn't been able to cushion the blows. One of the Saint Bernard's ears appeared to be dangling by no more than a string of flesh.

But it had regained its feet, little by little. She hadn't been able to believe her eyes . . . hadn't *wanted* to believe her eyes.

'*No!*' she had shrieked, totally out of control. '*No, lie down, you're supposed to be dead, lie down, lie down and die, you shit dog!*'

'Mommy, don't,' Tad had murmured, holding his head. 'It hurts . . . it hurts me . . .'

Since then, nothing in the situation had changed. Time had resumed its former slow crawl. She had put her watch to her ear several times to make sure it was still ticking, because the hands never seemed to change position.

Twenty past twelve.

What do we know about rabies, class?

Precious little. Some hazy fragments that had probably come from Sunday-supplement articles. A pamphlet leafed through idly back in New York when she had taken the family cat, Dinah, for her distemper shot at the vet's. Excuse me, distemper and *rabies* shots.

Rabies, a disease of the central nervous system, the good old CNS. Causes slow destruction of same – but how? She was blank on that, and probably the doctors were, too. Otherwise the disease wouldn't be considered so damned dangerous. Of course, she thought hopefully, I don't even know for sure that the dog *is* rabid. The only rabid dog I've ever seen was the one Gregory Peck shot with a rifle in *To Kill a Mockingbird*. Except of course that dog wasn't *really* rabid, it was just pretend, it was probably some mangy mutt they'd gotten from the local pound and they put Gillette Foamy all over him . . .

She pulled her mind back to the point. Better to make what Vic called a worst-case analysis, at least for now. Besides, in her heart she was sure the dog was rabid – what else would make it behave as it had? The dog was as mad as a hatter.

And it had bitten her. Badly. What did that mean?

People could get rabies, she knew, and it was a horrible way to die. Maybe the worst. There was a vaccine for it, and a series of injections was the prescribed method of treatment. The injections were quite painful, although probably not as painful as going the way the dog out there was going. But . . .

She seemed to remember reading that there were only two instances where people had lived through an advanced case of rabies – a case, that is, that had not been diagnosed until the carriers had begun exhibiting symptoms. One of the survivors was a boy who had recovered entirely. The other had been an animal researcher who had suffered permanent brain damage. The good old CNS had just fallen apart.

The longer the disease went untreated, the less chance there was. She rubbed her forehead and her hand skidded across a film of cold sweat.

How long was too long? Hours? Days? Weeks? A month, maybe? She didn't know.

Suddenly the car seemed to be shrinking. It was the size of a Honda, then the size of those strange little three-wheelers they used to give disabled people in England, then the size of an enclosed motorcycle sidecar, finally the size of a coffin. A double coffin for her and Tad. They had to get out, get out, get *out* –

Her hand was fumbling for the doorhandle before she got hold of herself again. Her heart was racing, accelerating the thudding in her head. *Please*, she thought.

It's bad enough without claustrophobia, so please . . . please . . . please.

Her thirst was back again, raging.

She looked out and Cujo stared implacably back at her, his body seemingly split in two by the silver crack running through the window.

Help us, someone, she thought. *Please, please, help us.*

Roscoe Fisher was parked back in the shadows of Jerry's Citgo when the call came in. He was ostensibly watching for speeders, but in actual fact he was cooping. At twelve thirty on a Wednesday morning, Route 117 was totally dead. He had a little alarm clock inside his skull, and he trusted it to wake him up around one, when the Norway Drive-In let out. Then there might be some action.

'Unit three, come in, unit three. Over.'

Roscoe snapped awake, spilling cold coffee in a Styrofoam cup down into his crotch.

'Oh *shitfire*,' Roscoe said dolefully. 'Now that's nice, isn't it? Kee-rist!'

'Unit three, you copy? Over?'

He grabbed the mike and pushed the button on the side. 'I copy, base.' He would have liked to have added that he hoped it was good because he was sitting with his balls in a puddle of cold coffee, but you never knew who was monitoring police calls on his or her trusty Bearcat scanner . . . even at twelve thirty in the morning.

'Want you to take a run up to Eighty-three Larch Street,' Billy said. 'Residence of Mr and Mrs Victor Trenton. Check the place out. Over.'

'What am I checking for, base? Over.'

'Trenton's in Boston and no one's answering his calls. He thinks someone should be home. Over.'

Well, that's wonderful, isn't it? Roscoe Fisher thought sourly. For this I got a four-buck cleaning bill, and if I do have to stop a speeder, the guy's going to think I got so excited at the prospect of a collar that I pissed myself.

'Ten-four and time out,' Roscoe said, starting his cruiser. 'Over.'

'I make it twelve thirty-four A.M.,' Billy said. 'There's a key hanging on a nail under the front porch eave, unit three. Mr Trenton would like you to go right on inside and look around if the premises appear deserted. Over.'

'Roger, base. Over and out.'

'Out.'

Roscoe popped on his headlights and cruised down Castle Rock's deserted Main Street, past the Common and the bandstand with its conical green roof. He went up the hill and turned right on Larch Street near the top. The Trentons' was the second house from the corner, and he saw that in the daytime they would have a nice view of the town below. He pulled the Sheriff's Department Fury III up to the curb and got out, closing the door quietly. The street was dark, fast asleep.

He paused for a moment, pulling the wet cloth of his uniform trousers away from his crotch (grimacing as he did it), and then went up the driveway. The driveway was empty, and so was the small one-car garage at the end of it. He saw a Big Wheels trike parked inside. It was just like the one his own son had.

He closed the garage door and went around to the

front porch. He saw that this week's copy of the *Call* was leaning against the porch door. Roscoe picked it up and tried the door. It was unlocked. He went onto the porch, feeling like an intruder. He tossed the paper on the porch glider and pushed the bell beside the inner door. Chimes went off in the house, but no one came. He rang twice more over a space of about three minutes, allowing for the time it would take the lady to wake up, put on a robe, and come downstairs . . . if the lady was there.

When there was still no answer, he tried the door. It was locked.

Husband's away and she's probably staying over with friends, he thought — but the fact that she hadn't notified her husband also struck Roscoe Fisher as mildly strange.

He felt under the peaked eave, and his fingers knocked off the key Vic had hung up there not long after the Trentons had moved in. He took it down and unlocked the front door — if he had tried the kitchen door as Steve Kemp had that afternoon, he could have walked right in. Like most people in Castle Rock, Donna was slipshod about buttoning up when she went out.

Roscoe went in. He had his flashlight, but he preferred not to use it. That would have made him feel even more like an unlawful intruder — a burglar with a large coffee stain on his crotch. He felt for a switchplate and eventually found one with two switches. The top one turned on the porch light, and he turned that one off quickly. The bottom one turned on the living-room light.

He looked around for a long moment, doubting what he was seeing — at first he thought it must be some trick of his eyes, that they had not adjusted to the light or something. But nothing changed, and his heart began to pump quickly.

Musn't touch anything, he thought. *Can't balls this up.* He had forgotten about the wet coffee splotch on his pants, and he had forgotten about feeling like an intruder. He was scared and excited.

Something had happened here, all right. The living room had been turned topsy-turvy. There was shattered glass from a knickknack shelf all over the floor. The furniture had been overturned, the books had been scattered every whichway. The big mirror over the fireplace was also broken – *seven years' bad luck for somebody*, Roscoe thought, and found himself thinking suddenly and for no reason about Frank Dodd, with whom he had often shared a cruiser. Frank Dodd, the friendly small-town cop who had just happened to also be a psycho who murdered women and little children. Roscoe's arms broke out in gooseflesh suddenly. This was no place to be thinking about Frank.

He went into the kitchen through the dining room, where everything had been swept off the table – he skirted that mess carefully. The kitchen was worse. He felt a fresh chill creep down his spine. Someone had gone absolutely crazy in here. The doors to the bar cabinet stood open, and someone had used the length of the kitchen like a Pitch-Til-U-Win alley at a county fair. Pots were everywhere, and white stuff that looked like snow but had to be soap powder.

Written on the message board in large and hurried block letters was this:

I LEFT SOMETHING UPSTAIRS FOR YOU, BABY.

Suddenly Roscoe Fisher didn't want to go upstairs. More than anything else, he didn't want to go up there. He had helped clean up three of the messes Frank Dodd had left behind him, including the body of Mary Kate Hendrasen, who had been raped and murdered on the Castle Rock bandstand in the Common. He never wanted to see anything like that again . . . and suppose the woman was up there, shot or slashed or strangled? Roscoe had seen plenty of mayhem on the roads and had even got used to it, after a fashion. Two summers ago he and Billy and Sheriff Bannerman had pulled a man out of a potato-grading machine in pieces, and *that* had been one to tell your grandchildren about. But he had not seen a homicide since the Hendrasen girl, and he did not want to see one now.

He didn't know whether to be relieved or disgusted by what he found on the Trentons' bedspread.

He went back to his car and called in.

When the telephone rang, Vic and Roger were both up, sitting in front of the TV, not talking much, smoking their heads off. *Frankenstein*, the original film, was on. It was twenty minutes after one.

Vic grabbed the phone before it had completed its first ring. 'Hello? Donna? Is that—'

'Is this Mr Trenton?' A man's voice.

'Yes?'

'This is Sheriff Bannerman, Mr Trenton. I'm afraid I have some rather upsetting information for you. I'm sor—'

'Are they dead?' Vic asked. Suddenly he felt totally

337

unreal and two-dimensional, no more real than the face of an extra glimpsed in the background of an old movie such as the one he and Roger had been watching. The question came out in a perfectly conversational tone of voice. From the corner of his eye he saw Roger's shadow move as he stood up quickly. It didn't matter. Nothing else did, either. In the space of the few seconds that had passed since he had answered the phone, he had had a chance to get a good look behind his life and had seen it was all stage scenery and false fronts.

'Mr Trenton, Officer Fisher was dispatched—'

'Dispense with the official bullshit and answer my question. Are they dead?' He turned to Roger. Roger's face was gray and wondering. Behind him, on the TV, a phony windmill turned against a phony sky. 'Rog, got a cigarette?' Roger handed him one.

'Mr Trenton, are you still there?'

'Yes. Are they dead?'

'We have no idea where your wife and son are as of right now,' Bannerman said, and Vic suddenly felt all of his guts drop back into place. The world took on a little of its former color. He began to tremble. The unlit cigarette jittered between his lips.

'What's going on? What do you know? You're Bannerman, you said?'

'Castle County Sheriff, that's right. And I'll try to put you in the picture, if you'll give me a minute.'

'Yes, okay.' Now he was afraid; everything seemed to be going too fast.

'Officer Fisher was dispatched to your home at Eighty-three Larch Street as per your request at twelve thirty-four this morning. He ascertained that there was no car in the driveway or in the garage. He rang the front doorbell repeatedly, and when there was no answer, he let himself in using the key over the porch eave. He found that the house had been severely vandalized. Furnishings were over-turned, liquor bottles broken, soap powder had been poured over the floor and the built-ins of the kitchen—'

'Jesus, Kemp,' Vic whispered. His whirling mind fixed on the note: DO YOU HAVE ANY QUESTIONS? He remem-bered thinking that note, regardless of anything else, was a disquieting index into the man's psychology. A vicious act of revenge for being dumped. What had Kemp done now? What had he done besides go through their house like a harpy on the warpath?

'Mr Trenton?'

'I'm here.'

Bannerman cleared his throat as if he were having some difficulty with the next. 'Officer Fisher proceeded upstairs. The upstairs had not been vandalized, but he found traces of – uh, some whitish fluid, most probably semen, on the bedspread of the master bedroom.' And in an unwit-ting comic ellipsis, he added, 'The bed did not appear to have been slept in.'

'Where's my wife?' Vic shouted into the phone. 'Where's my boy? Don't you have any idea?'

'Take it easy,' Roger said, and put a hand on Vic's shoulder. Roger could afford to say take it easy. His wife was home in bed. So were his twin girls. Vic shook the hand off.

'Mr Trenton, all I can tell you right now is that a team of State Police detectives are on the scene, and my own men are assisting. Neither the master bedroom nor your son's room appear to have been disturbed.'

'Except for the come on our bed, you mean,' Vic said savagely, and Roger flinched as if struck. His mouth dropped open in a gape.

'Yes, well, that.' Bannerman sounded embarrassed. 'But what I mean is that there are no signs of – uh, violence against person or persons. It looks like straight vandalism.'

'Then where are Donna and Tad?' The harshness was now breaking up into bewilderment, and he felt the sting of helpless little-boy tears at the corners of his eyes.

'At this time we have no idea.'

Kemp . . . my God, what if Kemp has them?

For just a moment a confusing flash of the dream he had the previous night recurred: Donna and Tad hiding in their cave, menaced by some terrible beast. Then it was gone.

'If you have any idea of who might be behind this, Mr Trenton—'

'I'm going out to the airport and rent a car,' Vic said. 'I can be there by five o'clock.'

Patiently, Bannerman said: 'Yes, Mr Trenton. But if your wife and son's disappearance is somehow connected with this vandalism, time could be a very precious commodity. If you have even the slightest idea of who might bear a grudge against you and your wife, either real or imagined—'

'Kemp,' Vic said in a small, strangled voice. He couldn't hold the tears back now. The tears were going to come. He could feel them running down his face. 'Kemp did it, I'm sure it was Kemp. Oh my Christ, what if he's got them?'

'Who is this Kemp?' Bannerman asked. His voice was not embarrassed now; it was sharp and demanding.

He held the phone in his right hand. He put his left hand over his eyes, shutting out Roger, shutting out the hotel room, the sound of the TV, everything. Now he was in blackness, alone with the unsteady sound of his voice and the hot, shifting texture of his tears.

'Steve Kemp,' he said. 'Steven Kemp. He ran a place called the Village Stripper there in town. He's gone now. At least, my wife said he was gone. He and my wife . . . Donna . . . they . . . they had . . . well, they had an affair. Banging each other. It didn't last long. She told him it was over. I found out because he wrote me a note. It was . . . it was a pretty ugly note. He was getting his own back, I guess. I guess he didn't like to get brushed off much. This . . . it sounds like a grander version of that note.'

He rubbed his hand viciously across his eyes, making a galaxy of red shooting stars.

'Maybe he didn't like it that the marriage didn't just blow apart. Or maybe he's just . . . just fucked up. Donna said he got fucked up when he lost a tennis match. Wouldn't shake hands over the net. It's a question . . .' Suddenly his voice was gone and he had to clear his throat before it would come back. There was a band around his chest, tightening and loosening, then tightening again. 'I think it's a question of how far he might go. He could have taken them, Bannerman. He's capable of it, from what I know of him.'

There was a silence at the other end; no, not quite silence. The scratching of a pencil on paper. Roger put his hand on Vic's shoulder again, and this time he let it stay, grateful for the warmth. He felt very cold.

'Mr Trenton, do you have the note Kemp sent you?'

'No. I tore it up. I'm sorry, but under the circumstances—'

'Was it by any chance printed in block letters?'

'Yes. Yes, it was.'

'Officer Fisher found a note written in block letters on the message board in the kitchen. It said, "I left something upstairs for you, baby."'

Vic grunted a little. The last faint hope that it might have been someone else — a thief, or maybe just kids — blew away. *Come on upstairs and see what I left on the bed.* It was Kemp. The line on the noteminder at home would have fit into Kemp's little note.

'The note seems to indicate that your wife wasn't there when he did it,' Bannerman said, but even in his shocked state, Vic heard a false note in the sheriff's voice.

'She could have walked in while he was still there and you know it,' Vic said dully. 'Back from shopping, back from getting the carb adjusted on her car. Anything.'

'What sort of car did Kemp drive? Do you know?'

'I don't think he had a car. He had a van.'

'Color?'

'I don't know.'

'Mr Trenton, I'm going to suggest you come on up from Boston. I'm going to suggest that if you rent a car, you take it easy. It would be one hell of a note if your people turned up just fine and you got yourself killed on the Interstate coming up here.'

'Yes, all right.' He didn't want to drive anywhere, fast or slow. He wanted to hide. Better still, he wanted to have the last six days over again.

'Another thing, sir.'

'What's that?'

'On your way up here, try to make a mental list of your wife's friends and acquaintances in the area. It's still perfectly possible that she could be spending the night with someone.'

'Sure.'

'The most important thing to remember right now is that there are no signs of violence.'

'The whole downstairs is ripped to hell,' Vic said. 'That sounds pretty fucking violent to me.'

'Yes,' Banner said uncomfortably. 'Well.'

'I'll be there,' Vic said. He hung up.

'Vic, I'm sorry,' Roger said.

Vic couldn't meet his old friend's eyes. *Wearing the horns*, he thought. *Isn't that what the English call it? Now Roger knows I'm wearing the horns.*

'It's all right,' Vic said, starting to dress.

'All this on your mind . . . and you went ahead with the trip?'

'What good would it have done to stay at home?' Vic asked. 'It happened. I . . . I only found out on Thursday. I thought . . . some distance . . . time to think . . . perspective . . . I don't know all the stupid goddam things I thought. Now this.'

'Not your fault,' Roger said earnestly.

'Rog, at this point I don't know what's my fault and what isn't. I'm worried about Donna, and I'm out of my mind about Tad. I just want to get back there. And I'd like to get my hands on that fucker Kemp. I'd . . .' His voice had been rising. It abruptly sank. His shoulders sagged. For a moment he looked drawn and old and almost totally used up. Then he went to the suitcase on the floor and began to hunt for fresh clothes. 'Call Avis at the airport, would you, and get me a car? My wallet's there on the nightstand. They'll want the American Express number.'

'I'll call for both of us. I'm going back with you.'

'No.'

'But—'

'But nothing.' Vic slipped into a dark blue shirt. He had it buttoned halfway up before he saw he had it wrong; one tail hung far below the other. He unbuttoned it and started again. He was in motion now, and being in motion was better, but that feeling of unreality persisted. He kept having thoughts about movie sets, where what looks like Italian marble is really just Con-Tact paper, where all the rooms end just above the camera's sight line and where someone is always lurking in the background with a clapper board. Scene #41, Vic convinces Roger to Keep On Plugging, Take One. He was an actor and this was some crazy absurdist film. But it was undeniably better when the body was in motion.

'Hey, man—'

'Roger, this changes nothing in the situation between Ad Worx and the Sharp Company. I came along after I knew about Donna and this guy Kemp partly because I wanted to keep up a front – I guess no guy wants to advertise when he finds out his wife has been getting it on the side – but mostly because I knew that the people who depend on us have to keep eating no matter who my wife decides to go to bed with.'

'Go easy on yourself, Vic. Stop digging yourself with it.'

'I can't seem to do that,' Vic said. 'Even now I can't seem to do that.'

'And I can't just go on to New York as if nothing's happened!'

'As far as we know, nothing has. The cop kept emphasizing that to me. You *can* go on. You can see it through. Maybe it'll turn out to have been nothing but a charade all along, but . . . people have to *try*, Roger. There's nothing else to do. Besides, there's nothing you can do back in Maine except hang out.'

'Jesus, it feels wrong. It feels all wrong.'

'It's not. I'll call you at the Biltmore as soon as I know something.' Vic zippered his slacks and stepped into his loafers. 'Now go on and call Avis for me. I'll catch a cab out to Logan from downstairs. Here, I'll write my Amex number down for you.'

He did this, and Roger stood silently by as he got his coat and went to the door.

'Vic,' Roger said.

He turned, and Roger embraced him clumsily but with surprising strength. Vic hugged him back, his cheek against Roger's shoulder.

'I'll pray to God everything's okay,' Roger said hoarsely.

'Okay,' Vic said, and went out.

The elevator hummed faintly on the way down – *not really moving at all*, he thought. *It's a sound effect.* Two drunks supporting each other got on at lobby level as he got off. *Extras*, he thought.

He spoke to the doorman – another extra – and after about five minutes a cab rolled up to the blue hotel awning.

The cab driver was black and silent. He had his radio tuned to an FM soul station. The Temptations sang 'Power' endlessly as the cab took him toward Logan Airport through streets that were almost completely deserted. *Helluva good movie set*, he thought. As the Temptations faded out, a jiveass dj came on with the weather forecast. It had been hot yesterday, he reported, but you didn't see *nuthin* yesterday, brothers and sisters. Today was going to be the hottest day of the summer so far, maybe a record-breaker. The big G's weather prognosticator, Altitude Lou McNally, was calling for temperatures of over 100 degrees inland and not much cooler on the coast. A mass of warm, stagnant air had moved up from the south and was being held in place over New England by hands of high pressure. 'So if you gas gonna reach, you gotta head for the beach,' the jiveass dj finished. 'It ain't goan be too pretty if you hangin out in the city. And just to prove the point, here's Michael Jackson. He's goin "Off the Wall".'

The forecast meant little or nothing to Vic, but it would have terrified Donna even more than she already was, had she known.

As she had the day before, Charity awoke just before dawn. She awoke listening, and for a few moments she wasn't even sure what she was listening for. Then she remembered. Boards creaking. Footsteps. She was listening to see if her son was going to go walking again.

But the house was silent.

She got out of bed, went to the door, and looked

out into the hall. The hall was empty. After a moment's debate she went down to Brett's room and looked in on him. There was nothing showing under his sheet but a lick of his hair. If he had gone walking, he had done it before she woke up. He was deeply asleep now.

Charity went back to her room and sat on her bed, looking out at the faint white line on the horizon. She was aware that her decision had been made. Somehow, secretly, in the night while she slept. Now, in the first cold light of day, she was able to examine what she had decided, and she felt that she could count the cost.

It occurred to her that she had never unburdened herself to her sister Holly as she had expected she would do. She still might have, if not for the credit cards at lunch yesterday. And then last night she had told Charity how much this, that, and the other had cost – the Buick four-door, the Sony color set, the parquet floor in the hallway. As if, in Holly's mind, each of these things still carried invisible price tags and always would.

Charity still liked her sister. Holly was giving and kindhearted, impulsive, affectionate, warm. But her way of living had forced her to close off some of the heartless truths about the way she and Charity had grown up poor in rural Maine, the truths that had more or less forced Charity into marriage with Joe Camber while luck – really no different from Charity's winning lottery ticket – had allowed Holly to meet Jim and escape the life back home forever.

She was afraid that if she had told Holly that she had been trying to get Joe's permission to come down here for *years*, that this trip had only occurred because of brutal generalship on her part, and that even so it had almost come down to Joe's strapping her with his leather belt . . . she was afraid that if she told Holly those things, her sister's reaction would be horrified anger rather than anything rational and helpful. Why horrified anger? Perhaps because, deep down in a part of the human soul where Buick station wagons, and Sony color TVs with Trinitron picture tubes, and parquet floors can never quite make their final stilling impact, Holly would recognize that she might have escaped a similar marriage, a similar *life*, by the thinnest of margins.

She hadn't told because Holly had entrenched herself in her upper-middle-class suburban life like a watchful soldier in a foxhole. She hadn't told because horrified anger could not solve her problems. She hadn't told because no one likes to look like a freak in a sideshow, living through the days and weeks and months and years with an unpleasant, uncommunicative, sometimes frightening man. Charity had discovered there were things you didn't want to tell. Shame wasn't the reason. Sometimes it was just better − kinder − to keep up a front.

Mostly she hadn't told because these things were her problems. What happened to Brett was her problem . . . and over the last two days she had come more and more to believe that what he did with his life would depend less on her and Joe in the final reckoning than it would on Brett himself.

There would be no divorce. She would continue to fight her unceasing guerilla war with Joe for the boy's soul . . . for whatever good that would do. In her worry over Brett's wanting to emulate his father, she had perhaps forgotten – or overlooked – the fact that there comes a time when children stand in judgment and their parents – mother as well as father – must stand in the dock. Brett had noticed Holly's ostentatious display of credit cards. Charity could only hope Brett would notice that his father ate with his hat on . . . among other things.

The dawn was brightening. She took her robe from the back of the door and put it on. She wanted a shower but would not take one until the others in the house were stirring. The strangers. That was what they were. Even Holly's face was strange to her now, a face that bore only a faint resemblance to the snapshots in the family albums she had brought with them . . . even Holly herself had looked at those photographs with a faint air of puzzlement.

They would go back to Castle Rock, back to the house at the end of Town Road No. 3, back to Joe. She would pick up the threads of her life, and things would continue. That would be best.

She reminded herself to call Alva just before seven o'clock, when he would be at breakfast.

It was just past 6 A.M. and the day was coming bright when Tad had his convulsion.

He had awakened from an apparently sound sleep around 5:15 and had roused Donna from a low doze, complaining of being hungry and thirsty. As if he had pressed a button deep down inside her, Donna had become aware for the first time that she was hungry too. The thirst she had been aware of – it was more or less constant – but she could not remember actually thinking of food since sometime yesterday morning. Now she was suddenly ravenous.

349

She soothed Tad as best she could, telling him hollow things that no longer meant anything real to her one way or another – that people would show up soon, the bad dog would be taken away, they would be rescued.

The real thing was the thought of food.

Breakfasts, for instance, take breakfasts: two eggs fried in butter, over easy if you don't mind, waiter. French toast. Big glasses of fresh-squeezed orange juice so cold that moisture beaded the glass. Canadian bacon. Home fries. Bran flakes in cream with a sprinkle of blueberries on top – bloobies, her father had always called them, another one of those comic irrationalities that had irritated her mother out of all proportion.

Her stomach made a loud rumbling sound, and Tad laughed. The sound of his laughter startled her and pleased her with its unexpectedness. It was like finding a rose growing in a rubbish heap, and she smiled back. The smile hurt her lips.

'Heard that, huh?'

'I think you must be hungry too.'

'Well, I wouldn't turn down an Egg McMuffin if someone threw it my way.'

Tad groaned, and that made them both laugh again. In the yard, Cujo had pricked up his ears. He growled at the sound of their laughter. For a moment he made as if to get to his feet, perhaps to charge the car again; then he settled wearily back on his haunches, head drooping.

Donna felt that irrational lift in her spirits that almost always comes with daybreak. Surely it would be over soon; surely they had passed the worst. All the luck had been against them, but sooner or later even the worst luck changes.

Tad seemed almost his old self. Too pale, badly used, terribly tired in spite of his sleep, but still indubitably the Tadder. She hugged him, and he hugged her back. The pain in her belly had subsided somewhat, although the scrapes and gouges there had a puffy, inflamed look. Her leg was worse, but she found she was able to flex it, although it hurt to do so and the bleeding started again. She would have a scar.

The two of them talked for the next forty minutes or so. Donna, hunting for a way to keep Tad alert and to also pass the time for both of them, suggested Twenty Questions. Tad agreed eagerly. He had never been able to get enough of the game; the only problem had always been getting one or the other of his parents to play it with him. They were on their fourth game when the convulsion struck.

Donna had guessed some five questions ago that the subject of the interrogation was Fred Redding, one of Tad's daycamp chums, but had been spinning things out.

'Does he have red hair?' she asked.

'No, he's . . . he's . . . he's . . .'

Suddenly Tad was struggling to catch his breath. It came and went in gasping, tearing whoops that caused fear to leap up her throat in a sour, coppery-tasting rush.

'Tad? *Tad*?'

Tad gasped. He clawed at his throat, leaving red lines there. His eyes rolled up, showing only the bottoms of the irises and the silvery whites.

'*Tad!*'

She grabbed him, shook him. His Adam's apple went up and down rapidly, like a mechanical bear on a stick.

351

His hands began to flop aimlessly about, and then they rose to his throat again and tore at it. He began to make animal choking sounds.

For a moment Donna entirely forgot where she was. She grabbed for the doorhandle, pulled it up, and shoved the door of the Pinto open, as if this had happened while she was in the supermarket parking lot and there was help close by.

Cujo was on his feet in an instant. He leaped at the car before the door was more than half open, perhaps saving her from being savaged at that instant. He struck the opening door, fell back, and then came again, snarling thickly. Loose excrement poured onto the crushed gravel of the driveway.

Screaming, she yanked the door closed. Cujo leaped at the side of the car again, bashing the dent in a little deeper. He reeled back, then sprang at the window, thudding off it with a dull cracking sound. The silver crack running through the glass suddenly developed half a dozen tributaries. He leaped at it again and the Saf-T-Glas starred inward, still holding together but sagging now. The outside world was suddenly a milky blur.

If he comes again –

Instead, Cujo withdrew, waiting to see what she would do next.

She turned to her son.

Tad's entire body was jerking, as if with epilepsy. His back was bowed. His buttocks came out of the seat, thumped back, rose again, thumped back. His face was taking on a bluish color. The veins in his temples stood out prominently. She had been a candy-striper for three years, her last two in high school and the summer following her freshman year at college, and she knew what was happening here. He had not swallowed his tongue; outside of the more purple mystery novels, that was impossible. But his tongue had slid down his throat and was now blocking his windpipe. He was choking to death in front of her eyes.

She grabbed his chin in her left hand and yanked his mouth open. Panic made her rough, and she heard the tendons in his jaw creak. Her probing fingers found the tip of his tongue incredibly far back, almost to where his wisdom teeth would be if they ever grew out. She tried to grip it and couldn't; it was as wet and slippery as a baby eel. She tried to tweeze it between her thumb and forefinger, only faintly aware of the lunatic race of her heart. *I think I'm losing him,* she thought. *Oh my dear God, I think I'm losing my son.*

Now his teeth suddenly clashed down, drawing blood from her probing fingers and from his own cracked and blistered lips. Blood ran down his chin. She was hardly aware of the pain. Tad's feet began to rattle a mad tattoo against the floormat of the Pinto. She groped for the tip of his tongue desperately. She had it . . . and it slipped through her fingers again.

(the dog the goddamned dog it's his fault goddam dog goddam hellhound I'LL KILL YOU I SWEAR TO GOD)

Tad's teeth clamped down on her fingers again, and then she had his tongue again and this time she did not hesitate: she dug her fingernails into its spongy top and underside and pulled it forward like a woman pulling a windowshade down; at the same time she put her other hand under his chin and tipped his head back, creating the maximum airway. Tad began to gasp again – a harsh, rattling sound, like the breathing of an old man with emphysema. Then he began to whoop.

She slapped him. She didn't know what else to do, so she did that.

Tad uttered one final tearing gasp, and then his breathing settled into a rapid pant. She was panting herself. Waves of dizziness rushed over her. She had twisted her bad leg somehow, and there was the warm wetness of fresh bleeding.

'Tad!' She swallowed harshly. 'Tad, can you hear me?'

His head nodded. A little. His eyes remained closed.

'Take it as easy as you can. I want you to relax.'

'. . . want to go home . . . Mommy . . . the monster . . .'

'Shhh, Tadder. Don't talk, and don't think about monsters. Here.' The Monster Words had fallen to the floor. She picked the yellow paper up and put it in his hand. Tad gripped it with panicky tightness. 'Now concentrate on breathing slowly and regularly, Tad. That's the way to get home. Slow and regular breaths.'

Her eyes wandered past him and once again she saw the splintery bat, its handle wrapped in friction tape, lying in the high weeds at the right side of the driveway.

'Just take it easy, Tadder, can you try to do that?'

Tad nodded a little without opening his eyes.

'Just a little longer, hon. I promise. I promise.'

Outside, the day continued to brighten. Already it was warm. The temperature inside the small car began to climb.

★   ★   ★

Vic got home at twenty past five. At the time his wife was pulling his son's tongue out of the back of his mouth, he was walking around the living room, putting things slowly and dreamily to rights, while Bannerman, a State Police detective, and a detective from the state Attorney General's office sat on the long sectional sofa drinking instant coffee.

'I've already told you everything I know,' Vic said. 'If she isn't with the people you've contacted already, she's not with anybody.' He had a broom and a dustpan, and he had brought in the box of Hefty bags from the kitchen closet. Now he let a panful of broken glass slide into one of the bags with an atonal jingle. 'Unless it's Kemp.'

There was an uncomfortable silence. Vic couldn't remember ever being as tired as he was now, but he didn't believe he would be able to sleep unless someone gave him a shot. He wasn't thinking very well. Ten minutes after he arrived the telephone had rung and he had sprung at it like an animal, not heeding the A. G.'s man's mild statement that it was probably for him. It hadn't been; it was Roger, wanting to know if Vic had gotten there, and if there was any news.

There *was* some news, but all of it was maddeningly inconclusive. There had been fingerprints all over the house, and a fingerprint team, also from Augusta, had taken a number of sets from the living quarters adjacent to the small stripping shop where Steven Kemp had worked until recently. Before long the matching would be done and they would know conclusively if Kemp had been the one who had turned the downstairs floor upside down. To Vic it was so much redundancy; he knew in his guts that it had been Kemp.

The State Police detective had run a make on Kemp's van. It was a 1971 Ford Econoline, Maine license 641-644. The color was light gray, but they knew from Kemp's landlord — they had routed him out of bed at 4 A.M. — that the van had desert murals painted on the sides: buttes, mesas, sand dunes. There were two bumper stickers on the rear, one which said SPLIT WOOD, NOT ATOMS and one which said RONALD REAGAN SHOT J. R. A very funny guy, Steve Kemp, the murals and the bumper stickers would make the van easier to identify, and unless he had ditched it, he would almost certainly be spotted before the day was out. The MV alert had gone out to all the New England states and to upstate New York. In addition, the FBI in Portland and Boston had been alerted to a possible kidnapping, and they were now running Steve Kemp's name through their files in Washington. They would find three minor busts dating back to the Vietnam war protests, one each for the years 1968–1970.

'There's only one thing about all of this that bothers me,' the A. G.'s man said. His pad was on his knee, but anything Vic could tell he had already told them. The man from Augusta was only doodling. 'If I may be frank, it bothers the shit out of me.'

'What's that?' Vic asked. He picked up the family portrait, looked down at it, and then tilted it so the shattered glass facing tumbled into the Hefty bag with another evil little jingle.

'The car. Where's your wife's car?'

His name was Masen — Masen with an 'e', he had informed Vic as they shook hands. Now he went to the window, slapping his pad absently against his leg. Vic's battered sports car was in the driveway, parked to one side of Bannerman's cruiser. Vic had picked it up at the Portland Jetport and dropped off the Avis car he had driven north from Boston.

'What's that got to do with it?' Vic asked.

Masen shrugged. 'Maybe nothing. Maybe something. Maybe everything. Probably nothing, but I just don't like it. Kemp comes here, right? Grabs your wife and son. Why? He's crazy. That's reason enough. Can't stand to lose. Maybe it's even his twisted idea of a joke.'

These were all things Vic himself had said, repeated back almost verbatim.

'So what does he do? He bundles them into his Ford van with the desert murals on the sides. He's either running with them or he's holed up somewhere. Right?'

'Yes, that's what I'm afraid—'

Masen turned from the window to look at him. 'So where's her car?'

'Well—' Vic tried hard to think. It was hard. He was very tired. 'Maybe—'

'Maybe he had a confederate who drove it away,' Masen said. 'That would probably mean a kidnapping for ransom. If he took them on his own, it was probably just a crazy spur-of-the-moment thing. If it was a kidnapping for money, why take the car at all? To switch over to? Ridiculous. That Pinto's every bit as hot as the van, if a little harder to recognize. And I repeat, if there was no confederate, if he was by himself, who drove the car?'

'Maybe he came back for it,' the State Police detective rumbled. 'Stowed the boy and the missus and came back for the car.'

'That would present some problems without a confederate,' Masen said, 'but I suppose he could do it. Take them someplace close and walk back for Mrs Trenton's Pinto, or take them someplace far away and thumb a ride back. But why?'

Bannerman spoke for the first time. 'She could have driven it herself.'

Masen swung to look at him, his eyebrows going up.

'If he took the boy with him—' Bannerman looked at Vic and nodded a little. 'I'm sorry, Mr Trenton, but if Kemp took the boy with him, belted him in, held a gun on him, and told your wife to follow close, and that something might happen to the boy if she tried anything clever, like turning off or flashing her lights—'

Vic nodded, feeling sick at the picture it made.

Masen seemed irritated with Bannerman, perhaps because he hadn't thought of the possibility himself. 'I repeat: to what purpose?'

Bannerman shook his head. Vic himself couldn't think of a single reason why Kemp would want Donna's car.

Masen lit a Pall Mall, coughed, and looked around for an ashtray.

'I'm sorry,' Vic said, again feeling like an actor, someone outside himself, saying lines that had been written for him. 'The two ashtrays in here were broken. I'll get you one from the kitchen.'

Masen walked out with him, took an ashtray, and said, 'Let's go out on the steps, do you mind? It's going to be a bitch of a hot day. I like to enjoy them while they're still civilized during July.'

'Okay,' Vic said listlessly.

He glanced at the thermometer-barometer screwed to the side of the house as they went out . . . a gift from Donna last Christmas. The temperature already stood at 73. The needle of the barometer was planted squarely in the quadrant marked FAIR.

'Let's pursue this a little further,' Masen said. 'It fascinates me. Here's a woman with a son, a woman whose husband is away on a business trip. She needs her car if she's going to get around very well. Even downtown's half a mile away and the walk back is all uphill. So if we assume that Kemp grabbed her here, the car would still be here. Try this, instead. Kemp comes up and trashes the house, but he's still furious. He sees them someplace else in town and grabs them. In that case, the car would still be in that other place. Downtown, maybe. Or in the parking lot at the shopping center.'

'Wouldn't someone have tagged it in the middle of the night?' Vic asked.

'Probably,' Masen said. 'Do you think she herself might have left it somewhere, Mr Trenton?'

Then Vic remembered. The needle valve.

'You look like something just clicked,' Masen said.

'It didn't click, it clunked. The car isn't here because it's at the Ford dealership in South Paris. She was having carburetor trouble. The needle valve in there kept wanting to jam. We talked about it on the phone Monday afternoon. She was really pissed off and upset about it. I meant to make an appointment for her to get it done by a local guy here in town, but I forgot because . . .'

He trailed off, thinking about the reasons why he had forgotten.

'You forgot to the make the appointment here in town, so she would have taken it to South Paris?'

'Yeah, I guess so.' He couldn't remember exactly what the run of the conversation had been now, except that she had been afraid the car would seize up while she was taking it to be fixed.

Masen glanced at his watch and got up. Vic started to rise with him.

'No, stay put. I just want to make a quick phone call. I'll be back.'

Vic sat where he was. The screen door banged closed behind Masen, a sound that reminded him so much of Tad that he winced and had to grit his teeth against fresh tears. Where were they? The thing about the Pinto not being here had only been momentarily promising after all.

The sun was fully up now, throwing a bright rose light over the houses and the streets below, and across Castle Hill. It touched the swing set where he had pushed Tad times without number . . . all he wanted was to push his son on the swing again with his wife standing beside him. He would push until his hands fell off, if that was what Tad wanted.

Daddy, I wanna loop the loop! I wanna!

The voice in his mind chilled his heart. It was like a ghost voice.

The screen door opened again a moment later. Masen sat down beside him and lit a fresh cigarette. 'Twin City Ford in South Paris,' he said. 'That was the one, wasn't it?'

'Yeah. We bought the Pinto there.'

'I took a shot and called them. Got lucky; the service manager was already in. Your Pinto's not there, and it hasn't been there. Who's the local guy?'

'Joe Camber,' Vic said. 'She must have taken the car out there after all. She didn't want to because he's way out in the back of beyond and she couldn't get any answer on the phone when she called. I told her he was probably there anyway, just working in the garage. It's this converted barn, and I don't think he's got a phone in there. At least he didn't the last time I was out there.'

'We'll check it out,' Masen said, 'but her car's not there either, Mr Trenton. Depend on it.'

'Why not?'

'Doesn't make a bit of logical sense,' Masen said. 'I was ninety-five percent sure it wasn't in South Paris, either. Look, everything we said before still holds true. A young woman with a child needs a car. Suppose she took the car over to Twin City Ford and they told her it was going to be a couple of days. How does she get back?'

'Well . . . a loaner . . . or if they wouldn't give her a loaner, I guess they'd rent her one of their lease cars. From the cheap fleet.'

'Right! Beautiful! So where is it?'

Vic looked at the driveway, almost as if expecting it to appear.

'There'd be no more reason for Kemp to abscond with your wife's loaner than there would be for him to abscond with her Pinto,' Masen said. 'That pretty well ruled out the Ford dealership in advance. Now let's say she takes it out to this guy Camber's garage. If he gives her an old junker to run around in while he fixes her Pinto, we're back at square one right away: Where's the junker? So let's say that she takes it up there and Camber says he'll have to keep it awhile but she calls a friend, and the friend comes out to pick her up. With me so far?'

'Yes, sure.'

'So who was the friend? You gave us a list, and we got them all out of bed. Lucky they were all home, it being summer and all. None of them mentioned bringing your people home from anywhere. No one has seen them any later than Monday morning.'

'Well, why don't we stop crapping around?' Vic asked. 'Let's give Camber a call and find out for sure.'

'Let's wait until seven,' Masen said. 'That's only fifteen minutes. Give him a chance to get his face washed and wake up a little. Service managers usually clock in early. This guy's an independent.'

Vic shrugged. This whole thing was a crazy blind alley. Kemp had Donna and Tad. He knew it in his guts, just as he knew it was Kemp who had trashed the house and shot his come on the bed he and Donna shared.

'Of course, it didn't have to be a friend,' Masen said, dreamily watching his cigarette smoke drift off into the morning. 'There are all sorts of possibilities. She gets the car up there, and someone she knows slightly happens to be there, and the guy or gal offers Mrs Trenton and your son a ride back into town. Or maybe Camber runs them home himself. Or his wife. Is he married?'

'Yes. Nice woman.'

'Could have been him, her, anyone. People are always willing to help a lady in distress.'

'Yeah,' Vic said, and lit a cigarette of his own.

'But none of that matters either, because the question always remains the same: Where's the fucking car?

362

Because the situation's the same. Woman and kid on their own. She has to get groceries, go to the dry cleaner's, go to the post office, dozens of little errands. If the husband was only going to be gone a few days, a week, even, she might try to get along without a car. But ten days or two weeks? Jesus, that's a long haul in a town that's only got one goddam cab. Rental car people are happy to deliver in a situation like that. She could have gotten Hertz or Avis or National to deliver the car here or out to Camber's. So where's the *rental* car? I keep coming back to that. There should have been a vehicle in this yard. Dig?'

'I don't think it's important,' Vic said.

'And probably it's not. We'll find some simple explanation and say *Oy vay, how could we be so stupid*? But it fascinates me strangely . . . it was the needle valve? You're sure of that?'

'Positive.'

Masen shook his head. 'Why would she need all that rigamarole about loaners or rental cars anyway? That's a fifteen-minute fix for somebody with the tools and the know-how. Drive in, drive out. So where's –'

'– her goddam car?' Vic finished wearily. The world was coming and going in waves now.

'Why don't you go upstairs and lie down?' Masen said. 'You looked wiped out.'

'No, I want to be awake if something happens –'

'And if something does, somebody will be here to wake you up. The FBI's coming with a trace-back system to hook up on your phone. Those people are noisy enough to wake the dead – so don't worry.'

Vic was too tired to feel much more than a dull dread. 'Do you think that trace-back shit is really necessary?'

'Better to have it and not need it than need it and not have it,' Masen said, and pitched his cigarette. 'Get a little rest and you'll be able to cope better, Vic. Go on.'

'All right.'

He went slowly upstairs. The bed had been stripped to the mattress. He had done it himself. He put two pillows on his side, took off his shoes, and lay down. The morning sun shone fiercely in through the window. *I won't sleep*, he thought, *but I'll rest. I'll try to, anyway. Fifteen minutes . . . maybe half an hour . . .*

But by the time the phone woke him up, that day's burning noon had come.

Charity Camber had her morning coffee and then called Alva Thornton in Castle Rock. This time Alva himself answered. He knew that she had chatted with Bessie the night before.

'Nope,' Alva said. 'I ain't seed hide nor hair of Joe since last Thursday or so, Charity. He brought over a tractor tire he fixed for me. Never said nothing about feeding Cujo, although I'd've been happy to.'

'Alva, could you run up to the house and check on Cujo? Brett saw him Monday morning before we left for my sister's, and he thought he looked sick. And I just don't know who Joe would have gotten to feed him.' After the way of country people, she added: 'No hurry.'

'I'll take a run up and check,' Alva said. 'Let me get those damn cacklers fed and watered and I'm gone.'

'That would be fine, Alva,' Charity said gratefully, and gave him her sister's number. 'Thanks so much.'

They talked a little more, mostly about the weather. The constant heat had Alva worried about his chickens. Then she hung up.

Brett looked up from his cereal when she came into the kitchen. Jim Junior was very carefully making rings on the table with his orange juice glass and talking a mile a minute. He had decided sometime during the last forty-eight hours that Brett Camber was a close relation to Jesus Christ.

'Well?' Brett asked.

'You were right. Dad didn't ask Alva to feed him.' She saw the disappointment and worry on Brett's face and went on: 'But he's going up to check on Cujo this morning, as soon as he's got his chickens tended to. I left the number this time. He said he'd call back one way or the other.'

'Thanks, Mom.'

Jim clattered back from the table as Holly called him to come upstairs and get dressed. 'Wanna come up with me, Brett?'

Brett smiled. 'I'll wait for you, slugger.'

'Okay.' Jim ran out trumpeting, 'Mom! Brett said he'd wait! Brett's gonna wait for me to get dressed!'

A thunder, as of elephants, on the stairs.

'He's a nice kid,' Brett said casually.

'I thought,' Charity said, 'that we might go home a little early. If that's all right with you.'

Brett's face brightened, and in spite of all the decisions she had come to, that brightness made her feel a little sad. 'When?' he asked.

'How does tomorrow sound? She had been intending to suggest Friday.

'Great! But' – he looked at her closely – 'are you done visiting, Mom? I mean, she's your sister.'

Charity thought of the credit cards, and of the Wurlitzer jukebox Holly's husband had been able to afford but did not know how to fix. Those were the things that had impressed Brett, and she supposed they had impressed her as well in some way. Perhaps she had seen them through Brett's eyes a little . . . through Joe's eyes. And enough was enough.

'Yes,' she said. 'I guess I've done my visiting. I'll tell Holly this morning.'

'Okay, Mom.' He looked at her a little shyly. 'I wouldn't mind coming back, you know. I do like them. And he's a neat little kid. Maybe he can come up to Maine sometime.'

'Yes,' she said, surprised and grateful. She didn't think Joe would object to that. 'Yes, maybe that could be arranged.'

'Okay. And tell me what Mr Thornton said.'

'I will.'

But Alva never called back. As he was feeding his chickens that morning, the motor in his big air conditioner blew, and he was immediately in a life-or-death struggle to save his birds before the day's heat could kill them. Donna Trenton might have called it another stroke of that same Fate she saw reflected in Cujo's muddy, homicidal eyes. By the time the issue of the air conditioner was settled, it was four in the afternoon (Alva Thornton lost sixty-two chickens that day and counted himself off cheaply), and the confrontation which had begun Monday afternoon in the Cambers' sunstruck dooryard was over.

Andy Masen was the Maine Attorney General's *Wunderkind*, and there were those who said that someday – and not too distant a day, either – he would lead the A. G.'s criminal division. Andy Masen's sights were set a good deal higher than that. He hoped to be Attorney General himself in 1984, and in a position to run for Governor by 1987. And after eight years as Governor, who knew?

He came from a large, poor family. He and his three brothers and two sisters had grown up in a ramshackle 'poor white trash' house on the outer Sabbatus Road in the town of Lisbon. His brothers and sisters had been exactly up – or down – to town expectations. Only Andy Masen and his youngest brother, Marty, had managed to finish high school. For a while it had looked as if Roberta might make it, but she had gotten herself knocked up higher than a kite following a dance her senior year. She had left school to marry the boy, who still had pimples at twenty-nine, drank Narragansett straight from the can, and knocked both her and the kid around. Marty had been killed in a car crash over on Route 9 in Durham. He and some of his drunk friends had tried to take the tight curve up Sirois Hill at seventy. The Camaro in which they were riding rolled over twice and burned.

Andy had been the star of the family, but his mother had never liked him. She was a little afraid of him. When talking to friends she would say, 'My Andy's a cold fish,' but he was more than that. He was always tightly controlled, always buttoned up. He knew from the fifth grade on that he was going to somehow get through college and become a lawyer. Lawyers made a lot of money. Lawyers worked with logic. Logic was Andy's God.

He saw each event as a point from which a finite number of possibilities radiated. At the end of each possibility line was another event point. And so on. This point-to-point blueprint of life had served him very well. He made straight A's through grammar school and high school, got a Merit Scholarship, and could have gone to college almost anywhere. He decided on the University of Maine, throwing away his chance at Harvard because he had already decided to start his career in Augusta, and he didn't want some piney-woodser in gumrubber boots and a lumberman's jacket throwing Harvard in his face.

On this hot July morning, things were right on schedule.

He put Vic Trenton's phone down. There had been no answer at the Camber telephone number. The State Police detective and Bannerman were still here, waiting for instructions like well-trained dogs. He had worked with Townsend, the State Police guy, before, and he was the sort of fellow Andy Masen felt comfortable with. When you said fetch, Townsend fetched. Bannerman was a new one, and Masen didn't care for him. His eyes were a little too bright, and the way he had suddenly come out with the idea that Kemp might have coerced the woman by using the kid . . . well, such ideas, if they were going to come, ought to come from Andy Masen. The three of them sat on the sectional sofa, not talking, just drinking coffee and waiting for the FBI boys to show up with the trace-back equipment.

Andy thought about the case. It might be a tempest in a teapot, but it might well be something more. The husband was convinced it was a kidnapping and attached no importance to the missing car. He was fixated on the idea that Steven Kemp had taken his people.

Andy Masen was not so sure.

Camber wasn't home; no one was home up there. Maybe they had all gone on vacation. That was likely enough; July was the quintessential vacation month, and they had been due to hit someone who was gone. Would he have taken her car in for a repair job if he was going away? Unlikely. Unlikely that the car was there at all. But it had to be checked, and there was one possibility he had neglected to mention to Vic.

Suppose she *had* taken the car up to Camber's Garage? Suppose someone *had* offered her a lift back? Not a friend, not an acquaintance, not Camber or his wife, but a total stranger? Andy could hear Trenton saying, 'Oh, no, my wife would never accept a ride from a stranger.' But, in the vernacular, she had accepted several rides from Steven Kemp, who was almost a stranger. If the hypothetical man was friendly, and if she was anxious to get her son home, she might have accepted. And maybe the nice, smiling man was some kind of a freak. They had had just such a freak here in Castle Rock before, Frank Dodd. Maybe the nice, smiling man had left them in the brush with their throats cut and had hied on his merry way. If that was the case, the Pinto would be at Camber's.

Andy did not think this line of reasoning *likely*, but it was *possible*. He would have sent a man up to the Cambers' anyway – it was routine – but he liked to understand why he was doing each thing he was doing. He thought that, for all practical purposes, he could dismiss Camber's Garage from the structure of logic and order he was building. He supposed she could have gone up there, discovered the Cambers were gone, and *then* had her car conk out on her, but Castle Rock's Town Road No. 3 was hardly Antartica. She and the kid had only to walk to the nearest house and ask to use the phone in that case, but they hadn't done it.

'Mr Townsend,' he said in his soft voice. 'You and Sheriff Bannerman here ought to take a ride out to this Joe Camber's Garage. Verify three things: no blue Pinto there, license number 218-864, no Donna and Theodore Trenton there, no Cambers there. Got that?'

'Fine,' Townsend said. 'Do you want—'

'I want only those three things,' Andy said softly. He didn't like the way Bannerman was looking at him, and with a kind of weary contempt. It upset him. 'If any of those three *are* there, call me here. And if I'm not here, I'll leave a number. Understood?'

The telephone rang. Bannerman picked it up, listened, and offered it to Andy Masen. 'For you, hotshot.'

Their eyes locked over the telephone. Masen thought that Bannerman would drop his, but he didn't. After a moment Andy took the phone. The call was from the State Police barracks in Scarborough. Steve Kemp had been picked up. His van had been spotted in the courtyard of a small motel in the Massachusetts town of Twickenham. The woman and the boy were not with him. After receiving the Miranda, Kemp had given his name and had since been standing on his right to remain silent.

Andy Masen found that extremely ominious news.

'Townsend, you come with me,' he said. 'You can handle the Camber place by yourself, can't you, Sheriff Bannerman?'

'It's my town,' Bannerman said.

Andy Masen lit a cigarette and looked at Bannerman through the shifting smoke. 'Have you got a problem with me, Sheriff?'

Bannerman smiled. 'Nothing I can't handle.'

Christ, I hate these hicks, Masen thought, watching Bannerman leave. *But he's out of the play now, anyway. Thank God for small favors.*

Bannerman got behind the wheel of his cruiser, fired it up, and backed out of the Trenton driveway. It was twenty minutes after seven. He was almost amused at how neatly Masen had shunted him off onto a siding. They were headed toward the heart of the matter; he was headed nowhere. But ole Hank Townsend was going to have to listen to a whole morning's worth of Masen's bullshit, so maybe he had gotten off well at that.

George Bannerman loafed out Route 117 toward the Maple Sugar Road, siren and flashers off. It surely was a pretty day. And he saw no need to hurry.

Donna and Tad Trenton were sleeping.

Their positions were very similar: the awkward sleeping positions of those forced to spend long hours on interstate buses. Their heads lolled against the sockets of their shoulders, Donna's turned to the left, Tad's to the right. Tad's hands lay in his lap like a beached fish. Now and again they would twitch. His breathing was harsh and stertorous. His lips were blistered, his eyelids a purplish color. A line of spittle running from the corner of his mouth to the soft line of his jaw had begun to dry.

Donna was in middle sleep. As exhausted as she was, her cramped position and the pain in her leg and belly and now her fingers (in his seizure Tad had bitten them to the bone) would let her sink no deeper. Her hair clung to her head in sweaty strings. The gauze pads on her left leg had soaked through again, and the flesh around the superficial wounds on her belly had gone an ugly red. Her breathing was also harsh, but not as uneven as Tad's.

Tad Trenton was very close to the end of his endurance. Dehydration was well advanced. He had lost electrolytes, chlorides, and sodium through his perspiration. Nothing had replaced them. His inner defenses were being steadily rolled back, and now he had entered the final critical stage. His life had grown light, not sunken firmly into his flesh and bones but trembling, ready to depart on any puff of wind.

In his feverish dreams his father pushed him on the swing, higher and higher, and he did not see their back yard but the duckpond, and the breeze was cool on his sunburned forehead, his aching eyes, his blistered lips.

Cujo also slept.

He lay on the verge of grass by the porch, his mangled snout on his forepaws. His dreams were confused, lunatic things. It was dusk, and the sky was dark with wheeling, red-eyed bats. He leaped at them again and again, and each time he leaped he brought one down, teeth clamped on a leathery, twitching wing. But the bats kept biting his tender face with their sharp little rat-teeth. That was where the pain came from. That was where all the hurt came from. But he would kill them all. He would –

He woke suddenly, his head lifting from his paws, his head cocking.

A car was coming.

To his hellishly alert ears, the sound of the approaching car was dreadful, insupportable; it was the sound of some great stinging insect coming to fill him with poison.

He lurched to his feet, whining. All his joints seemed filled with crushed glass. He looked at the dead car. Inside, he could see the unmoving outline of THE WOMAN's head. Before, Cujo had been able to look right through the glass and see her, but THE WOMAN had done something to the glass that made it hard to see. It didn't matter what she did to the windows. She couldn't get out. Nor THE BOY, either.

The drone was closer now. The car was coming up the hill, but . . . *was* it a car? Or a giant bee or wasp come to batten on him, to sting him, to make his pain even worse?

Better wait and see.

Cujo slunk under the porch, where he had often spent hot summer days in the past. It was drifted sleep with the decaying autumn leaves of other years, leaves which released a smell he had thought incredibly sweet and pleasant in those same other years. Now the smell seemed immense and cloying, suffocating and well-nigh unbearable. He growled at the smell and began to slobber foam again. If a dog could kill a scent, Cujo would have killed this one.

The drone was very close now. And then a car was

turning into the driveway. A car with blue sides and a white roof and lights on the top.

The one thing George Bannerman had been least prepared to see when he turned into Joe Camber's dooryard was the Pinto belonging to the missing woman. He was not a stupid man, and while he would have been impatient with Andy Masen's point-to-point kind of logic (he had dealt with the horror of Frank Dodd and understood that sometimes there *was* no logic), he arrived at his own mostly solid conclusions in much the same way, if on a more subconscious level. And he agreed with Masen's belief that it was highly unlikely the Trenton woman and her son would be here. But the car was here, anyway.

Bannerman grabbed for the mike hung under his dashboard and then decided to check the car first. From this angle, directly behind the Pinto, it was impossible to see if anyone was in there or not. The backs of the bucket seats were a bit too high, and both Tad and Donna had slumped down in their sleep.

Bannerman got out of the cruiser and slammed the door behind him. Before he had gotten two steps, he saw the entire driver's side window was a buckled mass of shatter-shot cracks. His heart began to beat harder, and his hand went to the butt of his .38 Police Special.

Cujo stared out at THE MAN from the blue car with rising hate. It was this MAN who had caused all his pain; he felt sure of it. THE MAN had caused the pain in his joints and the high, rotten singing in his head; it was THE MAN'S fault that the drift of old leaves here beneath the porch now smelled putrescent; it was THE MAN'S fault that he could not look at water without whining and shrinking away and wanting to kill it in spite of his great thirst.

A growl began somewhere deep in his heavy chest as his legs coiled beneath him. He could smell THE MAN, his oil of sweat and excitement, the heavy meat set against his bones. The growl deepened, then rose to a great and shattering cry of fury. He sprang out from beneath the porch and charged at this awful MAN who had caused his pain.

During that first crucial moment, Bannerman didn't even hear Cujo's low, rising growl. He had approached the Pinto closely enough to see a mass of hair lying against the driver's side window. His first thought was that the woman must have been shot to death, but where was the bullet hole? The glass looked as if it had been bludgeoned, not shot.

Then he saw the head move. Not much – only slightly – but it *had* moved. The woman was alive. He stepped forward . . . and that was when Cujo's roar, followed by a volley of snarling barks came. His first thought

(Rusty?)

was of his Irish setter, but he'd had Rusty put down four years ago, not long after the Frank Dodd thing. And Rusty had never sounded like this, and for a second crucial moment, Bannerman was frozen in his tracks with a terribly, atavistic horror.

He turned then, pulling his gun, and caught just a blurred glimpse of a dog – an incredibly big dog – launching itself into the air at him. It struck him chest-high, driving him against the Pinto's hatchback. He grunted. His right hand was driven up and his wrist struck the chrome guttering of the hatchback hard. His gun went flying. It whirled over the top of the car, butt-for-barrel and butt-for-barrel, to land in the high weeds on the other side of the driveway.

The dog was *biting* him, and as Bannerman saw the first flowers of blood open on the front of his light blue shirt, he suddenly understood everything. They'd come here, their car had seized up . . . and the dog had been here. The dog hadn't been in Masen's neat little point-to-point analysis.

Bannerman grappled with it, trying to get his hands under the dog's muzzle and bring it up and out of his belly. There was a sudden deep and numbing pain down there. His shirt was in tatters down there. Blood was pouring over his pants in a freshet. He lurched forward and the dog drove him back with frightening force, drove him back against the Pinto with a thud that rocked the little car on its springs.

He found himself trying to remember if he and his wife had made love last night.

Crazy thing to be thinking. Crazy –

The dog bored in again. Bannerman tried to dodge away but the dog anticipated him, it was *grinning*, at him, and suddenly there was more pain that he had ever felt in his life. It galvanized him. Screaming, he got both hands under the dog's muzzle again and yanked it up. For a moment, staring into those dark, crazed eyes, a swoony kind of horror came over him and he thought: *Hello, Frank. It's you, isn't it? Was hell too hot for you?*

Then Cujo was snapping at his fingers, tearing them,

laying them open. Bannerman forgot about Frank Dodd. He forgot about everything but trying to save his life. He tried to get his knee up, between him and the dog, and found he couldn't. When he tried to raise his knee, the pain in his lower belly flared to a sheeting agony.

What's he done to me down there? Oh my God, what's he done? Vicky, Vicky —

Then the driver's side door of the Pinto opened. It was the woman. He had looked at the family portrait Steve Kemp had stepped on and had seen a pretty, neatly coiffed woman, the sort you look at twice on the street, the second look being mildly speculative. You saw a woman like that and you thought that her husband was lucky to have her in the kip.

This woman was a ruin. The dog had been at her as well. Her belly was streaked with dried blood. One leg of her jeans had been chewed away, and there was a sopping bandage just over her knee. But her face was the worst; it was like a hideous baked apple. Her forehead had blistered and peeled. Her lips were cracked and suppurating. Her eyes were sunken in deep purple pouches of flesh.

The dog left Bannerman in a flash and advanced on the woman, stiff-legged and growling. She retreated into the car and slammed the door.

(cruiser now got to call in got to call this in)

He turned and ran back to the cruiser. The dog chased him but he outran it. He slammed the door, grabbed the mike, and called for help, Code 3, officer needs assistance. Help came. The dog was shot. They were all saved.

All of this happened in just three seconds, and only in George Bannerman's mind. As he turned to go back to his police cruiser, his legs gave out and spilled him into the driveway.

(Oh Vicky what's he done to me down there?)

The world was all dazzling sun. It was hard to see. Bannerman scrambled, clawed at the gravel, and finally made it to his knees. He looked down at himself and saw a thick gray rope of intestine hanging out of his tattered shirt. His pants were soaked with blood to both knees.

Enough. The dog had done enough to him down there.

Hold your guts in, Bannerman. If you're stepping out, you're stepping out. But not until you get to that fucking mike and call this in. Hold your guts in and get on your big flat feet —

(the kid jesus her kid is her kid in there?)

That made him think of his own daughter, Katrina, who would be going into the seventh grade this year. She was getting breasts now. Becoming quite the little lady. Piano lessons. Wanted a horse. There had been a day when, if she had crossed from the school to the library alone, Dodd would have had her instead of Mary Kate Hendrasen. When —

(move your ass)

Bannerman got to his feet. Everything was sunshine and brightness and all his insides seemed to want to slip out of the hole the dog had torn in him. The car. The police radio. Behind him, the dog was distracted; he was throwing himself crazily against the Pinto's buckled driver's side door again and again, barking and snarling.

Bannerman staggered toward the cruiser. His face was as white as pie dough. His lips were blue gray. It was the biggest dog he had ever seen, and it had gutted him. *Gutted* him, for Christ's sake, and why was everything so hot and bright?

His intestines were slipping through his fingers.

He reached the car door. He could hear the radio under the dash, crackling out its message. *Should have called in first. That's procedure. You never argue with procedure, but if I'd believed that, I never would have called Smith in the Dodd case. Vicky, Katrina, I'm sorry –*

The boy. He had to get help for the boy.

He almost fell and grabbed the edge of the door for support.

And then he heard the dog coming for him and he began to scream again. He tried to hurry. If he could only get the door shut . . . oh, God, if only he could close the door before the dog got to him again . . . *oh, God . . .*

(oh GOD)

Tad was screaming again, screaming and clawing at his face, whipping his head from side to side as Cujo thudded against the door, making it rock.

'Tad, don't! Don't . . . honey, please don't!'

'Want Daddy . . . want Daddy . . . want Daddy . . .'

Suddenly it stopped.

Holding Tad against her breasts, Donna turned her head in time to see Cujo strike the man as he tried to swing into his car. The force of it knocked his hand loose from the door.

After that she couldn't watch. She wished she could block her ears somehow as well, from the sounds of Cujo finishing with whoever it had been.

379

He hid, she thought hysterically. *He heard the car coming and he* hid.

The porch door. Now was the time to go for the porch door while Cujo was . . . was occupied.

She put her hand on the doorhandle, yanked it, and shoved. Nothing happened. The door wouldn't open. Cujo had finally buckled the frame enough to seal it shut.

'Tad,' she whispered feverishly. 'Tad, change places with me, *quick.* Tad? *Tad?*'

Tad was shivering all over. His eyes had rolled up again.

'Ducks,' he said gutturally. 'Go see the ducks. Monster Words. Daddy. Ah . . . ahh . . . *ahhhhhhh—*'

He was convulsing again. His arms flopped bonelessly. She began to shake him, crying his name over and over again, trying to keep his mouth open, trying to keep the airway open. There was a monstrous buzzing in her head and she began to be afraid that she was going to faint. This was hell, they were in hell. The morning sun streamed into the car, creating the greenhouse effect, dry and remorseless.

At last Tad quieted. His eyes had closed again. His breathing was very rapid and shallow. When she put her fingers on his wrist she found a runaway pulse, weak, thready, and irregular.

She looked outside. Cujo had hold of the man's arm and was shaking it in the way a puppy will shake a rag toy. Every now and then he would pounce on the limp body. The blood . . . there was so much blood.

As if aware he was being observed, Cujo looked up, his muzzle dripping. He looked at her with an expression (could a dog *have* an expression? she wondered madly) that seemed to convey both sternness and pity . . . and again Donna had the feeling that they had come to know each other intimately, and that there could be no stopping or resting for either of them until they had explored this terrible relationship to some ultimate conclusion.

It pounced on the man in the blood-spattered blue shirt and the khaki pants again. The dead man's head lolled on his neck. She looked away, her empty stomach sour with hot acid. Her torn leg ached and throbbed. She had torn the wound there open yet again.

Tad . . . how was he now?

He's terrible, her mind answered inexorably. *So what are you going to do? You're his mother, what are you going to do?*

What *could* she do? Would it help Tad if she went out there and got herself killed?

The policeman. Someone had sent the policeman up here. And when he didn't come back –

'Please,' she croaked. 'Soon, please.'

It was eight o'clock now, and outside it was still relatively cool – 77 degrees. By noon, the recorded temperature at the Portland Jetport would be 102, a new record for that date.

Townsend and Andy Masen arrived at the State Police barracks in Scarborough at 8:30 A.M. Masen let Townsend run with the ball. This was his bailiwick, not Masen's, and there was not a thing wrong with Andy's ears.

The duty officer told them that Steven Kemp was on his way back to Maine. There had been no problem about that, but Kemp still wasn't talking. His van had been given a thorough going-over by Massachusetts lab technicians and forensic experts. Nothing had turned up which might indicate a woman and a boy had been held in the back, but they had found a nice little pharmacy in the van's wheel well – marijuana, some cocaine in an Anacin bottle, three amyl nitrate poppers, and two speedy combinations of the type known as Black Beauties. It gave them a handy hook to hang Mr Kemp on for the time being.

'That Pinto,' Andy said to Townsend, bringing them each a cup of coffee. 'Where's that fucking Pinto of hers?'

Townsend shook his head.

'Has Bannerman called anything in?'

'Nope.'

'Well, give him a shout. Tell him I want him down here when they bring Kemp in. It's his jurisiction, and I guess he's got to be the questioning officer. Technically, at least.'

Townsend came back five minutes later looking puzzled. 'I can't get him, Mr Masen. Their dispatcher's tried him and says he must not be in his car.'

'Christ, he's probably having coffee down at the Cozy Corner. Well, fuck him. He's out of it.' Andy Masen lit a fresh Pall Mall, coughed, and then grinned at Townsend. 'Think we can handle this Kemp without him?'

Townsend smiled back. 'Oh, I think we can manage.'

Masen nodded. 'This thing is starting to look bad, Mr Townsend. Very bad.'

'It's not good.'

'I'm beginning to wonder if this Kemp didn't bury them in the ditch beside some farm road between Castle Rock and Twickenham.' Masen smiled again. 'But we'll crack him, Mr Townsend. I've cracked tough nuts before this.'

'Yessir,'Townsend said respectfully. He believed Masen had.

'We'll crack him if we have to sit him in this office and sweat him for two days.'

Townsend slipped out every fifteen minutes or so, trying to make contact with George Bannerman. He knew Bannerman only slightly, but he held a higher opinion of him than Masen did, and he thought Bannerman deserved to be warned that Andy Masen was on the prod for him. When he still hadn't reached Bannerman by ten o'clock, he began to feel worried. He also began to wonder if he should mention Bannerman's continued silence to Masen, or if he should hold his peace.

Roger Breakstone arrived in New York at 8:49 A.M. on the Eastern shuttle, cabbed into the city, and checked into the Biltmore a little before 9:30.

'The reservation was for two?' the desk clerk asked.

'My partner has been called home on an emergency.'

'What a pity,' the desk clerk said indifferently, and gave Roger a card to fill out. While he did so, the desk clerk talked to the cashier about the Yankee tickets he had gotten for the following weekend.

Roger lay down in his room, trying to nap, but in spite of his poor rest the night before, no sleep would come. Donna screwing some other man, Vic holding on to all of that — trying to, anyway — in addition to this stinking mess over a red, sugary kiddies' cereal. Now Donna and Tad had disappeared. Vic had disappeared. Everything had somehow gone up in smoke this last week. Neatest trick you ever saw, presto chango, everything's a big pile of shit. His head ached. The ache came in big, greasy, thumping waves.

At last he got up, not wanting to be alone with his bad head and his bad thoughts any longer. He thought he might as well go on over to Summers Marketing & Research on 47th and Park and spread some gloom around there – after all, what else did Ad Worx pay them for?

He stopped in the lobby for aspirin and walked over. The walk did nothing for his head, but it did give him a chance to renew his hate/hate relationship with New York.

Not back here, he thought. *I'll go to work throwing cartons of Pepsi on a truck before I bring Althea and the girls back here.*

Summers was on the fourteenth floor of a big, stupid-looking, energy-inefficient skyscraper. The receptionist smiled and nodded when Roger identified himself. 'Mr Hewitt has just stepped out for a few minutes. Is Mr Trenton with you?'

'No, he was called home.'

'Well, I have something for you. It just came in this morning.'

She handed Roger a telegram in a yellow envelope. It was addressed to V. TRENTON/R. BREAKSTONE/AD WORX/CARE OF IMAGE-EYE STUDIOS. Rob had forwarded it to Summers Marketing late yesterday.

Roger tore it open and saw at once that it was from old man Sharp, and that it was fairly long.

Walking papers, here we come, he thought, and read the telegram.

*   *   *

The telephone woke Vic up at a few minutes before twelve; otherwise he might have slept most of the afternoon away as well. His sleep had been heavy and soggy, and he woke with a terrible feeling of disorientation. The dream had come again. Donna and Tad in a rocky niche, barely beyond the reach of some terrible, mythical beast. The room actually seemed to whirl around him as he reached for the telephone.

Donna and Tad, he thought. *They're safe.*

'Hello?'

'Vic, it's Roger.'

'Roger?' He sat up. His shirt was plastered to his body. Half his mind was still asleep and grappling with that dream. The light was too strong. The heat . . . it had been relatively cool when he went to sleep. Now the bedroom was an oven. How late was it? How late had they let him sleep? The house was so *silent*.

'Roger, what time is it?'

'Time?' Roger paused. 'Why, just about twelve o'clock. What—'

'Twelve? Oh, Christ . . . Roger, I've been asleep.'

'What's happened, Vic? Are they back?'

'They weren't when I went to sleep. That bastard Masen promised—'

'Who's Masen?'

'He's in charge of the investigation. Roger, I have to go. I have to find out—'

'Hold on, man. I'm calling from Summers. I've got to tell you. There was a telegram from Sharp in Cleveland. We're keeping the account.'

'What? What? It was all going too fast for him.

Donna . . . the account . . . Roger, sounding almost absurdly cheerful.

'There was a telegram here when I came in. The old man and his kid sent it to Image-Eye and Rob forwarded it here. You want me to read it?'

'Give me the gist.'

'Old man Sharp and the kid apparently came to the same conclusion using different chains of logic. The old man sees the Zingers thing as a replay of the Alamo – we're the good guys standing on the battlements, standing by to repel the boarders. All got to stick together, all for one and one for all.'

'Yeah, I knew he had that in him,' Vic said, rubbing the back of his neck. 'He's a loyal old bastard. That's why he came with us when we left New York.'

'The kid would still like to get rid of us, but he doesn't think this is the right time. He thinks it would be interpreted as a sign of weakness and even possible culpability. Can you *believe* it?'

'I could believe anything coming from that paranoid little twerp.'

'They want us to fly to Cleveland and sign a new two-year contract. It's not a five-year deal, and when it's up the kid's almost sure to be in charge and we'll undoubtedly be invited to take a long walk off a short dock, but two years . . . it's enough time, Vic! In two years we'll be on top of it! We can tell them –'

'Roger, I've got to—'

'– to take their lousy pound cake and pound it up their asses! They also want to discuss the new campaign, and I think they'll go for the Cereal Professor's swan song, too.'

CUJO

'That's great, Roger, but I've got to find out what the Christ has been happening with Donna and Tad.'

'Yeah. Yeah. I guess it was a lousy time to call, but I couldn't keep it to myself, man. I would have busted like a balloon.'

'There's no bad time for good news,' Vic said. All the same, he felt a stab of jealousy, as painful as a silver sharpened bone, at the happy relief in Roger's voice, and a bitter disappointment that he couldn't share in Roger's feelings. But maybe it was a good omen.

'Vic, call me when you hear, okay?'

'I will, Rog. Thanks for the call.'

He hung up, slipped into his loafers, and went downstairs. The kitchen was still a mess – it made his stomach do a slow and giddy rollover just to look at it. But there was a note from Masen on the table, pegged down with a salt shaker.

Mr Trenton,

Steve Kemp has been picked up in a western Massachusetts town, Twickenham. Your wife and son are not, repeat, are not, with him. I did not wake you with this news because Kemp is standing on his right to remain silent. Barring any complication, he will be brought directly to the Scarborough S.P. barracks for charging on vandalism and possession of illegal drugs. We estimate him here by 11:30 A.M. If anything breaks, I'll call you soonest.

Andy Masen

'*Fuck* his right to remain silent,' Vic growled. He went into the living room, got the number of the Scarborough State Police barracks, and made the call.

'Mr Kemp is here,' the duty officer told him. 'He got here about fifteen minutes ago. Mr Masen is with him now. Kemp's called a lawyer. I don't think Mr Masen can come to the—'

'You never mind what he can or can't do,' Vic said. 'You tell him it's Donna Trenton's husband and I want him to shag his ass over to the phone and talk to me.'

A few moments later, Masen came on the line.

'Mr Trenton, I appreciate your concern, but this brief time before Kemp's lawyer gets here can be very valuable.'

'What's he told you?'

Masen hesitated and then said, 'He's admitted to the vandalism. I think he finally realized this thing was a lot heavier than a little nose candy stashed in the wheel well of his van. He admitted the vandalism to the Massachusetts officers who brought him over here. But he claims that nobody was home when he did it, and that he left it undisturbed.'

'You don't believe that shit, do you?'

Masen said carefully, 'He's quite convincing. I couldn't say that I believe anything right now. If I could just ask him a few more questions—'

'Nothing came of Camber's Garage?'

'No. I sent Sheriff Bannerman up there with instructions to call in immediately if Mrs Trenton had been there or if her car was there. And since he didn't call back in –'

'That's hardly definitive, is it?' Vic asked sharply.

'Mr Trenton, I really must go. If we hear any—'

Vic slammed the telephone down and stood breathing rapidly in the hot silence of the living room. Then he went slowly to the stairs and mounted them. He stood in the upstairs hall for a moment and then went into his son's room. Tad's trucks were lined up neatly against the wall, slant-parking style. Looking at them hurt his heart. Tad's yellow slicker was hung on the brass hook by his bed, and his coloring books were piled neatly on his desk. His closet door was open. Vic shut it absently and, barely thinking about what he was doing, put Tad's chair in front of it.

He sat on Tad's bed, hands dangling between his legs, and looked out into the hot, bright day.

Dead ends. Nothing but dead ends, and where *were* they?

(dead ends)

Now there was an ominous phrase if ever one had been coined. *Dead ends.* As a boy Tad's age he had been fascinated with dead-end roads, his mother had told him once. He wondered if that sort of thing was inherited, if Tad was interested in dead-end roads. He wondered if Tad was still alive.

And it suddenly occurred to him that Town Road No. 3, where Joe Camber's Garage stood, was a dead-end road.

He suddenly looked around and saw that the wall over the head of Tad's bed was bare. The Monster Words were gone. Now why had he taken those? Or had Kemp taken them for some weird reason of his own? But if Kemp had been in here, why hadn't he trashed Tad's room as he had those downstairs?

(dead ends and Monster Words)

Had she taken the Pinto up to Camber's? He remembered the conversation they'd had about the balky needle valve only vaguely. She was a little scared of Joe Camber, hadn't she said that?

No. Not Camber. Camber only wanted to mentally undress her. No, it was the *dog* she was a little scared of. What was his name?

They had joked about it. Tad. Tad calling the dog.

And again he heard Tad's phantom, ghostly voice, so hopeless and lost in this too-empty, suddenly creepy room: *Cujo . . . heere, Cujo . . . Coooojo . . .*

And then something happened which Vic never spoke of to anyone in the rest of his life. Instead of hearing Tad's voice in his mind he was *actually* hearing it, high and lonely and terrified, a going-away voice *that was coming from inside the closet.*

A cry escaped Vic's throat and he pushed himself up on Tad's bed, his eyes widening. The closet door was swinging open, pushing the chair in front of it, and his son was crying '*Coooooooooo—*'

And then he realized it wasn't Tad's voice; it was his own tired, overwrought mind making Tad's voice from the thin scraping sound of the chair legs on the painted plank floor. That was all it was and –

– and there were eyes in the closet, he saw eyes, red and sunken and terrible –

A little scream escaped his throat. The chair tipped over for no earthly reason. And he saw Tad's teddybear inside the closet, perched on a stack of sheets and blankets. It was the bear's glass eyes he had seen. No more.

Heart thumping heavily in his throat, Vic got up and went to the closet. He could smell something in there, something heavy and unpleasant. Perhaps it was only mothballs – that smell was certainly part of it – but it smelled . . . savage.

Don't be ridiculous. It's just a closet. Not a cave. Not a monster lair.

He looked at Tad's bear. Tad's bear looked back at him, unblinking. Behind the bear, behind the hanging clothes, all was darkness. Anything could be back there. *Anything.* But, of course, nothing was.

You gave me a scare, bear, he said.

Monsters, stay out of this room, the bear said. Its eyes sparkled. They were dead glass, but they sparkled.

The door's out of true, that's all, Vic said. He was sweating; huge salty drops ran slowly down his face like tears.

You have no business here, the bear replied.

What's the matter with me? Vic asked the bear. *Am I going crazy? Is this what going crazy is like?*

To which Tad's bear replied: *Monsters, leave Tad alone.*

He closed the closet door and watched, as wide-eyed as a child, as the latch lifted and popped free of its notch. The door began to swing open again.

I didn't see that. I won't believe I saw that.

He slammed the door and put the chair against it again. Then he took a large stack of Tad's picturebooks and put them on the chair's seat to weight it down. This time the door stayed closed. Vic stood there looking at the closed door, thinking about dead-end roads. Not much traffic on dead-end roads. All monsters should live under bridges or in closets or at the ends of dead-end roads. It should be a national law.

He was very uneasy now.

He left Tad's room, went downstairs, and sat on the

back steps. He lit a cigarette with a hand that shook slightly and looked at the gunmetal sky, feeling the sense of unease grow. Something had happened in Tad's room. He wasn't sure what it had been, but it had been something. Yeah. Something.

Monsters and dogs and closets and garages and dead-end roads.

Do we add these up, teacher? Subtract them? Divide? Fractionate?

He threw his cigarette away.

He did believe it was Kemp, didn't he? Kemp had been responsible for everything. Kemp had wrecked the house. Kemp had damn near wrecked his marriage. Kemp had gone upstairs and shot his semen onto the bed Vic and his wife had slept in for the last three years. Kemp had torn a great big hole in the mostly comfortable fabric of Vic Trenton's life.

Kemp. Kemp. All Steve Kemp's fault. Let's blame the Cold War and the hostage situation in Iran and the depletion of the ozone layer on Kemp.

Stupid. Because not everything was Kemp's fault, now, was it? The Zinger's business, for instance; Kemp had had nothing to do with *that*. And Kemp could hardly be blamed for the bad needle valve on Donna's Pinto.

He looked at his old Jag. He was going to go somewhere in it. He couldn't stay here; he would go crazy if he stayed here. He should get in the car and beat it down to Scarborough. Grab hold of Kemp and shake him until it came out, until he told what he had done with Donna and Tad. Except by then his lawyer would have arrived, and, incredible as it seemed, the lawyer might even have sprung him.

Spring. It was a spring that held the needle valve in place. If the spring was bad, the valve could freeze and choke off the flow of gasoline to the carb.

Vic went down to the Jag and got in, wincing at the hot leather seat. Get rolling quick. Get some cool in here.

Get rolling where?

Camber's Garage, his mind answered immediately.

But that was stupid, wasn't it? Masen had sent Sheriff Bannerman up there with instructions to report immediately if anything was wrong and the cop hadn't reported back so that meant —

(that the monster got him)

Well, it wouldn't hurt to go up there, would it? And it was something to do.

He started the Jag up and headed down the hill toward Route 117, still not entirely sure if he was going to turn left toward I-95 and Scarborough or right toward Town Road No. 3.

He paused at the stop sign until someone in back gave him the horn. Then, abruptly, he turned right. It wouldn't hurt to take a quick run up to Joe Camber's. He could be there in fifteen minutes. He checked his watch and saw that it was twenty past twelve.

The time had come, and Donna knew it.

The time might also have gone, but she would have to live with that — and perhaps die with it. No one was going to come. There was going to be no knight on a silver steed riding up Town Road No. 3 — Travis McGee was apparently otherwise engaged.

Tad was dying.

She made herself repeat it aloud in a husky, choked whisper: 'Tad's dying.'

She had not been able to create any breeze through the car this morning. Her window would no longer go down, and Tad's window let in nothing but more heat. The one time she had tried to unroll it more than a quarter of the way, Cujo had left his place in the shade of the garage and had come around to Tad's side as fast as he could, growling eagerly.

The sweat had now stopped rolling down Tad's face and neck. There was no more sweat left. His skin was dry and hot. His tongue, swelled and dead-looking, protruded over his bottom lip. His breathing had grown so faint that she could barely hear it. Twice she had had to put her head against his chest to make sure that he still breathed at all.

Her condition was bad. The car was a blast furnace. The metalwork was now too hot to touch, and so was the plastic wheel. Her leg was a steady, throbbing ache, and she no longer doubted that the dog's bite had infected her with something. Perhaps it was too early for rabies – she prayed to God it was – but the bites were red and inflamed.

Cujo was not in much better shape. The big dog seemed to have shrunk inside his matted and blood-streaked coat. His eyes were hazy and nearly vacant, the eyes of an old man stricken with cataracts. Like some old engine of destruction, now gradually beating itself to death but still terribly dangerous, he kept his watch. He was no longer foaming; his muzzle was a dried and lacerated horror. It looked like a gouged chunk of igneous rock that had been coughed out of the hotbed of an old volcano.

The old monster, she thought incoherently, *keeps his watch still.*

Had this terrible vigil been only a matter of hours, or had it been her whole life? Surely everything that had gone before had been a dream, little more than a short wait in the wings? The mother who had seemed to be disgusted and repulsed by all those around her, the well-meaning but ineffectual father, the schools, the friends, the dates and dances – they were all a dream to her now, as youth must seem to the old. Nothing mattered, nothing *was* but this silent and sunstruck dooryard where death had been dealt and yet more death waited in the cards, as sure as aces and eights. The old monster kept his watch still, and her son was slipping, slipping, slipping away.

The baseball bat. That was all that remained to her now.

The baseball bat and maybe, if she could get there, something in the dead man's police car. Something like a shotgun.

She began to lift Tad into the back, grunting and puffing, fighting the waves of dizziness that made her sight gray over. Finally he was in the hatchback, as silent and still as a sack of grain.

She looked out of his window, saw the baseball bat lying in the high grass, and opened the door.

In the dark mouth of the garage, Cujo stood up and began to advance slowly, head lowered, down the crushed gravel toward her.

It was twelve thirty when Donna Trenton stepped out of her Pinto for the last time.

*   *   *

Vic turned off the Maple Sugar Road and onto Town Road No. 3 just as his wife was going for Brett Camber's old Hillerich & Bradsby in the weeds. He was driving fast, intent on getting up to Camber's so he could turn around and go to Scarborough, some fifty miles away. Perversely, as soon as he had made his decision to come out here first, his mind began dolefully telling him that he was on a wild goosechase. On the whole, he had never felt so impotent in his life.

He was moving the Jag along at better than sixty, so intent on the road that he was past Gary Pervier's before he realized that Joe Camber's station wagon had been parked there. He slammed on the Jag's brakes, burning twenty feet of rubber. The Jag's nose dipped toward the road. The cop might have gone up to Camber's and found nobody home because Camber was down here.

He glanced in the rearview mirror, saw the road was empty, and backed up quickly. He wheeled the Jag into Pervier's driveway and got out.

His feelings were remarkably like those of Joe Camber himself when, two days before, Joe had discovered the splatters of blood (only now these were dried and maroon-colored) and the smashed bottom panel of the screen door. A foul, metallic taste flooded Vic's mouth. This was all a part of it. Somehow it was all a part of Tad's and Donna's disappearance.

He let himself in and the smell hit him at once – be bloated, green smell of corruption. It had been a hot two days. There was something halfway down the hall that looked like a knocked-over endtable, except that Vic was mortally sure that it wasn't an endtable. Because of the smell. He went down to the thing in the hall and it wasn't an endtable. It was a man. The man appeared to have had his throat cut with an extremely dull blade.

Vic stepped back. A dry gagging sound came from his throat. The telephone. He had to call someone about this.

He started for the kitchen and then stopped. Suddenly everything came together in his mind. There was an instant of crushing revelation; it was like two half pictures coming together to make a three-dimensional whole.

The dog. The dog had done this.

The Pinto was at Joe Camber's. The Pinto had been there all along. The Pinto and –

'Oh my God, Donna—'

Vic turned and ran for the door and his car.

Donna almost went sprawling; that was how bad her legs were. She caught herself and grabbed for the baseball bat, not daring to look around for Cujo until she had it tightly in her hands, afraid she might lose her balance again. If she had had time to look a little further – just a little – she would have seen George Bannerman's service pistol laying in the grass. But she did not.

She turned unsteadily and Cujo was running at her.

She thrust the heavy end of the baseball bat at the Saint Bernard, and her heart sank at the unsteady way the thing wiggled in her hand – the handle was badly splintered, then. The Saint Bernard shied away, growling. Her breasts rose and fell rapidly in the white cotton bra. The cups were blood streaked; she had wiped her hands on them after clearing Tad's mouth.

They stood staring at each other, measuring each other, in the still summer sunlight. The only sounds were her low rapid breathing, the sound of Cujo growling deep in his chest, and the bright squawk of a sparrow somewhere near. Their shadows were short, shapeless things at their feet.

Cujo began to move to his left. Donna moved right. They circled. She held the bat at the point where she believed the split in the wood to be the deepest, her palms tight on the rough texture of the Black Cat friction tape the handle had been wrapped with.

Cujo tensed down.

'Come on, then!' she screamed at him, and Cujo leaped.

She swung the bat like Micky Mantle going after a high fastball. She missed Cujo's head but the bat struck him in the ribs. There was a heavy, dull thump and a snapping sound from somewhere inside Cujo. The dog uttered a sound like a scream and went sprawling in the gravel. She felt the bat give sickeningly under the friction tape – but for the moment it still held.

Donna cried out in a high, breaking voice and brought the bat down on Cujo's hindquarters. Something else broke. She heard it. The dog bellowed and tried to scramble away but she was on it again, swinging, pounding, screaming. Her head was high wine and deep iron. The world danced. She was the harpies, the Weird Sisters, she was all vengeance – not for herself, but for what had been done to her boy. The splintered handle of the bat bulged and pumped like a racing heart beneath her hands and beneath its binding of friction tape.

The bat was bloody now. Cujo was still trying to get away, but his movements had slowed. He ducked one blow – the head of the bat skittered through the gravel – but the next one struck him midway on his back, driving him to his rear legs.

She thought he was done; she even backed off a step or two, her breath screaming in and out of her lungs like some hot liquid. Then he uttered a deep snarl of rage and leaped at her again . . . but as Cujo went rolling in the gravel, the old bat finally split in two. The fat part flew away and struck the right front hubcap of the Pinto with a musical *bong!* She was left with a splintered eighteen-inch wand in her hand.

Cujo was getting to his feet again . . . *dragging* himself to his feet. Blood poured down his sides. His eyes flickered like lights on a defective pinball machine.

And still it seemed to her that he was grinning.

'*Come on, then!*' she shrieked.

For the last time the dying ruin that had been Brett Camber's good dog Cujo leaped at THE WOMAN that had caused all his misery. Donna lunged forward with the remains of the baseball bat, and a long, sharp hickory splinter plunged deep into Cujo's right eye and then into his brain. There was a small and unimportant popping sound – the sound a grape might make when squeezed suddenly between the fingers. Cujo's forward motion carried him into her and knocked her sprawling. His teeth now snapped and snarled bare inches from her neck. She put her arm up as Cujo crawled farther on top of her. His eye was now oozing down the side of his face. His breath was hideous. She tried to push his muzzle up, and his jaws clamped on her forearm.

'Stop!' she screamed. *'Oh stop, won't you ever stop? Please! Please! Please!'*

Blood was flowing down onto her face in a sticky drizzle — her blood, the dog's blood. The pain in her arm was a sheeting flare that seemed to fill the whole world . . . and little by little he was forcing it down. The splintered handle of the bat wavered and jiggled grotesquely, seeming to grow from his head where his eye had been.

He went for her neck.

Donna felt his teeth there and with a final wavering cry she pistoned her arms out and pushed him aside. Cujo thudded heavily to the ground.

His rear legs scratched at the gravel. They slowed . . . slowed . . . stopped. His remaining eye glared up at the hot summer sky. His tail lay across her shins, as heavy as a Turkish rug runner. He pulled in a breath and let it out. He took another. He made a thick snorting sound, and suddenly a rill of blood ran from his mouth. Then he died.

Donna Trenton howled her triumph. She got halfway to her feet, fell down, and managed to get up again. She took two shuffling steps and stumbled over the dog's body, scoring her knees with scrapes. She crawled to where the heavy end of the baseball bat lay, its far end streaked with gore. She picked it up and gained her feet again by holding on to the hood of the Pinto. She tottered back to where Cujo lay. She began to pound him with the baseball bat. Each downward swing ended with a heavy meat thud. Black strips of friction tape danced and flew in the hot air. Splinters gouged into the soft pads of her palms, and blood ran down her wrists and forearms. She was still

400

screaming, but her voice had broken with that first howl of triumph and all that came out now was a series of growling croaks; she sounded as Cujo himself had near the end. The bat rose and fell. She bludgeoned the dead dog. Behind her, Vic's Jag turned into the Cambers' driveway.

He didn't know what he had expected, but it hadn't been this. He had been afraid, but the sight of his wife – could that *really* be Donna? – standing over the twisted and smashed thing in the driveway, striking it again and again with something that looked like a caveman's club . . . that turned his fear to a bright, silvery panic that almost precluded thought. For one infinite moment, which he would never admit to himself later, he felt an impulse to throw the Jag in reverse and drive away . . . to drive forever. What was going on in this still and sunny dooryard was monstrous.

Instead, he turned off the engine and leaped out. 'Donna! *Donna!*'

She appeared not to hear him or to even realize that he was there. Her cheeks and forehead were savagely welted with sunburn. The left leg of her slacks was shredded and soaked with blood. And her belly looked . . . it looked *gored*.

The baseball bat rose and fell, rose and fell. She made harsh cawing sounds. Blood flew up from the dog's limp carcass.

'*Donna!*'

He got hold of the baseball bat on the backswing and wrenched it out of her hands. He threw it away and grabbed her naked shoulder. She turned to face him, her eyes blank and hazed, her hair straggling, witchlike, any way. She stared at him . . . shook her head . . . and stepped away.

'Donna, honey, my Jesus,' he said softly.

It was Vic, but Vic couldn't be here. It was a mirage. It was the dog's sickening disease at work in her, making her hallucinate. She stepped away . . . rubbed her eyes . . . and he was still there. She stretched out one trembling hand, and the mirage folded strong brown hands over it. That was good. Her hands hurt dreadfully.

'Vuh?' she croaked in a whisper. 'Vuh – Vuh – Vic?'

'Yes, honey. It's me. Where's Tad?'

The mirage was real. It was really him. She wanted to cry, but no tears came. Her eyes only moved in their sockets like overheated ball bearings.

'Vic? Vic?'

He put an arm around her. 'Where's *Tad*, Donna?'

'Car. Car. Sick. Hospital.' She could now barely whisper, and even that was failing her. Soon she would be able to do no more than mouth words. But it didn't matter, did It? Vic was here. She and Tad were saved.

He left her and went to the car. She stood where he had left her, looking fixedly down at the dog's battered body. At the end, it hadn't been so bad, had it? When there was nothing left but survival, when you were right down to the strings and nap and ticking of yourself, you survived or you died and that seemed perfectly all right. The blood didn't seem so bad now, nor the brains that were leaking out of Cujo's cloven head. Nothing seemed so bad now. Vic was here and they were saved.

'Oh my *God*,' Vic said, his voice rising thinly in the stillness.

She looked over and saw him taking something out of the back of her Pinto. A sack of something. Potatoes? Oranges? What? Had she been shopping before all this happened? Yes, but she had taken the groceries into the house. She and Tad had taken them in. They used his wagon. So what –

Tad! she tried to say, and ran to him.

Vic carried Tad into the thin shade at the side of the house and laid him down. Tad's face was very white. His hair lay like straw on his fragile skull. His hands lay on the grass, seemingly without enough weight to crush the stems beneath their backs.

Vic put his head on Tad's chest. He looked up at Donna. His face was white but calm enough.

'How long has he been dead, Donna?'

Dead? she tried to scream at him. Her mouth moved like the mouth of a figure on a TV set the volume control of which has been turned all the way down. *He's not dead, he wasn't dead when I put him in the hatchback, what are you telling me, he's dead? What are you telling me, you bastard!*

She tried to say those things in her voiceless voice. Had Tad's life slid away at the same time the dog's life had slid away? It was impossible. No God, no fate, could be so monstrously cruel.

She ran at her husband and shoved him. Vic, expecting anything but that, fell over on his butt. She crouched over Tad. She put his hands above his head. She opened his mouth, pinched his nostrils shut, and breathed her voiceless breath into her son's lungs.

In the driveway, the somnolent summer flies had found the corpse of Cujo and that of Sheriff Bannerman, husband to Victoria, father to Katrina. They had no preference between the dog and the man. They were democratic flies. The sun blared triumphantly down. It was ten minutes of one now, and the fields shimmered and danced with silent summer. The sky was faded blue denim. Aunt Evvie's prediction had come true.

She breathed for her son. She breathed. She breathed. Her son was not dead; she had not gone through this hell for her son to be dead, and it simply would not be.

It would not be.

She breathed. She breathed. She breathed for her son.

She was still doing it when the ambulance pulled into the driveway twenty minutes later. She would not let Vic near the boy. When he came near, she bared her teeth and growled soundlessly at him.

Stunned with grief nearly to the point of distraction, deeply sure at the final bedrock level of his consciousness that none of this could be happening, he broke into Camber's house by way of the porch door at which Donna had stared so long and hard. The inner door beyond it had not been locked. He used the telephone.

When he came outside again, Donna was still administering mouth-to-mouth resuscitation to their dead son. He started toward her and then swerved away. He went to the Pinto instead and opened the hatchback again. Heat roared out at him like an invisible lion. Had they existed in there Monday afternoon and all day Tuesday and until noon of today? It was impossible to believe they had.

Underneath the hatchback's floor, where the spare tire was, he found an old blanket. He shook it out and put it over Bannerman's mutilated body. He sat down on the grass then, and stared out at Town Road No. 3 and the dusty pines beyond. His mind floated serenely away.

The ambulance driver and the two orderlies loaded Bannerman's body into the Castle Rock Rescue Unit. They approached Donna. Donna bared her teeth at them. Her parched lips formed the words *He's alive! Alive!* When one of the orderlies tried to pull her gently to her feet and lead her away, she bit him. Later this orderly would need to go to hospital himself for anti-rabies treatment. The other orderly came to help. She fought them.

They stood away warily. Vic still sat on the lawn, his chin propped in his hands, looking across the road.

The Rescue Unit driver brought a syringe. There was a struggle. The syringe was broken. Tad lay on the grass, still dead. His patch of shade was a little bigger now.

Two more police cars arrived. Roscoe Fisher was in one of them. When the ambulance driver told him that George Bannerman was dead, Roscoe began to cry. Two other policemen advanced on Donna. There was another struggle, short and furious, and Donna Trenton was finally pulled away from her son by four sweating, straining men. She nearly broke free again and Roscoe Fisher, still crying, joined them. She screamed soundlessly, whipping her head from side to side. Another syringe was produced, and she was injected successfully this time.

A stretcher came down from the ambulance, and the orderlies wheeled it over to where Tad lay on the grass.

Tad, still dead, was put on it. A sheet was pulled up over his head. At the sight of this, Donna redoubled her struggles. She freed one hand and began to flail about wildly with it. Then, suddenly, she was free.

'Donna,' Vic said. He got to his feet. 'Honey, it's over. Honey, please. Let go, let go.'

She did not go for the stretcher that her son lay on. She went for the baseball bat. She picked it up and began to bludgeon the dog again. The flies rose in a shiny green-black cloud. The sound of the ball bat making contact was heavy and terrible, a butcher-shop sound. Cujo's body jumped a little each time she struck it.

The cops began to move forward.

'No,' one of the orderlies said quietly, and a few moments later Donna simply collapsed. Brett Camber's bat rolled away from her relaxing hand.

The ambulance left five minutes or so later, siren howling. Vic had been offered a shot — 'to calm your nerves, Mr Trenton' — and although he felt utterly tranquilized already, he had accepted the shot to be polite. He picked up the cellophane the orderly had stripped from the syrette and examined the word UPJOHN printed on it carefully. 'We ran an advertising campaign for these guys once,' he told the orderly.

'That so?' the orderly asked cautiously. He was a fairly young man and he felt that he might throw up sometime soon. He had never seen such a mess in his life.

One of the police cars was standing by to take Vic to Northern Cumberland Hospital in Bridgton.

'Can you wait a minute?' he asked.

The two cops nodded. They were also staring at Vic
Trenton in a very cautious way, as if whatever he had might
be catching.

He opened both doors of the Pinto. He had to tug
long and hard at Donna's; the dog had dented it in a way
he wouldn't have believed. Her purse was in there. Her
shirt. The shirt had a jagged tear in it, as if maybe the dog
had taken a chomp out of it. There was some empty Slim
Jim wrappers on the dashboard and Tad's Thermos bottle,
smelling of sour milk. Tad's Snoopy lunchbox. His heart
gave a heavy, horrid wrench at the sight of that, and he
wouldn't allow himself to think of what that meant in
terms of the future — if there was any future after this
terrible hot day. He found one of Tad's sneakers.

Tadder, he thought. *Oh Tadder.*

The strength went out of his legs and he sat down
heavily on the passenger seat, looking between his legs at
the strip of chrome at the bottom of the doorframe. Why?
Why had something like this been allowed to happen?
How could so many events have conspired together?

His head was suddenly throbbing violently. His nose
closed with tears and his sinuses began to pound. He snorted
the tears back and passed a hand over his face. It occurred
to him that, counting Tad, Cujo had been responsible for
the deaths of at least three people, more than that if the
Cambers were discovered to be among his victims. Did
the cop he had covered with the blanket have a wife and
children? Probably.

*If I'd gotten here even an hour earlier. If I hadn't gone to
sleep —*

His mind cried: *I was so sure it was Kemp! So sure!*

If I'd gotten here just fifteen minutes earlier, would that have been enough? If I hadn't talked to Roger so long, would Tad be alive now? When did he die? Did it really happen at all? And how am I supposed to deal with it for the rest of my life without going mad? What's going to happen to Donna?

Another police car pulled up. One of the cops got out of it and conferred with one of the cops waiting for Vic. The latter stepped forward and said quietly. 'I think we ought to go, Mr Trenton. Quentin here says there are reporters on the way. You don't want to talk to any reporters just now.'

'No,' Vic agreed, and started to get up. As he did, he saw a bit of yellow at the very bottom of his field of vision. A bit of paper poking out from under Tad's seat. He pulled it out and saw it was the Monster Words he had written to ease Tad's mind at bedtime. The sheet was crumpled and ripped in two places and badly stained with sweat; along the deep creases it was nearly transparent.

> *Monsters, stay out of this room!*
> *You have no business here.*
> *No monsters under Tad's bed!*
> *You can't fit under there.*
> *No monsters hiding in Tad's closet!*
> *It's too small in there.*
> *No monsters outside of Tad's window!*
> *You can't hold on out there.*
> *No vampires, no werewolves, no things that bite.*
> *You have no business here.*
> *Nothing will touch Tad, or hurt Tad, all this ni—*

He could read no more. He crumpled the sheet of paper up and threw it at the dead dog's body. The paper was a sentimental lie, its sentiments as inconstant as the color in that stupid runny-dyed cereal. It was all a lie. The world was full of monsters, and they were all allowed to bite the innocent and the unwary.

He let himself be led to the police car. They drove him away, as George Bannerman and Tad Trenton and Donna Trenton had been driven away before him. After a while, a veterinarian came in a panel truck. She looked at the dead dog, then donned long rubber gloves and brought out a circular bone saw. The cops, realizing what she was going to do, turned away.

The vet cut off the Saint Bernard's head and put it in a large white plastic garbage bag. Later that day it was forwarded to the State Commissioner of Animals, where the brain would be tested for rabies.

So Cujo was gone, too.

It was quarter to four that afternoon when Holly called Charity to the telephone. Holly looked mildly worried. 'It sounds like somebody official,' she said. About an hour earlier, Brett had given in to Jim Junior's endless supplications and had accompanied his young cousin down to the playground at the Stratford Community Center.

Since then the house had been silent except for the women's voices as they talked over old times – the *good* old times, Charity amended slightly. The time Daddy had fallen off the haytruck and gone into a great big cowflop in Back Field (but no mention of the times he had beaten them until they couldn't sit down in payment for some real or imagined transgression); the time they had snuck into the old Met Theater in Lisbon Falls to see Elvis in *Love Me Tender* (but not the time Momma had had her credit cut off at the Red & White and had backed out of the grocery in tears, leaving a full basket of provisions behind and everybody watching); how Red Timmins from up the road was always trying to kiss Holly on their walk back from school (but not how Red had lost an arm when his tractor turned turtle on him in August of 1962). The two of them had discovered it was all right to open the closets . . . as long as you didn't poke too far back in them. Because things might still be lurking there, ready to bite.

Twice, Charity had opened her mouth to tell Holly that she and Brett would be going home tomorrow, and both times she had closed it again, trying to think of a way she could say it without leading Holly to believe they didn't like it here.

Now the problem was momentarily forgotten as she sat at the telephone table, a fresh cup of tea beside her. She felt a little anxious – nobody likes to get a telephone call while they're on vacation from someone who sounds official.

'Hello?' she said.

Holly watched her sister's face go white, listened as her sister said, 'What? *What?* No . . . no! There must be some mistake. I tell you, there must—'

She fell silent, listening to the telephone. Some dreadful news was being passed down the wire from Maine, Holly thought. She could see it in the gradually tightening mask of her sister's face, although she could hear nothing from the phone itself except a series of meaning-less squawks.

Bad news from Maine. To her it was an old story. It was all right for her and Charity to sit in the sunny morning kitchen, drinking tea and eating orange sections and talking about sneaking into the Met Theater. It was all right, but it didn't change the fact that every day she could remember of her childhood had brought a little piece of bad news with it, each piece a part of her early life's jigsaw, the whole picture so terrible that she would not really have minded if she had never seen her older sister again. Torn cotton underpants that the other girls at school made fun of. Picking potatoes until her back ached and if you stood up suddenly the blood rushed out of your head so fast you felt like you were going to faint. Red Timmins – how carefully she and Charity had avoided mentioning Red's arm, so badly crushed it had to be amputated, but when Holly heard she had been glad, so *glad*. Because she remembered Red throwing a green apple at her one day, hitting her in the face, making her nose bleed, making her cry. She remembered Red giving her Indian rubs and laughing. She remembered an occasional nourishing dinner of Shedd's Peanut Butter and Cheerios when things were particularly bad. She remembered the way the outhouse stank in high summer, that smell was *shit*, and in case you should wonder, that wasn't a good smell.

Bad news from Maine. And somehow, for some crazed reason she knew they would never discuss even if they both lived to be a hundred and spent the last twenty old-maid years together, Charity had elected to stick with that life. Her looks were almost entirely gone. There were

wrinkles around her eyes. Her breasts sagged; even in her
bra they sagged. There were only six years between them,
but an observer might well have thought it was more like
sixteen. And worst of all, she seemed totally unconcerned
about dooming her lovely, intelligent boy to a similar
life . . . unless he got smart, unless he wised up. For the
tourists, Holly thought with an angry bitterness that all
the good years had not changed, it was Vacationland. But
if you came from the puckies, it was day after day of bad
news. Then one day you looked in the mirror and the
face looking back at you was Charity Camber's face. And
now there was more dreadful news from Maine, that home
of all dreadful news. Charity was hanging up the telephone. She sat staring at it, her hot tea steaming beside
her.

'Joe's dead,' she announced suddenly.

Holly sucked in breath. Her teeth felt cold. *Why did
you come?* she felt like shrieking. *I knew you'd bring it all
with you, and sure enough, you did.*

'Oh, honey,' she said, 'are you sure?'

'That was a man from Augusta. Name of Masen. From
the Attorney General's office, Law Enforcement Division.'

'Was it . . . was it a car accident?'

Charity looked directly at her then, and Holly was
both shocked and terrified to see that her sister did not
look like someone who has just received dreadful news;
she looked like someone who has just received *good* news.
The lines in her face had smoothed out. Her eyes were
blank . . . but was it shock behind that blankness or the
dreamy awakening of possibility?

If she had seen Charity Camber's face when she had

checked the numbers on her winning lottery ticket, she might have known.

'Charity?'

'It was the dog,' Charity said. 'It was Cujo.'

'The dog?' At first she was bewildered, unable to see any possible connection between the death of Charity's husband and the Camber family dog. Then she realized. The implications came in terms of Red Timmins's horribly mangled left arm, and she said, in a higher, shriller tone, 'The *dog*?'

Before Charity could reply — if she had meant to — there were cheery voices in the back yard: Jim Junior's high, piping one and then Brett's, lower and amused, answering. And now Charity's face changed. It became stricken. It was a face that Holly remembered and hated well, an expression that made all faces the same — an expression she had felt often enough on her own face in those old days.

'The boy,' Charity said. 'Brett. Holly . . . how am I going to tell Brett his father is dead?'

Holly had no answer for her. She could only stare helplessly at her sister and wish neither of them had come.

RABID DOG KILLS 4 IN BIZARRE THREE–DAY REIGN OF TERROR, the headline on that evening's edition of the Portland *Evening Express* blared. The subhead read: *Lone Survivor at Northern Cumberland Hospital in Guarded Condition*. The headline on the following day's *Press-Herald* read: FATHER TELLS OF WIFE'S DOOMED STRUGGLE TO SAVE SON. That evening the story had been relegated to the bottom of page one: MRS TRENTON RESPONDING TO RABIES TREATMENT, DOCTOR

SAYS. And in a sidebar: DOG HAD NO SHOTS: LOCAL VET. Three days after it had ended, the story was inside, on page four: STATE HEALTH AGENCY BLAMES RABID FOX OR RACCOON FOR DOG'S CASTLE ROCK RAMPAGE. A final story that week carried the news that Victor Trenton had no intention of suing the surviving members of the Camber family, who were said to be in 'deep shock'. This intelligence was scant, but provided a pretext upon which the entire tale could be rehashed. A week later, the front page of the Sunday paper carried a feature story on what had happened. A week after that, a national tabloid offered a fervid synopsis of what had happened, headed: TRAGIC BATTLE IN MAINE AS MOM BATTLES KILLER SAINT BERNARD. And that was really the end of the coverage.

There was a rabies scare in central Maine that fall. An expert attributed it to 'rumor and the horrifying but isolated incident in Castle Rock.'

Donna Trenton was in the hospital for nearly four weeks. She finished her cycle of treatments for the rabid dog bites with a good deal of pain but no serious problems, but because of the potential seriousness of the disease – and because of her deep mental depression – she was closely watched.

In late August, Vic drove her home.

They spent a quiet, showery day around the house. That evening as they sat in front of the television, not really watching it, Donna asked him about Ad Worx.

'Everything's fine there,' he said. 'Roger got the last Cereal Professor commercial on the rails single-handed . . . with Rob Martin's help, of course. Now we're involved in a major new campaign for the whole Sharp line.' Half a lie; Roger was involved. Vic went in three, sometimes four days a week, and either pushed his pencil around or looked at his typewriter. 'But the Sharp people are being very careful to make sure that none of what we're doing will go beyond the two-year period we signed for. Roger was right. They're going to dump us. But by then it won't matter if they do.'

'Good,' she said. She had bright periods now, periods when she seemed very much like her old self, but she was still listless most of the time. She had lost twenty pounds and looked scrawny. Her complexion was not very good. Her nails were ragged.

She looked at the TV for a while and then turned to him. She was crying.

'Donna,' he said. 'Oh babe.' He put his arms around her and held her. She was soft but unyielding to his arms. Through the softness he could feel the angles of her bones in too many places.

'Can we live here?' she managed in an unsteady voice. 'Vic, can we live here?'

'I don't know,' he said. 'I think we ought to give it a damned good shot.'

'Maybe I should ask if you can go on living with me. If you said no, I'd understand. I'd understand perfectly.'

'I don't want anything else but to live with you. I knew that all along, I think. Maybe there was an hour – right after I got Kemp's note – when I didn't know. But that was the only time. Donna, I love you. I always have.'

Now she put her arms around him and hugged him tight. Soft summer rain struck the windows and made gray and black shadow patterns on the floor.

'I couldn't save him,' she said. 'That's what keeps coming back on me. I can't get rid of it. I go over it again . . . and again . . . and again. If I'd run for the porch sooner . . . or gotten the baseball bat . . .' She swallowed. 'And when I finally did get up the guts to go out there, it was just . . . over. He was dead.'

He could have reminded her that she'd had Tad's welfare in mind above her own all the time. That the reason she hadn't gone for the door was because of what would have happened to Tad if the dog had gotten to her before she could get inside. He could have told her that the siege had probably weakened the dog as much as it had Donna herself, and if she had tried Cujo with the baseball bat earlier on, the outcome might have been terribly different; as it was, the dog had almost killed her in the end. But he understood that these points had been brought to her attention again and again, by himself and by others, and that not all the logic in the world could blunt the pain of coming upon that mute pile of coloring books, or seeing the swing, empty and motionless at the bottom of its arc, in the back yard. Logic could not blunt her terrible sense of personal failure. Only time could do those things, and time would do an imperfect job.

He said, 'I couldn't save him either.'

'You—'

'I was so sure it was Kemp. If I'd gone up there earlier, if I hadn't fallen asleep, even if I hadn't talked to Roger on the phone.'

'No,' she said gently. 'Don't.'

'I have to. I guess you do too. We'll just have to get

along. That's what people do, you know? They just get along. And try to help each other.'

'I keep feeling him . . . sensing him . . . around every corner.'

'Yeah. Me too.'

He and Roger had taken all of Tad's toys to the Salvation Army two Saturdays ago. When it was done, they had come back here and had a few beers in front of the ballgame, not talking much. And when Roger went home, Vic went upstairs and sat on the bed in Tad's room and wept until it seemed the weeping would pull all his insides apart. He wept and wanted to die but he hadn't died and the next day he had gone back to work.

'Make us some coffee,' he said, and slapped her lightly on the rump. 'I'll light a fire. Chilly in here.'

'All right.' She got up. 'Vic?'

'What?'

Her throat worked. 'I love you too.'

'Thanks,' he said. 'I think I needed that.'

She smiled wanly and went to make the coffee. And they got through the evening, although Tad was still dead. They got through the next day as well. And the next. It was not much better at the end of August, nor in September, but by the time the leaves had turned and began to fall, it was a little better. A little.

She was wired with tension and trying not to show it.

When Brett came back from the barn, knocked the snow from his boots, and let himself in the kitchen door, she was sitting at the kitchen table, drinking a cup of tea. For a moment he only looked at her. He had lost some weight and had grown taller in the last six months. The total effect was to make him look gangling, where he had always before seemed compact and yet lithe. His grades during the first quarter hadn't been so good, and he had been in trouble twice – scuffles in the schoolyard both times, probably over what had happened this last summer. But his second-quarter marks had been a lot better.

'Mom? Momma? Is it—'

'Alva brought him over,' she said. She set the teacup on the saucer carefully, and it did not chatter. 'No law says you have to keep him.'

'Has he had his shots?' Brett asked, and her heart broke a little that this should be his first question.

'As a matter of fact, he has,' she said. 'Alva tried to slip that over on me, but I made him show me the vet's bill. Nine dollars, it was. Distemper and rabies. Also, there's a tube of cream for ticks and ear mites. If you don't want him, Alva will give me my nine dollars back.'

Money had become important to them. For a little bit she hadn't been sure if they would be able to keep the place, or even if they should try to keep it. She had talked it over with Brett, being level with him. There had been a small life insurance policy. Mr Shouper at the Casco Bank in Bridgton had explained to her that if the money was put in a special trust account, it plus the lottery money would make nearly all the outstanding mortgage payments over the next five years. She had landed a decent job in the packing and billing department of Castle Rock's one real industry, Trace Optical. The sale of Joe's equipment – including the new chainfall – had brought them in an additional three thousand dollars. It was *possible* for them to keep the place, she had explained to Brett, but it was apt to be a hard scrabble. The alternative was an apartment in town. Brett had slept on it, and it had turned out that what he wanted was what she wanted – to keep the home place. And so they had stayed.

'What's his name?' Brett asked.

'Doesn't have a name. He's just weaned.'

'Is he a breed?'

'Yes,' she said, and then laughed. 'He's a Heinz. Fifty-seven Varieties.'

He smiled back, and the smile was strained. But Charity reckoned it better than no smile at all.

'Could he come in? It's started to snow again.'

'He can come in if you put down papers. And if he piddles around, you clean it up.'

'All right.' He opened the door to go out.

'What do you want to call him, Brett?'

'I don't know,' Brett said. There was a long, long pause. 'I don't know yet. I'll have to think on it.'

She had an impression that he was crying, and restrained an impulse to go to him. Besides, his back was to her and she couldn't really tell. He was getting to be a big boy, and as much as it pained her to know it, she understood that big boys often don't want their mothers to know they're crying.

He went outside and brought the dog back in, carrying it cradled in his arms. It remained unnamed until the following spring, when for no reason either of them could exactly pinpoint, they began to call it Willie. It was a small, lively, short-haired dog, mostly terrier. Somehow it just looked like a Willie. The name stuck.

Much later, that spring, Charity got a small pay raise.

She began to put away ten dollars a week. Towards Brett's college.

Shortly before those mortal events in the Camber door-yard, Cujo's remains were cremated. The ashes went out with the trash and were disposed of at the Augusta waste-treatment plant. It would perhaps not be amiss to point out that he had always tried to be a good dog. He had tried to do all the things his MAN and his WOMAN, and most of all his BOY, had asked or expected of him. He would have died for them, if that had been required. He had never wanted to kill anybody. He had been struck by something, possibly destiny, or fate, or only a degenerative nerve disease called rabies. Free will was not a factor.

The small cave into which Cujo had chased the rabbit was never discovered. Eventually, for whatever vague reasons small creatures may have, the bats moved on. The rabbit was unable to get out and it starved to death in slow, sound-less misery. Its bones, so far as I know, still remain there with the bones of those small animals unlucky enough to have tumbled into that place before it.

> *I'm tellin you so you'll know,*
> *I'm tellin you so you'll know,*
> *I'm tellin you so you'll know,*
> *Ole Blue's gone where the good dogs go.*
> — FOLK SONG

September 1977–
March 1981

STEPHEN KING
PET SEMATARY

A pet isn't just for life . . .

The house looks right, feels right, to Dr Louis Creed. Rambling, old and comfortable. A place where the family can settle; the children grow and play and explore. The rolling hills and meadows of Maine seem a world away from the fume-choked dangers of Chicago.

Only the occasional big truck out on the two-lane highway growls out an intrusive threat. But behind the house there's a carefully cleared path up into the woods where generations of local children have processed with the solemn innocence of the young, taking with them their dear departed pets for burial.

A sad place maybe, but safe. Surely a safe place. Not a place to seep into your dreams, to wake you, sweating with fear and foreboding . . .

'King can make the flesh creep half a world away'
– *The Times*

HODDER

**Don't miss the following
iconic chillers**

**To find out more about Stephen King's books,
audio and electronic editions, as
well as news, Reading Group Notes,
competitions, videos and lots more please visit
www.hodder.co.uk**